# EVIE GRACE

# Her Mother's Daughter

arrow books

1 3 5 7 9 10 8 6 4 2

Arrow Books
20 Vauxhall Bridge Road
London SW1V 2SA

Arrow Books is part of the Penguin Random House group of companies whose addresses can be found at global.penguinrandomhouse.com.

First published in Great Britain by Arrow Books in 2018

www.penguin.co.uk

A CIP catalogue record for this book is available from the British Library.

ISBN 9781784756239

Typeset in 10.75/13.5 pt Palatino by Jouve (UK), Milton Keynes
Printed and bound in Great Britain by Clays Ltd, St Ives Plc

To Rich

# 1853

# Chapter One

## *A Small Miracle*

The sound of hooves slipping and scraping on the stones outside announced the arrival of an unexpected visitor at the Berry-Clays' residence early on a cold February morning.

Agnes was eating at the table in the nursery while Nanny, wrapped in a heavy woollen shawl, sat in the straight-backed mahogany chair beside the fireplace, flicking through the pages of a book. With a quick glance to see if she was looking, Agnes abandoned her porridge and hurried to the window.

'Miss Agnes, where are you?'

Hearing Nanny's voice, she sat down quickly on the window seat, pulled her legs up and drew the heavy drapes closed behind her. She breathed on the ice inside the glass and rubbed at it with her sleeve, making a clear circle through which she could make out Papa's groom holding on to a dark horse. Its rider, a man dressed in a hat and dark overcoat, dismounted and detached a brown leather bag from the saddle.

What business did he have at such an isolated place as Windmarsh Court? she wondered.

'Good morning, Miss Treen,' came another voice. 'I've come to lay the fire if it isn't too late. I would 'ave bin up before, but the mistress asked that I did the rooms in a different order this morning with the nursery last. The word is that the doctor's bin summoned for.'

'Thank you, Miriam, but we should mind our tongues when it comes to the family's affairs,' Nanny said.

'It hasn't gone unnoticed that the mistress has bin unwell for some time.'

Mama was sick? Agnes looked out across the yard and the walled garden where the gardener and his boy faced a constant battle to keep the surrounding marsh at bay. She could see the Swale estuary and the Isle of Sheppey on the far side of the water, clothed in its winter ochres, greys and greens, and a barge with its brown sails unfurled, heading between the mudflats towards the coast. Agnes felt a twinge of guilt that she hadn't noticed her mother was ill, but then how could she when she hardly saw her? She hardly saw anyone, apart from the servants. She had no friends her own age. She only had Nanny for company.

She rearranged her velvet skirt and pinafore over her petticoat and hugged her knees, shivering with cold.

'It would be a miracle if Doctor Shaw confirms our suspicions,' Miriam went on.

'It isn't for us to speculate,' Nanny said firmly. 'Do go ahead with your duties, for we are about to freeze to death.'

'I've never known a winter like it.' Agnes heard the swish of the brush and the scrape of the shovel as Miriam began to clear the ashes from the grate. 'Where is Miss Berry-Clay?'

'It seems that she has completely disappeared.' Agnes suppressed the giggle that rose in her throat as Miss Treen continued, 'You don't happen to have seen her? I'm beginning to wonder if she's gone and found the tunnel this time, and got herself lost.'

'I 'aven't sin her,' Miriam said, 'although . . . can you

see the curtain, the way it trembles without the slightest draught to disturb it?'

Agnes caught her breath. Was she about to be found out?

'I think your imagination has got the better of you.'

'I believe that it has.' Miriam chuckled and Agnes began to relax.

'Oh, but perhaps you're right. Your eyes don't deceive you after all.' Agnes froze as she heard footsteps draw close. 'The tunnel is said to be haunted.'

The drapes flew open and a grey skein of silk fell from the ceiling and landed on Agnes's head. She screamed. She couldn't help it.

'It's only a cobweb,' Nanny said, helping her brush the offending item from her hair. 'I believe that our talk of the tunnel has given you an attack of the frights.'

'No, not at all,' Agnes said, collecting her wits. She was fourteen years old, not a child. She wasn't scared. Not much.

'The spirits of the smugglers haunt the schoolrooms of impressionable young ladies who don't admit the truth at all times,' Nanny said chidingly. She was smiling, though, and Agnes realised that Nanny and Miriam had known exactly where she was all along. It wasn't surprising, because Agnes had used up all the hiding places on the top floor of the house many times over.

'Oh dear, the poor little soul will 'ave nightmares after this,' Miriam said.

'I will not,' Agnes said adamantly. She gazed at the two women. At five foot and one inch in height, Agnes was taller than the maid and shorter than Nanny, who was wearing her uniform of a dark serge dress and black slippers. Nanny's eyes were hazel and ringed with dark lashes, while her hair, the colour of the sienna in Agnes's paintbox, was coiled in a plait around her head with a white cap on top.

Miriam was hardly the epitome of neatness. She had a smut on the end of her upturned nose, her apron was grubby and strands of her blonde hair had fallen from her bun. She was about twenty-five, and Miss Treen had once let slip that she was thirty-seven.

'May I have a go at lighting the fire?' Agnes asked.

'Oh no, miss.' Miriam chuckled. 'That's maid's work. You'll never 'ave to know how to light a fire in your life.'

'But I should like to learn all the same.'

'Nanny wishes you to stick to l'arning from books, don't you, Miss Treen?'

'Indeed I do. Our little miss is to become a lady with more servants than she needs. Although . . .' Nanny paused for a moment. 'It doesn't hurt to know enough to make sure that one's maids are doing the job properly.'

'So I can light it?' Agnes asked, watching Miriam place some dry sticks in the grate.

'No,' Nanny said. 'You will soil your dress.'

Agnes was disappointed.

'I wonder how long the doctor will spend with the mistress,' Miriam said, taking the tinderbox from the mantelpiece and striking the flint. 'Do you think that it's possible after all this time?' The flint sparked and soon a curl of smoke rose from the kindling in the box. Miriam blew on it gently and transferred the flame on a thin taper to the sticks in the grate.

'It's no use asking me – I'm not a medical man,' Nanny said briskly.

'I thought you might 'ave some idea. You are the most l'arned person of my acquaintance.' Agnes, Nanny and Miriam watched as the flame took hold of the sticks.

'That'll do,' Miriam said eventually, and she tipped the coal from the scuttle on top.

'Thank you. Please remove the breakfast dishes.' Nanny

looked towards the mantel clock. 'This will not do. We are already five minutes late for our lessons. Agnes, sit down at your desk. You will practise your letters first.'

As the maid left the room with the tray of breakfast dishes, Agnes sat down and opened the lid of the desk, a miniature version of Papa's, and took out her writing materials: paper, pencil and pen, ink and a wooden rule. She pulled up the upholstered stool, blew on her fingers and began to draw lines across the page. The second line wasn't quite parallel with the first, and in a fit of annoyance she scribbled it out.

'Oh dear,' Nanny sighed. 'It's going to be one of those days. It's only natural to be concerned about your mama, but you mustn't let it get in the way of your lessons. Is there anything you'd like to ask me? I shall answer if I can.'

'Well, yes, I'd like to know if Mama is going to die.'

'My dear child, of course she isn't! There's no danger of that.' Nanny smiled as she placed an open book on the desk. Mama's opinion was that she was suitably plain, but Agnes thought her quite pretty when she smiled. 'I should like you to copy this poem in your best copperplate and curlicue, before committing Mr Wordsworth's verse to memory.'

'Why?' Agnes said. 'Why should I have to learn it when I could read it straight from the book?'

'Really, you are becoming quite rebellious.' Nanny cocked one eyebrow, making Agnes smile. 'Suffice to say, we all have to do things we don't want to do. You would be wise to practise obedience until it becomes a habit. When you marry, you will be required to carry out the duties of the lady of the house without question or complaint.' She walked over to the window seat and sat down to do some sewing.

Agnes tried to concentrate, but the clock was ticking

and the lace on her collar was pricking at her neck. She ruled lines on a second piece of paper, wrote an 'I', and was halfway through 'wandered' when she became aware of a shadow falling across her work. She looked up.

'Are you ready to recite this poem to me? No, I thought not. Make haste, or we will have no time to study geography this week.'

She looked towards the cupboard on the far side of the room where Miss Treen kept the globe locked away. Papa had brought it home with him one day in payment of a debt owed to the brewery and Agnes had fallen in love with it: the colours of the lands and oceans; the names of the magical-sounding places far away. Mama disapproved of geography – she said that young ladies had no need of such knowledge. Their horizons should be limited to accomplishments suitable for the drawing room, such as painting, music and deportment.

Perhaps it was for that reason and because she was always cooped up at Windmarsh Court that geography had become Agnes's favourite subject. The threat of missing out was enough to ensure that she became familiar with Mr Wordsworth's daffodils very quickly. When the clock struck ten, Agnes recited the poem, keeping to the rhythm of the beat of Miss Treen's rule against the desk.

'You spoke that beautifully,' Nanny said when she had finished. 'You will do it again for your parents this evening to demonstrate your progress.'

They were her adoptive parents, not her mother and father by blood. Papa had never kept it a secret from her. He had taken pity on a poor orphan infant dressed in rags whose mama couldn't look after her and brought her back to Windmarsh Court, where he had kept the names Agnes Ivy that had been given to her by her true mother, and honoured her with the surname of Berry-Clay.

'I think they will be very proud of me,' Agnes said.

Nanny frowned and shook her head. 'What did we talk about the other day?'

'Paris?' Agnes said, her thoughts drifting back to the globe.

'We discussed the importance of being humble.'

'Did we?' Agnes felt her forehead tighten as she tried to remember. It was all very well, but what was the point of being deferential when she was only speaking the truth? 'Isn't the truth more important than being humble?'

'My dear child, people warm to those who don't brag about their accomplishments.'

'Mama isn't humble,' Agnes said.

'It isn't our place to offer that opinion,' Nanny corrected her gently, and for that tiny indiscretion, she condemned Agnes to a discussion of etiquette for a whole hour before luncheon.

'This instruction will serve you well in the future,' Nanny said, as though reading her mind. 'I hope that one day you will recall fondly how your nanny taught you how to be the perfect hostess, for I am sure that when you are married, you will entertain all kinds of interesting guests at your house.'

'I don't wish to be married. I should like to become a nanny and governess like you.'

'You are destined for better things.' Nanny smiled ruefully.

'Don't you like being a governess, then?'

'Oh, I like it very much. I have loved you since I first set eyes on you when you were a baby.' Nanny stopped abruptly. 'That's enough. I believe you are trying to distract me from my purpose.' She ran her finger down one of the pages in her book and began to read again. 'A gentleman may take two ladies upon his arms, but under no circumstances should a lady take the arms of two gentlemen.'

'Why should that be so? We are all blessed with two arms,' Agnes said lightly.

'It would be improper for a lady to conduct herself in such a manner. Ladies are expected to behave with decorum. Gentlemen, especially the younger ones, are allowed more latitude when it comes to how they deport themselves.'

'I don't think that's fair.'

'Life isn't always fair, my dear.' She put the book down beside her with its cover facing upwards and its pages spread out. Agnes reached out to pick it up and close it properly as she had been taught, so as not to break its spine. What was wrong with Nanny today?

'Oh, I can't concentrate on etiquette either,' Nanny admitted. 'Why don't you fetch the globe and we will look for the capital city of Italy?'

'Italy?' A frisson of excitement ran down her spine. Mama owned a piece of Italian glass from Murano, a vase that glinted in the sunshine and cast rays of different colours across the windowsill in the drawing room. Its exotic appearance hinted at royal palaces and shimmering heat, far away from the ditches and dykes of the bleak Kentish marshes.

'We will learn about the history of Rome and the canals of Venice.'

'How do you know so many things?'

'I was attentive in lessons at school.'

'Was that the school for downtrodden ladies?' Agnes said, even though she had heard Nanny's stories before.

'It was a charity school run by Mrs Joseph for young ladies whose families had fallen upon hard times.' Nanny touched the corner of her eye as if she was pressing back a tear. 'My poor father lost everything through no fault of his own, God rest his soul.'

Agnes didn't ask about Nanny's mother. She had

broached the subject once before and Miss Treen had become very upset.

'You have an uncle still living. Is he well?'

'Oh yes. I shall visit him and my cousins once removed quite soon.' Miss Treen's mood brightened again. 'Samuel – Mr Cheevers – paid for my education. I'll always be grateful to him for making sure that I acquired the means to make my own way in the world.' She took a key from her pocket and handed it to Agnes, who went to unlock the cupboard.

Her heart beat faster as she wheeled the globe on its brass castors and mahogany stand to the centre of the schoolroom. Nanny lit one of the oil lamps and held it up close to the magnificent painted sphere, illuminating the text inside a circle in the middle of the Atlantic Ocean: *The new Terrestrial Globe, exhibiting the tracks and discoveries made by Captain Cook; Together with every other improvement collected from Various Navigators to the present time.*

'Can you find Italy?' Nanny asked, lighting up the northern hemisphere.

Agnes pointed at the toe of Italy's boot which had kicked Sicily into the Mediterranean Sea.

'You have remembered well,' Nanny said, before going on to tell her about Venice and Rome, the Sistine Chapel, the mountains and lakes.

'May I look at another place?' Agnes asked when they had exhausted Italy.

'One more.'

Agnes spun the globe and stopped it with her fingers straddling the Indian and Pacific oceans. She leaned in close and read the names of the nearest countries.

'Australia,' she said slowly, 'and Tasmania.'

'Oh no.' Nanny leaned across and forcibly turned the globe back with Europe uppermost. 'We won't be studying those. They are too far away to be of interest.'

'I think I should find them at least as fascinating as Italy,' Agnes protested. Even more so now that Nanny had drawn her attention to them by her reaction.

'No, I have very little knowledge of those' – Nanny flicked her hand as if to push the globe away – 'distant lands.' Agnes stepped back, astounded. It was the first time that Miss Treen had ever admitted to a gap in her learning. 'We must put the globe away. Immediately.'

They wheeled it back into the cupboard, then Nanny locked the door and put the key around her neck. Miriam delivered soup, ham and bread to the schoolroom.

Agnes returned to the nursery next door to wash her hands, catching sight of her reflection in the mirror above the washstand. Sometimes her eyes looked green, sometimes hazel, depending on the light. Her mouth, she thought, was too wide, but her nose was small and her cheekbones high and well shaped. She ran a brush through her wavy dark brown hair, wishing that it was lighter, more like Miriam's. She yearned for some womanly curves and a time when she didn't have to wear her skirts to just below the knee.

As she returned to the schoolroom she overheard Nanny and Miriam talking.

'The master has sent for a second doctor, would you believe?' the maid said, and Agnes's throat tightened. Mama had to be very sick to require the services of more than one medical man.

'But why? Cannot Doctor Shaw give an opinion?' Nanny demanded.

'Apparently, the mistress is not satisfied with his diagnosis.'

'What did he say?'

'We don't know.' Miriam's voice dropped to a whisper. 'Mrs Catchpole has bin plotting to find out.'

'I beg you not to be part of the housekeeper's plan,' Miss Treen said. 'I'm sure we will find out what was said soon enough.'

Miriam left the schoolroom and Nanny said grace. She and Agnes ate in silence then rested for half an hour to aid the digestion before going for a walk across the marsh. The sun was already low in the sky and the light was growing dimpsy when they set out by the back door, crossed the yard and entered the kitchen garden.

Agnes glanced back towards the imposing mass of Windmarsh Court with its brick walls, tiled roof and numerous chimney pots. The southern aspect of the house, on the advice of the architect who had designed it many years ago, had no windows to prevent the Black Death gaining entry on the prevailing winds. Fortunately, he had compensated for the lack of light by including tall arched windows to the grand rooms on the first floor on the other three sides in his plans.

At the far end of the kitchen garden, beyond the rows of winter cabbages and raspberry canes, they passed through the gate in the wall and stepped on to the path. The tang of salt and cold air caught Agnes by the throat, making her cough.

She tucked her hands inside her fur muff and set out along the embankment across the marsh. They went through the hamlet of Windmarsh, passing the church, two houses and a row of cottages built from grey Kentish ragstone and flint on the way, and back along the road beside the long, reed-lined ditch of brackish water to the house. They took the same route every day since her parents forbade any deviation from it. Mama had a fear of strangers. She didn't like open spaces and crowds. In fact, she rarely left the house. Papa said they should keep to familiar paths to avoid mishaps, whatever those might be. Nanny had explained that he was being protective of his daughter, just as any other father would.

They returned indoors. Agnes left her outdoor shoes in the boot room and put on her slippers, then caught up with Nanny in the kitchen. The oak dresser held an abundance of plates, fish kettles and a colander, and a meat chopper and a brass pot of skewers glinted from the table. Cook was standing red-faced over a pan that threatened to bubble over on the range, while the scullery maid wielded the bellows over the flames in the hearth.

'How was your walk, miss?' Mrs Nidget said, looking up from the pan.

'It was very cold,' Agnes said. 'I should like some hot chocolate.'

'A "please" wouldn't go amiss,' Nanny muttered from beside her.

'Please,' Agnes added petulantly.

'Of course you can, ducky. I'll send it up to the nursery with some freshly baked scones and lemon curd.' Mrs Nidget had eyes like raisins, set deep above her doughy cheeks. She was almost as wide as she was tall, but Agnes had privately concluded that her ample figure bore no relation to the quality of her cooking.

'I fear that you are spoiling the child,' Nanny said, removing her gloves.

'It isn't me. If you want my opinion, it's the way she's being brought up. She has everything she can possibly need, and more, but no friends her own age.'

'I didn't ask for your views, thank you,' Nanny said.

Mrs Nidget shrugged.

Not for the first time, Agnes noticed the tension between the two women. She felt sorry for Nanny, who didn't quite fit in with either the servants or the family. It wasn't her fault – it was due to her position in the household, not her character.

'I was wondering if there was any news – the doctor?'

'Oh, that?' Cook scooped up some stew and sucked it noisily out of her ladle. 'I should 'ave thought you would 'ave bin the first to know, the way the family favours you.' She smiled, but it wasn't a friendly smile, Agnes thought. 'If the rumours are true, your position here will be secure for many years to come. I don't know what it will mean for our young lady here.'

'It won't change anything. She will be loved just the same for her disposition, which never fails to bring sunshine to a dull day and a smile to everyone's faces,' Nanny said. 'So it is true, Mrs Nidget? The doctor has confirmed it?'

'Mr Turner overheard the master congratulating the mistress on her news.' Turner was the butler who did everything from managing the indoor servants to ironing Papa's newspapers in the morning. He was also in charge of the safe.

Mrs Catchpole, the housekeeper, was supposed to be responsible for running the household, subject to the mistress's instructions, but it was Turner and Mrs Nidget who ruled the roost at Windmarsh Court.

'I don't know how it is possible after all this time, and at her age,' Cook said. 'She is forty years old.'

'God has answered her prayers at last.'

'I don't think He had much to do with it.' Mrs Nidget gave a coarse laugh.

Nanny frowned with displeasure as Cook went on, 'I'm planning some new dishes to help the mistress keep her strength up. I've ordered oranges and lemons for a posset served with a dainty sugared almond shortbread. What do you think of that?'

'I think that you will bankrupt the Berry-Clays,' Nanny said.

'They are made of money. It pours into the master's hands on tap like the beer that flows from the brewery. We aren't doing anything wrong. The mistress doesn't like to be worried by trivial matters. She trusts us to do right by the family. She's never complained, not once.' Cook gave Nanny a long, hard stare. 'You'll keep your nose out of my business if you know what's good for you.'

Agnes shrank back, shocked at the way Mrs Nidget had spoken to her governess.

'I thought Cook was rather impolite,' she ventured as she and Nanny made their way upstairs to the schoolroom on the third floor.

'She is no lady. She is without manners, breeding or education,' Nanny agreed. 'You, however, should have more delicacy than to criticise your elders. Children should be seen, not heard.'

Agnes sighed inwardly at the expectation that she should behave like one of her dolls, sitting in perfect silence on the shelf in the schoolroom. Nanny was much stricter than anyone else she knew.

After the hot chocolate and scones, she practised reciting the poem she had learned in the morning and read quietly for a while before a meal of chicken and potato stew that didn't taste of anything at all.

The mantel clock chimed five and then six.

'Look at the time!' Nanny exclaimed. 'Wash your hands and face, and brush your hair. Quickly. We mustn't keep your mama and papa waiting.'

Agnes didn't take a second bidding.

She loved all the rooms on the middle floor of the house, their extravagant decoration in marked contrast to the starkness of the nursery and schoolroom. In the drawing room, a fire danced in the marble hearth, bringing the cherubs carved into the mantel above to life. Gold and turquoise brocade drapes hung across the tall windows and rich tapestries decorated the walls. There were chairs with sumptuous upholstery, a chaise longue for Mama, a gleaming piano and all kinds of trinkets and curios that Papa's grandfather had brought back from the voyages he made around the world upon his retirement from the brewery.

The precious Italian glass vase had been removed to the safety of a side table when the drapes had been closed for the evening, and the candle that flickered in the sconce above scattered rainbow fragments on to the cloth on which it stood.

Dodging the clutter and ignoring Miss Treen's pleas for decorum, Agnes made straight for her father who was sitting in his leather armchair, dressed in a jacket and patterned cravat. He was tall with wide shoulders, flamboyant copper hair and a beard.

She threw her arms around his neck, catching his scent of malt and cigar smoke.

'Agnes, you are getting far too old for that,' her mother sighed. She reminded Agnes of the Snow Queen in a fairy tale Nanny had once read to her. Her long fair hair was caught back from her thin face by two silver combs and she was wearing a pale grey bodice and skirt, lace undersleeves and an ivory shawl with a sparkling silver thread running through it. She was very beautiful, but her frozen features rarely softened to a smile, and her touch was like ice.

'Mama, are you sick?' Agnes asked.

'I'm so sorry, Mrs Berry-Clay. Please, miss, come here,' she heard Nanny say in vain.

'Don't worry, my dearest child. Your mother is quite well,' Papa said. 'Nanny, let her be a child for a little while longer. She'll have to grow up all too soon.'

Reassured as to Mama's state of health, Agnes pulled away from her father and took up position in the middle of the room.

'I'm going to recite a poem for you,' she said, and without hesitation, she straightened her spine, took a deep breath and plunged in.

'Never was the word "daffodil" enunciated in such a clear and enthusiastic way,' said Papa admiringly when she had finished. Agnes smiled at his glowing praise. She knew he was exaggerating, but that was what he always did, as though he was deliberately compensating for Mama's more critical appraisal of her talents.

'It was decidedly average,' Mama said, patting her hair into place. 'What would Mr Wordsworth think upon hearing his delightful words put through the mangle like that? I'm sure I would have taught you to recite with far more expression.'

But you didn't, Agnes thought. Mama had this way of hurting her feelings, implying that she wasn't good enough to be her daughter.

'How can you say that?' Papa said. 'How can two pairs of ears hear so differently? I heard the voice of an angel.'

'Really, James. You do exaggerate.' Mama pouted.

Papa stood up and walked across to his wife. He stood beside the chaise and rested his hand on her shoulder.

'There, my dear Louisa, you have every reason to be distracted. Why don't you tell Agnes our wonderful news?'

'What is it?' Agnes said. 'Are we going to Italy?'

'Where did you get that idea from, you peculiar creature?' Mama said.

'Perhaps I should leave,' Nanny said.

'You may stay,' Mama said. 'This announcement concerns you.'

'There will soon be a new arrival in the house,' Papa said, beaming.

'A puppy?' Agnes had always wanted a lapdog.

Mama touched her stomach where the sides of her bodice met at a point at the front.

'I have had my suspicions for a while, and now not one, but two doctors have confirmed that I am with child.' She had dark circles beneath her eyes and her complexion, which was always fashionably pale, looked whiter than ever, but a smile played on her lips. 'I never thought I would live to see this day. I thank God for this miracle.'

'In a few months' time, Agnes, you will have a baby brother or sister,' Papa explained, but it didn't help.

Mama said she was with child, but Agnes couldn't see a child anywhere. She was confused. Having led such a sheltered life at Windmarsh Court, she had no idea about babies and where they came from.

'Pay attention to your father,' Mama said.

'I said, you'll have a brother or sister,' Papa repeated.

'Oh, I'd like a sister, please.' She clapped her hands together with delight.

'No, it is a boy. I am certain of it,' Mama said.

'It would be better all round if that was the case,' Papa said.

'Indeed.' Mama's voice was suddenly brittle with resentment. 'My husband has put me in a situation where, if he should die without a son, the brewery will pass to his brother and then his brother's elder son, and I shall be dependent on their generosity and a small annual income given to me by my parents upon my marriage. It is a sorry state of affairs which has caused me much anxiety in the past.'

'I have no intention of dying for a very long time, but if anything should happen, our son will inherit the brewery. Don't fret. I am but fifty-two years old. My father was hale and hearty until he was eighty-three.' Papa slapped his thigh with delight. 'My brother will be one of the first to congratulate us, I'm certain.'

'May I offer you my felicitations,' Nanny said calmly.

'Felicitations accepted,' Papa guffawed. 'Of course, we will continue to require your services until the boy is eight, when he will go to school.'

'Thank you, sir.' Agnes could hear the relief in her governess's voice.

'Can I go to school?' she asked.

'No, Agnes,' Mama said.

'Why not, Mama?'

'What sensible young lady would wish to go to school in preference to remaining here at Windmarsh Court with her mama and papa and Nanny's excellent teaching?' Papa said, but no one gave her time to reply.

'Nanny, remove Agnes to the nursery,' Mama said. 'Mr Berry-Clay and I have much to discuss.'

'Kisses first.' Papa pointed to his whiskery cheek. Agnes stepped up and kissed him as she always did. She walked across to kiss Mama, who turned away as she always did, and then she followed Nanny back to the nursery.

'Where is the baby now?' Agnes asked when she was getting ready for bed. 'How do they know it will be a boy?'

'They don't,' Nanny said sternly. 'It is wishful thinking. It's just as likely to be a girl.'

'Who will bring it to the house?' Agnes thought she recalled one of her cousins telling her that there was a stork that delivered babies.

'It is far too delicate a subject for a young lady's ears and one that shouldn't be discussed until the day of her marriage.'

'I imagine it is painful.'

'I beg your pardon?' Nanny's eyes widened with apparent shock, quickly veiled.

'I mean the way that the baby is dropped down the chimney. I'm glad that we don't remember that part.' Agnes changed the subject. 'Will Mama and Papa still love me?'

'Of course they will. What a strange thing to say! They have always loved you as their daughter, and always will. That will never change. When they adopted you as a baby, they took you on as their own. No one could have been more delighted with you than your papa.'

'And Mama?'

'She was happy too.'

'How could she be when she really wanted a boy?'

'She would have loved a boy or a girl equally.' Agnes wasn't sure that Nanny was convinced. 'Goodnight, Agnes. Sweet dreams.'

As soon as her head touched the fragrant, lavender-scented pillow, she fell asleep, reassured that she would soon have a companion in the nursery, someone she could call her brother, and her life would carry on as before, but with more joy in it.

# Chapter Two

## *The Golden Linnet*

Winter turned into spring and Nanny's enthusiasm for geography did not return. In spite of Agnes's entreaties the globe remained locked in the cupboard. The weather grew warmer, the marsh turned green, and the sheep grazed with their lambs gambolling around them. In May, preparations began in earnest for the birth of the son who would eventually inherit Windmarsh Court.

Agnes and Nanny were obliged to move to freshly whitewashed bedrooms, converted from the attic storage area where Papa had stowed unused furniture and possessions that were too precious to throw away, yet too ugly or damaged to put on display. The schoolroom remained the same, but the original night and day nurseries were redecorated, and a cot installed with soft cotton sheets and knitted blankets.

One morning at the beginning of June, Miriam was delivering breakfast while Agnes was getting dressed. She could see her across the landing, wiping her hands on her apron.

''Ave you heard the gossip?'

'You know I don't listen to telltales.' Nanny was smiling as Miriam continued anyway.

'You may recall that the doctor was sent for last week.'

'And the week before that, if I remember rightly,' Nanny

said. 'The doctor has been called out every time the mistress has sneezed or suffered the slightest alteration in her nerves.'

'She is better now. Doctor Shaw blamed her illness on Cook for serving up undercooked chicken pie, and now Cook is up in arms. Apparently, the master has heard that the French style of cooking is in fashion. He's most determined that the mistress will not 'ave to suffer food poisoning for a second time and wishes his son to 'ave the best start possible. To that end he has found a French cook. If the monsieur is agreeable, then Cook will be dismissed forthwith.'

'A monsieur?' Nanny gasped. 'A man in the kitchen? That is most improper. That won't do. The mistress will never allow it.'

'He has bin employed in the best kitchens in Paris.'

'Why on earth would he choose to come to Windmarsh, then, if not to cause trouble among the maids?' Agnes frowned, wondering what kind of trouble Nanny meant. 'What is Mr Berry-Clay thinking of? Children require plain fare, not fancy foods that will inflame their tempers and palates. No confectionery, fresh fruit or puffed pastries.'

'Well, I'm looking forward to something other than dry roasts and soggy cabbage,' Miriam said. 'I like a bit of fat on my meat and the juice left running through it.'

Agnes began to feel hungry as Miriam went on, 'I don't know what poor Mrs Nidget will do.'

'She has a sister in Faversham. I expect she will stay with her until she finds another position, which may depend upon the mistress providing her with a character,' Nanny said. 'Is the monthly nurse here yet?'

'She arrived from London late last night. She is sleeping in one of the guest rooms until her room is ready. Her name is Mrs Pargeter.'

'I shall find it hard to have another woman sharing my domain,' Nanny murmured.

'I'd better go before Mrs Catchpole starts wondering where I am,' Miriam said. 'By the way, don't let Miss Agnes stir the porridge today – it's burned to a crisp underneath.'

Agnes wished for a breakfast like Papa's: fillets of beef and game pies, boiled eggs; bread, jams, orange marmalade and fruits in season. She wondered what a French breakfast would be like.

She asked Papa the question later that day when she met him for their customary hour in the drawing room. Mama was there as well, having been absent on the previous two occasions. Agnes sat down on one of the Chesterfield fireside chairs opposite her father while her mother reclined on the chaise, her figure draped with layers of skirts and a pleated bodice that appeared to have been let out to accommodate her belly.

'Nanny said that it would be café au lait and petits pains or bavaroises.'

'Did she? Well, I'm not sure what those things are, apart from the coffee. I regret that I didn't take full advantage of my education. School was something which had to be endured.' Papa turned away and called for the butler, who appeared from the room beyond in his white gloves, carrying a large object covered with a black cloth. 'I have bought you a present. I saw it on my way through the market today and thought of you.'

'Oh, Papa, thank you.'

'You haven't seen what it is yet. You might not like it,' he chuckled. 'Turner, place it on the table.'

'What is it?'

Papa nodded to the butler who took the top of the cloth and whisked it away with a flourish to reveal a brass cage with a scalloped top, and a small bird perched on a twig inside it.

'Oh, how pretty!' Agnes's heart filled with joy and gratitude.

'For you, my dear child.' She noticed how Papa didn't call her his dearest child as he'd used to. 'It is a golden linnet,' he added as she peered at the bird. She – she wanted it to be a girl – was brightly coloured with red, white and black feathers on her head, a golden body and white belly and her wings were adorned with bands of yellow. The bird chirruped and sang. 'Listen to how sweetly it sings.'

'Oh, James, you spoil that child,' Mama complained. 'Don't forget that you will have a son to buy gifts for soon.'

Agnes felt hurt at her mother's comment. She had been mean to her many times before, but she was beginning to make her feel distinctly unwanted.

'I hope you aren't suggesting that I treat them any differently, apart from giving presents that are appropriate for their sex,' Papa said.

'They are different, by virtue of Agnes being an adopted child. The infant will be ours through and through.'

Papa's beard seemed to bristle with resentment.

'We will consider them as full brother and sister, the Master and Miss Berry-Clay. Please don't strain yourself by making yourself disagreeable to your husband. Remember the infant that grows inside you and treat him with some consideration, or he will be born with a sour look on his face.'

Mama fell silent, but she sat sucking on her lip as if she still had plenty that she wanted to say.

'We have never hidden the fact that you are adopted from you, Agnes,' Papa went on. 'Can you remember what we've told you?'

'Yes. You chose me to be your daughter, Papa. The lady who was my mama couldn't look after me so you gave me a home at Windmarsh.'

'That is correct,' Papa said.

'Where is my other mama?' The promise of a new sibling had made Agnes think about her own parents. No one had ever talked about the mother and father who had given her up. When she had asked, the conversation had always been broken off or the subject abruptly changed.

'She is gone. Dead, my dear Agnes,' he said softly. 'I'm sorry.'

'Oh?' She was overwhelmed with a wave of sadness. 'And my other papa?' She assumed that she had one.

'Both of your parents are dead and buried. You have us now. Let's have no more thought of them.'

'But who were they?' She needed to know who these mysterious people were.

'It doesn't matter. Suffice to say that you could be the daughter of a baronet or descended from royalty, but whatever the circumstances of your birth, you are being brought up to be a lady.'

'And shall I marry a prince?' she said, smiling. She felt a vague sadness that her other parents were gone, but they had left her the legacy of intelligence, good humour and the knowledge that she had been high born, because Papa had said so.

He smiled. 'You will need to wed a prince to keep you in the lifestyle to which you have become accustomed. Your mother has expensive tastes and a profligate manner of spending.' His voice hardened when he turned to Mama. 'I saw the bills from the tradesmen today. Don't you think that the cost of refitting the nursery was somewhat extortionate? I'm sure that it could have been done for less.

Why did you need wallpaper from London when a fresh coat of whitewash would have sufficed?'

'Cream damask is quite the rage,' Mama countered.

'For a fleeting moment until printed flowers or Flemish tapestries become à la mode. I noticed that Cook was wearing a rather pretty lace collar – it reminded me of one I'd seen you wearing recently.'

'I gave some of my old things to the servants.'

'It looked brand new.'

Mama shrugged. 'I can't help it if my preference for a particular style has altered. James, I'm finding this talk of money quite vulgar.'

'I'm asking you to make small economies where and when you can, that is all. I'm not telling you to go around in rags. We have a good income, but there are investments to be made in new machinery and adaptations to the brew house.'

'Are you saying the brewery is no longer profitable?'

'No, I'm not.' Papa sounded exasperated. 'Oh, how I hate to talk about business at home! This is supposed to be my haven of peace and repose. But it is important. Let's speak of this again after our son has been safely delivered into the world. I remember that the doctor has said that your nerves must be made a priority.'

'So has Mrs Pargeter. If she had her way I would be locked away in my room. She has been here less than one day and she is driving me to distraction with her attentions – the windows have had to be sandbagged against draughts, the baby clothes have had to be laundered three times and Mrs Catchpole has to direct all her enquiries about the running of the household through her,' Mama said sulkily.

Agnes smiled to herself. She had thought that her mother would have been delighted to have an excuse for laying abed all day.

'Talking of household matters,' Mama went on, 'is there any news of the French cook?'

'I have sent him a letter inviting him to meet me at the brewery at the end of the week to discuss terms.'

'I do hope he will agree. You have persuaded me that French cuisine is much superior to the English way of cooking.'

'Nanny says that it is all garlic and snails,' Agnes said, wrinkling her nose at the thought.

'Hush,' Nanny whispered, reminding her of her presence. She seemed to have blended into the background like part of the furniture, and the Berry-Clays weren't at all concerned about speaking in front of her.

'We must hold a dinner party soon for your brother and his wife, and our neighbours,' Mama said.

Agnes felt ignored. Rejected.

'Let us not be in too much of a rush. Monsieur hasn't accepted my offer yet. And you must consult with the guard dog—' Agnes noticed how Mama raised one eyebrow and Papa corrected himself, 'Mrs Pargeter – the occasion of hosting a dinner party is too much for your constitution at the best of times.'

Agnes sat in silence, listening to her parents and watching the bird. This was supposed to be their time for her, but Mama and Papa seemed too wrapped up in their own affairs. She felt quite cross with them.

Eventually, the clock on the mantel chimed seven times, signalling that it was time for her to leave. Papa called for the butler to carry the birdcage upstairs.

'Thank you again, Papa, but I wonder if you should take it back to the market,' Agnes said.

'What are you saying?' He frowned. 'Don't you like it after all?'

'No, I love it, but wasn't it rather expensive? I shouldn't

like to end up poor. I heard you talking to Mama about the brewery.'

Papa's lips curved into a smile before he broke into loud laughter.

'Oh, don't let that conversation worry your head. It's very thoughtful of you, offering to return my gift, but we have more than enough riches to cover the price of a bird and gilded cage. You will never be poor, I promise. Goodnight, Agnes.'

'Goodnight, Papa.' She wished Mama the same and returned to the nursery, reassured by her father's words, but her peace of mind was soon broken, for in the middle of the night, the whole house awoke to the sound of an eerie scream.

She scrambled out of bed, her first thought being that it was one of the ghostly smugglers come to haunt them. Her second was that something terrible had happened to the bird. She made her way to the schoolroom where the butler had left the cage. As her eyes grew accustomed to the darkness, she saw that the linnet was asleep on her perch with her head to one side and her feathers fluffed up. She sprinkled some of the seed that the butler had left on a plate on the mantel and placed the cloth back over the cage as Nanny, looking flustered and dressed in her nightgown, joined her. The candle she was carrying flickered and went out.

Another scream pierced the darkness, making Agnes almost jump out of her skin.

'What's that noise?' she whispered.

'I believe that it was one of Heaven's angels heralding the arrival of the mistress's son.'

'Oh? How does that happen?'

'You will find out one day,' Nanny said as Miriam came hurrying in to the room with a small lantern.

'Everything is upside down and inside out,' she exclaimed. 'Mrs Pargeter has the whole household on its feet, running errands. Turner has sent Mr Noakes with the carriage for the doctor, and the footman to the cellar for fresh supplies of brandy. Cook is making gruel and the other maids are collecting clean sheets and hot water. Oh my, I can't for the life of me remember what I'm here for.' She paused for a moment. 'That's it. Mrs Pargeter wants me to light the fire in the mistress's room and I've come to look for spills.'

'That seems rather wasteful, a fire in June, but I suppose that these are exceptional circumstances,' Nanny said. 'Please, let me light my candle.'

'Of course.' Miriam opened the door on the lantern. Nanny placed the wick of her candle in the flame where it sputtered back to life. 'The mistress is about to deliver her child.'

'I fear that it may take some time. My dearly departed mama laboured for two whole days—' Nanny stopped abruptly.

'The poor lady,' Miriam said. 'I don't wish for children of my own.'

'The gift of a child is a blessing. If I could marry and bear a child, I would undergo any trial or tribulation.' Nanny touched the corner of her eye.

She was crying, Agnes realised with astonishment. Nanny had mastered the art of controlling her emotions to such an extent that her pupil had wondered if she actually ever felt anything at all. She suppressed an impulse to reach out and comfort her.

'I'm sorry to 'ave upset you,' Miriam said quickly.

'It's all right. I'm content with looking after other people's children, but there are occasions such as this when I wish . . . Oh, what does it matter? There is nothing that can be done.' Nanny cleared her throat. 'There will be much joy and celebration when Agnes's brother is here. We are all looking forward to having an infant at Windmarsh Court.'

'I had better be on my way,' Miriam said, hurrying off.

'Dearie me, she has forgotten the spills after all that,' Nanny said. 'Run after her with them, will you?'

Agnes grabbed a handful of twisted papers from the spill-box and caught up with the maid at the end of the landing.

'Here you are,' she said, placing them in Miriam's hand.

'Thank you, miss. I'm all of a flap.'

There was another bloodcurdling scream that sent Agnes fleeing back to the schoolroom.

'Mama is dying,' she sobbed.

'Calm yourself,' Nanny said. 'She is quite well. It is perfectly natural.'

'She is in pain. Why? It is inhuman.'

Agnes couldn't help wondering if Queen Victoria had suffered in the same way when she had produced her eighth child a couple of months earlier. It didn't seem possible to contemplate having one child – let alone an eighth – if it caused such agony.

'We should go out for a walk,' Nanny decided. 'Make haste. Get dressed and meet me downstairs.'

'It is dark,' Agnes observed.

'Dawn is about to break.'

Agnes didn't even brush her hair. She put on her clothes and ran down the first flight of stairs, her heart pounding. In spite of Nanny's reassurances, she was convinced that both Mama and the infant were going to die. She hadn't wanted a brother, but now that God was about to take him up to Heaven, she was distraught.

As she reached the landing, she caught the sound of a

stranger's voice coming from the doorway into Mama's room.

'You look as though you are in need of some medical attention for yourself, Mr Berry-Clay.'

'Please don't concern yourself with me, Doctor Shaw. I'm worried for my wife and child. I wish I had done as Mrs Pargeter asked and stayed at my place of business overnight, leaving this to the women.'

'It is a worrying time for all, especially when labour accelerates precipitously as it has in this case, but be assured that I shall do all that I can.'

'Is there anything that can be done for the pain? She is suffering terribly. I can't bear to hear her like this. She is normally very self-contained.'

'There are some obstetric surgeons who are beginning to recommend chloroform, but it is my firm belief that we should not interfere. If God had wished labour to be painless, he would have created it so. Mr Berry-Clay, I suggest that you retire to your study, take a draught of brandy and wait.'

'What do you think the outcome will be? Please tell me. I'm not going to lose them, am I?'

'I cannot say. Let me go and attend to your wife.'

'Yes, of course. I'm sorry. I mustn't delay you for a moment longer.'

Feeling guilty for eavesdropping and panicked further by her father's exchange with the doctor, Agnes hurried on down the second flight of stairs and the third to the ground floor. She met Nanny outside the boot room. She was holding a pair of outdoor shoes. Agnes took them and put them on, her fingers trembling as she tied the laces.

They went out together and walked in silence as the sky turned pastel blue and the sun began to spread its golden rays across the surface of the water of the estuary. What were they going to find on their return?

'Can you hear anything?' Agnes asked when they arrived at the rear of the house where the ivy had taken a firm grip on the brickwork around the back door and sent suckers crawling up to the first-floor windows.

Nanny paused to listen and shook her head. She pushed the door open. Agnes stepped inside, hardly daring to breathe. She could hear the sound of voices from the kitchen along the corridor: laughter; the whistle of a kettle; the chinking of glasses.

'Well, I never did.' Nanny's lips curved into a smile, and Agnes's breast flooded with relief.

They hastened to the kitchen where they found Cook and the maids in high spirits.

'Please, someone put us out of our misery,' Nanny said. 'It's good news?'

'The mistress has bin delivered of a son – they are both doing well.' Cook placed a tray of loaves fresh from the bread oven on the table, and raised a glass.

'Thanks be to God,' Nanny exclaimed. She turned to Agnes and embraced her, temporarily forgetting to behave with restraint.

'I have a brother.' Agnes couldn't stop smiling. 'I can't wait to meet him.'

'All in good time.' Nanny took a step back. 'Mrs Nidget, we would like eggs on toast and slices of cake served in the schoolroom. And some tea, please.'

'It's a little inconvenient – we are celebrating. Mr Turner thought the master would be more than happy to let him serve a little wine on this occasion.'

'We cannot wait. Agnes is growing pale for want of sustenance. She didn't have breakfast because of the excitement of the morning.'

'I will see what I can do.' Cook sighed and called the

scullery maid who was chopping vegetables to stop and put some eggs on to boil.

'I don't want to eat,' Agnes said. 'I wish to meet my brother.'

'You will have to wait until your mama says that you can.'

'Oh?' Her heart sank. She was aching to see him and could only pick at the rubbery eggs on toast when it was brought upstairs.

Nanny gave her a long, hard stare.

'Be patient,' she said. 'Life will return to normal soon enough.'

But it didn't.

Later the same afternoon, Mrs Pargeter came bustling into the schoolroom.

'That bird can't stay in here – it is injurious to health. Miss Treen, I should have thought you would have known better.'

'Mr Berry-Clay thought fit to give the bird to Agnes yesterday and we have remained quite well.' Nanny was being sarcastic, Agnes decided.

'Please don't question my authority – the nursery is my domain while I'm at Windmarsh Court. I have full responsibility for what goes on in here. The infant is my priority and he will be moving to his quarters tonight. The mistress needs her rest. No, this will not do.' She swept through in her wide skirts, and within half an hour, Agnes found herself and Nanny and the bird removed to a spare guest room where they spent the rest of the afternoon making it their own, with the help of the butler and the footman who were charged with moving the furniture to the new schoolroom.

'I suppose we will have to make do,' Nanny said crossly as she yanked at the curtains and forced the windows open.

Agnes was torn between siding with Nanny and the frisson of excitement that she felt about their move. She liked the idea of a change of scene to counter the dull routine of her daily life.

'If Mrs Pargeter is bringing the infant to the nursery, we will be able to meet him,' she said hopefully.

'I don't think she will allow it. She will make some excuse that she needs time and space to establish baby's routines. She will say the doctor has ordered peace and quiet.'

'When is she leaving Windmarsh?'

'Soon, I hope. Oh, don't listen to me. I am a little out of sorts. She is here for at least one month, but who knows what your parents will decide? They are already gone quite mad, talking of this French chef – rich food is unsuitable for a child's digestive system as well as his morals.' She turned to where Mr Turner and the footman were carrying the globe into the room. 'You could have left that behind, but now that it's here, it can go beside Agnes's desk.'

'We'll be able to travel the world again,' Agnes said, delighted. She ran and sent it spinning, but there was something wrong with it: someone had stuck a piece of brown paper across the southern hemisphere. 'Oh, what has happened to it?'

'I've covered the places that we don't need to study,' Nanny said. 'I didn't want them to remain a distraction.'

Agnes frowned. What was the point in hiding them when she remembered exactly what they were?

'We will review Paris,' Nanny said, but Paris no longer held any magic. All Agnes wanted was to meet her brother. She heard him crying at night when she was trying to sleep. She heard him crying during the day when Mrs Pargeter was running him back and forth to Mama's room. She saw him once, just the copper glint of his hair peeking out from his white swaddling clothes, as the nurse carried him past her on the stairs.

*

It was a whole week after her baby brother's birth and Agnes was wondering if her parents had completely forgotten her, when they called her to the drawing room.

'I told you to be patient,' Nanny said when they went downstairs at the allotted time, but it was easy for her to say, Agnes thought. She was pretty sure that Nanny had managed to slip away and see the new arrival on the sly.

She rushed straight into the drawing room without knocking.

'Good evening,' Papa said jovially, standing up from his fireside chair to greet them. 'Come and meet your brother, Henry James Robert Berry-Clay.' He held out his hand towards Mama, who was sitting in the chair opposite with the sleeping infant in her arms.

'Oh!' Agnes suppressed a cry of joy, not wanting to wake him. She had thought she would hate him, but he was the sweetest-looking creature she had ever seen with his shock of carroty hair and pale lashes that gleamed like pure gold. With his snub nose, pouty lips and smooth skin, he reminded her of the cherubs that were carved into the mantel. She turned back to her governess. 'Isn't he adorable?'

'He is very handsome indeed,' Nanny agreed before making an excuse to leave the room.

'Can I hold him?' Agnes asked.

'I don't think so – I fear that you might drop him,' Mama said.

'Mama, please,' she begged.

'No. Don't argue with me, Agnes. It's unseemly.'

The baby yawned and opened his eyes.

'James, ring for Mrs Pargeter,' Mama said quickly. 'She must take him now. I can't stand to hear him cry. You know how it upsets me.'

'I wish you would comfort the infant in your arms,

Louisa, as you used to do with Agnes at the beginning,' Papa said. 'Even at the Union I've seen mothers cleaving to their children with deep affection. And in the poorest homes, the people seem happier than us, the children running about freely and engaging at will with their parents. The interaction isn't always loving, but more often than not there is laughter and demonstration of a deep attachment between all members of the family.'

'You spend too much time with those wretches,' Mama said, giving Agnes a sideways glance. 'Don't let their base behaviour bring you down to their level. We have standards, and I should like to maintain them in the proper manner. The child will return to the care of Mrs Pargeter immediately.'

Papa looked downcast. He picked up a brass bell from the side table and shook it. Its deep jangle brought Mrs Pargeter into the room within an instant. As the baby began to sob, she scooped him from Mama's faltering grasp and took him away.

'I should have liked to have spent more time with Henry,' Agnes said.

'There will be plenty of time for that,' Papa said before turning to Mama. 'I wish you would take more rest. Doctor Shaw recommended that you remain in bed for a full two weeks.'

'I should like to dine with my husband this evening. That Pargeter woman is tiresome. I don't think I can put up with her for much longer.'

'You are happy enough to hand Henry over to her,' Papa pointed out. 'Her being here enables you to recover and not be overburdened. She will stay until Henry is old enough to pass into Miss Treen's capable hands.'

'She is a treasure,' Mama said. 'Do you think she will manage with the baby and the older one?'

The older one? She means me, Agnes thought.

'I know of nannies who look after several children at once. She shouldn't find it too arduous.'

'That's true. She has had it easy for a long while, and it would benefit Agnes. She has become quite self-absorbed recently.'

Papa turned to Agnes. 'You don't mind sharing your governess when Henry's a little older, do you?'

It was a statement rather than a question. Agnes shook her head, not wanting to defy her dear father, but she did mind. Very much. In her opinion, Henry should have had his own nanny. Why should she share Miss Treen with anyone else?

She soon found that she had no choice. From then on life revolved around Henry's comfort, not hers. She had been displaced and hidden from view – as far as Mama was concerned, at least. Papa still loved her, she thought, but he had to share his affection between his children. It was hard for her to accept.

Even the bird seemed unhappy about the new situation. The more that Agnes listened to her song and watched her fluttering around the cage, a few tiny feathers floating down to the cage floor each time she flew into the bars, the less sure she was that she could describe the bird's frantic trilling as pretty. It made her uneasy to hear another living creature singing her heart out as though she was calling to the other finches outside, begging for her freedom.

In spite of all the care and attention lavished upon him, Henry didn't stop crying. One evening when he was four weeks old, Agnes was trying to sleep with him bawling from the nursery across the landing. When she slipped out of bed to see if there was anything that could be done, she found Nanny and Mrs Pargeter having a difference of opinion at the nursery door.

'I wish the mistress hadn't given him up to be fed by bottle,' Nanny was saying. 'It is never satisfactory and this only goes to prove it. He has terrible colic, the poor little mite. I've heard that a little gin and rosehip syrup helps to improve matters.'

'You are quite wrong in your opinion. From my extensive experience, infants do just as well whichever way they are nursed. As for the suggested remedy, I wouldn't recommend it.'

Henry continued to cry from his crib.

'One of us should go to him,' Nanny insisted. 'I can't stand to hear him cry like that.'

'I forbid you to attend to him. The moral duty must be taught early – when baby cries, he must be left to cry, not learn to demand.'

'Would the bird soothe Henry's nerves with her singing?' Agnes interrupted.

'He is too young to have nerves,' Mrs Pargeter said scathingly.

'Go back to bed, young lady,' Nanny said.

Agnes returned to her room and lay under the covers with her hands over her ears, but nothing could block out the infant's cries. How she wished he would stop! What ill wind had brought him to Windmarsh? She prayed for a hawk to fly down, snatch him up from his perambulator and carry him far out to sea. She sat up again, biting back tears of frustration.

Babies were supposed to be gifts from Heaven according to Nanny. This one was a squalling monster from Hell.

She got up for a second time and crept across the landing, wondering if there was any way she could quieten him. She pushed the door to the old schoolroom open and paused. Mrs Pargeter was snoring from her bed in the room that had been Nanny's. The baby was sobbing.

Mrs Pargeter must be wrong, she thought. He sounded distressed, lonely . . . She recognised his pain.

She took a step inside and another, testing each floorboard before she put her full weight on it. There was a creak. She froze, but Mrs Pargeter's snoring continued unabated. She tiptoed past the door to her room and into the nursery where she could just make out Henry's shape in the crib.

She looked in from above. His blanket had fallen away, revealing his tiny body, dressed in a robe with short sleeves. His eyes were wide open, and his mouth turned down at the corners. His shoulders heaved with another heart-wrenching sob.

'Oh, my poor little brother,' she whispered, leaning down to touch his arm. 'You are cold.'

She glanced behind her. Did she dare pick him up?

She leaned into the crib and slid her hands underneath him, cupping his head as she lifted him out. She carried him carefully over to the nursing chair and sat down, holding him in her arms. He stared at her.

'You have no idea who I am, have you?' she whispered as a rush of love and pride flooded her breast. 'I'm your sister.'

He smiled a brief, toothless smile – at least, it looked like a smile, although Nanny had told her that babies didn't smile properly until they were a few weeks old. Then he closed his eyes and fell asleep. Very slowly and quietly, she laid him back in the crib, covering him with the blanket.

'Goodnight, dear, sweet Henry,' she whispered before she returned to bed.

For the first time in her life, she didn't feel alone.

# Chapter Three

## *Consommé and Garlic*

'It's going to be a social gathering the like of which hasn't been seen at Windmarsh for many years.' Nanny picked up the hairbrush from the dressing table and its silver back glinted in the morning sunshine. 'Let me put your hair up for you.'

Agnes had already visited the schoolroom to feed the golden linnet with extra seed and thistle tops. Now she sat down and submitted to Nanny's ministrations.

'I expect Mama and Papa will require me to play the piano or recite a poem.'

'I'm afraid not,' Nanny said crisply. 'It is Henry's day. They don't want anything or anyone to take attention from him. You must promise to be seen and not heard. Think of it as an opportunity to practise your good manners.'

It was early July, and Henry was eight weeks old.

'It is a most unsatisfactory arrangement,' Agnes said, disappointed. 'I shall be bored witless.'

'You will behave like a young lady and not let your feelings show,' Nanny scolded. 'I thought you were looking forward to today.'

'I was, but . . .' Her voice trailed off.

'You can't be the centre of attention any more. Your brother will always be put first because of his sex. That is the way it is. There's nothing that can be done about it.'

The bristles of the hairbrush caught her scalp as Nanny pulled her hair overly tight.

'Ouch! That hurt.' Agnes put her hands up to her head, but she was more upset by Nanny's harsh words than her actions.

'I'm sorry. You must be brave.'

There was a knock at the door.

'Do come in,' Nanny called, and the lady's maid entered with the clothes Mama had chosen for Agnes to wear for the occasion. The maid laid them on the bed and left the room just as Miriam arrived with breakfast. She put the tray on the dressing table in front of Agnes.

'Oh, there is such a to-do in the kitchen.' She smiled. 'Monsieur has sent out a cold breakfast, saying he can't do hot because he is too busy preparing luncheon. We 'ave seven house guests to look after and more visitors on their way, and the master has taken the footmen aside to help with the surprise he has arranged for after the baptism.'

'What is it?' Agnes lifted the lid on the teapot, releasing a bitter fragrance into the air.

'We don't know yet.' Miriam chuckled. 'That's why it's going to be a surprise, miss.'

Agnes recoiled. 'What is that smell?'

'It is coffee, made the French way,' Miriam said. 'I agree – it has the fago of smoked herring about it.'

'I don't think our young lady should be drinking coffee for breakfast. It is too stimulating,' Nanny said. 'Please bring us some tea instead, and poached eggs on toast. We cannot start the day with pastries. What is the master thinking of?'

'I believe he is giving Monsieur the benefit of the doubt. I don't like to talk ill of anyone, but he is the most dreadful little man. He has passed over the usual tradesmen, bin rude to Mr Turner and the scullery maid, and made the gardener's boy cry.'

The gardener's boy was eighteen, older than Agnes. It seemed strange that he should cry without good reason. She wondered what the Frenchman had said to him.

'I must go, or we won't be ready for the vicar at eleven.' Miriam disappeared downstairs and Agnes never did get her tea, but she did get to wear white just like Mama. She wore a dress down to her ankles, new shoes with jewelled buckles, white kid gloves and a silver ribbon in her hair, and pantaloons that were made from the finest broderie anglaise adorned with lace frills.

She felt as if she was floating on air as she glided down the steps to the hall, where she caught sight of her full glory in the great mirror on the wall opposite the walnut long-case clock. Its gilded hands gleamed as they crept slowly towards the hour of eleven.

'Slow down, Agnes. Please show a little decorum,' Nanny said, following along behind her in her Sunday best, but Agnes carried on in a rush to meet Uncle Rufus, who was waving to her from just inside the front door.

'Agnes, is that really you?' he said, walking over to her. He handed his coat to the footman. 'Well, I never did. You're turning out to be quite as I expected, rather unremarkable.' He leaned on a stick with a silver fox's mask for the handle. 'What do you think, Mrs Berry-Clay?' He turned to his wife, a short, plump woman who was wearing a green satin dress stitched with gold, and a matching bonnet adorned with ostrich feathers.

'Oh, there must be something wrong with your eyes. She's always been a pretty girl. Agnes, you haven't seen your cousins for a while. Look at how they have grown up in the last few months. When were we last here all together? For the New Year, if I remember rightly. Philip?

Edward?' Smiling, Aunt Sarah looked behind her, but her sons had vanished. 'Where are the boys? Where have they gone?'

'To make mischief, no doubt,' Uncle Rufus said proudly. He was shorter than Papa but he had the same red hair, just less of it, and he didn't wear a beard, only side-whiskers and a moustache. He was younger than Papa but looked several years older, Agnes thought. She didn't like him. He made her flesh creep.

'The young gentlemen are heading to the drawing room,' Nanny said disapprovingly. 'Come this way.'

The party walked up the stairs together, following the sound of voices to the drawing room, where the furniture had been moved against one wall to make space for more seating and a font, decorated with white flowers and ferns. A long table had appeared beside the tall arched windows to accommodate the christening gifts: knife, fork and spoon sets; a tooth-cutter; knitted items and bottles of port to be laid down for the future.

There were two boys at the table, attracted like magpies by the shiny silver cups and rattle.

'You may look but not touch, Miss Agnes,' Nanny said in a very loud voice, but the two boys ignored her, and their parents said nothing.

Her cousins were very odd with their rather large skulls and peg teeth, Agnes thought as she watched the older one picking up the cups and dropping them back on the table, and the younger one shaking the rattle. Philip was about fourteen and Edward was eight. Philip with his stoop and bowed legs was the most unfortunate of the brothers in appearance.

Mama and Papa arrived in the drawing room with Mama's parents – Agnes hadn't seen them since the New Year and she was sure they were shrinking with age.

Mama's unmarried sister Caroline, some of their neighbours and a few of Papa's business associates and their wives, turned up too. Apart from her cousins, there was no one near Agnes's age.

'Congratulations,' Uncle Rufus said, stepping towards his brother. In the light from the window, Agnes noticed the extra ball of flesh at the side of his nose – she had always been fascinated by it. Nanny gave her a nudge.

'It's rude to stare,' she whispered. Agnes tried to look away, but although she did her best, her gaze kept drifting back to her uncle's face.

'You must be relieved that at last you have a child who wasn't born within sight of the gravel pits,' he went on.

'Not now,' Papa said sharply.

'I'm sorry, James. My observation was uncalled for.'

'Apology accepted.' Papa touched his brother's arm. 'I'm very grateful to you for agreeing to sponsor my son.'

'It will be a pleasure to be Henry's godfather. I shall look forward to mentoring him as you mentor my sons.' Uncle Rufus smiled. 'Aren't they growing up to be as handsome as their father?'

'Indeed,' Papa said, but there was something in the tone of his voice that made Agnes wonder if he didn't believe what he was saying.

'I wanted to talk to you about the architect,' Rufus said.

'Please, let's have no talk of business,' his wife said.

'What else is there?' Rufus said.

'It is Henry's day,' she went on firmly.

'Indeed.' Uncle Rufus looked a little cowed, but not for long.

'I've planned a surprise for this occasion, something memorable for our guests at the end of dinner,' Papa said.

'Ah, I've been looking forward to a decent port.'

'It is far better than that. And far more expensive.'

'Why do you always feel the need to impress other people?' Uncle Rufus asked. 'Isn't it enough that you're showing off your French cook?'

'I like to share my good fortune,' Papa retorted. 'There is nothing wrong in that.'

'Your generosity could be construed as gloating.'

'What is wrong with you?' Papa exclaimed. 'You are jealous. That's it, isn't it? I've put your nose out of joint by producing a son. You should be happy for me. Imagine how I have felt over the past fourteen years, watching you produce one child after another.'

'And lose them one by one,' Uncle Rufus said quietly. 'Do not pity me for it.'

'I shall not. Let's not speak of it again. We are supposed to be celebrating.' Papa shook hands with his brother. 'Why don't you take a seat? The vicar will be here shortly.'

Uncle Rufus sat down beside his wife, Papa greeted the other guests and Turner showed them to their seats. Agnes sat quietly at the back of the room with Nanny.

At ten past eleven, the vicar took his place at the font. Mama and the godparents stood up beside him, and Mrs Pargeter whisked into the room with Henry in her arms. The baby looked rather ridiculous in the long white embroidered gown that had been passed down through the family, Agnes thought. The sleeves were tied around his chubby arms with satin ribbons, and his bonnet had slipped down over his eyes.

She recognised the vicar from the rare occasions when she had attended church. Mama had never been 'good at open spaces', as she put it, and their trips away from Windmarsh Court had gradually dwindled over the years. As a consequence, Papa had engaged the vicar to carry out the baptism at home – for a substantial honorarium, no doubt.

The elderly priest celebrated Henry's birth with a long, booming speech, during which Agnes gathered that her brother was about to enter the kingdom of God from unbelief to Christian faith, from darkness into light. When the moment arrived for Mrs Pargeter to pass the baby to Uncle Rufus, who then passed him into the vicar's arms, Henry screamed. He bawled so loudly that no one could hear the name he had been given as the vicar sprinkled holy water over his head. Mama frowned with displeasure while Papa seemed embarrassed.

'He has strong lungs,' he kept saying. 'He is his father's son.'

The vicar said a final prayer and handed Henry back to his godfather, who handed him back to Mrs Pargeter. As they reached the conclusion of the ceremony, she gave up trying to pacify him and took him back to the nursery.

After the formalities, the guests mingled in the drawing room, awaiting the bell to summon them for luncheon. With Henry gone, Agnes saw her chance to impress. Glancing towards Nanny, who was safely engaged in conversation with Mrs Rufus Berry-Clay, she stepped up to the pianoforte which had been pushed to the end of the room. She moved the piano stool, which had legs shaped like staves, and sat down. She reached for the keys and took a deep breath, marking time with one foot before playing a few bars of introduction and breaking into song.

'She wore a wreath of roses—'

And that was as far as she got because Nanny was straight over to her.

'Miss Agnes, you must stop immediately.' She caught hold of her arm, bringing her performance to a halt. 'Everyone is staring at you.'

'But I am singing,' she snapped.

'No one wants to hear you sing of sorrow and young widows at a time like this. Move away from the piano.'

Reluctantly and with the music still running through her head, Agnes stood up and glared at her governess.

'You must apologise to your parents later for your disobedience. This is what happens when you indulge a child like your papa has done. It ruins even the sweetest, most even-tempered of young ladies.' Agnes's face burned as Nanny marched her out of the room. 'I realise that it's painful to find out that you've been put aside in favour of your brother, but you must learn to accept your new place in the family with grace and gratitude, not behave like a brat. Remember who you are.'

Agnes turned away as Turner rang the bell for luncheon. She wasn't sorry. What had been the point of music lessons if she wasn't allowed to use her talents to entertain guests? She felt that she had to stand up for herself. She had been brought up with expectations that were gradually being whittled away, thanks to Henry. It seemed that if she didn't make herself noticed, her parents would forget that she existed.

Everyone poured out of the drawing room and hastened across the hall to the dining room.

Agnes could hear the French cook yelling from the kitchen downstairs.

'He is rather temperamental,' Papa said, making excuses for him to no one in particular.

'It isn't his fault – he's a perfectionist,' Mama said.

'I hope the food lives up to its reputation,' the vicar said, having been invited to dine in return for saying grace.

'He is a very fine-looking man.' Mama drifted on past Agnes without acknowledging her at all. 'He is a little small, perhaps, but I find his accent most intriguing.'

The guests took their places in the dining room and

Turner escorted the two cousins, Philip and Edward, over to Nanny.

'The mistress says they are to dine in the nursery,' he said.

'That is not possible,' Nanny said. 'She has forgotten that we have been displaced from the nursery by Mrs Pargeter.'

'A picnic could be arranged,' Turner said.

'Oh no. It isn't right that we should be banished to the garden. What impression would that give the master's guests? That Windmarsh Court is so small that it cannot accommodate his own daughter?'

'All right,' Turner said grudgingly. 'I suppose they can eat in the servants' hall just this once.'

'Thank you. I shall supervise them at all times.'

'Make sure that you do. You have to have eyes in the back of your head with those little tykes. The last time they were here, the mistress found one of her ornaments broken and put back together on the shelf. She blamed one of the maids, which wa'n't fair on the girl.'

Philip stared at the butler in defiance while Edward looked down at his shiny shoes.

'A gentleman would offer his apologies,' Turner went on, 'but whoever did it can't have bin a gentleman, but a youth with bad manners and an attitude.'

'I shall ask my father to reimburse you.' Philip's face turned red. His voice was shrill.

'If you would,' Turner said smoothly. 'The mistress will be much obliged.'

Agnes was astounded by Philip's confession. She'd thought he was going to get away with it. He would have done if he'd only held his nerve.

She followed Nanny and the boys down the back stairs. They passed the kitchen where she could hear clattering pans, panicky voices and the monsieur shouting in French, and then the scullery, where she caught a glimpse of the scullery maid up to her elbows in the sink with a piece of wet sacking tied around her middle to protect her skirt. They continued past the entrance to the cellar, the butler's pantry and the housekeeper's room, and entered the servants' hall, the room where the servants dined and did the mending and polishing.

'Why did you confess to the crime, Cousin Philip?' Agnes asked when Nanny was distracted with counting out four sets of cutlery and napkins from the dresser. She knew which ornament it was – the Staffordshire one of Diana, the goddess of hunting, wearing a crescent head-dress, a gown decorated with delicate, hand-painted flowers, and sandals. Its arm had fallen off when Miriam had picked it up for dusting. She recalled how Miriam had cried when Mrs Catchpole had rounded on her and threatened her with dismissal. 'Papa can easily afford to buy a new one.'

'You cannot necessarily replace something that is of sentimental value,' Philip said.

She thought him very wise and felt a little ashamed that she hadn't thought of that.

'You could still have kept quiet.'

'That Turner fellow knew that one of us had done it, and I wanted to protect my brother. He isn't well, you see. The doctor says that he has inflammation of the lungs and might not last another winter if the chill settles back on his chest. I have already lost three sisters very young.' He looked Agnes in the eyes. 'I'd like to be a medical man one day and now that Uncle James – your papa – has a son to take on the running of the brewery, I think that I shall be allowed to pursue my studies to their full conclusion.'

Agnes saw Philip in a new light. She had thought him rather dull, associating ugliness with a lack of intelligence, and lacking in consideration for others and their property, but he had been generous, taking the blame for his brother.

'May we sit now, Nanny?' She pulled out the chair at the head of the table that stood in the centre of the room.

'You may, but not there. That's Mr Turner's place.'

'He isn't here.'

'He wouldn't like it. Sit down beside me.' Nanny laid the table and pulled out another chair. 'Philip and Edward, you sit opposite us. That's right. Now, who will say grace? Philip?'

Blushing, he mumbled a few words.

'Amen,' he said and then they waited, looking at each other.

'Where is the first course?' Nanny muttered.

'I'm hungry,' Edward said, swinging his legs against the table.

'Please, remember your manners,' Nanny said.

He stopped, but only for a few minutes.

'Edward, stop,' Philip said.

Edward stared at his brother. 'I will not.'

'It would serve you well to listen to your elders and betters,' Nanny said, as Miriam came into the servants' hall with the first course. She placed the plates on the table.

'What is the meaning of this?' Nanny said.

'It is – let me see if I can remember – an entrée.'

Agnes stared at the pile of green leaves adorned with a tomato cut into the shape of a flower.

'It's salad,' Philip said.

'It is not at all nutritious,' Nanny said. 'What does Monsieur think we are? Rabbits?'

'The mistress is of the same opinion, but the master insists that everyone eats the French way. We are serving the second course shortly. It's a consommé de volaille, served with sherry,' Miriam said slowly, concentrating on the pronunciation, 'but it's really just a soup. I'll be back to clear your plates.'

'You can take mine now.' Edward pushed his plate away. 'I'm not eating that.'

Agnes ate a mouthful of leaves, but all she could taste was vinegar and salt. Nanny, Philip and Edward left theirs.

Eventually, Miriam brought the soup. Agnes felt sick at the first sip. It was so strong that the game might just as well have been crawling from the dish.

'It is made from pheasant,' Nanny said. 'You are not accustomed to such strong flavours.'

Miriam smiled. 'Monsieur insists on hanging the birds by the feet until they drop off. I've sin them in the larder, as green as green can be.'

Nanny turned pale and held a napkin to her mouth. Edward and Philip grimaced.

'The mistress and some of the other ladies 'ave 'ad to leave the dining room,' Miriam continued. 'Shall I clear the dishes?'

'Yes, please, straight away,' Nanny said. 'Dare I ask what is next?'

'The pièce de resistance. Roast beef.' Miriam collected the bowls on to a tray and carried them away for the scullery maid. At that moment a fracas broke out from the kitchen along the corridor.

'Where is Monsieur? He is nowhere to be found.' Agnes thought she heard Mrs Catchpole's voice.

'He has gone down to the cellar to source a Bordeaux,' someone else said. 'He doesn't approve of the wine that the master ordered to be served on this occasion.'

'Well, we can't wait – the guests are about to rebel.' Mrs Catchpole called for one of the footmen to fetch the trolley to carry the beef. 'Miriam, you will have to help bring the vegetables. Oh, where is the insufferable little

Frenchman? I wish he'd stayed on the other side of the English Channel.'

Fortunately, the roast beef was a great improvement on the previous dishes. Edward fell silent, shovelling food into his mouth while Nanny frowned. Meanwhile, Agnes found herself making conversation with Philip.

'The meat is not too messed about with,' he said, smiling.

'It is most acceptable.' Being unused to company, Agnes didn't know what else to say.

'Everyone will look up to your papa for his choice of cook.' There was a long silence before Philip started again. 'I wonder how the drayman is – the one at the brewery who fell from the ladder when he was loading the barrels and broke his head. Didn't your father mention it?'

'No,' Agnes said. 'He doesn't discuss business with me.' She recalled how he preferred to keep his work and home life completely separate.

'Oh? What do you have to talk about, then?'

She glanced towards Nanny, hoping for guidance, but she was trying to ignore the banging and clattering and breaking of glass from along the corridor.

'What is that?' Edward couldn't contain his curiosity. He jumped down from his seat and ran out of the room. Philip wiped his mouth and followed. Agnes joined them. She couldn't resist, and it seemed that neither could Nanny.

Turner was at the top of the steps leading down into the cellar.

'What is the commotion?' Nanny asked.

'It is the monsieur. Young man' – the butler turned to Philip – 'will you help me?'

'Yes, of course.'

'Come with me.' Turner and Philip disappeared down to the cellar and reappeared shortly afterwards, half dragging, half carrying the Frenchman back up the stone steps.

*'Tu es si beau,'* Monsieur said, turning and planting a kiss on the butler's cheek.

'Keep your hands to yourself and we will get along,' Turner said sternly. 'We'll leave him in the scullery to sober up.'

'Shall we fetch him a chair?' Philip said.

'He can sit on the floor.'

'Come away, Miss Agnes, and you, Edward. I'm sorry to have exposed you to such a sight. He has partaken of too much wine. His behaviour is beyond the pale,' Nanny said, ushering them away.

'What about Philip?' Agnes said. 'He is a guest, not a servant.'

'He will join us shortly. This way, children. I should be grateful if you would each forget what you have just seen. That man is a disgrace. We are going to the dining room where Philip will join us for the surprise.'

'What can it be?' Agnes hurried on ahead.

'Hush. Remember that this is in Henry's honour, not yours.' When they reached the dining room, Nanny directed them to pass by the guests who were at their tables, and made them stand in the corner by the sideboard. 'Don't stare.'

It was hard to avoid staring, Agnes thought. The guests seemed restless. Aunt Sarah was sitting with her lips pursed as though she had been sucking on bones.

'What is this surprise, James?' Uncle Rufus said loudly. Agnes noticed that he had left soup on his whiskers. 'I hope it isn't more garlic – it lingers on the breath and skin.'

'You have no taste, no refinement,' Papa said.

'How can you say that? It is you who has no taste. Either that, or you are making some pretence that you prefer this foreign food to good old English fare. I like my beef well done, not raw.'

'Please, stop sparring like a pair of coxcombs,' Mama said, interrupting them. 'James, won't you have Monsieur summoned to the dining room so he may be congratulated?'

'That is an excellent idea, my darling. Where is Turner?' Papa looked around the room. 'Where is the damned man when you want him?'

'I'm here, sir.' The butler came rushing into the dining room with Philip, who made his way to stand next to Agnes. He gave her a smile and she smiled back.

Papa whispered something into Turner's ear.

'The monsieur is unfortunately indisposed,' Turner said quietly, but clearly enough for everyone – apart from Mama's mother, who was a little deaf – to hear.

'He's been overcome by fumes – of garlic,' Uncle Rufus joked.

Papa didn't laugh.

'Where are the footmen?'

'They are outside the door,' Turner said.

'Send them in when I give word.'

'Yes, sir.' Turner bowed.

Papa took to his feet, and tapped his glass.

'Ladies and gentlemen, Louisa and I are very grateful that you could attend our son's christening today and we thank you for the gifts you have brought. I hope that you have enjoyed sampling the art of dining executed in the French style.' He paused to clear his throat. 'As one final gesture of our hospitality, I would like to introduce you to the surprise of the day: the miracle of creation that is . . .' Papa nodded and gestured to the butler, who was at the door. 'The word, Turner,' he hissed. 'I have given the word.'

'Have you, sir?'

'Yes, indeed I have.'

'I'm sorry, it's completely slipped my mind which word it was.'

'Creation,' Papa muttered. 'The miracle of creation that is . . .'

Turner opened the door with a flourish. The two footmen walked into the room, carrying a large silver tray between them. On top of it, nestled among a mound of under-ripe strawberries from the kitchen garden, was an object that looked like a brown and yellow pine cone with a crown of ragged spiky leaves rising from the top.

' . . . the pineapple,' Papa went on.

'What is it?' Agnes whispered.

'This is a very rare thing, a fruit from the tropics. Feast your eyes upon it, because it may be the only one you ever see.'

'Will we be able to partake of it?' Uncle Rufus asked.

'Oh no. I have rented it for the occasion. I believe that it is rather unpleasant to eat: musty to the taste and overly fragrant.'

'It looks as if it is affected by rot to me.'

'It is a curiosity,' Papa said hotly. 'Tomorrow you will be able to tell everyone of your acquaintance that you have seen a pineapple in the flesh.'

'Why should I wish to do that?' Uncle Rufus started bickering with Papa again as the footmen carried the surprise around the room so everyone could marvel at it.

It had been a good day on the whole, except for not being allowed to sing, Agnes thought later when she retired to bed. She had sampled French cuisine, worn a longer skirt and been able to make conversation, albeit rather stilted, with someone other than the usual inhabitants of Windmarsh Court. Thanks to Henry, her parents were letting her grow up at last, whether by accident or design, she wasn't sure. She couldn't help suspecting that it was the latter and they wanted rid of her so they could lavish all their attention on their son.

However, the christening had left some people, including Nanny, feeling a little out of sorts. Agnes met her in the new schoolroom the morning after to find her sitting quietly on her chair, holding a ceramic hot-water bottle wrapped in cloth to her stomach, and sipping tea.

'Good morning, Nanny.'

'It's morning. That's all I can say about it,' she said, looking pained. 'Please go ahead and feed the bird.'

Agnes lifted the cloth from the bird's cage. Her black crown was fading, the yellow band across her wings was ragged, and she'd lost some of her tiny feathers from her chest. She was sickening, Agnes thought. She offered her the top of a thistle, some birdseed, and a piece of yellow groundsel that Papa had suggested was good for birds, but the bird didn't want it.

She stood the cage in the window and the linnet began to trill, calling to the other birds that flew free outside. Was she unhappy? Agnes wondered. Was it right to keep her in a cage all the time when she wanted to spread her wings and reach the sky?

'What do you think I should do?' she asked.

'We'll go and pick some more thistle on our walk this afternoon.' Nanny pressed her hand against her forehead and moaned.

'After lessons? Can't we go now?'

'No, lessons first. At the moment, I am indisposed.'

'Should I ask Papa to call for the doctor?'

'No, dear. I'm suffering from an overindulgence of garlic. I shall recover without medical assistance.'

'I meant for the bird,' Agnes said. 'She is sick.'

'Oh, really, child.'

I'm not a child, Agnes wanted to say, but she bit her tongue. She had displeased Nanny by putting the health of the linnet before hers, but it was only because the bird couldn't help herself, whereas her governess was wise and knew what to do in every situation – except how to treat avian ailments.

'Be patient. The bird will be well – listen to her singing.'

When Nanny slipped out of the room for a while, Agnes opened the window. She could see the gardener weeding the flower beds. No one was looking.

'Go on, little bird,' she whispered, opening the door at the front of the cage. 'Fly free.'

The bird hopped out of the cage on to the sill and looked out, tipping her head to one side. Suddenly, she fluttered away, disappearing into the hedge below, and in spite of Agnes's rather romantic idea that the golden linnet would reappear on a bough to give her a bob of thanks, she didn't see her again.

'Who is that? To whom are you talking?' she heard Nanny saying.

Agnes turned sharply, tugging at the curtain to hide the empty cage, but it was too late. Nanny with her unerring eye for trouble was at her side.

'Oh, Agnes, what have you done?'

'She flew away.' Her heart thudded dully in her chest. What she had thought was right now felt very wrong. 'The door must have come open.'

'You opened it. The bird couldn't have done it herself. Oh, Agnes, what are you thinking of, lying to me? What is your papa going to say when he hears of this?'

'Oh, don't tell him. Please.' She felt sick, hollow to the stomach.

'He is bound to find out.' Nanny shook her head. 'I cannot keep this from him. You will be punished.'

Agnes felt a tear prick at her eyelid and roll down her cheek.

'There's to be no weeping over spilled milk. I should be thinking about what I was going to say to my father who gave me such a lovely present in the expectation that I was going to care for it, and then lied to her nanny about what she did.'

Agnes made excuses not to go down to the drawing room that evening. She had a headache. She'd eaten too much garlic. But Nanny wouldn't hear of it. Her charge was going to face the music, and sooner rather than later.

For once, as she sat in the drawing room with her hands in her lap, Agnes hoped that her parents' attention would be on Henry whom Mrs Pargeter had brought to join them.

'Here is the young Master Berry-Clay come to see his mama and papa,' Mrs Pargeter said. 'Look how he is growing.'

'Has he been more settled today?' Mama asked.

'He hasn't cried once.'

Agnes frowned, because she had heard him whimpering and wailing throughout the day.

'Has he fed?'

'Several times and with great gusto.'

'Ah, that's my son.' Papa smiled as he leaned down and touched the baby's cheek. Henry cried. 'You soothe him, Louisa. He wants his mother.'

'Oh no, Mrs Pargeter does a much better job,' Mama said. 'Please, take him away and put him to bed. Bring him again this time tomorrow. Don't look at me like that, James. You are always saying that we mustn't expose Henry to any unpleasantness at this tender age, so it is better that he isn't here while you speak to Agnes.'

Her chest tightened so she could barely breathe. Papa knew about the golden linnet. Nanny must have told him.

She glanced towards where she stood beside the window, looking out. She wondered if she was hoping to catch a glimpse of the bird.

'Come here, Agnes,' Papa said, turning to her. 'Where is my kiss?'

'I'm sorry, Papa.' Heavy-legged, she walked across to him and kissed his beard.

'Ungrateful child,' Mama exclaimed.

'Why did you let the bird go?' Papa asked.

'I wanted to set her free. I thought she'd come back.'

'You let it go in a fit of pique,' Mama said. 'How could you when it was a gift?'

She didn't say that a gift couldn't buy affection and good behaviour, or make her feel any differently about her baby brother. She had loved the bird, let her go and she hadn't come back. Wasn't that punishment enough?

'I understand why you felt you had to do something to help the poor little creature, but not why you hid the truth afterwards. You have caused great disappointment to your mother and to God,' Papa said gravely.

'She is bitter and jealous!' Mama exclaimed. 'She has a bad character. What if you are wrong, James, and your little experiment is a failure? You haven't got the outcome you desired. You have the one I expected. I said it wouldn't work – you cannot bring them out of their temperaments.'

'You didn't say that when I brought the child home.'

'I had faith in my husband. Why should I question your opinion?'

'You've done that often enough since then.' Papa drank a glass of sherry in one gulp. 'You aren't normally so restrained in yours.' He turned to Agnes. 'Your behaviour has made me reflect upon my actions. I've done everything in my power to bring you up as a respectable and good-natured young lady. You have wanted for nothing, yet the way you've treated my gift shows a distinct lack of gratitude. You've become very selfish, and I blame myself in part for not exposing you to the outside world. It's time that you saw how other children suffer – I believe that would go some way to reforming your character.'

'I don't think I should like that.'

'Quiet,' Mama interrupted. 'Let your father speak. James, you may take her to Faversham so she may visit the workhouse.'

'No, not there,' Papa said quickly. 'I have a meeting in Canterbury very soon. Miss Treen will accompany us.'

'There are poor people there too?' Mama asked.

'Indeed. There is poverty everywhere you look. Many of Canterbury's citizens are wealthy and genteel, and there are several clergy of superior rank who reside within the precincts of the great cathedral. However, there are many parts of the city that have turned into slums where families are crammed into poor housing: mothers, fathers and children living in the same room. The drains regularly overflow, causing a stink, and the place is overrun with rats.'

Agnes had prayed to leave the confines of Windmarsh Court, but not this way.

'I will acknowledge that you were right when you said that she had been overindulged, but one look at those poor unfortunates will persuade her to examine her conscience and change her attitude,' Papa went on.

'It's all very well, but she won't change. She can't. She has but half a heart,' Mama said.

'May I venture to suggest that Agnes accompanies me to Canterbury on my next visit to see my relatives?' Nanny said.

'Oh? Yes.' Mama raised her thin eyebrows at the thought that Miss Treen had relatives. It was strange how they had let her bring up their children, Agnes mused, yet didn't seem to know anything about her. 'What do you think, James?'

He hesitated.

'They are respectable people,' Nanny said. 'My uncle, Mr Cheevers, owns one of the tanneries on the River Stour. He has brought up my cousins once removed, Master Oliver and Miss Temperance, for the past ten years, with the assistance of his housekeeper. He employs a boy from a disadvantaged family, and he's also a founder and member of various charities. If it reassures you further, I shall not let Miss Agnes out of my sight.'

'It sounds like the ideal situation,' Papa said. 'I give my permission for you to take Agnes with you.'

'I shall write a letter to my uncle,' Nanny said.

Agnes returned to her room to get ready for bed. Mama had said she had but half a heart and she couldn't help believing her. She was looking forward to an outing to Canterbury to meet Nanny's relatives. She didn't care all that much about the suffering children, but she worried about the fate of the golden linnet. She prayed that she was safe, but a few days later, the gardener found a set of yellow feathers drifting across the lawn, and the linnet's mortal remains between the jaws of one of the cats.

Agnes couldn't understand why, if she had but half a heart, it could break so painfully with sorrow.

# Chapter Four

## *Kid Gloves and Canterbury Brawn*

Agnes felt a thrill of anticipation as she stepped outside. It was supposed to be a punishment, but it didn't feel like one. The horses, four big bays, shining like conkers fresh from their shells, were champing on their bits and tossing their heads, impatient to move on. Mr Noakes, the coachman, was already in his place, his hands tight on the reins. The stable boy was at their heads and the groom stood to one side holding the carriage door open. Turner helped Agnes then Nanny on board. The groom slammed the door shut and the carriage jolted forwards.

Nanny caught Agnes's eye as the horses broke into a trot. 'We are off,' she said.

They passed the cottages and church of Windmarsh, and turned on to the turnpike road towards Canterbury and London. The flat land gave way to wooded hillsides and then to a rolling landscape of hop gardens, orchards and fields of corn where the barley was beginning to ripen, turning gold in the sunshine.

'It looks as if there will be a good harvest this year,' Nanny said. 'Your papa will be pleased – there will be plenty of malt for making beer.'

Agnes assumed that meant that the brewery would remain in profit, and her father would not be worrying about money.

She glanced down at the fresh pair of pure white kid gloves that she'd taken from her glove box that morning. She'd had to powder her hands with alum before she could get them on. She fidgeted with the clasp on the knitted silver purse that Papa had given her to contain the coins she was carrying to give to the poor.

'Do calm down,' Nanny said.

'But I am impatient to reach Canterbury.'

'Let me have the purse. I'll look after it for you.' Nanny took it and placed it in her canvas bag for safekeeping.

'When will we get there?' Agnes asked. Having rarely left Windmarsh, she had little concept of how long it would take to cover the miles to the city.

'It isn't much further. This is Golden Hill where the pilgrims told Chaucer's last tale, and if you look out of the window on this side now, you can see the stone pinnacles and towers of the cathedral coming into view.'

'It seems a very long way.'

'It does,' Nanny agreed lightly. 'I always find that the more you look forward to something, the more slowly the time seems to pass until a second becomes a full minute, and a minute becomes an hour.'

'What are you looking forward to most?' Agnes dared to ask.

'Freedom. A whole day released from routine and obligation.' It seemed from Nanny's broad smile that she was casting off the shackles of Windmarsh. 'There are the ruins of St Augustine's, St Dunstan's church – and look how the river meanders through the meadows.'

It was a pastoral idyll, Agnes thought, with cattle grazing among the grasses and brown sedge.

'There are the Westgate Towers,' Nanny said, pointing to the rather forbidding grey building which consisted of a pair of towers with arrow slits and battlements, and an arch between them. It reminded Agnes of a castle.

The coachman drove the carriage along the street to one side of the towers, where they were stopped by two carts carrying goods to market, a pair of cows and a young man who was trying to catch a rooster which had escaped from the basket on his tricycle. Eventually, Mr Noakes lost patience and forced the carriage past, sending the rooster and its feathers scattering.

The horses trotted on, crossing a bridge over the river before the carriage came to a halt.

'This is the High Street,' Nanny said, as the stable boy who had accompanied the coachman opened the door to allow them to disembark.

Agnes stepped aside as a cart laden with milk churns rattled past. She caught snippets of conversation from passers-by and heard men shouting in the distance over the sound of church bells. She closed her eyes. The noise, the hustle and bustle and the smells of unwashed clothes and foul water were overwhelming. Part of her wanted to jump back in the carriage and go straight home, but Nanny took her arm and led her across the street.

'Come, my dear. I've arranged for the carriage to collect us from my uncle's house at four o'clock sharp. Don't worry. You will become accustomed to the crowds.'

'I'm not sure that I shall,' she muttered. There were people everywhere. She had never seen so many.

'We will go and find some peace inside the cathedral – no trip to Canterbury can be complete without a visit there. But we won't stop for long because I'd rather spend the time with my uncle and cousins.' Nanny gave Agnes a look. 'I trust that I can rely on your discretion.'

'You mean you don't want me to tell Papa about how long we spend at the cathedral?'

'That's right. If he asks, we took the time to see every nook and cranny. Don't look so shocked.' She guided her into Mercery Lane and Agnes stared up at the old timber-framed shops that belonged to various outfitters, linen drapers and bootmakers. The upper storeys of the row to her left seemed to lean in towards the ones opposite, almost blocking out the sky.

'Look where you're going.' Nanny chuckled as Agnes tripped over her own feet. 'Just along here is Christchurch gate which takes us into the cathedral precincts.'

'You know Canterbury well?' Agnes asked as they walked past West's Dining House.

'Of course. I was brought up here, and I visit regularly on my days off.'

Agnes felt guilty for not having given a moment's thought to how her governess spent her spare time.

'It's a wonderful place, with a theatre and two public libraries, and two market days every week for poultry, butter and vegetables. There's always something going on, whereas there's precious little entertainment to be found in the country. I should like to live here again one day.'

'Don't you like Windmarsh Court?' It had never occurred to her that Miss Treen might not be happy there.

'There are times when I wish I lived in a larger household. The life of a governess can be lonely when she is neither family nor servant, but never mind. That's the way it is and I'm grateful for my situation. I'm looking forward to when Mrs Pargeter leaves and we have Master Henry to ourselves.' She changed the subject. 'It's nearly time for an early tea at my uncle's house, and I have a fancy for some Canterbury brawn.'

'What is that?'

'It's the meat from a pig's head set in jelly,' Nanny said, and Agnes wished that she hadn't asked.

They walked around the cathedral, visiting the chapel where the martyr Thomas à Becket's shrine had been, an empty space since Henry VIII ordered its destruction during the Reformation. A single candle was aflame on the floor, across which the light from the stained-glass windows cast streaks of many colours.

'I like to come here when I need space to think,' Nanny said. 'I find that the presence of God restores the tranquillity of the soul.'

Agnes wasn't so sure. She found the atmosphere unnerving. The cathedral was filled with tombs and memorials, and the stone steps down into the shadowy crypt had been worn down by the feet of many pilgrims over the centuries. It was a relief to emerge into the bright sunlight once more where she found the sight of the displays in the jewellers' shop windows much more to her taste.

'We haven't come here to buy trinkets,' Nanny said, drawing her away. 'I wish you wouldn't dawdle. My uncle is expecting us.'

They progressed past the Westgate and turned along a street that followed the course of the river. There was a row of terraced cottages to one side, built from brick with an upper storey clad in timber. The windows were small and dirty, and the doors opened straight on to the street. Opposite the cottages was another row of homes, the buildings made from a mixture of materials – stone, brick, wattle and daub – thrown up together all higgledy-piggledy so Agnes couldn't tell where one ended and another began.

An overflowing drain ran down the middle of the street, spilling black water across the stones.

'Mind where you put your feet.' Nanny hitched up her skirts.

'Why is everything so dirty?' Agnes wrinkled her nose at the stench of effluent and rot. 'Why don't the people who live here send their servants to clean it up? I would.'

Nanny laughed wryly.

'My dear child, you have led a sheltered life. This isn't Windmarsh Court. The people who live here don't have the luxury of servants.'

'Surely they are a necessity, not a luxury. How does anyone manage without a cook and a maid at the very least?'

'The people who live here can barely feed and clothe themselves and their families. Work is hard to come by. The landowners and farmers who used to employ men and women as labourers in the fields introduced machinery to do the threshing, for example, in their stead. They were laid off and moved into the city to seek employment, but there isn't enough to go round.'

'How do they survive then?' Such poverty seemed incomprehensible to Agnes.

'They beg or steal, or live off charity, which I believe can be permanently injurious to a man's pride.'

'Then there is a simple solution – the landowners should get rid of their machines and go back to the old ways.'

'It's too late for that. All these people who live in our cities need food that's cheap and plentiful. Without the machines, they can't produce enough to go round.' Nanny waved her hand towards the broken windows nearby which had been stuffed with rags. 'This is the price of progress.'

A horse and cart splashed through the water. The horse's bones were showing through its skin and its coat was dull, while the cart was made of pieces of wood knocked together with rough nails, and had wheels which didn't match. The driver slapped the horse on the rump with a long stick to keep it moving with its load of kettles, pots and pans, which clanged with every jolt.

'Which way do we go now?' Agnes asked. 'Are we lost?'

'Of course not.' Nanny laughed. 'We go right here.'

They turned down another street that ran towards the river, where the stench grew more intense. Nanny stopped outside a pair of high gates with a sign reading, 'Cheevers' Tannery: Estd 1798 for the best Leather, natural and dyed. Enquire within.' To their left was an alleyway with a five-barred gate fronting a pebbled drive.

Agnes watched her governess ring the brass bell that was set on the wall beside it.

'This is Willow Place, my uncle's establishment,' she said as a small, slender woman dressed in black emerged from the house at the top of the drive and came to open the gate for them.

'Good afternoon, Mrs Hill,' Nanny said, but the woman remained silent. She raised one arm and pointed towards the house, a black and white timber-framed house from medieval times with three storeys stacked unevenly on top of each other, giving the impression that they might topple over at any moment. She escorted them past the lawn where a pair of ducks nestled in the grass, and into the house. Agnes copied Nanny in removing her shoes inside the front door and adding them to the row already present: fine boots for a man, a set of lady's shoes and slippers, and some waders.

They followed the woman, whom Agnes assumed was the housekeeper, through to a study with shelves stacked with leather-bound books, and a desk where an old man sat reading some correspondence. He looked up and smiled.

'Marjorie, how wonderful to see you.' He stood up, massaging his hip with one hand and reaching for a stick with the other. His tall frame was curved into a stoop, and he had waves of white hair and a grey beard, dark eyes and a hooked nose. His ears were large with pendulous lobes, making Agnes think of a friendly goblin. 'I'm so glad you have come.' He embraced his niece warmly before turning to Agnes. 'And who is this?'

'This is Miss Berry-Clay, my charge,' she said. 'Agnes, this is Mr Samuel Cheevers, my uncle.'

Agnes greeted him with a small curtsey.

'I'm delighted to meet you,' she said.

'And I you. Marjorie has told me much about you – within the normal bounds of discretion, of course.' He turned back to his niece. 'Let us go and sit outside. I believe that Mrs Hill is preparing tea and cake.'

Marjorie. The name was a surprise to Agnes. She followed them through the house to put their shoes back on again before they went outside. Why, she had never heard anyone call her governess by her first name. She was always Nanny or Miss Treen.

They settled in the garden that sloped down behind the house to a low wall with the river behind it and a row of willow trees that trailed their branches like long fingers in the water. The stench of rot was fainter, partially obscured by the scent of roses and honeysuckle that scrambled over the wrought-iron veranda.

They were joined by a young lady and gentleman as they took their seats at a small table.

'Allow me to introduce you to my grandchildren, Miss Temperance and Master Oliver Cheevers,' Mr Cheevers said.

'Good afternoon,' Agnes said politely. The young gentleman was probably two or three years her senior and the lady was older than that, about twenty, she guessed.

Temperance was a pretty creature with chestnut curls,

an upturned nose and rosebud mouth, and Agnes wished they could be friends, but she didn't know how. When Temperance greeted her uncle's guests, her mouth was smiling, but her eyes were not.

Master Cheevers was more welcoming – and very handsome. He was tall with loose curls of dark hair down to his shoulders and a hint of side-whiskers. He was dressed in corduroy breeches and a clean linen shirt with the sleeves rolled up to show off his muscular arms. His brown eyes were soft and ringed with dark lashes, and Agnes could hardly keep herself from staring.

He pulled up a chair for his sister and helped the housekeeper with the trays of tea, sandwiches, a whole brawn and cake.

'That will be all for now, thank you,' Mr Cheevers said, and Mrs Hill retreated without saying a word, making Agnes wonder if she was permanently mute. 'The brawn is especially for you, Marjorie. I know it is your favourite.'

'You do spoil me,' she said with a smile as she poured the tea, and Oliver sliced the meat jelly.

'Somebody has to.' Mr Cheevers smiled back. 'What do you think of our little oasis, Agnes?'

'It's lovely,' she said, comparing it with the dirty, bustling streets that were less than a stone's throw away. 'It is very different from Windmarsh Court. Everything is so much smaller.'

'Smaller?' said Temperance. 'Is your home really that grand?'

'Oh, it is,' Agnes said.

'It is the people within it who make a house a home, not its size or the number of treasures within its walls,' Nanny cut in sternly.

Agnes realised that she had spoken out of turn. Chastened, she nibbled on a brawn sandwich, dropping a few crumbs on the table. As her companions made conversation, she watched a little bird, a robin redbreast, fly down on to a nearby rose. It cocked its head and gazed at her through beady eyes just like the golden linnet had used to do. Her heart began to beat faster. Had she been forgiven for what she had done? She held her breath as the robin flew on to the edge of the table, inches from her hand, and pecked at the crumbs before pausing to look up at her, cock its head once more and flutter away.

'You seem to have a way with God's creatures,' Mr Cheevers remarked.

To her relief, Miss Treen did not enlighten him as to the fate of the linnet, although perhaps she already had.

'Shall we forget this strange mission set up by the young lady's father?' he went on, addressing Nanny. 'It's rather demeaning to parade people in front of her as some kind of moral lesson about poverty. I think she will find it distressing. She is a sensitive girl and very young for her age.'

'Her naivety comes from living in the wilds of Windmarsh during her formative years. I have done my best to expose her to the outside world through my teaching, but her actual experience is limited. Her mother suffers from a fear of the outdoors and unfamiliar faces – she doesn't go out herself, or let us travel too far from home. I'm afraid that the sights and odours will upset Agnes's constitution, but I cannot go against my employer's instructions in this matter. He has given her money to hand to a person who is in need.'

Agnes felt her neck and face grow hot as she noticed both Temperance and Oliver gazing at her with evident curiosity.

Mr Cheevers sighed. 'If you insist on following this

plan, Oliver will take you along to the tannery and introduce you to the boy who works for us.'

'That is a very sound idea,' Nanny agreed.

'Except that our guest isn't wearing suitable clothes,' Oliver interrupted. 'The yard is dirty. They will get soiled.'

'It is no matter,' Nanny said, although Agnes thought otherwise.

'His name is Bert, and he's eight years old,' Mr Cheevers continued. 'I thought he could tell his story, and if Agnes is in accord, she can give him the contents of her purse.'

How could such a young boy be at work? Agnes wondered, recalling Papa's plans to send Henry away to school. She continued to pick at her food, anxious about what exactly she was about to be confronted with.

When they had finished their tea, she walked down to the tannery with Nanny and Master Cheevers. The stench of rot grabbed her by the throat as Oliver opened the gates into the yard. She held her hand over her mouth, fighting the urge to be sick.

'Here, have this,' Nanny said, searching her bag and finding a vinaigrette of smelling salts. She opened the lid of the silver box and handed it over. Agnes held it to her nose and inhaled the scent of hartshorn and lavender oil. 'Is that better?'

She nodded, and handed it back.

'Perhaps we should turn around,' Oliver suggested.

'I shall be all right, thank you,' Agnes said firmly, not wishing to come across as weak in front of him.

A cart swung past them into the yard. It was loaded with hides with horns still attached, piled high and roped down. The wheels were splashed with flesh and blood. The mare pulling it snorted and fidgeted as though she hated the smell. Agnes couldn't help it. She retched.

'Really, this isn't a good idea. Marjorie, take her back to the house.'

'No, I will stay and do this.' Agnes looked around the yard which had buildings on all sides. There was a gap ahead of them from which a muddy track led down to the riverbank, and to their right was a row of pits filled with black liquid.

'The state of the place disgusts you,' Oliver said with a mocking smile. 'Where do you think your lovely shoes and gloves come from?'

She stared at her hands, at the immaculate white kid gloves. How could it be possible that they came from a place such as this? Nanny had taught her the proverb about it taking three kingdoms to make a glove: Spain to provide the leather, France to cut it out and England to sew it. There had been no mention of any blood and gore being involved.

When she didn't answer him, Oliver turned to Nanny and chuckled.

'Have you not l'arned her anything useful?'

'You are most impertinent,' Nanny said, giving him a withering look. 'What would be the purpose of educating her in the process of tanning when she will marry into a wealthy family and have not a care in the world? She is being brought up for a life very different from this. She is as unfamiliar with your way of existence as you are with hers.'

'I'm sorry, Marjorie. I should have thought,' he said. 'My apologies, miss. No offence taken, I hope.' She shook her head as he went on, 'When I look around the tan-yard, I see opportunity. I'm an alchemist who turns stinking hides into gold. The leather we produce here is the best in Can'erbury, and we sell it to the craftsmen – the curriers and saddlers – to make harnesses for horses, and shoes for ladies like yourself. Allow me to show you,' he said. 'Let me take you by the arm so that you don't slip. And you, Marjorie.'

Agnes recalled the manual of etiquette and how a gentleman was permitted to take two ladies on his arms, but a lady could not accept the arms of two gentlemen at the same time. She relaxed a little at the thought, and then worried that she might slip in spite of Oliver's assistance, because the whole yard seemed to be awash with water, limy waste and residues of flesh.

'I shall wait for you here,' Nanny said.

Mustering her courage, Agnes put her arm through Oliver's and the two of them moved around the tannery under his guidance. He showed her the office, the weighing room for the hides and the cool room for storage.

'It takes many weeks to make good leather. The fresh hides that have just arrived will be washed in the river then immersed in the lime pits to remove the outer layers of the skin. After a few weeks, we'll take them out and throw them over beams in the beam house over there to remove any flesh or hair roots that are left. The flesh goes for glue, and the hair roots are bought by plasterers or upholsterers for cheap felt.' He gazed earnestly into her eyes.

She blushed, unused to being in close proximity to a young gentleman.

'We move the treated hides into the mastering pits to remove the lime, then cut them up into butts – smaller pieces for tanning in the leaching pits, which are filled with a liquor made from ground oak bark and water.'

Oliver took her right up close to the pits of black liquid, where two men wearing stained clothing, rawhide aprons and gaiters, were moving the hides or butts from one pit to another by trolley. The evil-smelling butts slopped and dripped across the yard.

Agnes stood well back, afraid of splashing her clothes.

'Good afternoon, Mr Hale and Mr Jones,' Oliver said.

'Afternoon, sir,' one said. 'Where's the gaffer?'

'Mr Cheevers will be here later,' Oliver replied.

The other man, who had a pipe in his mouth, touched his cap, his respectful attitude making Oliver seem much older than his years. He might be only sixteen years of age and of a lower class than herself, Agnes thought, but he had a surprising air of authority and confidence.

'We move the butts from pit to pit, then take them out and dry them in the loft.'

She followed Oliver's gaze to the building which had a first floor clad with louvred weatherboard.

'All in all, it takes a year and a half until it's ready to make boot soles or go to the currier for cleaning and softening. It's a long process requiring much patience,' Oliver said. 'You are not very forthcoming, Agnes.'

'What do you mean?' she said, uncertain. She wasn't used to speaking to people outside of Windmarsh Court.

'Well, young ladies of my experience are usually full of chatter. You're very quiet.'

'I have been taught not to speak unless spoken to.'

He frowned. 'Is that the custom when you are living in a big house?'

She wondered if he might be teasing her. 'I believe it is a matter of good manners.'

'You can say what you like when you're here.' He smiled gently. 'My grandfather encourages me and Temperance to express our opinions freely.'

She thought of her meetings with Mama and Papa in the drawing room as he continued, 'I don't think I should like to live by the same constraints as you do. You have never been swimming?'

She shook her head.

'What do you do when you aren't studying?' he asked.

'I walk and paint a little and play the piano. I like to learn about geography.'

'What is Windmarsh like? It's over Faversham way, isn't it? I have never been there.'

'It's wild and windswept. You can walk across the marshes without seeing another soul.'

'I've always lived in Can'erbury. I went to school for a while – I can read and write, and add up – but my grandfather needed me to help him with the tannery so I left, and continued my education at home. Samuel deals with the contracts, the buying and selling, while I oversee the yard and work with the men when and where I'm required.'

'It seems a rather unpleasant occupation,' she offered.

'Ah, but my family have done well out of it, thanks to old Boney picking a fight. There were thousands of troops stationed here and they all needed boots. Even now the war's over, we make more than enough profit to support our family and allow my grandfather to engage in good works.' A small boy in a torn shirt and trousers who was darting around the cart with the hides caught his eye. 'Ah, there's Bert.'

At the mention of his name, the boy paused from where he was cutting off snippets of meat left on the hides with a knife, and dropping them into a metal bucket. Oliver led Agnes back across the yard to where Nanny was waiting, and Agnes reluctantly relinquished his arm.

'Over here, lad,' Oliver called.

The boy dropped his knife in the bucket and sauntered over.

'Good afternoon, Master Cheevers.' He grinned.

'This is Miss Berry-Clay,' Oliver said. 'She is my Aunt Marjorie's charge.'

'Good afternoon.' The boy removed his cap to reveal a shock of grubby blond hair and a pair of hazel eyes. His clothes, his face and hands were filthy, smeared with blood and grime. His jacket was stiff with dirt, and looked as if it would stand up on its own if he took it off. His boots were patched and the sole tied on with an extra knotted lace.

Agnes shifted from one foot to the other as he stared at her.

'Why, miss, you look very fine,' he mumbled.

What should she do? In polite society, one was supposed to pay a compliment in return, but she couldn't think of one. And besides, she was here as a punishment for lying, and Oliver was hovering at her side as though expecting her to speak. Flustered, she said the first thing that came into her head, which happened to be the truth.

'While you are disgusting and dirty.' The words spilled from her mouth. 'You could have at least had a wash.'

'That is a cruel thing to say,' Oliver said gruffly.

'But you are very fine,' the boy repeated.

'She looks that way,' Oliver said, 'but her temper leaves a lot to be desired.'

She burned with fury at herself for being so insensitive and at Oliver for his censure, even though it was perfectly justified. She turned to Nanny for moral support, but she was frowning.

'I'm sorry. This young lady had the benefit of a good education, but has as yet learned nothing of the world beyond the schoolroom and the marshes. It is regrettable – because she was a sweet child in the beginning – that her temperament has been moulded by her class. I have tried to instil a softness and generosity of spirit within her, but she has disappointed me today.'

Agnes's heart plunged at the thought that she had let her governess down. She was deeply hurt to discover Nanny's true feelings.

'I fear that it is impossible to break this sense of superiority that she has. Her father sent her here to meet you in the hope that it would set her on the path of making charitable endeavours, but I think that her attitude is too entrenched. She has been spoiled with rich food, fine clothes and gifts. He panders to her every whim.'

'It is a pity when you have told us that he is a renowned philanthropist himself,' Oliver said.

'He can afford to be,' Nanny said with a hint of bitterness.

Agnes had hurt the boy's feelings, but her upbringing prevented her from apologising. Part of her felt that she should, but her sense of superiority overruled it. Why should she apologise to such an inhuman creature? Mama wouldn't. She wanted to make it up to Nanny, though, who seemed embarrassed. And for some reason she was unsure about, she wanted to make it up to Oliver, to show him that she had more than half a heart.

'Young Bert here works all day from when he's woken by the knocker upper until six or whenever it gets dark in the winter. He has no spare clothes. Tell the ladies what you do with the meat that you take from the hides,' Oliver said.

'I sell it for wittles.'

'Nothing is wasted. These people can't afford to throw anything away, no matter how small and insignificant. Tell the young lady where you live.'

The boy flushed hot and angry.

'I shan't. I shan't say where or how we live,' he said rudely. 'I 'ave my pride. That's what Ma says – even when we have nothing left, we will always 'ave our pride and nobody can take that away from us. Can I go now, sir? She needs me back to help her deliver the laundry.'

'Of course,' Oliver said, and the boy picked up his bucket and knife and walked away as fast as his legs could carry him.

'My purse,' Agnes said quickly, turning to Nanny. 'I have a purse of coins from my father.'

As her governess handed her the silver reticule, it slipped from her fingers and fell with a splat in the muck by her feet. Oliver bent down, picked it up and gave it back to her. Agnes grimaced as she opened the clasp, her beautiful white gloves becoming smeared with a greenish-brown liquor. She wanted to cry. She did cry. A tear rolled down her cheek and she couldn't dash it away because she would have dirtied her face. Keeping her eyes down, she tipped the coins into Oliver's outstretched palm.

'I thank you on Bert's behalf,' Oliver said. 'I'll use the money to buy him a new pair of boots and supply his mother with a parcel of food. It isn't wise for a small boy to carry coins on his person – there are muggers and pick-pockets about.'

Agnes felt upset, embarrassed and naive all in good measure. Oliver was a man of the world. She was a rich young lady, insulated from ordinary life by her privileged upbringing. She wished she hadn't offended Bert. So much for not having any feelings, she thought. She felt the boy's distress at being singled out all too much.

Oliver walked Agnes and Nanny back to Willow Place, where he excused himself and returned to his business at the tannery. When the carriage arrived to take them back to Windmarsh, Samuel and Temperance bade them farewell and wished them a safe journey.

'What did you think of our day in Canterbury?' Nanny said as they travelled at breakneck speed, the horses impatient to get home.

'Your uncle and cousins were most hospitable, but I didn't like the tannery.' She had folded her gloves in half and dropped them accidentally on purpose into the gutter as they had climbed into the carriage. She didn't want them now that they were soiled. 'When I see how Henry will grow up surrounded with everything he needs and more, I can't help thinking how unfair it is on someone like Bert.'

'The world isn't fair,' Nanny said. 'We are all born to our respective places in society and we have to learn to live with it. Men like your father and my uncle are committed to helping the poor. They do what they can, but it's a drop in the ocean.'

'Don't you think that it's demeaning for those who receive such charity?' Agnes asked. 'Shouldn't donations be given anonymously?'

'I think people should be given the chance to express their gratitude to their benefactors,' Nanny said. 'Where are all these questions coming from?'

'I have one more.'

'What is that?'

'Do you really think I'm spoiled?'

'Perhaps I shouldn't have expressed my opinion in such strong language in front of my uncle.'

'So it's true? You spoke your mind.'

'Don't let it trouble you.'

'But it does trouble me. How can I improve myself?'

Nanny considered for a moment.

'I think you have learned a valuable lesson today – that all people from high to low have feelings.' She shut her eyes. 'I think I have eaten too much brawn.' Agnes knew what she meant. The conversation was closed.

Back at Windmarsh, she bathed and changed her dress before meeting with her parents in the drawing room. Mrs Pargeter was present as well, walking up and down with Henry in her arms. She was rocking him back and forth rather too violently for Agnes's liking.

'Oh, Papa, I should have liked to have helped all the poor people of Canterbury. I wish I could invite the boy to Windmarsh Court so he can taste hot chocolate and wash with rose-scented soap.'

'It would not be a good idea to introduce the poor to our kind of life,' Mama said. 'It would encourage envy and discontent.'

'I think it's quite the opposite,' Papa said. 'It would give them something to aspire to. It would ignite the flame of ambition in those poor souls' breasts, making them work harder to raise themselves from poverty.'

'So may Bert pay us a visit?' Agnes said.

Her father seemed to reconsider. 'I don't think so. It wouldn't be fair on the others in his situation – his mother, for example.'

'They can all come,' she said. 'We have plenty of room.'

'I'm sorry, we must think of Mama's nerves.'

Agnes couldn't help thinking that Papa was deferring far too much to her mother's state of health. Surely that poor boy's future was more precarious.

'I've been thinking about what else I can do, and I've decided that I should like to give up the globe and my jewellery to the poor.'

'You must leave it to men like me and Mr Cheevers, and the politicians. The way forward is to give these people help to enable them to work and support themselves and their families. If you provide them with everything they need, they will become lazy and dependent on donations,' Papa said. 'Now, let me speak with Mrs Pargeter. How has my son been today? Has he smiled? And fed? Is he growing?'

Agnes sat back in silence. Windmarsh Court felt oddly cold and empty compared with Willow Place. She thought of Oliver and his grandfather and for the first time in her life she felt a little disappointed in Papa – the Cheeverses weren't the kind of men who would feel the need to rent a pineapple to impress their acquaintances.

# 1857

# Chapter Five

## *While the Cat's Away, the Mice Will Play*

Agnes stood at the schoolroom window, watching a flock of seabirds rise, wheel away and settle again on the marsh. It was late October, a few weeks away from her nineteenth birthday, and she couldn't help wondering if the occasion would cause a stir of any kind at Windmarsh Court. She doubted it. Very little had recently disturbed the tranquillity of the house. The monsieur had been dismissed and Mrs Nidget re-employed on a higher salary soon after she and Nanny had returned from Canterbury the first time. Mrs Pargeter had left when Henry was two, and Nanny had taken over his care, meaning that Agnes had had fewer lessons and more time to pursue her own activities.

She wrote poetry, painted pictures, and read books. Sometimes she thought she would die of boredom.

Henry clambered up and knelt on the window seat. She reached out to stroke his soft copper curls. He was four years old.

'Agnes, that tickles,' he chuckled.

'I'm sorry.' She smiled.

Her cousins came to disturb the peace of Windmarsh every few months. She looked forward to talking to Philip. He brought a welcome breath of fresh air with his conversation about school and the boys with whom he associated.

Agnes accompanied Nanny to Willow Place twice more before Papa, perhaps alarmed by her reformed character and evangelical desire to help the poor, forbade any further expeditions to Canterbury. Her experiences there had changed her. They had made her appreciate what she had.

After that, Nanny brought news of the Cheeverses two or three times a year. She said that Mr Cheevers, Oliver and Temperance always asked after her and recalled her fondly. It was polite of them to say so, Agnes thought, when she had been unkind to the boy on the first occasion of meeting them. She had tried to make up for her behaviour, but she still felt that she hadn't done enough to deserve their high regard.

'Look,' Henry exclaimed, bringing her back to the present.

'What is it? What can you see?' she said.

'A boat.'

'I wonder where it's going. Come on, the clock has struck nine. It's time for lessons.'

'I don't want to learn my letters,' he grumbled. Even frowning, he managed to look angelic, dressed in his wool knickerbockers, nansook shirt and belted tunic which had brass buttons down the front. One of them had come off when he had put it in his mouth, a habit that Nanny was trying hard to break.

'It's essential for a gentleman to be able to read and write, if he is to be a success.' Agnes smiled to herself, wondering when she had begun to sound like her governess. She turned and pulled Henry's chair up to the desk, scraping the legs across the floorboards.

'Oh, please keep the noise down.' Nanny winced. 'I have the most terrible head.' She was sitting beside the fire, sipping hot water. She had been suffering from a headache since one of the footmen had delivered a letter for her to the nursery the day before. Whatever its contents, they had unsettled her.

'You may go to your room,' Agnes said. 'I can look after Henry.'

'That is a kind offer but it would be most improper. I cannot abandon my responsibilities just like that.'

'I am eighteen, more than capable.'

Nanny thought for a moment. 'I suppose there would be no harm in it for an hour or two.'

'I shan't say anything to Mama.'

'I'm not entirely comfortable with that proposal.'

'You aren't well,' Agnes argued.

'You are right. I am about to faint with the pain.' Nanny struggled up from her chair, pressing her hand against her temple. Agnes pitied her for having to spend her life looking after people, without having someone to look after her. 'Make sure Henry does his lessons and wake me when the clock strikes twelve – I shall leave the door open in case of emergency.'

'Of course.' Agnes's heart leapt. She couldn't wait for Nanny to leave the schoolroom so she could be free to be herself for two joyous hours. She had an idea to occupy her brother. 'Henry, I need your help.'

Together, they turned the table upside down.

'Stay there. Don't move or make a sound. I'll be back.' Agnes ran downstairs to the linen cupboard, opened the door and pulled out a bedsheet. It was neatly folded and ironed, but bore the faint scent of damp. She picked up a newspaper from the hall table and returned to the schoolroom, where she set up a sail, tying the sheet between two of the table legs.

'Go and fetch the cushions from Nanny's chair, Henry,' she said as she began to open up the newspaper and turn it into a hat. He picked up the cushions and dropped them into the upturned table. 'Who is going to be captain of this ship?'

'Me,' he said with a giggle.

Agnes dropped the hat on to his head.

'Thanking you kindly,' he said with a bow. She laughed.

'We will sail across the water to Italy. You are obliged to help me aboard because I am a lady.'

He took her hand and helped her on to the cushions before he set sail, looking out for trouble while shading his eyes from the reflection of the sun on the sea. There were adventures: pirates, sharks, a shipwreck and treasure on the way, and they had only just reached the shores of Italy when the clock chimed the agreed hour and she had to go and wake Nanny.

'We must pack up,' she said.

'No.' Henry's face crumpled.

'Don't be a crybaby,' she said short-temperedly. She was tired of playing now. She couldn't understand how Nanny coped with looking after him all day every day. It was exhausting. She gave him a consoling hug before she began to clear the evidence of their adventures, but it was too late.

Nanny had woken by herself.

'What has been going on here?' she said severely. 'It appears to me that you have disobeyed my orders and been playing games.'

'Henry has been learning at the same time,' Agnes said. 'We have been studying geography.'

'Is that a bedsheet?' Miss Treen said.

'It came from the linen cupboard. I'll put it straight back.'

'No, don't. It will be covered with dust.' Her eyes focused on Henry's hat. 'Is that your father's newspaper?' Nanny pulled it off his head and started to unfold it so she could read the date. 'This is today's. He won't have read it yet. Oh dear . . . He will have our guts for garters when he finds out.'

'I'll put it back together again,' Agnes said.

'You can try – I'm not sure that you will have any success.' Nanny sighed. 'I suppose this is what happens when the cat's away.'

'What is that, Nanny?' Henry asked.

'The mice will play. Never mind. I'll thank you for not mentioning this to your parents this evening. Would you oblige me by tidying up here, Agnes, and looking after Henry for a little while longer? I wish to have a private conversation with the mistress.'

Agnes felt her forehead tighten.

'It's all right. It's nothing serious, just an idea that I've had.' Nanny bustled away, returning about ten minutes later.

'Were you well received?' Agnes dared to ask.

Nanny nodded carefully. 'I think so. Mama requests the pleasure of your company – both of you – in the drawing room at six o'clock as usual. She has something to tell you.'

'What can that be?'

'Patience, Agnes.'

If Papa noticed the extra creases in his newspaper later that day, he didn't say so.

Henry sat beside Mama on the chaise. Agnes perched on the chair opposite Papa's. Nanny had retired to her room.

'She will be nineteen in December. It won't be long before we have to turn our thoughts to her marriage,' Mama said. 'Miss Treen is right. How is she to make a good match if she never meets any eligible young men? Or old ones for that matter?'

Marriage? Agnes sat up straight.

'Sometimes I wonder if we have sheltered her a little too well,' Mama went on. 'She has had little opportunity to put her accomplishments to the test. What do you think of holding a party here at Windmarsh to celebrate her birthday?'

'I think that is a wonderful idea,' Papa said. 'What do you think, Agnes?'

'You have taken me by surprise. Thank you.' A social gathering in her honour? She was eighteen years old, and restless. She hadn't wandered further than two miles from Windmarsh Court for months. She had read every book in the library, walked every inch of the gardens, and painted a series of watercolours of the marsh birds and landscape. She yearned for passion and adventure. Perhaps this could be the start of it.

'It would be the perfect opportunity to introduce her to a wider social circle,' Mama said. 'I could write to the Seddons at Sittingbourne, the Norths and the Throwleys. How about inviting some of the other members of the Board? They are gentlemen of stature and influence. Some of them must have sons of a suitable age, surely?'

Papa was on the Board of Guardians, responsible for managing the Union in Faversham. He took his role of helping the poor in the workhouse very seriously, even though Mama didn't approve.

'I don't think so,' he said.

'Are you trying to tell me that your associates have been blessed only with daughters?' Mama said, her tone scathing. 'Really, James.'

'You know I don't like to bring business – and that includes my charitable works – into the sanctuary of our home,' Papa said, sounding annoyed. 'Let me consider your suggestion. I will give you an answer tomorrow.'

'Nanny has observed that the girl will need new clothes for such an occasion,' Mama said, apparently satisfied with Papa's response.

'Then arrange for the dressmaker to call,' Papa said more cheerfully.

'Oh, Mama, can't I go to Mrs Roache's shop in person?' Agnes asked.

'Absolutely not,' Papa said. 'No, I forbid it.'

'James, she can go with Nanny as chaperone – she has already offered. Miriam can look after Henry. It's time that she experienced a little of the world beyond Windmarsh Court,' Mama continued as Papa stroked his beard.

'Anyone would think you were in a hurry to see her married,' he said slowly.

'Well, she can't stay here for the rest of her life. I couldn't contemplate having her here to look after us in our old age as my sister cares for my parents. She will require her own establishment.'

Mama flicked her fan open and started fanning furiously. Not for the first time, Agnes felt that she was nothing more than an inconvenience.

'I wonder how your cousin Philip will find you when he comes to Windmarsh for the celebrations,' she began again.

Agnes frowned.

'He is not spoken for as yet,' Mama went on. 'He would make a suitable husband.'

'Oh, Mama, you cannot be suggesting—'

'You could do worse.'

'Over my dead body, Louisa. It's too soon to think about Agnes leaving us,' Papa interrupted. 'I should miss her far too much. Besides, much as I admire Philip for his determination in opposing my brother regarding his choice of profession, he isn't for our daughter. She will marry up as we planned from the beginning.'

Agnes smiled, relieved that even if Mama was plotting a match between her and her cousin, there was no way her father would ever allow it.

Papa returned to the subject of Agnes's birthday. 'I'll make the arrangements in advance for Agnes and Miss Treen to accompany me to Faversham in the carriage.'

'I should like to see the brewery,' Agnes said.

'There is no need for you to worry your head about the brewery,' he said with a smile. 'It will fall to Master Henry to manage the family business in the future. Your destiny is to marry well, bear children, and oversee the running of a grand household, just like your mother.'

Why was Nanny teaching her about Italy and poetry if she was to become a wife like Mama? she wondered.

'I wish that you would come with us too, Louisa,' Papa went on.

'I couldn't possibly countenance travelling to Faversham – you know what effect it has on my nerves. I shall spend the day quietly at home.'

'As you always do,' Papa said, downcast. He turned his eyes to the flames that flickered in the fireplace, obviously irritated by his wife's decision, but Agnes wondered if there was something else troubling him. Was he unwell, or worrying about the brewery?

It wasn't long before she was tasked with taking Henry back to the nursery.

'We are going to Faversham,' she told Nanny as she started putting Henry to bed. 'Papa has agreed. What did you say to persuade Mama that we should have a party at Windmarsh?'

'I reminded her of your birthday.'

'Had she forgotten?' Nanny didn't comment. Of course she had forgotten, Agnes thought.

The next few days were taken up with making arrangements for the trip to Faversham and the gathering at Windmarsh Court two weeks after that. Papa agreed to Mama's guest list, including the gentlemen of the Board and their families. Agnes wrote the invitations and posted them – along with letters that Nanny had written – one day while she, Nanny and Henry were out on their usual walk. Mama met with Mrs Catchpole and Cook to choose the menu for the guests and decorations for the table. For the first time in ages, the house was a hive of activity.

Papa sat opposite Agnes in the carriage on the way to Faversham on a freezing late November morning. He was dressed in a silk hat and heavy coat with silver buttons that matched the silver top of his ebony cane. His beard was bushier than ever, but the coppery colour had been toned down by the appearance of a smattering of white hairs. Outside the carriage, a biting wind swept across the marsh.

'You are cold,' said Papa. 'Would you like a blanket?

'No, thank you, Papa.' She had arranged her foot warmer – a wooden box containing a tray of hot coals – at her feet with her skirt hanging over it to trap the heat. If she had shivered, it was with excitement and anticipation, not from the chill in the air.

'I shall take advantage of it then,' Nanny said from beside her. She was past forty now and although she looked much younger, unworn by the trials of marriage and childbirth, she complained frequently of pains in her knees. She was wearing her Sunday best and had scrubbed her face so hard for the occasion that her cheeks were high with colour.

Papa handed her the blanket.

Agnes looked back at the house and waved to Henry,

who was standing at the nursery window where he had been left to spend the day with Miriam.

As they travelled, Agnes gazed at the passing scenery while Nanny kept her eyes firmly closed and Papa occupied himself with looking at some papers. When the spire of the parish church came into view, he put down his work and drew the curtains.

'Oh, Papa,' Agnes sighed.

'It's best not to draw attention to ourselves,' he said.

She opened her mouth to question him, but thought better of it as Nanny gave her a nudge with her elbow. It wasn't her place to question the authority of her father, but it seemed a strange precaution to take, unless it was because he was in a hurry to get to business at the brewery and didn't want to be waylaid by anyone. She frowned. Surely, everyone recognised the carriage as belonging to the Berry-Clays anyway. Unless, she thought, he didn't want anyone to know she had accompanied him. Was he ashamed of her for some reason?

'Are you quite well, Miss Treen?' Papa enquired.

'It is the motion of the carriage, Mr Berry-Clay. I shall be better when we are back on terra firma.'

'Which won't be long. We are just arriving at the brewery,' he said as the carriage lurched around a corner and pulled up on the cobbles. Noakes yelled at the horses to stand still and the door came open.

'Good morning, sir.' One of the draymen lowered the step. Papa alighted first, followed by Nanny who looked as if she was about to faint. Agnes stepped down behind them and took a deep breath of hot malt, yeast and bitter hops.

The brew house and tower were in front of her, the date 1745 inscribed in stone above the entrance. To her left were offices, a malt house and cooperage, and to her right was another building that held the stalls for the dray horses. Behind her was the rear of the tap house where the Berry-Clays sold beer direct to the public.

'It is quite an enterprise, is it not?' Papa said, his voice filled with pride.

'It is indeed,' Agnes said, listening to the sounds of the brewery: a blacksmith, hammering a shoe on to a horse's hoof; the low vibration of the machinery operating the leather conveyor belt which carried the fine malt grist sixty feet to the top of the tower; a cooper laughing with one of the draymen as he overhauled a damaged barrel; a horse whinnying from its stall.

'I shall go to my office while you ladies spend the family fortune.' Papa's eyes twinkled with amusement. 'Look at how I wear myself out to keep the dressmakers of Faversham in clover.'

Agnes buried her gloved hands deep inside her fur muff. She had no idea what dresses cost. Nanny had taught her that it was vulgar for a lady to discuss money. Finance was a gentleman's responsibility.

'Miss Treen, it will take me several hours to conduct my business – I suggest that you meet me back here at three o'clock. Promise me that you'll keep to the main streets and take luncheon at the Ship Hotel – I have an account there. Mention my name and they will find you a private room where you will be safe from unwanted attention. Many people pass through this town: revenue and excise men, all kinds of journeymen, couriers, the military, preachers . . . Some are respectable fellows, but many are scoundrels.' He smiled again and wished them good day before turning and walking towards the brew house.

'Your father is the most considerate gentleman in all of Kent,' Nanny said. 'Let us walk before we freeze to death.'

They attended the dressmaker first. It was a spacious establishment, Agnes thought as they stepped inside. It smelled of lavender, roses and fresh linen, and there was a counter with an archway behind it, and shelves containing rows of materials: silks, satins, muslins and cottons of every colour of the rainbow.

A woman who was about the same age as Mama, wearing a blue dress with elaborate ruffles and under-sleeves, stepped through the arch from the back of the shop. Agnes had met her when she had visited Windmarsh Court in the past. She was tall with dark hair, a widow's peak and pale – almost white – eyebrows and lashes.

'Good morning, Mrs Roache,' Nanny said. 'I believe you are expecting us.'

'Miss Berry-Clay and Miss Treen, I'm delighted to renew our acquaintance. Come this way.' The dressmaker showed them to an alcove to one side of the counter, and called for a girl to take their coats. 'Please, take a seat so that we can discuss your exact requirements,' Mrs Roache continued. 'Your mama sent word that a pale grey or deep green silk would suit your complexion, and that she isn't keen on red. You require three dresses à la mode, laced corsets and petticoats.'

'I believe that is Mama's wish,' Agnes said, although she coveted the scarlet velvet that she had seen on the shelves. She wasn't sure about her mother's knowledge of current fashions and she certainly didn't want to dress like her any longer in pale hues that sapped the complexion.

'What do you think of this?' Mrs Roache showed her a drawing from a pattern book of a woman with acres of skirt and a tightly laced bodice. 'I can see that in a French silk – we have this beautiful shade of pale grey, almost white.' She nodded at the girl, who spread the end of a roll across the table.

'I think your mama would be happy with that one,' Nanny said. 'It is suitably demure for a young lady.'

Agnes sighed inwardly. She didn't want to be demure. She wished to be noticed. She had a vague, romantic notion that if she did ever have the chance of attending a party where there were young men present, her style of dress would do as much to attract their attention and interest as her conversation, singing voice and knowledge of geography.

'So we are agreed on that one.' Mrs Roache asked the girl to put the roll of material and the pattern aside. 'Let's examine the green silks next.'

Agnes noticed that Nanny kept glancing at the clock.

The girl fetched two shades of green, one deep like a wine bottle, the other brighter, like emeralds.

'I prefer the lighter shade,' Agnes said quickly.

'It is perfect for you,' Mrs Roache said, holding it up to Agnes's face. 'It complements your eyes.'

'I'm not sure,' Nanny began.

'Yes, that is my second choice,' Agnes said quickly, cutting her off.

Mrs Roache smiled. 'An excellent decision. You have an eye for colour, Miss Berry-Clay.'

'I should like to see the scarlet velvet next, if I may,' she said politely but firmly.

'Of course you may. You are the customer, and the customer may request whatever she wants,' Mrs Roache said with humour.

'Oh no, miss, I would counsel you not to go against your mama's direction,' Nanny said.

'It's my decision. I will take responsibility for my choices. I should like to see the scarlet,' Agnes repeated, in defiance of her governess's disapproving frown.

'Are you sure that a practical navy serge like mine wouldn't be more appropriate for the third dress?'

'Surely you know that you don't wear serge to parties.

These outfits are for social occasions, not every day. You are supposed to be my chaperone, not my fashion adviser.' Agnes felt a little guilty for being sharp with her dear governess, who was only trying to help her avoid any unpleasantness with Mama, but she adored the scarlet cloth. She could picture it made into the most delectable dress with a low-cut bodice and lace to protect her modesty. 'I like this very much.'

'In that case, I shall take your measurements in preparation for making your dresses. If you'd care to step this way.' Mrs Roache showed them into the room at the rear of the shop.

There was a doorway leading into another room behind that where she could see four women at work. One was laying out a pattern on to a piece of fabric at a large table. Another was pinning and cutting. The third and fourth were sewing.

'That is the workshop where everything is done by hand with great precision and care,' Mrs Roache said. She proceeded to measure Agnes with a tape, writing down the length of her arms, width of her shoulders and circumference of her waist in a notebook. Eventually, she decided that she had enough information to work with and printed out the details of the order.

'You are welcome to return for a fitting once the order is completed, or I can arrange to call at Windmarsh Court with the items.'

'Oh, I should like to come back to the shop,' Agnes said.

'I think it best that you call at the house,' Nanny said. 'It's what your father would prefer.'

Reluctantly Agnes agreed and confirmed the order with her signature.

When she and Nanny were back outside the shop, she wondered briefly if she could give her the slip and explore on her own, but she knew that if she stepped out of line, she would never be allowed to forget it and there would be no chance of keeping the red velvet dress.

'I had planned to show you the creek, but your papa has asked me to keep to the main streets,' Nanny said, glancing over her shoulder as if she was expecting to find someone staring down her neck.

'You're as nervous as a bird,' Agnes observed.

Nanny turned and took her by the hands.

'Listen to me,' she said in a low voice. 'This is very important. You have to promise me that you can keep a secret.'

'That's a strange request. What kind of secret?'

'I have to know that I can trust you not to breathe a word of this to anyone, not Henry, not Miriam, not your parents, not Mrs Catchpole.'

'Well, I don't know.' As far as she knew, keeping secrets and telling lies had a habit of getting one into trouble.

'Promise me,' Nanny repeated.

Agnes nodded. 'Is it about a gentleman?' she asked.

'What on earth are you talking about?'

'I thought with the letter that came and all the secrecy, you might have been arranging a clandestine meeting. I don't mind. It's wonderfully romantic. Although Henry and I will miss you when—'

'Agnes, you have got hold of the wrong end of the stick. I am not being courted, more's the pity, and if I were, I would never risk my place by indulging in the pursuit of love while at work and holding responsibility for the moral welfare of a susceptible young lady. There are many who have lost their incomes through their indiscretions, and I shall not be one of them,' Nanny said. 'I will explain when there are fewer pairs of ears around to hear us. This has nothing to do with me, and everything to do with you.'

# Chapter Six

## *Half a Sixpence*

'What is it?' Agnes followed her governess along the street. 'Please don't keep me in suspense.'

'Hush,' Nanny said. 'Hold your tongue.'

They passed the timber-framed Guildhall which stood on stilts. Beneath it the market traders were busily selling butter, cheese, fruit and other provisions.

'The freshest dabs you've ever sin,' crowed the man at the fish stall, which was piled high with flatfish, cod, cockles and whelks. The fish seemed to stare at her with their dead eyes, Agnes thought, hurrying past to avoid the smell of stale seaweed. 'They're cheap at the price, ladies. I promise you, you won't be disappointed.'

'No, thank you,' Nanny said, hurrying along.

They crossed the iron footbridge and made their way past the tall quayside buildings to Crab Island, where there was a partially built timber hull and several boats lined up for maintenance and repair in the shipyard.

'I think it's safe to talk here.' Nanny stopped.

Was it? Agnes wondered. 'You're frightening me.'

'Steel yourself, my dear. I received a letter recently from a woman whom I had thought long dead. In fact, your father had informed me of that fact, so imagine my surprise when I heard she was alive and well.'

'Do stop talking in riddles.'

'I am speaking of your mother, not Mama, the other one.'

'How can that be?' Agnes's hands were shaking. 'That can't be right. She is dead. Papa says so.'

'I'm afraid I have no doubt that the woman who wrote the letter is telling the truth and she is who she says she is.'

'Papa wouldn't lie. He is an honest man.' He was her hero, her protector. He adored her. It wasn't possible.

'I'm sorry, this must be a terrible shock to you, but I assure you that it's true.'

'Is this why you went to so much trouble to get me here? You planted the idea of a party in Mama's head and offered to chaperone me? I can't believe it. I didn't think you were capable of such a devious and underhand plot. How could you? I am . . .' Agnes touched her mouth ' . . . speechless.'

'Oh dear, this seemed so straightforward, but now we are here . . . I wish that I'd burned the letter and kept my silence.'

'So do I,' Agnes said bitterly.

'I have searched my conscience many times since she made contact with me,' her governess continued, 'and decided that it was right that you two should meet, albeit briefly.'

'But why? What good will it do?'

'I lost my dear mama and I wish for you to know yours. Your mother wrote such a sweet, considerate letter, and it revived my guilt for my part in what happened. Let me tell you the story—'

'Is this the truth or more lies?' Agnes interrupted, the words grating in her throat.

'I was looking for a position with a respectable family,' Nanny went on. 'There was an advertisement in the newspaper asking for an educated, well-mannered young lady of Christian beliefs and good moral standing to take up the position of nanny. I answered it. Your father interviewed me, and having decided that all was in order, he introduced me to your mama, who gave her approval for me to look after their child. They didn't send for me straight away. They paid me a retainer for about a month before they contacted me again to inform me that they had hopes of adopting an infant.'

'That was me?' Agnes said.

'Yes. I tore you from your loving mother's arms when you were no more than eight months old. The look on her face as you screamed for her will haunt me for ever. I hope that arranging this meeting will go some way in making amends.'

'Isn't it rather too late for that?' Agnes felt numb. 'Why did she contact you now? Why not years ago if she felt so much love for me, her child?'

'I'm sure she will be able to explain.'

A horse and cart passed by laden with baskets of oakum caulking, and a young man in dirty clothes with a tattoo of an anchor on his arm sauntered along, whistling out loud.

'Where did Papa meet my mother?'

'She was one of the inmates at the Union.'

'The workhouse?' Agnes bit back tears. How could that be? There was only one explanation. She had come from lowly stock. She was not descended from a baronet or even a country squire. Papa had misled her in more ways than one. She had thought herself above Nanny and the servants at Windmarsh Court, yet here she was in reality brought lower than anyone she knew by her birth.

How could she now be a person of consequence, knowing her true origins? How could she walk the drawing rooms of society with confidence? How would she ever marry a prince?

'You know that your father is on the Board of Guardians,' Nanny went on.

She nodded.

'Your mother was young and unmarried, and she applied for the Union's support – your papa authorised it.'

So he had taken pity on her out of kindness, but it wasn't a kind thing that he had done, Agnes thought. She was devastated.

'You were the prettiest child with a sunny disposition in spite of the trials you had been through. Once I'd spent a while consoling you over parting from your mother, it soon became clear that you were willing to love and be loved, which is exactly what Mrs Berry-Clay desired at the time, having been unable to produce a child in the first years of her marriage.'

'Which is strange, because I can't remember her ever showing me any affection,' Agnes observed.

'She adored you at first. She took you in her arms and wouldn't let you go, but after a few months, she returned to her old self,' Nanny said. 'I have great respect for her, but I can't help thinking that she's incapable of deep and lasting affection. The novelty of having a daughter wore off. She couldn't love a child who wasn't truly hers. I don't blame her – I believe she was brought up in a very strict household.'

'Stricter than Windmarsh?'

'Oh yes. Your father once mentioned when he was giving me instructions on the methods of discipline he wanted me to employ with you, that the nanny there used to tie the children to their chairs and lock them in cupboards to punish them for the most minor misdemeanours. Your mama's nerves never recovered.'

What else was her beloved governess going to reveal today? A storm of confusion and resentment raged inside Agnes's mind. It seemed that she had been rejected twice – by her true mother first, and then by Mama. It was all too much for her to take in.

'I want to go home,' she decided. 'I have no wish to meet this woman.'

'You can't blame her. This situation was not of her making.'

'She wasn't married,' Agnes said. 'That makes her a whore, doesn't it?'

'That is a wicked judgement to make. I'm disappointed in you.'

Agnes recalled the last time she had fallen in Nanny's estimation. She remembered Oliver and the boy at the tannery, and how one's fate was not always of one's own making.

'I'm sorry. You're right, but it makes no difference,' she said.

'I realise this is rather distressing for you, Agnes—'

'I will not meet her,' she interrupted.

'Please keep your voice down and your emotions in check. Don't make a scene.'

Agnes hadn't realised that she had raised her voice. She glanced around her, obedient to her governess from force of habit. One of the boat builders had paused with a hammer in his hand, but otherwise from where she was, everyone appeared to be carrying out their business in a normal manner. Why should they notice her? She was nobody.

'I promise that she would have kept you if she could,' Nanny whispered.

'How do you know that?' Agnes said hotly.

'I saw the look in her eyes. She could hardly bear to let you go.'

'Oh?' Agnes wasn't sure how to respond. The stench of fish filled her nostrils. A boy was washing fish guts and scales from the deck of a barge moored alongside. A young woman ran by, dressed in a tattered yellow dress pricked out with pink flowers, a shawl and grubby shoes.

Nanny took a firm grip on Agnes's arm.

'Walk this way. Briskly. There are things that are not suitable for a young lady's eyes.' Nanny caught her breath. 'What is he doing here? Don't tell me he is here carrying out charitable works.'

'Who? Who is it?'

'Hush. Turn your face away.'

Agnes was about to disobey, but there was something in her governess's voice that stopped her. She looked down at her feet, but not before she caught sight of her uncle, dressed in a hat and long coat, and carrying his stick.

'I expect he came to take the air. Yes, I'm sure that's it,' Nanny said. 'I don't believe that he saw us. Our secret is safe.'

Agnes wasn't sure from the tone of her voice that Nanny was convinced, but, she reasoned, her uncle was supposed to be at the brewery with Papa, so he might not wish to reveal his whereabouts by exposing theirs. If they could leave now and return to Windmarsh without anything more being said, she might be able to forget this episode and the circumstances of her birth, even if she wasn't sure she could ever forgive her governess for putting her into this situation, and Papa for lying to her. The fact that he had hesitated over Mama's suggestion that they should invite the gentlemen of the Board of Guardians made sense now. He didn't want to be reminded of where his daughter had come from.

'Let us go home,' Agnes said quickly, but Nanny

ignored her, her eyes on the figure of a woman who had slipped out of the shadows cast by the barge.

Agnes tried to get away, but her governess had caught her behind the elbow, pinching her fingers into the soft flesh there to cause her maximum pain as she had when Agnes had been younger and about to blurt out something unwanted in front of her parents.

'You will stand here and meet your mother,' Nanny said through gritted teeth.

The figure approached, her face shaded. She stopped in front of them and pulled the hood of her cloak back to reveal her wavy dark hair. She was almost as tall as Agnes, and – she had to allow – quite handsome, although her complexion was weathered and her hands were chapped and swollen with chilblains. She was a countrywoman, Agnes thought, unable to stop staring at the stranger who seemed somehow familiar. There was no doubting her identity. She saw the shape of her cheekbones and curve of her chin every day in the mirror in her room at Windmarsh Court.

The woman turned to Nanny who seemed overwhelmed at the sight of the two, mother and daughter, together.

'Good morning, Miss Treen,' she said softly. 'I remember you.'

'As I do you.' She held a handkerchief to her nose. 'I shall keep watch at a distance.'

'No, you will wait here,' Agnes said, but Nanny had already taken up a position a short distance away.

'Thank you for agreeing to meet me,' the woman said.

'I did not choose to do this. Make it brief,' Agnes said curtly.

'I'm sorry for your inconvenience.' A shadow crossed the woman's eyes. 'Let me take your hands and look at you awhile. Let me absorb your features into my memory.'

'I've dreamt of this moment every day since we were parted,' she went on in a coarse Kentish accent.

'I don't know you.' Agnes took a step back, afraid of getting her new kid gloves dirty. She thought of Papa and how she would have to lie to him. 'I shouldn't be here. It is a mistake. My governess has made a terrible error of judgement.'

The woman's eyes filled with tears.

'I won't keep you for long. I have just one request – in a few days' time, it will be your nineteenth birthday.'

Agnes nodded.

'I have something for you—'

'I don't want anything from you.'

'It is a memento of your true father.' The woman's voice quavered. 'It holds the deep sentiments of the man who loved you before you were born. I've held it on his behalf until now, but it's time I passed it on to you. You can decide when to hand it on to your children in turn.'

'I don't want anything of yours, thank you, Mrs—' Agnes pushed her hand away.

'My name is Mrs Carter, Mrs Catherine Carter.' She grasped Agnes's hand firmly and pressed a small object into her palm. 'You must take it. I insist.'

Agnes stared at it as it glinted in the pale winter sun. It was a roughened and stained piece of a coin, not a whole sixpence, just half of one, set on a silver chain.

'What would I want with that?'

'Your father gave it to me – he must have cut the original coin in half when he was on the ship, waiting for passage. It is yours, my dear Agnes. It belongs to you.'

Agnes trembled uncontrollably as the woman continued, 'The half a sixpence is a lucky charm. Promise me that you'll keep it safe to keep the memory of your loving father alive.'

'I shall not promise anything,' Agnes said stubbornly. 'This man of whom you speak is not my father, just as you are not my mother.' She didn't mean to sound so disdainful, but she was still reeling with shock at discovering her deceased mother was actually alive, and that she had been born out of wedlock to a woman who had been forced into the workhouse by poverty. It was all too much.

'I can't – I don't expect you to feel fondly towards me, but your true father was a good man. We were about to be married, but on our wedding day, he was arrested and charged with a crime he didn't commit. I expect you have heard of the battle of Bossenden' – she pronounced it Bozenden – 'your governess will have taught you about it. It happened in the year you were born.'

In spite of her determination not to be drawn into further conversation, Agnes shook her head. She hadn't heard of it. Why had Nanny deemed the history of Italy more important than local events?

'Sir William Courtenay, also known as plain Mr Thom, was a liar and a lunatic who led a gang of farm labourers into an uprising near Dunkirk. He persuaded them to fight, promising them riches when they had defeated the wealthy farmers and landowners who were the cause of their oppression. It didn't end well.'

'What happened to my father?' Agnes asked, her curiosity getting the better of her.

'He was convicted of murder at the Maidstone Assizes and transported to the other side of the world.'

Agnes felt her blood drain to her feet. On top of everything else, she was the daughter of a convicted murderer?

'He was innocent. He wouldn't hurt a fly.' The woman

caught Agnes by the arm. 'I'm sorry, but I thought you should know.'

'Is he still alive?'

'I did hear from him once – he had served his sentence and was making a life for himself in Tasmania. He asked me to join him, but it was too late.' She took a moment to regain her voice. 'You look very well. I did right by you even though it was against my instincts. And now – well, I made a promise that I wouldn't try to find you – I have already breached it by coming here. Remember, my darling daughter, I have never stopped loving you.' She reached out and brushed her fingers against Agnes's cheek. 'Always and for ever.'

She pulled up her hood, turned and hurried away, leaving Agnes standing on the wharf, her mind welling up with questions, and her eyes filling with tears. She glanced down at her clenched fist and opened her palm. The half a sixpence glittered.

She raised her arm to throw it into the water, but something stopped her: the image in her head of a young man about to become a husband and father, shackled and imprisoned. Even then in his despair, he had thought of his family and created the love token, because that was what it was. It was worth nothing, yet it had meant everything to him.

She slipped the half a sixpence and chain inside her glove.

'You look very pale,' Nanny observed as she returned to Agnes's side.

'Oh, leave me alone.'

'You know I can't do that. Come along now. Let's go to the inn to recover our wits.'

'I have not lost my wits,' Agnes protested.

'Wipe your eyes.' Nanny tried to give her a handkerchief, but Agnes refused to take it.

In that morning, her true mother's revelations had dragged her from her privileged and rather dull existence and forced her abruptly into adulthood. She was not an orphan. She did not hail from the higher echelons of society. She was the illegitimate daughter of a countrywoman and a man who had been transported to the other side of the world for a crime he hadn't committed.

'I don't expect you to understand why I brought you here. You may never understand, but to know yourself, you need to know where you came from. One day, if by some mischance you find yourself facing adversity, you'll be able to look back and think of your mother and remember how she had the strength to carry on and come through hard times. She is no longer in the workhouse. She is married and living quietly in the country.'

'She looked quite unkempt. Didn't you notice her clothes? The mud on her boots? The way she spoke . . .' Agnes felt a little sorry for being so abrupt with the poor woman now.

'She is comfortably off, I believe,' Nanny said. 'Didn't you want to ask her more questions? Weren't you curious?'

'No,' Agnes said firmly. 'I want nothing more than to put this behind me. I will not hear any talk of this again.'

'That's very wise.' Nanny cleared her throat. 'You will be sure not to say anything? If your father finds out that I have betrayed his trust after all these years, I will lose my place. You will have your dresses and your party. Who knows what will happen to me?'

'I won't betray you.' Who had comforted her when she

had woken from a nightmare? Who had read to her and mopped her brow when she had been sick? Who had taught her to draw and paint? Her governess was more of a mother to her than anyone else. 'I promise.'

'Then I'm most grateful.'

'Just one thing,' Agnes said. 'Did you know of my true father's fate? Is that why you were so determined that we wouldn't study Australia and Tasmania?'

'I had an inkling,' Nanny admitted. 'I'm sorry, I didn't want to expose you, an innocent child with a sensitive nature, to the subject of criminals and imprisonment.' She forced a smile. 'When you were young, you were terrified of the idea that the spirits of the smugglers from long ago were haunting the house. I didn't want to add to your anxieties, or remind myself of mine. When I attended the school for the daughters of distressed gentlefolk, one of the teachers would threaten us with transportation.'

'How cruel!' Agnes exclaimed.

'I never forgot it.' Nanny changed the subject. 'Let us look forward, not back. We will make our way to the Ship Hotel to take refreshment.'

They walked back into the middle of the town and made their way to the hotel where the landlord showed them through to a private room and arranged for them to be served a dish of roasted lamb and vegetables.

'That was a most enjoyable luncheon, even more so as your father is paying,' Nanny said, wiping her mouth delicately with a napkin.

Agnes looked down at her dish – she had hardly touched her food.

'It seems a shame to waste it when it costs all of one shilling and six. May I?' Without waiting for permission,

Nanny exchanged their dishes, and continued to eat. It appeared that the meeting with Agnes's true mother had settled her conscience and revived her appetite, because by the time they arrived back at the brewery to meet Papa, her health seemed fully restored.

It was her father who did not seem well during their journey in the carriage. He looked weary, Agnes thought.

'Well, did you order plenty of new dresses?' he asked.

'Yes, Papa,' she said rather curtly. She wasn't sure she could forgive him for his deception.

'And Nanny showed you the market?'

She nodded. 'We enjoyed our luncheon at the hotel.'

'I thought you would. It is good hearty fare. I had hoped to meet you there, but I had business to attend to. One of the men was mixing hot water and grist in the mash tun – I don't know how he managed it, but the water got into his boots.' Papa grimaced. 'I have never heard a man scream like that. I sent him home on one of the drays, and called for the doctor. I hope that he'll be able to return to work in a while. In the meantime, I shall have to continue to pay his wage so he can support his family. He has a wife and five children. But that's enough talk of the brewery. What did you learn from your trip to Faversham?'

Agnes glanced at her governess. Part of her wanted to confess so she could challenge her father over his lies, but she remembered what Miss Treen had said. She couldn't bear it if she lost her place, and she and Henry never saw her again.

'Nanny taught me some history,' she said lightly. It was true – she had learned the history of her other family and where she had come from.

# Chapter Seven

## *Many a Slip Twixt Cup and Lip*

'We'd better make sure you're ready in plenty of time,' Nanny said as she brushed Agnes's hair on the evening of the birthday celebration. It was December and a fire burned in the grate.

'How about you?' Agnes gazed at their reflections in the mirror on the dressing table. 'You are invited to dinner.'

'I'm bringing Henry to meet the guests, then I'll put him to bed before I come back down. Now, which dress did you and Mama decide upon?'

Mrs Roache had delivered the new dresses the day before, and although Agnes had been a little afraid of Mama's reaction to the scarlet one, she had in fact been delighted with it.

'Can't you guess?' Agnes smiled as Nanny finished putting her hair up.

'You're right. Of course I can. Answer a fool according to his folly, lest he be wise in his. Now, mind you don't spoil my handiwork while you're dressing.'

Agnes stood up and put on a long chemise and a corset of whalebone over white cotton bloomers and dark stockings. Next, she added a petticoat and an underskirt with a ruffled hem, and a corset cover before Nanny helped her with the dress. She picked up a mother-of-pearl fan from the dressing table.

'What about one of your necklaces to complete the picture?' Nanny said.

'The gold one?' Agnes opened her rosewood box and there on top of her other jewellery was the half a sixpence. She picked it up and rolled it between her fingers, remembering the pain she'd felt on meeting her true mother. 'What if Uncle Rufus did see us and he reports to Papa while he's here tonight?'

'Don't you think he would have done that by now? They see each other almost every day at the brewery. You know I'm right,' Nanny said. 'It's important to know where you came from, but now you must put that knowledge aside and make the best life that you can. Put the coin away. Keep it safe.'

Agnes hid it in the compartment beneath the velvet liner at the bottom of the box. She had thought of little else the past few days, and managed to gain some perspective on what she had found out about her past. Her mother had loved her. She had no doubt that she had done her best in her straitened circumstances. She wondered what her life would have been like if her parents had married. Would she have been brought up on the land and lived in a tiny cottage? Would she have had lots of brothers and sisters? She would have liked to have been part of a large family, but there was no point in wishing that things had been different.

Nanny was right. It was time to shut away the past, and move on. It was her birthday. She could still be the daughter of a baronet, she could still marry a prince, as long as nobody else knew her secret. Her true mother's existence and the revelation of her father's past had been a shock, but there was no need for them to affect her future.

For the first time in her life, she felt true gratitude: to

Nanny for bringing her up to be a lady, and most of all to her dear papa who had taken her in and stood by her, and loved her as his own daughter.

She took her chosen necklace from the box and handed it to her governess who reached round and fastened the clasp at the back of her neck. Touching the jewelled pendant at her throat, Agnes glanced into the mirror again. Her eyes were flashing in the light of the candle and her cheeks were pink with anticipation.

'Where has my little girl gone?' Nanny grew tearful. 'You are quite grown up. Soon, you will get married and leave us, then what will I do?'

'You will come with me, of course,' Agnes said, unable to contemplate being without her. 'You will be nanny to my children.'

'That's very sweet of you. When Henry is sent away to school, I'll be done here.'

'I wonder when I'll meet my handsome prince.'

'Handsome is as handsome does, and a prince is just as likely to turn out to be a rogue as an ordinary man.'

'I shan't marry an ordinary man.'

'I'm sure you won't.' Nanny smiled. 'It's time you went downstairs. Your mama has expressed a wish that you sit with her to greet the guests.'

Agnes went to the drawing room and her mother stared at her from the chaise. She was wearing one of her pale grey dresses with a hooped skirt, and white flowers in her hair which she wore in barley curls, long ringlets which she thought the height of fashion, although Agnes begged to differ.

'The red suits your colouring, although it would not be my preference,' she said eventually. She patted the chaise beside her. 'Come and sit here. You are looking well.'

'Thank you, Mama.' Agnes took her place as a bell

rang from downstairs, announcing the arrival of the guests.

'I wish you a happy birthday,' Mama said as the visitors filed into the drawing room. Papa, wearing one of his colourful silk waistcoats, made the formal introductions. There were her uncle and his family, two sets of near neighbours, an earnest young man who was a friend of her cousin Philip, and Aunt Caroline and Agnes's grandparents. The Seddons, the Norths and the Throwleys arrived, along with several acquaintances of Papa's linked with his business and charitable endeavours. They were accompanied by their wives, and two of the couples brought their sons and daughters.

'Allow me to introduce our beautiful daughter, Miss Agnes Berry-Clay,' Papa kept saying. A sheen of perspiration shone on his forehead.

If Mama had imagined that this was a good way of introducing her into society, Agnes was a little disappointed, but when she thought of the alternative, what low class of person she would have met if she had been brought up by her true mother and father, she felt somewhat mollified. Her prince wasn't here this evening, but she had no doubt that one day he would appear. Or the baronet, she corrected herself in case she was aspiring too high. A baronet would suit her just as well.

'She is grown up to be quite the young lady,' one of the neighbours said. Agnes didn't like the way the husband kept staring at her, his eyes sweeping her figure.

She stood up and took her father aside.

'You look very beautiful tonight,' he said. 'I'm very proud of you, my dear.'

'Thank you. Are you well, Papa?' she asked quietly. 'You seem a little out of sorts.'

'I am perfectly well, thank you. It is rather close in here, that's all. The fire . . .' He gestured towards the fireplace where a fairy could have extinguished the sputtering flame with a single breath. It wasn't warm. She hadn't put on a shawl, wanting to show off the dress, but she could have done with one.

'Maybe it's a touch of dyspepsia. Don't worry your head about it. It will pass. I won't let anything spoil your evening.' He paused before going on, 'I have a surprise for you after dinner.'

'What can that be?' she asked, recalling the pineapple. Why did Papa always wish to show off? 'Is it a baronet wrapped up in brown paper and string?' she said lightly.

'Oh, Agnes.' He chuckled. 'Not tonight, but I will find you a suitable match, a man of stature with an estate of at least one hundred acres, and not too far away so that you can visit us often.' He turned to face the door. 'Ah, here is my son,' he said with a smile as Nanny led Henry and Cousin Edward into the drawing room. Henry stood shyly at Nanny's side, wearing a sailor suit, a blouse and navy bell-bottoms which Mama had had Mrs Roache make up for him because she wanted him to look like the little Prince of Wales.

'Where is the young lady of the moment?' The sound of Uncle Rufus's voice made Agnes start. 'Oh, there she is.' He pushed in between her and Papa, and took both her hands. 'What a wonderful occasion this is.' He had a blob of spittle on his lip and the ball of flesh at the side of his nose seemed to swell as he flared his nostrils, making her wonder if he had already partaken of too much sherry.

'It is indeed, uncle,' she said, trying to extricate herself from the unwanted contact without appearing rude.

'You will accompany me to the dining room,' he said, taking her by the arm instead. 'I hope there is no garlic.'

'Will you never forget?' Mama interrupted from the chaise.

'It kept the vampires away for a few days,' he chuckled as he held out his other arm, inviting Mama to join them. She stood up and walked across to them.

Agnes was aware that Nanny was frowning as though she wished to throw the manual of etiquette at him.

'I hope that Cook is well prepared. I gave her the menu to practise several days ago,' Mama said.

Which explained why they'd had roast venison in varying states from pink to cindered for three days in a row, Agnes thought, amused.

Nanny removed the two younger boys to the nursery and the rest of the party proceeded to the dining room, where the ladies and gentlemen sat down to dine. Agnes found herself seated between Papa and Philip.

Turner, who was dressed smartly in black, poured the wine. She noticed how he served Uncle Rufus sparingly with a nod from Papa. She turned to Philip, who smiled. He kept his mouth closed and it wasn't until he spoke that she noticed he'd lost two of his teeth at the top.

'This is a happy occasion, my dear cousin,' he said.

'How is Faversham?' she asked. 'I went there only ten days ago.'

'I doubt it has changed much since then,' he said seriously. 'Did you find much to occupy yourself with on your outing?'

'I visited the dressmaker, and Nanny and I went—' She bit her tongue, remembering that her governess had gone against Papa's orders. 'How are your studies?' she asked, changing the subject. 'Are you still planning to enter the medical profession?'

'Of course, but I'm still trying to obtain my father's blessing' – he smiled again – 'and a contribution to the expenses that I'd incur. I've left school and have no occupation, apart from going to the brewery every day to sit in the office and stare at the walls. It is tedious.'

'Why does he thwart you?'

'He is of the opinion that a gentleman should not work with his hands. I've told him that I can be a physician – I wouldn't be required to perform any procedures or surgeries as a surgeon does – but I can't convince him. I thought I'd speak to your father at some stage to see if he'll put a good word in for me.'

'My papa is tired,' Agnes said.

'And mine is a forceful and opinionated man, although his mind isn't as sharp as it used to be. I will not sacrifice my ambition for the brewery, so if the situation can't be resolved, I will walk away. I have some money put aside, and I can work while I'm studying.'

'Could you really do that, change your life in that way?'

'I don't know. I'm a coward at heart, too fearful of being cut off from my family to take that step.'

'It would be even harder for a member of the fairer sex,' Agnes observed. She looked around the table. Nanny, who had returned from the nursery and taken her place at the end of the table alongside Mama's parents, flashed her a glance of warning.

'We'd better keep our voices down, Cousin Philip. Our conversation is too animated for the dinner table.' Agnes suppresed a chuckle. It's giving Nanny concerns about our digestion.'

They went on to eat in silence.

Agnes barely tasted the fish course, or the venison, or the chartreuse of oranges and dariole pudding, because the memory of the small boy and the bucket of trimmings he had snipped from the hides at the tannery sprang to her mind as she watched her privileged family and acquaintances pushing food into their mouths to excess.

She wondered what 'wittles' Bert and his nearest and dearest were eating this evening. She wasn't sure why she had thought of him and the Cheeverses after all this time. Perhaps it was because Philip's honesty, which she admired, had reminded her a little of Oliver Cheevers.

'Shall we retire to the drawing room?' Mama said at the end of the meal. 'The gentlemen may stay and smoke if they wish.'

'Oh no,' Papa said immediately. He didn't smoke, but Uncle Rufus enjoyed a pipe. 'We will have some music – Agnes, will you sing to us, while Miss Treen plays the piano? I have a fancy to sit and listen for a while.'

'Are you sure you wish me to sing, Papa?' she said, recalling the occasion at Henry's christening many years before when her attempts at entertainment had been rebuffed.

'Of course,' he said. 'This is your day.'

Nanny moved to Agnes's side as they entered the drawing room. Agnes glanced towards Philip, who was standing beside his earnest friend with his back to the fireplace. He smiled and she smiled back.

Nanny sat down at the pianoforte.

'What would you like to begin with, Agnes?'

'"The Mistletoe Bough", I think.'

Nanny raised one eyebrow. 'Are you sure?'

Agnes nodded. The song was a little downhearted, about a missing newlywed bride who locked herself in a trunk while playing hide and seek with her wedding party, and died before she could be found, but it was in a key that suited her voice and she carried it off with aplomb. The audience clapped and cheered.

'Louisa, she is not only a beauty, she is a clever and artistic young lady,' said Aunt Sarah. 'She is a credit to you.'

'They have been practising for many hours and given me quite a headache.' Mama sighed, but she appeared to be enjoying the attention of the guests.

'I expect you have been standing over them with a horsewhip,' Uncle Rufus said cheerfully.

'Not at all,' Mama said. 'I have better ways of occupying my time.'

Agnes smiled to herself. Her upbringing had nothing to do with her adoptive mother, and everything to do with her father and governess.

'I do believe that is enough for now. You can have too much of a good thing, don't you think?' Mama went on.

'Not when she sings so sweetly, like a bird.' Uncle Rufus turned to Papa. 'I didn't realise that Agnes and Miss Treen had accompanied you to Faversham the other day. I was most surprised to see them on the wharf.'

Agnes froze. A chill ran down her spine as her uncle curled his mouth into a challenging smile.

'The wharf?' Papa said.

'I'm not mistaken,' Uncle Rufus said. 'Look how the guilty party blanches and trembles.'

'My instructions were to keep to the main streets,' Papa said, addressing Nanny.

'We took a wrong turn,' she said, keeping her eyes warily on the younger Mr Berry-Clay.

'And just happened to run into a mutual acquaintance of ours to ask her for directions, I assume,' he said.

'Which acquaintance?' Mama said. 'Do tell.'

Papa was bristling with fury. His face turned a deep scarlet.

'My daughter and her governess have no acquaintances in Faversham.'

'I thought as much, James. I feel it is my duty to report that I have seen your daughter and her chaperone in the company of the woman we once met at the Union, the whore whose child you took in.'

Silence fell upon the room. Everyone – the neighbours, friends, the gentlemen of the Board of Guardians, the Seddons, the Norths and the Throwleys – stared at the Berry-Clay brothers.

'Oh dear, have I said too much?' Uncle Rufus said.

Of course he had, Agnes thought, her jaw dropped open. To accuse someone's daughter of being born from the belly of a prostitute was disgraceful conduct when the mere sound of a belch in company could lead to the offender being ostracised by society. Her uncle's comment was absolutely unforgivable, and from the shocked silence that ensued, everyone in the room thought the same.

'Is this true?' Papa turned to Nanny.

'Don't listen to my husband,' Aunt Sarah stepped into the fray, reaching for her husband's sleeve. 'I'm afraid that he has taken leave of his senses.' She turned to the rest of the company. 'He is in his cups, thanks to the butler being overly generous with the contents of the cellar.'

It wasn't fair to blame Turner, Agnes thought, her heart pounding with apprehension.

'Rufus, we should send for our carriage and make our way home immediately.'

'What, and spoil the party?' he barked.

'You are doing that by yourself,' Aunt Sarah muttered. 'I am mortified.'

Turner cleared his throat to draw attention. 'I shall arrange for some strong coffee and tobacco to be sent up to the dining room. Gentlemen, come this way.' He tried to divert the brothers from the drawing room, on to the landing outside, but they refused to continue their argument in private, as though years of sibling rivalry and antagonism had bubbled over into outright war.

'I saw what I saw with my own eyes,' Uncle Rufus slurred. 'It is the absolute truth. I mean, why would I make it up?'

'For the same reason as you failed to mention this before,' Papa said sadly. 'To make a stir, to embarrass me in front of our friends and neighbours, to get back at me for some imagined slight from our childhood? You have always been jealous of me being the elder son. It has always brought you a perverse joy to humiliate me or cause me pain.' He turned back to Nanny. 'You have disobeyed my orders and broken my trust. I have no choice but to ask you to leave Windmarsh Court at first light.'

'No, Papa. You cannot send her away. I will not allow it.' Agnes confronted her father. 'Nanny didn't know where we were going or whom we were to meet. She is entirely innocent.'

'Then how did this come about? Tell me,' her father said sternly.

'I-I-I received a letter,' she stammered. So much for social convention and virtue! Her governess's reputation was at stake and she would do anything to defend it.

'And nobody thought to mention this to me? As master of this house?' Papa looked at the butler and the other servants, who kept their eyes averted.

'No, sir,' Turner said. 'I can speak for all the servants when I say that no such letter arrived at the house.'

'So how did it get here?'

'I intercepted it,' Agnes said.

'Are you in the habit of intercepting the post?'

She nodded. 'It was addressed to me. I didn't see why I shouldn't open it.'

'I can't express how disappointed I am.' His eyes glittered with sudden tears and her heart broke for having let him down. 'Miss Treen, I wish you had told me of this, but I suppose this headstrong young woman persuaded you not to.'

Nanny's expression was one of complete consternation. For a moment, Agnes thought she was going to counter her lie with the truth, but her governess maintained her silence. Perhaps she would have changed her mind again, but for Mama who stood up from her place on the chaise.

'You said she was dead,' she said slowly. 'James, you said the mother was dead and the infant was an orphan.'

A gasp echoed around the room. Agnes couldn't believe her ears. Papa and Nanny had been party to the truth, while Mama had been excluded.

'What could I do? She needed help to get back on her feet. The child was beautiful, an endearing little soul. And I knew I could help them, and us at the same time. Look at how we were suffering, my darling. Remember how desperately sad you were before I brought the little girl home?' Papa corrected himself. 'How sad we were. She has brought us great joy.'

'At the beginning,' Mama said fiercely.

'You said without a child, you had no role in society. Agnes's arrival gave you hope for the future and a purpose. It was the right thing to do for all of us.'

'You lied to me.'

'I'm your husband. I did what I thought for the best. I had the unfortunate mother sign a document in which she waived her rights to her daughter and promised not to contact her again.'

'But you didn't trust her. You thought she might come along and snatch her back into the bosom of her family. That's why you've kept Agnes here out of sight, not because you didn't want her to fall sick and die like her true mother. How could you do this to me?'

'To protect you, my love. I didn't want you worrying. You had been through enough pain and disappointment.' He turned to his brother. 'Why did you think it necessary to tell tales, knowing how it would upset my wife's state of mind? And yours too, for we all know what you were doing on the wharf.'

'How dare you. I was on a charitable mission.'

'To save the poorest, most desperate women of Faversham. Yes, I can believe that,' Pa said sarcastically.

Rufus shrugged.

'I should call you out,' Papa hissed. White froth adorned his beard.

'Papa, no,' Agnes said, stepping in between the two men. 'You are doing yourself no good at all. Please, sit down. Turner, fetch the brandy.'

Philip took it upon himself to place his arm around Papa's back and support him to a chair while the butler sent one of the footmen to fetch a fresh glass.

'Let me have a moment to regain my self-control.' Papa was breathing hard. 'Then we will go outside and have this out.'

'James, no,' Mama said. 'This is shameful.'

'You cannot tell me what to do. You are my wife,' Papa said, his mouth twisting as though he was in pain. 'Turner, fetch my pistol.'

The butler frowned. 'I shall see what I can do, sir, but let me serve you a nip of brandy first.'

'I don't know why you are so sensitive about the situation,' Uncle Rufus said, his malice unabated. 'We have always known and others have suspected of Agnes's shadowy background.'

'You will take that back,' Papa snapped. 'She is one of us.'

'You have Henry for your son and heir. She is superfluous.'

Is that what other people think of me? Agnes wondered, as Papa stood up.

'Take that back,' Papa repeated. 'Apologise or I shall . . . I shall . . .' His complexion turned from scarlet to royal purple as he clutched at his chest.

'Or you'll what?' Rufus sneered. 'You've always been too much of a gentleman in all of your dealings, business and private. Even when you were a boy you couldn't say boo to a goose.'

'Rufus, pray silence!' his wife interrupted. 'Can't you see? He isn't well.'

'He's fooling around.' Rufus gazed at his brother, and something in his expression changed. 'You are play-acting?'

A shiver of panic ran down Agnes's spine as Papa toppled forwards. Rufus caught him and dragged him, almost unconscious, to the chaise where Philip helped him lie him down with a cushion beneath his head.

'He is overheating – I'll open the curtains,' Nanny said as Mama uttered a small scream. 'Someone attend to Mrs Berry-Clay. Turner, send for the doctor.'

Aunt Sarah took Mama aside.

'We need more brandy, and the smelling salts,' she called.

Agnes turned her attention to her father. Philip was kneeling at his head, loosening his necktie and unfastening his collar.

'Go on then, my son. If you're so set on becoming a doctor, you help him,' his father urged.

'I'll do what I can.' Philip checked Papa's wrist for a pulse, but he began to shudder and convulse and seemed to gain the strength of ten men as they tried to keep him from falling on to the floor. Philip and Rufus pinned him to the chaise, and all of a sudden, he took a gasp of air and lay still with pink foam trickling from the corner of his mouth.

'What is happening?' Mama exclaimed from the far side of the room. 'Oh, he has gone!'

'Stay here with us,' Nanny said. 'The men will revive him.'

'Rufus, you have surely killed him!'

'No, mistress, he is far from dying,' Nanny went on, trying to calm her.

'Why should I believe you? Why should I believe any one of you?'

'Please, take some more brandy for the sake of your nerves,' Aunt Sarah said.

'Agnes, fetch a mirror,' Philip whispered.

Frowning, she went out to the landing and removed the gilded mirror from the wall above one of the side tables.

'Thank you, cousin,' Philip said on her return. 'Hold it in front of his nose and mouth.'

She did as he asked and together they watched and waited for the shadow of condensation that would confirm the presence of life. Agnes held her breath, and eventually it came, a faint misting of the glass along with a soft, shallow sigh.

'He is still with us,' she exclaimed gratefully. 'Thank God.' She knelt down and held her father's hand.

Doctor Shaw arrived an hour after Papa's collapse. He addressed Agnes and Philip because Mama was unfit to speak and Uncle Rufus was standing in isolation by the fire. The other guests had retreated, while the butler organised their carriages and rooms for those who were staying overnight.

'How is he?' Philip enquired.

'I cannot say yet.' The doctor turned to the other people

in the drawing room. 'I must have quiet while I examine the patient. Please clear the room.'

Agnes released her father's hand and went across to reassure her mother that she would let her know the doctor's opinion as soon as he had given it.

'I think it best that you put Mama to bed,' she said, addressing Nanny and Aunt Sarah. 'And Uncle Rufus, you must leave us. You can wait in the parlour.'

'I need to stay,' he muttered.

'I insist,' she said sternly. 'You've done enough damage—' A lump formed in her throat. 'There are no words to describe the level of my censure against you. I find your behaviour to be appalling beyond belief. Now, go!'

Her uncle bowed his head and left the room, following behind the women. Agnes returned to her father's side, taking his hand again. His fingers were limp, but warm to the touch.

'How did this begin? Did he suffer some kind of excitement or shock?' the physician asked.

'He had a heated exchange with my father, his brother. They had a disagreement' – Philip looked at Agnes – 'over a family matter on the occasion of my cousin's birthday. He held his chest, complaining of pain and foamed at the mouth before falling down.'

'It appears that he has suffered from apoplexy as a consequence of heart disease. Mr Berry-Clay to my knowledge has always been a man of passion, and such men in my experience are more prone to afflictions of the heart. They are ambitious, hard-working and under strain.'

Agnes thought it was odd. She had always thought of her father as a jovial man without a care in the world, but then she remembered how he worried about the brewery and the poor. Perhaps it had all been too much for him.

Doctor Shaw opened his bag and took out his stethoscope, a wooden trumpet with an ivory earpiece.

'Please, undo his waistcoat,' he said.

'I'll do it,' Philip said and Agnes watched as he unfastened Papa's buttons, parting his waistcoat and then his shirt to reveal his hairy chest. Agnes was shocked – she hadn't realised that men had hair beneath their shirts.

The doctor placed the stethoscope against her father's chest and listened intently before straightening up.

'We must have brandy warmed and administered with water, and a mustard plaster is to be placed over the patient's lungs to support respiration,' he pronounced. 'Firstly, though, he should be moved to a bed where he can receive the care he requires. Can we call for assistance with that?'

Agnes got up to call for Turner and the footmen to help carry her father to his chamber, and for Mrs Catchpole to organise the treatments, and for Miriam to be at hand. She wanted her in particular because she knew she could rely on her.

A few minutes passed as the men struggled to move Papa to his bedroom, but eventually they managed to put him to bed.

'Thank you. That will be all for now,' Agnes said, taking charge. 'Mrs Catchpole, you have the mustard, cloths and hot water?'

'Yes, miss,' she said, her expression grim. 'Is there anything else?'

'I'll call if I need you,' Agnes said. 'Oh, wait. Perhaps Doctor Shaw would like some refreshment.'

'There is some venison left over. I'll 'ave a plate made up.'

'I am most grateful for your consideration,' Doctor Shaw said.

Mrs Catchpole left while the doctor explained to Agnes and Miriam how to wrap the patient's feet in cloths soaked in hot water and mustard, and gave him laudanum and camphor from his bag.

'Everything is designed to reduce pain and assist the heart and circulation,' he said. 'It will alleviate the symptoms.'

'That's all very well,' Agnes said. 'Will it cure him?'

'I cannot say. Medicine is an art, not a science.' Agnes saw how Philip listened to the doctor, taking in every word. 'The spasms often return when the laudanum and camphor have worn off.'

'What about digitalis?' Philip asked. 'Would that be of use in this situation?'

'What do you know of it, young man?' Doctor Shaw asked.

'I've been studying medical texts – I'm hoping to go into medicine.'

'Then you know that we don't want to overwhelm the body in this situation. We will see how he is tomorrow. In the meantime, the room should be kept quiet and moderately warm to maintain his circulation.'

'I shall sit with him,' Agnes said. 'Miriam will stay with me.'

'Of course, miss, but are you sure that it's your place to be in the sickroom?'

'Where else would I be? He is my father.'

She wondered briefly if she should have insisted that Mama came to be with him as well. They were husband and wife, after all, but she doubted that her nerves could stand it.

It was up to her to care for Papa and make sure that everything that could possibly be done was done. It was the first time she had felt real responsibility for anyone but herself, and it was a heavy burden. If only Nanny had decided against a meeting with her true mother. If only Uncle Rufus hadn't happened to be on the quay that day. If only Papa's heart had been strong.

The doctor excused himself, promising to return the following morning.

Agnes turned to Philip. 'I'm most grateful for how you have assisted my father this evening.'

'It is what anyone would have done,' he said, his cheeks turning a deep shade of pink. 'I will pray for him. Goodnight, my fair cousin. I hope that we can be friends in spite of our fathers' quarrel.'

'I hope so too,' she said.

'Will you permit me to return to the sickroom in the morning? I believe that we are staying here tonight.'

'Of course. I have no objection.' She wished him good-night.

Miriam moved two chairs close to the bed when Philip had left the room.

'Sit down, miss,' she said.

Agnes did as she was bid. She glanced down at her dress. It seemed a much duller red in the lamplight, more the colour of blood than a scarlet rose. She tried to ignore the haunting sound of the wind howling across the marshes and rattling the windows.

'Let us pray for your dear papa,' Miriam said softly.

Agnes prayed for her father to be well. She prayed forgiveness for her uncle, and for herself and Nanny.

# Chapter Eight

## *A Cuckoo in the Nest*

'I don't understand it. The master's always bin as fit as a fiddle,' Miriam said as she and Agnes replaced the mustard plaster that had cooled on his chest. 'It's a terrible worry. Oh, I'm sorry, miss. I'm upsetting you. It's gone midnight. Wouldn't you like to go and get some sleep? I can stay and watch him.'

'I couldn't sleep if I tried.' Agnes rinsed out the cloth. The scullery maid had brought a ewer of freshly boiled hot water up from the kitchen at Miriam's request. 'Thank you, though. How is Mama, I wonder?'

'When I went out last, I met Nanny on the landing. She said that the doctor gave her some sleeping drops and they've had the desired effect. Why don't you go and change out of that lovely dress at least?'

'You promise you won't leave him?'

'You can rely on me, miss.'

Agnes thanked Miriam, took a quick look at her father who seemed about the same, and left the room. There was a lot of quiet activity in the house. Uncle Rufus was pacing the landing below – she glanced down through the banisters to see who it was. Turner appeared to have taken it upon himself to patrol the corridor outside her father's room. He nodded in acknowledgement then asked her how the master was.

'There's no change,' she said.

'We are all praying for him.'

She thanked him and went upstairs to the next floor landing. As she opened her bedroom door, Nanny stepped up behind her, making her start.

'I thought you were a ghost,' she exclaimed, her hand on her throat.

'Is there any news?' Nanny whispered.

Agnes shook her head.

'He is no worse, then?'

'And no better either. How is Henry? Does he know anything of this yet?'

'I want to keep it from him for as long as possible.'

'He'll guess that there's something wrong as soon as he gets out of bed,' Agnes said. Why did her elders and so-called betters think that it was preferable to keep bad news to themselves? She recalled Miriam once sweeping some dirt under the carpet in the nursery and Nanny finding out. It hadn't been a pretty picture.

'I wish to thank you for your discretion this evening, not that I condone your interjection,' Nanny said. 'I'm afraid that it will rebound on us if your father is not much recovered by morning. Are you nursing him?'

'Yes, I want to,' Agnes said. 'If we hadn't gone to Faversham, he wouldn't be in this state.'

'It isn't your fault,' Nanny exclaimed. 'This is down to me, and your uncle. Anyway, what's done is done. I will look in on Henry. Goodnight, my dear.'

Agnes changed into one of her everyday dresses and pulled a shawl around her shoulders before returning to her father's room. Miriam looked up when she walked through the door.

'How is he?' she whispered.

'His breathing is slower. I hope that's a sign that Doctor Shaw's medicine is working.'

'As long as he is out of pain.' Agnes tiptoed back to the bed, and took her seat. Miriam passed her a blanket and stoked the fire.

Agnes wrapped herself up and sat watching and waiting. This wasn't how she was expecting to spend her first night, having turned nineteen. She and the maid dozed and drank sweet tea on and off until dawn came, murky, pale and cold.

Miriam pulled the curtains open.

'I don't think this can be good for an invalid. There is ice on the inside of the windows.' She moved across to the patient and checked his hand. 'I'll fetch a hot water bottle.'

'What can I do?' Agnes asked.

'By rights, you shouldn't be doing anything. You're the daughter of the house, not a servant.'

'I want to help. I need him to get better.' She couldn't bear the thought of Windmarsh Court without Papa. 'I'll do anything.'

'I know you will, dear.' The sound of knocking interrupted her.

'It's me.' Philip put his head around the door. 'How is he?'

'About the same, thank you,' Agnes said. 'He hasn't woken at all.'

'That could be down to the medicine.'

'I hope so. We're waiting for the doctor to call to give his opinion.'

'I will leave you then,' Philip said. 'Good day, cousin. I hope to see you again soon in better circumstances. We're leaving now because my father says he can't bear to stay any longer – he hasn't slept a wink. I hope that you will send word to us in Faversham.'

'Of course,' she said. 'Goodbye, Philip.'

He closed the door behind him and another hour passed before there was another knock, and Mama entered the room, followed by Turner and Doctor Shaw.

Agnes stood up to take her mother by the arm and lead her over to the bed.

'My poor husband.' Mama reached out and touched his face. 'Do you think he hears us? Doctor Shaw,' she demanded, 'tell me what you think. Does he know I'm here?'

The doctor lifted Papa's eyelids and peered into his eyes. He took a needle from his bag and touched it to his hands and feet. He pinched his fingers and toes. There was no response. Nothing at all. Agnes's heart began to beat faster. She wasn't a medical man, yet she could tell something was badly wrong. It was as if the person who was her father had been extinguished, his character snuffed out like a candle.

Doctor Shaw straightened and took Mama's hands.

'I'm sorry, Mrs Berry-Clay,' he said gently. 'Your husband is in a state of insensibility from which I doubt that he will ever recover. I'm afraid it is only a matter of time. His heart is failing. There is fluid on his lungs.'

Mama uttered a scream.

'Sit down,' the doctor said. He looked towards Agnes, not recognising her as the daughter of the house. 'Fetch your mistress a glass of water.'

She went down to the kitchen where she was confronted by Mrs Catchpole, Cook, one of the footmen and the scullery maid, who were clearing up after the breakfast they had provided for the remaining house guests.

She shook her head at their silent questioning.

'He is gone,' Mrs Catchpole gasped. 'The master is dead.'

She could hardly bring herself to speak.

'No, no, not yet, but the doctor doesn't seem to think

that there's any room for hope.' She cleared her throat. 'Mama needs a glass of water.'

'Would she like some brandy with that?' Mrs Catchpole said. 'For medicinal purposes, of course.'

'Just the water.'

Cook filled a glass and called for the scullery maid to fetch a tray and carry it up to the mistress.

'I'll take it.' Agnes took the glass and returned to her father's room to find the doctor attending to Mama, checking her pulse.

'The mistress fell into a faint,' Miriam explained.

'She is better now,' the doctor said. 'Offer her some water, a sip at a time.'

Agnes handed the glass to the maid and returned to her father's side. Something drew her there, an ice-cold sensation, a draught whisking down the back of her neck. She touched his hand – it was blotchy in appearance and cold to the touch. While the doctor had been with Mama, Papa had stopped breathing.

'He's gone,' she said quickly, falling to her knees at the bedside. How dare he slip away like this, without saying goodbye?

'He has passed,' the doctor confirmed, at which Mama uttered a loud wail and fainted again.

'This cannot be happening,' Miriam said.

'Papa,' Agnes said, her voice breaking with grief. She prayed to God who had taken her dear father up to Heaven. Why, though? What use had He possibly got for him that was more important than him being head of the family, owner of the brewery, and member of the Board of Guardians? What had Papa done wrong? What sin had he ever committed? She recalled the warmth of his smile, his sense of fun, and his kindliness to Mama, in spite of her temperament and her nerves.

She stood alongside the bed later while Miriam and Mrs Catchpole washed and dressed Papa's body for the funeral. Miriam placed coins on his eyes to keep them closed. Mrs Catchpole opened the windows to allow his soul to fly away.

'I wish you would leave us to it, miss,' the maid said gently, but Agnes couldn't bring herself to abandon him when neither Mama nor Henry could be present. It was a mark of her respect for the man who had saved her from a life in the workhouse.

The household went into mourning. The thought of wearing the scarlet dress didn't cross her mind. Instead, Agnes wore an old black dress of her mother's. The servants wore black as well, and Mama had her husband's portrait in the hall turned to face the wall because it made her cry to look at it.

Mr James Berry-Clay's funeral was packed with people paying their respects: family, friends, those with whom he'd worked in business, including landowners, farmers and maltsters, the architect who was designing new buildings for the brewery, and others whom he'd helped with donations for housing and hospital bills.

Agnes hadn't realised how much he had been loved.

Mama didn't attend the church. Nanny stayed at home with the grieving widow and Henry.

'I hope your mother will treat you kindly now that your father is gone,' Nanny said when Agnes arrived home from the church. 'You are the cuckoo in the nest. She will want you to fledge and fly away.'

She stood alongside the bed [illegible] Miriam and Mrs [illegible] crossed Pyrah's body in the [illegible] Nurse [illegible] [illegible]

[illegible]

[illegible] Miriam [illegible]

[illegible]

[illegible]

[illegible] with the [illegible]

[illegible] from the [illegible] want you to [illegible]

# 1858

# Chapter Nine

## *Desperate Times*

Time passed slowly as winter turned to spring. Four months after Papa's demise when the trees in the orchards were laden with blossom, Mama called for her. Agnes went to the drawing room where her mother was sitting in her usual place, dressed in black with the curtains pulled across the windows. A candle flickered on the table beside her.

'You asked for me,' Agnes said.

'Come and sit down.'

She moved towards the big leather wingback chair opposite the chaise.

'Not that one,' Mama cut in. 'It is Papa's.'

'I'm sorry.' Agnes remained on her feet, feeling uncomfortable in the shrine her mother had created. Everything had been laid out as if she was merely waiting for her husband to come home from the brewery. A newspaper lay folded on the arm of the chair. His day slippers were in front of the fireplace with a brandy bottle and glass on a silver tray.

'What is it? What do you want?' she asked, aware that her mother could barely bring herself to look at her.

'I wish to inform you of my recent conversation with your uncle. Oh, he is a most unpleasant man, but one whose presence has to be endured since he is family. If he were not, I should banish him from the house for his role in recent events.' Mama bit her lip before continuing, 'Anyway, he has come up with a proposition, an idea to assuage his guilt.'

'Mama, you can't still believe that Uncle Rufus had a hand in Papa's passing? You heard what Doctor Shaw said. That it could have happened at any time. He died from angina pectoris caused by changes in his heart, anxiety and mental strain. The events of that day may have hastened his collapse, but they didn't trigger them.'

'Rufus says that if he had kept his own counsel, then my husband – his dear brother – would still be with us.' Mama choked back a sob. The doctor's opinion didn't matter to her – she needed someone to blame.

'I beg you not to distress yourself again.' Agnes moved across and rested her hand on her mother's shoulder. 'Didn't the vicar say when he called on you that he is always with us in spirit?'

'It is no comfort. I want him here in body and soul. I would give anything to see him, hear him laugh, feel his touch . . . I loved him.'

'Oh, Mama,' Agnes sighed. She remembered how Nanny had once said that she thought Mama incapable of deep and lasting affection. It seemed that she had been proved wrong, because her mother had sunk to the depths of grief over Papa. It was hard to watch.

'Anyway, nothing can be done about it,' Mama said. 'I've decided that it is time you were married.'

'I beg your pardon.' She hadn't met anyone whom she wished to marry so far, and, due to recent events, she hadn't given the future more than a passing thought.

'Your uncle thinks that it would be a great help to me if you were off my hands – he has someone suitable in mind.'

'Who?'

'Your cousin Philip.'

'That isn't possible,' Agnes exclaimed. 'He isn't at all handsome.'

'Don't be too hasty. He is of the right age and disposition, and your uncle believes that he wouldn't be averse to taking you as his wife. Philip is fond of you – we saw you talking to each other. You are both bookish.'

'He hasn't yet made his way in life,' Agnes countered. 'He's going to study to become a doctor. He will be ill-equipped to take a wife until he's qualified.'

'I know he has a bee in his bonnet about it, but his father will not let him. He is part of the Berry-Clay dynasty – even when Henry takes over, there will be room for Philip at the brewery. I have your uncle's assurance on that.'

He was kind – she knew that from the way he had looked after her father when he'd collapsed on that fateful evening, and how he had sent her a letter afterwards to offer his condolences, but friendship wasn't enough. She craved love and romance, and a title.

'I should die rather than marry my cousin. Papa wouldn't have approved.'

'He isn't here,' Mama said acidly, 'and your background, now well known, will hold you back. There will always be someone willing to dredge it up in an attempt to ruin your reputation. I'd always hoped you might make a match with one of the Throwleys or the Seddons, but your options for marriage are limited now that everyone knows who you are and where you came from.'

Agnes couldn't help wondering if that had been part of her uncle's plan – to bring up her history so she would have to marry Philip, there being no other eligible and willing suitors.

'It is a sensible match that will benefit everyone,' Mama went on. 'It will be many years before Henry is old enough to run the brewery. In the meantime, Philip will continue to run it with his father, and you will have a household of your own in Faversham. Your uncle has his eye on a small establishment, a townhouse. With a careful juggling of the books, the brewery will buy it as an investment. It is better than you could have expected, considering your circumstances. You will be able to afford a cook and a maid, at least. All this about Philip wishing to become a physician is a young man's whim.'

Agnes's heart sank. Nanny had encouraged her to think for herself, but now it seemed there had been no point. She felt sick at the thought that she had no say in whom she would marry.

'I would rather be an old maid.'

'Don't be ridiculous,' Mama said. 'You would be bored witless.'

'Why can't I stay at Windmarsh to look after you when you are old?'

'Why should I need you to do that? I have servants and my dear Henry who looks more and more like his papa every day.'

'What will you do when he goes to school?'

'He will be home for the holidays, and you may call upon us now and again when you are settled with Philip. I married your father for his establishment in the first place because I knew I would have a comfortable life with a role to play, but I did grow fond of him. Very fond.'

'I don't like Philip in that way.'

'Of course you don't. No girl likes her intended at first. It's perfectly normal.'

'You don't understand how wrong this would feel for me.'

'It doesn't matter how you feel about him.'

'Papa would never have made me marry a man who is repellent to me.' She felt lost without her protector.

'He is not here and I have had to take advice from your uncle.'

'Why would you take advice from a man whom you blame for your husband's death?' Agnes exclaimed.

'Because this is the only way to get you off my hands,' Mama said, her eyes flashing with angry tears. 'I can hardly bear the sight of you after what's happened. Yes, I blame Rufus, but I can't forget your part in this.'

'Mama! I loved Papa. He was my father.' This wasn't fair. She had been an innocent child when she'd been brought to Windmarsh Court. She hadn't been mistress of her destiny then and she certainly wasn't now.

Agnes trembled as Mama took a deep breath and began to speak in a calm and controlled manner.

'Your uncle has made this offer as he sets out to redeem himself in the eyes of this family and God. He is arriving from Faversham at midday so that we can confirm the engagement. I thought it correct that Philip should ask for your hand, but we decided he shouldn't come with his father. God forbid you should turn him down.'

Agnes was devastated, but she still had hope. For a start, she doubted that her cousin would willingly offer a proposal, considering the circumstances.

'Why have you sprung this upon me? It's all so sudden.' She had dreamed of someone strong and forceful, sharp of wit and bathed in wisdom. She wanted more than poor Philip could provide.

'I will turn him down,' she said adamantly. 'I will brook no further discussion.'

'You have no choice. Marry Philip, or I will turn you out of the house. Go upstairs and put on your dress, the scarlet one, and join me and your uncle for luncheon at one o'clock.'

'Oh no, I couldn't.' She couldn't bear to see the dress

again – it was a painful reminder of her birthday – and she wasn't hungry. The idea of marrying Philip had quite put her off her food.

'That is an order, not a request. It won't take long. I have no intention of spending more time with Rufus than I have to.'

'I will not join you.'

'Remember, duty comes before personal happiness. We are trapped by our sex, birth and position in society. You will be married. You will not have to work, or worry about money. You will be very comfortable as Philip's wife.'

'I will go upstairs and not come down.'

'Then I will invite your betrothed to Windmarsh in the near future, and send him to your room so you can become better acquainted. The threat of ruination is a straightforward way of progressing an unwanted union.'

'How could you? That's blackmail.'

'Is that so?' Mama ran one fingernail across the arm of the chaise, making a deep gouge in the wood. 'I prefer to consider it as being cruel to be kind.'

'You would really set out to ruin my reputation?'

'I will if you don't consent to this marriage. Philip will be most disappointed if you are not willing.'

'You're lying. He doesn't want to marry me any more than I wish to marry him. That's why my uncle isn't bringing him with him today. Oh, Mama, I'm not stupid.' She turned and fled out of the room and up the stairs. She closed her bedroom door behind her and slid the bolt across before pulling the metal trunk away from the end of the bed, and the bags from her wardrobe. She began to pack her belongings.

How was she going to get away from Windmarsh? She could hardly borrow the carriage without anyone's knowledge. She soon realised too that she couldn't possibly remove all her possessions even if she had twenty carriages. She would have to make some painful decisions about which of her precious things to leave behind.

She sat down at her dressing table and opened her rosewood jewellery box, and cried as she picked out the half a sixpence. How could it be a good luck charm when it had done her so much harm?

She threw it across the room, and it bounced and rolled under the bed.

Good riddance, she thought.

She glanced through the rest of her jewellery, the necklace of garnet flowers and the gold rope bracelet, pretty trinkets that Papa had bought for her and memories of happier times that made her feel sadder than ever. Riches didn't necessarily bring happiness. It was the little things that counted: a pink dawn on a frosty morning; the call of the curlew; a charm of golden linnets.

A knock at the door distracted her.

'Please, I beg you to let me in,' she heard Nanny whisper. 'I do not deceive you. There is no one else here.'

'Mama hasn't sent you to winkle me out?'

'Trust me.'

Agnes relented and unlocked the door.

'You are running away?' Nanny said as she walked in.

'I have no choice. I cannot marry Philip. Papa would never have made me.' She didn't know what happened in the marital bed, but she didn't want to lie in it with him. He was a kind man, but she couldn't get past his bow legs and the way he was losing his teeth.

'I'm willing to help you if I can.'

'How? I'm powerless now that Papa has gone.'

'One question: are you absolutely sure you cannot tolerate him? I only say this because—'

'It would have its advantages in that I'd have a wealthy

husband, Mama would be taken care of, and I'd still have the approval of my adoptive family, the Berry-Clays?' Agnes finished for her. 'I'm very much aware of what I would be giving up.'

'And you have no idea of what fate will befall you as an alternative.'

'That is true, but I am willing to take the risk. You have your independence. You've done well for yourself by your own merits.'

'When you say I have done well, what exactly do you think I've achieved?'

'The satisfaction of earning your own income. Of teaching me to think for myself. Those lessons you've taught me are invaluable.'

'Maybe they have spoiled you, though. If you had been led like a sheep, you might have been perfectly content to marry your cousin. Agnes, don't be too hasty – delay your journey, put your belongings away so as not to arouse suspicion, and take time to reconsider your decision.'

'I have very little time. My uncle is arriving shortly for luncheon with Mama – they want to confirm my engagement to cousin Philip. They are determined to marry me off as soon as possible.'

'If you insist on following this course of action, at least let me see what I can do to set you up with some means of bringing in an income. The banns haven't been read yet. That gives us at least three weeks, if not more. They will not try to subvert the church – you know how they like to keep up appearances.'

'Nanny, it is you who is being subversive,' Agnes exclaimed. 'This isn't like you.'

'You will have to work for your living. If you run away, your mother won't send anyone to bring you back. She won't tell you that all is forgiven and you don't have to marry Philip after all. She will disown you, I'm certain of it.'

'I cannot possibly work. I'm not accustomed to it.'

'Then you will starve to death,' Nanny said sharply.

'What can I do?' She thought of Miriam laying the fires and emptying the piss pots, and shuddered. 'I couldn't be a maid.'

'There aren't that many opportunities for a woman to make her own way in the world. There's marriage where one loses one's autonomy. Or there's working as a domestic servant, or nannying. Or, being frank, there's the option of selling one's body like the poor woman we saw on the wharf.'

'No!' She was shocked to the core.

'I am sorry if that idea offends your sensibilities, but I am trying to jolt you out of complacency. Running away isn't necessarily the best answer. If you leave, you will have to stand on your own two feet. No one will help you.' Her voice softened. 'It's what I've had to do.'

'You've done well enough, haven't you?'

'I have very little, my dear. I have no children, no husband. I have a little money tucked away, but no establishment that I can call my own. I shall be condemned to work into my old age, unless I can acquire enough savings to retire.'

There must be something she could do, Agnes thought.

She was clever and accomplished – Papa had said so. But after all the lessons she had both enjoyed and endured, depending on the subject, she wondered if she was qualified for any job in particular. She could sing and play the piano, but not well enough to make her living from music. She had made a thorough study of geography, but what good was that? She could read and write, and add up. Did that qualify her to apply for a position as a clerk like the ones who worked for the brewery? She wasn't sure if gentlewomen were accepted for that kind of work.

She was proficient at needlework, but she remembered the dressmaker's shop and the girls working in the back room, straining their eyes and sewing non-stop to make dresses as quickly as possible to meet the demands of the wealthy women who had ordered them.

She suddenly realised the enormity of her decision and its consequences.

'I could be a governess, couldn't I?' Agnes said, hope returning to her breast. 'Do you think I could pass myself off as a nanny?'

'I'm not sure. You are well qualified to teach young ladies, but you are not worldly wise. There are perils.'

Agnes almost laughed. 'What threats lie await to catch a governess?'

'Ah, you may mock, but I have been in what I can only describe as situations before. In my first place, I was pursued relentlessly by the father of my charges. It was unpleasant and awkward. I had to repel his advances in a polite manner that would not invoke his wrath. Eventually, he grew bored with my rejections and persuaded the mistress to employ another governess in my place. He didn't give her the real reason, of course, just that he would prefer someone of a prettier countenance and a more even temperament about the house.' Nanny smiled wryly, then took Agnes's hand in her own and continued earnestly, 'You have been like a loving daughter to me and I would do anything for you. I wish to help you, but you must promise to keep it to yourself.'

Agnes nodded.

'We need to find some excuse to get you away from Windmarsh, a visit to Canterbury, perhaps. I doubt your mother will be as protective as your dear papa. In the meantime, you must wash your face, brush your hair, put on your dress and come down and act like a young lady who is sweet on her cousin.'

Agnes thanked her. She wasn't sure what she was most afraid of – marrying Philip or casting herself adrift from the security of Windmarsh Court.

# Chapter Ten

## *Desperate Measures*

'You seem in better spirits than when we had luncheon with your uncle,' Mama commented at dinner the next day. 'I'm glad to see you have come to your senses. I shall call for Mrs Roache to bring samples of dresses for the wedding. None of yours are suitable. We should put on some kind of a show.' This was the first time she had seen Mama smiling since Papa's passing, she thought, but the smile soon vanished from her face as she wondered aloud about who would give Agnes away.

'I will ask your uncle for advice,' she decided.

Agnes was concerned that her mother was seeking the opinions of Uncle Rufus in lieu of her father's.

'I think Henry would look rather sweet dressed in a suit,' Mama continued.

'Thank you, Mama.' Agnes supposed that she would have to go through with the pretence for as long as possible. 'I wonder if I could go to Canterbury for a day – I should like to buy some new gloves for the wedding. Nanny will chaperone me.'

'I don't know,' Mama sighed. 'Oh, why not? I don't see that it can do any harm. A trip out might put some colour in your cheeks – mourning dress does drain the colour from one's complexion. Arrange it with Nanny. Miriam can look after Henry.'

She began to pick at a loose thread on her cuff, her wrists slender and delicate. 'There are things you should know about your wedding night.'

'No . . . I do not wish to know.'

'It is better to be prepared. The sight of a naked man is quite shocking.'

'Mama, stop!'

'Oh, Agnes, just do as your husband says and all will be well. It is nothing to worry about and is over quickly.'

Agnes prayed that she would not have to endure it, but it seemed more than likely that the wedding would go ahead.

She and Nanny spent time together in the schoolroom – Nanny allowed her to plan and teach Henry's lessons to prepare her for the role of governess. It seemed far-fetched, she thought, but, having reviewed all the possibilities several times, it was the only work she was qualified to do.

'You must be firm with him,' Nanny chuckled when Henry refused to concentrate on his letters one morning.

'I don't want to write today.' Henry folded his arms and swung his legs, kicking against the desk. 'It's the dullest thing ever.'

'You have to do it,' Agnes said, trying to sound stern. 'A gentleman has to learn his letters, or he will not be able to carry out his business.'

'I don't want to do business.' Henry scowled.

'It is your duty.' She felt a little two-faced talking about duty when she was the one trying to run out on hers. 'One day, you will run the brewery.'

'I don't want to. I'm going to be a sailor.'

'Mama wouldn't like that, and neither would you in reality. All you would have to eat and drink is ships' biscuits, and rum and lime. There would be no cherry cake.'

His eyes widened. 'Really?'

'Really,' she said calmly, although inside, her heart was racing at the way her brother was testing her authority. If she couldn't teach, what could she do? There was precious little else left, apart from marry Philip. 'Now, pick up your pencil and write. The sooner you are finished, the sooner we can go out and watch the boats.'

'Very good,' Nanny said. 'Now, while Henry's completing the task you've set him, we must continue with your education, Agnes.'

She knew what she meant. They were being careful to talk in riddles so that Henry couldn't report back to Mama.

She was unconvinced that Nanny's plan would work when it depended on a series of circumstances that had to be in place within a few weeks, the date of the wedding having been set for the middle of May. The servants weren't happy about it. It was too soon to make the preparations, and May was an inauspicious month for a wedding. Miriam quoted the rhyme, 'Marry in the month of May, and you'll surely rue the day.' She said that September would be better. 'Marry in September's shrine and you'll have a living that's rich and fine.'

'Agnes, are you listening?' Nanny clicked her fingers.

'No, I'm sorry. I was distracted.'

Nanny sighed. 'I'm not surprised. These are tense times. Now, show what you have written.'

Agnes took a piece of paper from the cupboard and handed it to her. She reread her words over Nanny's shoulder.

*GOVERNESS – A young lady wishes for a situation as resident governess. She is competent to teach English, French, geography, painting and pianoforte (without master). She can give the most satisfactory references. She has no objection to the country. Address, post paid, at Mr S. Cheevers of Canterbury.*

'This is excellent,' Nanny opined. 'We will take it to Canterbury with us, place it in the local newspapers and apply to any suitable responses.'

'What about the references, though? I haven't got any.'

'I'll copy out my own character and sign it with another name. It's a daring plan, but desperate times mean desperate measures.'

'What are you two whispering about?' Henry asked.

'Nothing that concerns you, dear Henry,' Nanny said cheerfully. 'How are you getting on with those letters?'

'Very well, Nanny,' he said with a sigh.

'Of course you are, my little angel,' she said, bustling over to him. Agnes smiled to herself. Her brother was turning out to be a very spoiled young gentleman who could wrap Nanny and Mama around his little finger. He was growing quite tubby on Cook's treats, and looked more like Papa every day.

One morning later that week, Agnes and Nanny embarked on a trip to Canterbury, leaving Henry behind. Mama gave Agnes some sovereigns with which to make her purchases.

'Choose wisely,' she said.

'I'll try, Mama,' Agnes said, feigning obedience. 'Should I ask for black? We are in mourning, are we not?'

Mama frowned. She had taken to wearing black wool gloves, considering that kid was too shiny to be suitable.

'You will not marry in black. Your papa wouldn't have liked that. It would be in poor taste. Oh, I wish that I felt well enough to accompany you, but my nerves . . . I can't risk disturbing them further before your wedding day. I'm already overcome with weakness whenever I talk to Mrs Catchpole and Cook about the menu for the wedding breakfast, but it will be worth it – for all of us. I look forward to welcoming Philip to Windmarsh Court as my son-in-law. There is one thing, though.'

'What is that?' Agnes sighed.

'The house will not be ready – your uncle sent word yesterday. I didn't want to disturb your peace of mind by mentioning it before, but I have to warn you that you will be obliged to stay at your uncle's house for the first weeks of your married life. It will be no trial, I think, no trial at all.'

'I was hoping that I would have my own establishment right from the start,' Agnes said, trying to look upset at the news.

'I know. I'm sorry to disappoint you, but you will look forward to it even more.'

'Yes, Mama.'

'Run along then. I expect Nanny is waiting for you. No doubt she will call upon her uncle today.'

'He has written to her to say that he's unwell,' Agnes said, preparing the ground to enable them to put their plan into action.

'I hope he is better soon,' Mama said – generously for her, Agnes thought. 'Have a lovely day.'

Agnes travelled with Nanny in the carriage, where they were able to discuss their plans in depth without danger of being overheard.

'I feel I ought to write to Philip to warn him that I'm going to break the engagement,' she said. What if he'd grown used to the idea of their marriage? She didn't like the idea that he'd be disappointed.

'I understand why you wish to do so. I can't stop you, but I'd advise you strongly against it. The more people who know about our plot, the more likely it is that it will be exposed, and a stop put to it.'

Agnes chewed her lip. Her governess had a point.

'We will order the gloves first,' Nanny said. 'Then we will place the advertisement at the newspaper's office before we go to my uncle's house. It will give you time to make sure you are certain about this course of action that we're taking. Be under no illusion. You are casting yourself off.'

'I realise that.' Agnes watched the cathedral coming into view.

'I don't think that you can understand it until you've been there. You will have to earn your living, manage your money and live within your means. You will be at the beck and call of your pupils from dawn till dusk.'

'I will live frugally.'

'You don't know the meaning of the word, my dear.' Nanny patted her arm.

'Maybe I will save up and buy a house in the future so I can run a school for young ladies.'

Nanny smiled. 'That is a dream too far. You may be able to put aside enough money to retire and take up other interests in the future, but the riches and rewards of being a governess come from the pride one has in one's pupils' achievements, not in guineas. Now, we are almost there.'

Shortly afterwards, the coachman pulled the coach up on the bridge over the Stour. The stable boy opened the door and helped Agnes and then Nanny out on to the street.

'Thank you, Mr Noakes,' Nanny called. 'We will meet you outside Willow Place as arranged.'

'I'll be there, don't you worry, Miss Treen,' he called back.

The stable boy slammed the door shut and sprang up beside the coachman, who whipped the horses back into a lazy trot.

'Well,' said Nanny, 'we have made it this far.'

'Which way is it to the glovers?' Agnes asked.

'My uncle has given me the address of a shop in St Peter's. He knows the currier who supplies the leather.'

They walked to the shop where a gloveress greeted them and measured Agnes's hands.

'We can make them from kid or calf, or suede,' she said.

'What do you think, Agnes?' Nanny said.

It didn't matter – she didn't need them. She had four pairs of kid gloves still in her glove box at home. Not home, she reminded herself. It wouldn't be home for much longer.

'I think the calf leather would be suitable,' she said. 'I like the blue.'

'That's an excellent choice, madam,' the gloveress said.

'Miss Berry-Clay will be wearing them for her wedding – she is still in mourning, but she can't wear black for the ceremony. Yes, the blue is perfect,' Nanny agreed.

'I'd recommend a four-button style that covers the wrist and reaches a couple of inches up the forearm.'

Agnes nodded. She would agree to anything. She wished to hurry on and place her advertisement before she changed her mind. Every so often a wave of panic would wash through her, making her doubt her ability to change her life. Occasionally, she would wonder if marrying Philip was the better option, but she couldn't go through with it. It wouldn't be fair on either of them.

'We can have them sewn with the highest quality silk thread, and finished within two weeks. You may collect or we can deliver.'

Agnes cast Nanny an enquiring glance.

'I shall collect them,' Nanny said. 'We should take four pairs, I think. Send the bill to . . .' She gave Mama's name and address. Nothing was to be left to chance. Nothing must raise suspicion.

They went to the local newspaper's office to place the advertisement, then walked to Willow Place where Nanny rang the bell at the gate. As before, Mrs Hill opened the gate for them. She showed them up the drive to the house, and directed them to the study. Nanny knocked on the door.

Oliver answered it. He smiled broadly in welcome.

'Come in,' he said. 'My grandfather is expecting you.'

'Agnes, wait out here for a moment,' Nanny said. 'There are things my uncle and I need to discuss in private.'

'I shall wait with you,' Oliver said, letting Nanny through and pushing the door closed behind her. 'How are you, Agnes? Are you well? Oh no, I'm sorry. You're in mourning. Marjorie brought word of—' He broke off as she bit back a tear. 'I wish I knew what to say to comfort you.'

'There is nothing,' she muttered, noticing that the study door had swung ajar.

'Let me ask Mrs Hill to make us some tea,' he said softly, and he disappeared off into the depths of the house.

Agnes overheard snatches of the conversation between Nanny and Samuel.

'It is a kind deed that you do for your charge,' he said, 'but I do not condone it. There is already too much dishonesty in the world. I'm on a mission to improve society's moral standards, to which end I'm setting up an organisation to rid the streets of the thieves and pickpockets, and the screevers who set up their offices to write false words to cheat and embezzle well-meaning people out of their money.'

'The problem is that I can't stand by and let it happen,' Nanny countered. 'My heart fails me when I think of it, the poor girl being forced into a marriage with a young man for whom she has little affection.'

'What about him, though? What does he think of the matter?'

'I believe that he's equally unenthusiastic. He has ambitions to go to medical school, but his father wants him to marry and go into business at the brewery. He did what he could to try to save Mr Berry-Clay's life, something he has no need to be ashamed of, considering that the doctor in attendance couldn't save him either. Uncle, which is worse? To bind two people together in holy matrimony and break their spirits, or free them both from this contract?'

Agnes's heart sank again as she thought of the future. Why, she would rather marry Oliver than Philip. It was impossible, of course. They were from very different backgrounds, and he was no baronet with a large estate and an income of twenty thousand a year. He was fairly handsome and kindly, but, as the heir to the tannery, the stench of curing hides would always cling to his skin and clothing.

'You make a good case, but how do you intend to pursue this aim of yours?' Samuel said as Oliver returned along the hallway, carrying a rattling tray of teacups, saucers and a teapot.

Agnes pushed the door open for him.

'Thanking you kindly,' he said. 'Grandpa, we have tea.'

'Then bring it in,' Samuel said cheerfully.

The four of them sat and talked for a while before Samuel suggested that Agnes and Oliver should go to see Bert.

Agnes hesitated, unsure that she wanted to return to the tannery.

'He would like to see you again,' Samuel said. 'He often

talks about the time the young lady came and he had new boots.'

'He has grown considerably,' Oliver commented. 'Come with me.'

Agnes made her mind up and walked across to the tannery with him.

'I regret taking up your time,' she said, as the stench began to take her by the throat. It was a little easier to deal with this time. She managed to maintain her dignity by not retching in front of her host.

'No, don't. It's a pleasure to see you again. Marjorie has called on us many times since we last saw you, and each time we hoped you'd come with her. My grandfather looks forward to having visitors – he isn't always well, and the company of others cheers him up. He suffers terribly from gout and the rheumatics.' He smiled wryly. 'I hope he will feel better when summer comes.'

'How is your sister?' Agnes asked.

'Temperance is married – did Marjorie not mention it to you?'

Agnes shook her head. It had probably slipped her mind.

'I am delighted for her. Who is the lucky young man?'

'He is a few years older than her. He is pleasant enough, I think, but they are struggling to settle to married life. He married my sister thinking she was young enough that he could change her, and make her such a wife as he chose. Unfortunately she felt the same of him – that she could wreak some alteration of his character.' He paused. 'Forgive me if I am overstepping the mark, but I have the impression that there is something going on. Marjorie is good at keeping secrets, but I overheard her speaking to my uncle. There is some problem? I am willing to help you if I can.'

'I'd prefer not to discuss it,' she said rather sharply. 'I'm sorry. I cannot say anything. It is a delicate situation, but thank you for offering.' She felt embarrassed by his kindness. 'Where will we find Bert?'

'I'll show you. You will hardly recognise him. He's fourteen years old and working full-time at the tannery. His younger brother, Arthur, who is six, works here too.'

Agnes felt chastened as she thought of Henry's life of ease. It didn't seem right or fair.

'Their mother is still taking in laundry to make ends meet,' Oliver went on. 'In fact, my uncle sends our laundry to her, but it often comes back dirtier than when it left the house.'

They moved along the yard where two men were lifting a hide from one of the tan-pits. They let the initial rush of water drain across the cobbles, then carried it to the next pit where they submerged it into the black liquor.

'Bert, can you come over here for a moment?' Oliver called.

One of the two men turned and smiled.

'Afternoon, sir,' he said, doffing his cap as he walked across to them.

He had changed out of all recognition, Agnes thought. He had been a boy when she'd last seen him, and now he was a young man.

'This is Miss Berry-Clay, whom you met many years ago,' Oliver said.

Bert gazed at her, his eyes wide with curiosity. 'You've altered a bit, miss.'

'I hope that I have.' Even though she had seen him since, she blushed at the memory of being unkind to him when she had first met him, carrying the purse of coins from her papa.

'Are you still a stuck-up—'

'That's enough,' Oliver interrupted.

'That's what you called her in the past,' Bert said.

'Really, Bert. I might have expressed that sentiment, but I didn't use those words.'

'I'm sorry, sir. I take them back. It is a pleasure to see you again, miss.'

'You may go,' Oliver said. 'Oh, one more thing. Is your brother here?'

'He was here.' Bert looked around the yard. 'I 'aven't sin him recently. Arthur!' he shouted. 'Arthur, show yourself.' He cursed aloud. 'Oh, where are you? My ma will kill me. I'm supposed to be minding him.'

'We've had this discussion before,' Oliver said, his voice scolding. 'How many times have I told you that it isn't safe? You can't concentrate on tanning hides and mind your brother at the same time.'

'It would help if he wasn't such a varmint, disappearing off and hiding himself.' Bert was almost in tears.

'Calm down,' Oliver said, although from his tone he sounded anything but calm, Agnes thought. A six-year-old boy could easily come to harm in the tan-yard.

'Hey, over here!' There were shouts coming from the gap in the wall leading down to the river. 'There's a body in the water!'

Oliver and Bert set off at a run. Agnes followed, holding up her skirts from the flood of liquor that was washing across the cobbles. Her heart was pounding. Her breath was short. She waded through the mud to the edge of the river. Further downriver towards the mill and the bridge, she spotted a small dark mass floating on the surface. Bert was wading towards it, the water up to his waist. Oliver was ahead of him, up to his neck.

'Stop there, Bert! You can't swim,' he yelled back. 'Let me go.'

Bert was screaming out his brother's name.

'Oliver, take care!' Agnes joined in as she watched him dive into the murky, fast-flowing water.

'They'll both be drownded.'

She glanced to one side to find one of the other tannery workers with her.

'Oliver can swim?' she asked, feeling frantic.

'He can, but there's currents out there, and silt to catch a man unawares. I don't know how many times I've told young Arthur to stay away from the water, but will he listen?'

Agnes's feet began to hurt. It was early April and cold for the time of year. The water was freezing. If they survived the drowning, they'd die from exposure, she thought. As Oliver tried to reach the boy, she turned and ran back to the house. She flew up the drive and hammered at the door. Mrs Hill opened it.

'Where is Mr Cheevers?' she gasped.

The housekeeper pointed to the study. Agnes left her boots on and pushed past her. Nanny and Samuel looked up as she burst into the room.

'Oliver and Arthur are in the river,' she said quickly. 'We need hot water and towels. Hurry, or we will be too late.'

Samuel grasped his stick, stood up and hastened across the room. He bellowed instructions to Mrs Hill, slipped his feet into his boots, leaving the laces untied, and strode across to the tannery and down to the river with Agnes. Nanny caught up with them.

Oliver was wading out of the shallows with the limp body of a small boy in his arms. Bert was at his side, begging his brother to wake up.

'Arthur,' he kept saying, 'Arthur. Stop playing silly beggars. Wake up!'

'I'll take him,' Samuel said, dropping his stick.

Oliver handed him over as Mrs Hill appeared with an armful of towels and a kettle of hot water.

'Let's go into the office,' Oliver said, his teeth chattering. 'The fire is lit.'

They piled into a small room. Agnes and Nanny pushed the heavy mahogany desk and chairs back to give more space in front of the fire. Agnes moved the fire-screen, and Mrs Hill placed a towel around Oliver's shoulders while Samuel laid the boy on the rug.

'He is dead,' Bert sobbed. 'It's all my fault.'

'No, wait,' Samuel said.

Oliver stepped in, lifted the boy by his ankles and shook him. All of a sudden, he coughed and water poured from his lungs.

'Yes!' Bert exclaimed as Oliver lowered him back on to the rug. 'You saved 'is life, sir. Listen, everyone, the gaffer saved 'is life.' He fell to his knees and embraced his little brother, who opened his eyes. His skin was blue and his teeth were chattering.

'Mrs Hill, strip him down and wrap him in the towels. Rub his arms and legs to invigorate his circulation,' Oliver said.

'What about you?' Agnes said. 'Are you in need of medical attention?'

'I will be fine,' he said with a smile. With trembling fingers, he unfastened the buttons on his shirt and took it off, revealing his muscular torso. Agnes turned away, shocked by the sight of his nakedness. When she looked back, he had pulled a towel over his shoulders.

'Mrs Hill, make some hot sugary tea, please,' Nanny said. 'And find some brandy.'

'There's a bottle in the desk,' Samuel said. 'I keep one there for emergencies.'

Gradually, the party regained their spirits, warmed by the tea and an excellent brandy.

When Arthur was recovered enough to try to get up, Oliver picked him up and sat him on one of the office chairs. Bert stood over his brother, stroking his face.

'Why didn't you do as you was told and stay away from the water?' he muttered. 'I thought I'd lost you.'

'I'm sorry,' Arthur said weakly. 'I should 'ave listened. I'll never do it again, I promise.'

At three, Agnes and Nanny took their leave as Mr Noakes had brought the carriage round for them.

'Oliver was a hero,' Nanny said when they were heading away from Canterbury. 'If Arthur had remained in the water for even another minute, I think the outcome would have been very different. We will keep this little episode from your mother, though. It wouldn't be good for her nerves. We have made great progress today.'

We have set the scene, Agnes thought. She and Nanny had created good reasons to return to Canterbury: to collect the gloves and to call on the Cheeverses to enquire about Samuel's health. All she had to hope for now was that someone would respond to her advertisement. What were the chances of that?

For someone used to certainty in all things – the appearance of hot chocolate in a fine bone china cup whenever she wished, freshly laundered sheets on a Wednesday and the daily hour spent with Mama in the drawing room – the unpredictability of the future scared and invigorated her at the same time.

Oliver's bravery was an inspiration. If he was willing to risk his life for another, she could find the strength to break away from her old life and make her own way in the world.

# Chapter Eleven

## *All that Glisters is not Gold*

The vicar was due to read the banns for the first time on Sunday. Agnes dressed dutifully in her mourning clothes to accompany Nanny to the church in Windmarsh. Naturally, Mama declined to attend, but the other servants of the house went along as was their custom.

Agnes and Nanny left separately from the others. Turner closed the front door behind them, and they trudged down the drive to the road. They continued alongside the ditch towards Windmarsh, and the cedar-shingled spirelet of the bell tower came into view. The marsh harriers wheeled and tumbled across the clear blue sky and the reed warblers sang their churring song. The spring breeze tugged at the ribbons of Agnes's dark satin bonnet as they passed the cottages and two houses to reach the church.

Nanny placed her arm through hers and guided her up the pathway, past the gravestones and overhanging yews.

'Come on, Agnes. You must be brave, my dear.'

'I will do my best,' she said.

'I know you will,' Nanny said. 'I'm sorry you have to do this, but you must show your face if we are to convince everyone of your willingness to marry your cousin.'

'It's all right.' Agnes wanted to be absolutely sure that her instincts were correct.

The vicar welcomed them at the steps leading up to the church door.

'Good morning, Miss Berry-Clay. I'm delighted that you are willing to join our congregation in celebrating the reading of the banns for your imminent marriage. I told your mother how honoured I was to be asked to officiate at your wedding.'

He seemed quite touched, Agnes thought, but she knew very well why Mama and her uncle had chosen the church at Windmarsh above the grander St Mary of Charity Church in Faversham. The marriage was to be conducted quickly and discreetly, thanks to the revelations of her origins.

'Do go inside,' he said, and they entered the church. Agnes was thrown into confusion because the Berry-Clays' lack of regular attendance meant that they didn't have a defined place.

'This way,' Nanny said, ushering her along the aisle towards the front, where cousin Philip stood and raised his hand, gesturing her towards the seat beside him. She wasn't sure how to react to his smile of pleasure at seeing her. He was friendly, but she thought she detected a touch of resignation in the way he greeted her.

'Cousin, we meet again,' he said, not 'my love', or 'my dear'. He was wearing a dark brown suit and a starched cravat tied in a horizontal bow. His shirt collar was so high it looked as if it might strangle him, she thought.

'Thank you for saving me a seat,' she whispered as she sat down. 'It's most kind of you.'

'It's the least he can do, considering you are soon to be his wife.'

Agnes looked past Philip to find his father staring at her with a mocking expression on his face.

'Good morning, uncle,' she said stiffly. 'How are my aunt and cousin Edward?'

'Your aunt has sent her apologies – she has been forced to remain at home with Edward, who has had an attack of the faints. She is looking forward to being present at your nuptials. She wouldn't miss that for the world.'

Agnes didn't believe him. Perhaps Aunt Sarah had stayed away as a tacit expression of her disapproval of their union.

The vicar seemed to consider that slow and ponderous repetition would reinforce the message of his sermon, but at last the service ended and the congregation left the church. Agnes walked slowly along the path between the graves, hanging back to speak to Philip, who was rubbing his back as if to iron out his stoop.

'Ah, let the young lovebirds spend a moment together, Miss Treen,' Uncle Rufus said with a lecherous expression on his face. Nanny gave Agnes a knowing smile.

'Agnes, I want you to know that I have always been fond of you,' Philip said. 'I've thought this through – in fact, I've thought of little else since my father spoke to me about our marriage.'

This wasn't what she had been expecting. Was Philip saying that he wanted to marry her, in spite of knowing where she came from?

'I'm willing to abandon all hope of entering the medical profession to make you happy.' He gazed down at the ground. 'I think we can be happy in time.'

'In time,' she echoed. She wanted to tell him of her plan which would mean they wouldn't have to marry at all, freeing him to pursue his ambition, but she knew that she had to remain silent. As Nanny had said, the fewer people who knew of it, the better. At least now she was convinced that she was doing the right thing. 'Good day, cousin,' she said.

'Until next Sunday,' he said, looking up again.

'Yes, of course.' She forced a smile. She didn't expect to see him again. Next week and the Sunday after, she would feign a headache.

Nanny went back to Canterbury on her half-day the following week to visit her uncle, who was still ailing – at least, that was the case that she set before Mama. She stayed for three days.

The wedding dress was ready, safely delivered to the house, and the wedding breakfast had been arranged. Surely there was not enough time, Agnes thought when she saw the carriage returning with her governess.

She ran downstairs to the kitchen to greet her with Henry at her heels.

'We've missed you,' she said. 'What news? How is your uncle?'

'I had to stay longer than I first intended, but there is progress, Agnes – more of that later. My uncle is improving too, thank you. The doctor says he is on the mend.'

'Sit down and rest your feet for a while, Miss Treen,' Cook said. 'The kettle's just boiled.'

'It is very kind of you.' Nanny turned to Henry. 'What have you learned today?'

'Lots,' he said, grinning.

Agnes smiled. He had been an excellent pupil. They had played hide and seek in the house and grounds, composed songs and laughed together.

''Ave a sultana cake, Master Henry,' Cook said.

'I would prefer a cherry one,' he said.

'Henry, you should be grateful for what you have,' Agnes said repressively.

'Oh, let him 'ave what he wants,' Cook said. 'I'll see if

there are any cherry ones left in the pantry.' She scurried away and returned with a tin. 'I'll 'ave to make some more tomorrow. In the meantime, there's a sponge here with jam through the middle and sugar on the top. I'm sure I can find some cream to go with it.'

By the time she had finished spoiling him, he was feeling quite sick, and Agnes couldn't help thinking that it served him right. She wondered at the change in her attitude. She had been a spoiled child and had spoken forthrightly about her wishes, yet here she was feeling critical of Henry's demanding tone of voice. It didn't mean she didn't love him. She adored him. He was like a miniature of Papa with his copper curls, quick eyes and beautiful smile. How could she possibly think of leaving him?

She met with Nanny in her room after Henry had been put to bed.

'I have a letter for you. It is only one, I'm afraid. I'm awaiting two other replies. I hope you don't mind, but I wrote on your behalf – I am a fair copy of your handwriting.'

Agnes smiled ruefully at her governess's cunning.

'It is a little harder with you being so young, but I think we can overcome that – you are mature for your age, and I have stated that you have been two years in your last place and can produce a good character for your honesty, morals and education. It crossed my mind to mention remuneration in my original letter of application, but it is thought vulgar to raise such a topic at least until we have secured an interview with the lady of the house.'

Agnes held the envelope, studying the name and address. Miss Linnet? It was the name they had agreed on, but it looked so strange. With trembling fingers, she opened the seal.

*Roper House, near Harbledown, Canterbury*

*Dear Miss Linnet*

*Bring your character to the house tomorrow. I think very likely you would suit. My daughters are most keen to practise the art of conversation and acquire a certain polish in playing pianoforte to impress in the drawing room.*

*However, absolute discretion and personal neatness are two things which I expect of all those in my service and if you are not in the habit of practising both, it is needless for you to come.*

*Lady Faraday*

She wanted to throw her arms up in the air with joy and relief that their plan had succeeded thus far, but her heart began to sink at the thought of the practicalities.

'How will I get away?'

'As you see, I have forgotten to collect the gloves. It completely slipped my mind.' Nanny had a small smile on her face. 'I've spoken to your mama and told her that they were not quite ready, and that we would have to go into town tomorrow to fetch them. And furthermore that my uncle wished to present you with a small gift in honour of your wedding.'

'What did she say?'

'She seemed distracted, laid low again in her distress – something had reminded her of your father's passing, their wedding anniversary, I think. It wasn't hard to press her into agreeing to let us take the carriage tomorrow afternoon. I will ask Mr Noakes to drop us off on the outskirts of town. We can then take a cab to the house and return to meet him as soon as you are finished.'

'What about going to call on your uncle?'

'Ah, we will not disturb him. It was merely an excuse.'

Agnes felt a little disappointed. She would have liked to have seen the Cheeverses again. They were the nearest she had to having friends.

Nanny held her gaze. 'You can change your mind. You don't have to go through with it.'

'Of course I do,' she said, thinking of the alternative.

'Then you must make your preparations tonight, but be discreet. If anyone hears of this plot, we will both suffer for it.'

'Thank you, Nanny. I'm sorry that you are risking your position here for my sake.'

'It will be worth it,' she said. 'You don't have your father to protect you now. It's up to me.'

Agnes slid the bolt on her bedroom door, laid out her clothes for the morning and copied out Nanny's character in her neatest writing. She had to make a good impression so a little forgery and sleight of hand seemed a small price to pay, although it did make her feel bad, writing lies about herself. She had been brought up to tell the truth, even though others around her had not always practised what they preached.

*To whomsoever it may concern, regarding Miss Agnes Linnet.*

*I am glad to be able to recommend you a good and honest governess. She is neat in her appearance and has a nice manner, is thoroughly respectable and well conducted. She is capable of performing all tasks within and without the schoolroom with a cheerful disposition. I think she will suit any establishment very well. She can read well and clearly, and is fluent in French.*

*Mrs Clive Norbert at—*

She gave an address in Wandsworth and rewrote it, omitting the comment about the French speaking, not wanting to make too much of herself.

The next day, Mr Noakes dropped Agnes and Nanny at St Dunstan's, where they managed to hail a cab to give them a lift to Upper Harbledown, and wait for Agnes to complete her business there.

'Take a deep breath and remember what I told you,' Nanny said when Agnes disembarked at the end of the drive to Roper House. 'Be expansive about your education, but as for your personal details, the less said the better. Take courage, child. I have taught you well. You have nothing to fear.'

Agnes turned and walked along the long drive past the iron railings, and the rough pasture and tall trees covered in unfurling leaves. The house stood at the top of the hill, its rows of sash windows looking out across the parkland. It was built in the Queen Anne style with a central triangular pediment and four of the tallest chimneys she had ever seen.

She made her way up the sweep of steps to the front door, then lowered her parasol and rang the bell, the sound reminding her of home. This was the kind of house where she would like to live and work. Although it was older and a little less cared for than Windmarsh Court, it would suit her very well.

She waited for a while but no one came, which put her in a quandary. Was it correct to ring the bell a second time?

As she hovered on the top step in a torment of indecision, the door opened to reveal a middle-aged man with dark hair slicked back against his head, and dressed in tails. His white collar appeared stained as if he had over-indulged in Macassar oil. He looked her up and down, staring in a most inappropriate way. She opened her mouth to correct him, but, remembering that even though she was superior to him in every way, she had to pretend that she wasn't. She wasn't used to being treated like a servant.

'Madam.' He was in his fifties, she guessed, and he had grown flabby on the good living provided by his employers. His jowls wobbled like one of Cook's jellies when he spoke. 'May I ascertain the purpose of your visit?'

'My name is Miss Linnet. I have an appointment with Lady Faraday about the position of governess.'

'This way.'

'Thank you,' she said as he showed her into the hall, his footsteps echoing across the black and ivory tiles. Several stuffed deer with glassy eyes stared down from the walls, and a pair of cloven hoofs sat on the marble-topped side table. Papa hadn't approved of hunting and Mama would have gone into a faint if she'd seen the household's trophies.

'May I take your coat?'

'I should be much obliged.' She let the butler take her coat and hang it on the stand in the corner behind the foot of the staircase, before following him past the ebony chiffonier, several portraits in oil of finely dressed men and women and a stuffed boar, into a corridor. He stopped at a door and knocked.

'Come in,' a voice said.

The butler held the door open and Agnes entered a small parlour where an older woman with grey hair looked up from a letter she was reading. She removed her pince-nez and gazed at Agnes, her expression one of cool appraisal which soon turned to suspicion.

A pulse began to beat at her temple. She wasn't worried that Lady Faraday would find her qualifications inadequate for the position – she was more than qualified to act as a governess. She was afraid that she would be found out for who she really was, but she had to go through with it, no matter how uncomfortable she felt, because time was running out. If she failed this interview, she would be forced into marrying Philip.

'My lady, allow me to introduce Miss Linnet. I believe you are expecting her,' the butler said.

'Thank you, Pell.' The layers of silk in Lady Faraday's dress matched the blues and yellows on the wall, which in turn coordinated with the darker hues in the brocades of the drapes and upholstery. 'Have some tea sent up.'

'Very good, my lady. Is there anything else?'

'That will be all for now.'

The butler nodded and reversed from the room.

'It is a pleasure to make your acquaintance, Lady Faraday,' Agnes said, noticing the burnished steel fire irons and the warm glow of the fire. The ornaments and clock on the mantel were all under glass domes to protect them from the dust and smoke.

'Would you be so kind as to take a turn around the room? Pause at the window, if you will. I wish to study your features.'

It wasn't what Agnes had been expecting. She walked from one corner to the other, then stopped at the window.

'Turn to the light, just a little.' Lady Faraday stood up and moved closer, taking time to examine her face and her dress. 'You have fine hands. Your features are rather too beautiful and your figure is above average.'

Was that a good thing for a governess? Agnes wondered, aware of the critical tone of Lady Faraday's voice. Was she comparing her appearance with that of her daughters? Did she not want to employ someone who would outshine them in beauty, or was she more concerned about the effect the presence of an attractive young lady might have on the gentlemen of the house?

'Now come and sit and we can discuss your reference. It is most complimentary but you seem very young to be a governess. In fact, it hardly seems possible that you were employed for long enough to have demonstrated all the attributes stated here.' Agnes opened her mouth to speak, but Lady Faraday cut her off. 'I suppose it's possible that you are one of those most fortunate of ladies who appears younger than she is. You don't mention your family.'

'I'm sorry. I find it distressing to talk of them. My mama died when I was quite young, and my dear papa lost his business through grief.' She'd practised her story until she was word perfect. 'I was brought up with my cousins at a house on the coast.' She hoped that the more convoluted her tale, the less likely it was that any potential employer would investigate.

'Whereabouts on the coast? I'm particularly fond of Dover.'

'A little further east,' she said, not wishing to be too precise.

Suddenly, a fracas broke out. A pair of muddy gun dogs, big black creatures with their tongues hanging out and dripping spittle, came running into the room. One jumped on the furniture and ran across the chairs. The other rushed to the far corner sniffing and snuffling at the carpet. They were closely followed by a large gentleman dressed in tweeds and carrying a stick.

'Sir Richard, what is the meaning of this?' Lady Faraday made to get out of her seat, then sat back down again.

'I've come to chase out the rat. Pell reported there'd been a rat giving the maids the frights.'

'How many times? Oh, you are infuriating. When I married a baronet, I expected him to have some manners.'

'Who is this young lady?' he said, spotting Agnes.

'That's what I'm trying to find out,' Lady Faraday said sharply. 'Get yourself and those filthy hounds out of here.'

'It's only mud. It'll wash off,' Sir Richard said in a booming voice. He whistled for the dogs and stomped off in his outdoor boots.

'I apologise for the interruption,' Lady Faraday said, turning back to Agnes as though nothing had happened. 'Now, where were we? Oh, yes. Did you attend school?'

'We had an excellent governess.'

'You say that your previous position was in London with a Mr and Mrs Clive Norbert. I don't believe that I have met them, but then London is a large city, I suppose.' Her voice faded then returned. 'Why did you leave your place?'

'Because the dear young ladies were quite grown up, and had no more need of my guidance and teaching.'

'I see. Do sit down.'

Agnes was glad to sit down and take some of the tea that the maid delivered and poured into delicate china cups decorated with hand-painted flowers. She realised that the drinking of tea wasn't a social offering, but a test of her manners and deportment.

'You do not say if you can speak French?'

'Yes, I am quite fluent,' she said.

'I see. I believe that French conversation is considered to be a fashionable accomplishment at present.'

'I am also proficient in geography, singing, piano and painting.

'You do paint in watercolour?'

'Naturally.' She was about to go on to explain that she could paint with oils too, when Lady Faraday nodded and said, 'It would be rather vulgar for a lady to paint in anything else. Watercolours are far more delicate and suitable for the feminine sex than any other medium. Tell me, how would you plan my daughters' days?'

'I would fit their lessons into the family's routine with time allocated to reading, writing and arithmetic in the mornings, and the afternoons devoted to the other subjects.'

'Miss Faraday is already most accomplished at music. Her sister will need more attention to her deportment. She is a little wild, while the elder needs to be brought out of her shell. Our last governess was careless in the way she talked of the family in the presence of others. As I stated in my letter, I require complete discretion.'

'I am used to encouraging the shyest of young ladies to speak with quiet confidence and deport themselves correctly in the presence of others. As to the latter point, I keep my own counsel when it comes to matters that don't concern me.'

Lady Faraday frowned.

'I am still concerned that you are very young and too close in age to my daughters. How long did you say you were with the Norberts?'

Agnes began to sense the position slipping away.

'I was there for a full two years and left through no fault of my own, as you can see from my reference. I am young, that is true, but youth is no barrier to proficiency. I have enthusiasm, vigour, and an empathy with young ladies, more so, dare I venture, than an older governess would have.'

'You are very sure of yourself.'

'A teacher must be able to inspire confidence in her pupils by setting a good example.'

'You have answered well, but I still believe that I should be taking a risk if I should hire you. I shall write to you when I have met the other applicants, Miss Linnet. Good day. Pell will see you out.' She picked up a bell from the table and rang it, bringing the butler scurrying in to escort Agnes away.

'If a letter should come for me, I fear that we will not have the time to pick it up from your uncle's,' Agnes said once they were seated in the cab on the way back to Canterbury to meet Mr Noakes with the carriage.

'I will have to call on him again when I have my half-day,' Nanny said.

'I wish you didn't have to go to so much trouble on my behalf.'

'We've gone this far. We must continue this business to its conclusion.' Nanny glanced at her pocket watch. 'I hope the driver will hurry. We are due to meet Mr Noakes shortly at the Rose Inn. And collect the gloves.'

Agnes wished she had asked Lady Faraday when she could expect her answer. Her wedding was arranged for two weeks' time at the beginning of May. She didn't hold out much hope.

'So Nanny has gone to Canterbury again?' Mama said. It was the evening before the wedding, and Agnes had taken Henry to the parlour to sit with her for a while. 'I can't help wondering if she has become acquainted with a gentleman other than her uncle.'

'It is nothing of the sort, Mama. Mr Cheevers is unwell.'

'Why does she feel obliged to keep visiting him?'

'Because he took her in when she lost her parents. He paid for her to attend school.'

Mama raised one eyebrow. 'I did not know.'

Agnes knew that her mother would never have had the slightest interest in Nanny's history. A governess might be a valued member of staff in some households, but here at Windmarsh she was just one of the servants. She prayed that Mama wouldn't ask any more questions. She was afraid that her nerves would give her away.

'You are ready for tomorrow?'

'Yes, Mama.' She bit her lip.

'I will not attend the ceremony. I do not wish to make myself ill.'

'I understand,' Agnes said softly. She wondered with a pang of renewed grief what her wedding day would have been like if Papa had still been alive. He would have come to the church with her. More importantly, he wouldn't have arranged for her to be affianced to her cousin. She glanced at the clock. The hands of time seemed to be standing still. Where had Nanny got to? When was she going to discover her fate?

She heard the sound of the carriage and the banging of a door. Nanny was home. She returned to the nursery with Henry, and Miriam gave him a glass of milk and helped him get ready for bed. Agnes said goodnight and retired to her room. She walked inside to find a lamp burning and a shadow sitting at the dressing table.

'Oh!' She touched her throat. 'I wasn't expecting to see you there.' She moved closer and caught sight of the letter lying beside her hairbrush and comb. Her heart beat faster as Nanny picked it up and handed it to her.

'Open it,' she said softly.

With trembling fingers, Agnes opened it up.

'Well?'

'It appears that Lady Faraday has no expectation that I will decline her offer,' Agnes said. 'She has stated the time that I should arrive – tomorrow morning – and enclosed details of my wages and conditions. I will have half a day off on Sunday, and half on a weekday, and two weeks a year.'

'Oh, that's wonderful. I've been so worried.' Nanny

stood up and embraced her. 'Congratulations, my dear. We have done it, and in the nick of time. You'll have a roof over your head, financial security and company. But' – she traced the tear that ran down Agnes's cheek – 'you are upset. Have you changed your mind? It is not too late.'

'Oh no. I'm relieved and sad at the same time.'

'So you will go and leave your old life behind?'

Agnes nodded. 'I have no choice. My feelings for Philip are unchanged, and I know he will thank me for letting him have his freedom.' She hesitated. 'You don't think they will come after me for breaking the engagement?'

'I doubt it. They will have to find you first, and I shan't let on where you are. My lips are sealed.' Nanny went to her room and returned with a package. 'I have something for you in the expectation that it will be of help when I'm not there for you to ask – I wrapped it in advance.'

Agnes tore off the brown paper, revealing the dreaded manual of etiquette.

'It is the most useful weapon to be found in a governess's armoury,' Nanny went on.

Agnes couldn't help smiling.

'This is very kind of you. What a thoughtful gift.' She hugged the book to her breast. 'I shall treasure it – it will always remind me of you and all you've done for me.'

'I have three pieces of advice for you. Do not on any account consider yourself a friend of the family, or even part of it. Make sure you are beyond suspicion in the confidence which is naturally reposed in you. Finally, look out for unwanted attentions by the master and grown-up sons of the family and turn them down in no uncertain terms. That is all. We will meet again one day.'

'I shall write to you every day,' Agnes exclaimed.

'It is too risky to exchange letters. It only takes one

person to investigate a name or address and one or both of us will be exposed.'

'I hadn't thought of that.'

'While I have thought of little else,' Nanny sighed. 'Although we won't be in touch, I will keep you in my prayers. I wish you well.' She took the book, placed it on the table and clasped Agnes's hands. 'Pack what you need and travel before dawn.'

'But it will be dark,' Agnes said nervously.

'It will be convenient – you will be able to slip away unnoticed, travelling by Shanks's pony. I will cover for you if anyone asks.'

'What about Miriam? She will see that I'm missing when she comes to lay the fire.'

'I will say you have gone out early for some fresh air – for your complexion. Oh, I don't know. I'll think of something. Now, I must leave you to it.'

'Won't you stay? I shan't sleep a wink.'

'We can't do anything to arouse suspicion. I will return to my room as usual. You will retire as you always do.'

'I haven't said goodbye to Henry,' Agnes said, remembering.

'I wouldn't advise it,' Nanny said.

'But what will he think?' She pictured his face when he found out she was gone.

'I will reassure him that his sister still loves him,' Nanny said tearfully.

'And always will,' Agnes said, breaking down completely.

'It is still not too late to change your mind.'

'No, I've come this far.'

'Goodnight then, my dearest girl. Good luck. We will meet again, I'm sure.'

'Goodnight,' she muttered, hardly able to speak. 'Thank you for everything you've done for me.'

'One more thing,' Nanny said before she slipped away. 'All that glisters is not gold. If something seems too good to be true, it probably is.'

Agnes sat on the edge of the bed, the mattress sinking beneath her. What had she done? She felt as if she was about to wade into a river, not knowing if she would sink or swim.

# Chapter Twelve

## *The Faradays*

When Pell opened the front door to her, he didn't seem to recognise her at first.

'I was to come all the way by carriage, but it lost a wheel and I thought it best that I walk the rest of the way so as not to be late. I know how Lady Faraday dislikes tardiness.' It had taken Agnes over four and a half hours to cover the distance between Windmarsh and Harbledown, carrying her luggage along the muddy roads and tracks in the rain. She must look a fright, she thought, regretting the appearance of her boots and the hem of her coat.

'Ah yes, Miss Linnet. Come in. I'll show you to your room so you can change,' he said, looking down his nose at her. 'I will ask one of the maids to bring up a tray with refreshment. You look dead on your feet.'

'Thank you for your kind consideration.'

He called for one of the footmen to carry her bags, and she followed Pell through to the rear of the house, up several narrow flights of stairs and on to a dark landing.

'This is your room.' He opened a door and showed her inside. 'The young ladies have their bedchambers at the end of this corridor. Dinner is served in the dining room at seven o'clock. You will normally dine with the family, not in the servants' hall, but this evening, her ladyship thought you would prefer to dine alone in your rooms rather than be forced to mingle with her guests.'

She felt a small stab of disappointment that she wasn't going to meet her pupils.

'She suggests that you begin the young ladies' education first thing tomorrow morning as they are otherwise occupied today.'

'I wonder if you could let them know that I'll meet them in the schoolroom at nine o'clock,' Agnes said, not wanting to delay.

Pell's lips curved into a wry smile.

'They haven't used the schoolroom for a long while. I'll send word to Mrs Cox to make sure that it is aired. I shall inform them on your behalf.'

'Thank you, Pell,' she said.

'Good luck to you, Miss Linnet.' He gave her a long stare, then ordered the footman to leave her bags beside the window before the two men left her to make herself at home.

The room was adequately furnished, she thought, trying to be optimistic about the threadbare carpet which showed but a trace of its original colour. There was a scratched mahogany table with a writing slope on top to one side of the fireplace and a wardrobe with a mirror to the other. There was a washstand, chair and bed. She checked the mattress – it was stuffed with horsehair and smelled of the stables. She had a basin and ewer, a soap-dish with a bar of cheap soap, a water bottle and glass. For her comfort, there was also a chamber pot and hip bath behind a screen.

It wasn't quite the luxury she had expected, and certainly not what she had been used to at Windmarsh Court. The room faced north and the weather was cold for May.

She investigated the fire which hadn't been lit. There

was coal in the grate and more in the scuttle, and she spotted a tinderbox on the mantel. She took the tinderbox down and knelt beside the grate. She took out the flint and steel and struck them over the tinder – some charred rag – in the box, catching her knuckles in error. How many times had she watched Miriam do it? And yet she still couldn't get it right.

Maybe it was damp, she thought.

She blew on the tinder again and again. It refused to ignite.

Frustrated, she tried once more. The rag glowed, just enough for her to kindle a brimstone match and transfer the flame to one of the candles that had been left out on the table.

'Well done, Agnes,' she muttered to herself as she lit the fire with the burning wick. She would be all right here – as long as no one found out her secret.

She unpacked her few personal items, her jewellery which she'd carried in a bag, a brush and comb, and pincushion. She put her folded clothes into the trunk at the end of the bed and hung her coat and cloak from the pegs in the back of the wardrobe.

Someone delivered tea, cold pie and bread on a tray which they left outside her door, and later someone brought her dinner. Twice, she went out on to the corridor, but she didn't see a soul. She heard voices, laughter, and horses and carriages coming and going outside. She smelled the scent of cooking – hot beef, cabbage and steamed pudding – wafting up the stairs while she sat alone at her table, planning lessons for the following day to keep herself occupied.

This should have been her wedding day. She felt terribly homesick, but she knew that she couldn't possibly have gone through with a marriage to Philip. She hoped he was well, and happy now that she'd freed him to go ahead with his studies. As for her, she had won her independence, but she had never felt so scared and lonely.

In the morning, after a fitful night's sleep, she managed to catch the maid as she knocked at the door. She was about the same age as Agnes – eighteen or nineteen years old – and wore uniform, a dark twill dress with a wide white Holland apron over the top and a crochet cap on her head.

'Please, come in. The tray can go on the table,' Agnes said.

The maid wished her a good morning, but otherwise appeared tongue-tied as she delivered the tray and filled the ewer with hot water for washing. Agnes wondered if she was a country girl with her big arms and scarlet cheeks. She had long brown hair tied back with a dark ribbon, and deep blue eyes.

'Can you tell me where to find the schoolroom?' Agnes asked.

'It's on the next floor, directly above. I'll clean your room later.'

'You may stay and do it now, if you wish. I don't mind.'

'Oh no, Lady Faraday wouldn't like that. Good day, Miss Linnet.'

'Good day, Miss . . . ?'

'Evie. My name is Evie Potts.' The maid closed the door behind her, leaving Agnes to her breakfast and toilette. She dressed as modestly as she could before heading up with her lesson plans to find the schoolroom half an hour before her meeting with her pupils.

She pushed the door open and her heart sank. She was prepared, but the schoolroom was nowhere near to being ready to receive the young ladies. It was dark and neglected, the wallpaper unfurling from a patch of mould above the window. She opened the shutters to let in the daylight, and scanned the unfamiliar view across the lawns and parkland. She could just see the smoke coming from the chimney of the gatehouse at the end of the drive through the trees, and the red-brick cottages in the distance.

She looked around for something to sweep the floor with. She found a broom in a cupboard and swept the dust into one corner. No one had thought to clean the ashes from the fireplace and light a fire to take the damp chill from the air.

How could she expect anyone to learn in these conditions?

She made her way downstairs, looking for the servants' quarters and kitchen, where her appearance was met with a wall of silence that made her feel distinctly unwelcome.

'I'm Miss Linnet, the new governess,' she began, her mouth running dry as she addressed the small group of staff. 'I should like to introduce myself to the housekeeper.'

A woman looked up from the table where she was sitting with a cup of tea.

'I'm Mrs Cox, the housekeeper,' she said.

'I'm delighted to meet you.' From the expression on the older woman's face, Agnes didn't think the feeling was mutual. 'I should like to borrow one of the maids to clean the fireplace in the schoolroom.'

'Well, I don't know about that. It's most irregular. The maids are taken up with clearing up after last night's dinner. I'm not sure I can spare even one of them, and besides, I take my orders from her ladyship.'

'I don't see why we need to trouble her over such a small matter.' Agnes frowned, unused to being in the position of an employee not a master. 'You will do as I say.'

'I will not. Who are you coming in here and throwing

your weight around?' The housekeeper's eyes flashed with irritation, but Agnes felt that she was entitled to the help. She would have her way.

'It is for the young ladies' benefit, not mine.' The hairs on the back of her neck bristled with antagonism as she stared at Mrs Cox's small nose and mean features, which seemed to match the woman's temperament. 'I shall go and speak to Lady Faraday.'

'That isn't necessary on this occasion.' Mrs Cox relented. 'You can 'ave Evie for half an hour and no longer.'

Agnes thanked her and returned to the schoolroom, where she was soon joined by the maid.

'I'm sorry for taking you away from your other chores,' she said.

'I shouldn't be talking to you. The others won't like it. They say you 'ave ideas above your station.'

'Oh dear.' Agnes felt hurt.

'I'm sure you're nothing of the sort,' Evie backtracked. 'It's just the way you're put above the rest of the servants, being a governess and all that. You don't 'ave to share a room in the attic, or sleep in the closet next to the scullery. You 'ave your food delivered to your door while we are condemned to eat in the servants' hall, which is a terrible ordeal, because Pell eats so fast, gulping his dinner down like a dog. As soon as he's finished, he expects us to put our knives and forks down. One day, we will all starve and it will be down to him.'

'I feel that I'm very much disliked, yet I have done nothing to deserve it. It is expected that I dine in my room and on occasion with the family.'

'I hardly know the Faradays,' Evie said. 'I can count on the fingers of one hand the number of times I've seen Sir Richard since I started work here. You speak proper, miss. Where do you come from?'

She explained, just as she had to Lady Faraday at her interview.

'I can't imagine having no family,' Evie said. 'I 'ave a mother and father and five sisters who are all but one in service.' She knocked the coal from the scuttle that she had carried up the stairs. 'Oh, I'm such a clodpole. I'll get it cleaned up.' She wiped soot across her cheek and then got on with rolling up the hearth rug and laying down canvas in front of the fireplace, while Agnes arranged the furniture: a table, two desks and some bentwood chairs.

Evie raked the ashes, swept them up and brushed the fireplace, using some black-lead for the back and sides, then she scoured the stone hearth with soap, sand and cold water.

Agnes found paper and pens, but there was no ink. The wells were dry.

'When you have laid the fire, would you be able to find some ink for the young ladies' lessons?' she asked.

'I'll try the master's study.' Evie piled the coals in the grate and lit the fire, blowing on the tinder to coax the flame alight. Once the coals were smoking, she dried the hearth with a cloth and left the room, returning with a bottle of ink – which was lucky, Agnes thought, because there was precious little else to aid her teaching, apart from one novel, a Bible, a poetry book and a muddied tray of watercolour paints.

'The young ladies haven't had a governess for the past two or three years. There was some unpleasantness, a scandal. Apparently, the lady in question revealed secrets about the family and allowed Miss Elizabeth to run riot. There, I've said too much. Good day, Miss Linnet,' Evie added with a shy smile.

Agnes thanked her for her trouble, and secretly hoped that she and the maid could be friends in the future.

She checked the clock on the mantel. It was already close to ten o'clock and there was no sign of the young ladies. Had there been some kind of misunderstanding with Pell? She expected people to do her bidding, and now she had to learn that she should have no expectations. It appeared that lessons at Roper House were not a priority.

She went downstairs and found Pell in the butler's room that faced out towards the front of the house, which meant he could see visitors on the drive, and therefore answer the door without delay. He was at the table, holding a lighted candle behind the neck of a bottle of red wine which he was pouring slowly into a cut-glass decanter. He stopped and looked up.

'Your presence has disturbed the sediment, Miss Linnet. I thought you were in the schoolroom.'

'I'm sorry. I have been waiting for the young ladies to join me.'

'Oh, I believe they are in the parlour with their mother. You know your way.' He placed the candle back in the holder on the table and put the bottle down. The silver plate shone from the cabinets behind him.

She nodded. 'Yes, thank you.'

'I'm afraid that you'll find they aren't much taken with the idea of lessons. They will find any excuse to avoid their studies and you don't have the authority to bring them into line. I suggested to Lady Faraday that she should employ someone older with more experience. I tell you, Miss Linnet – you won't last a week. In fact, you might as well pack your bags right now.'

'Thank you for your honesty, Pell, but I can assure you that I don't give up that easily.'

'I don't suppose you can afford to. I have made many contacts in the area over the years and so far nobody has said they have heard of you. It seems rather peculiar, don't you think?'

She wouldn't let him intimidate her, she thought. He couldn't know anything.

'I have recently worked in London. It is a vast city, far more expansive than Canterbury, in case you were unaware,' she added. 'It's impossible to know everyone.'

'It's all rather convenient if you ask me,' Pell said, his complexion colouring. He didn't like being made to look a fool, she realised. She would have to tread carefully.

'If you say so,' she retorted.

'You are not that much of a mouse, then. Maybe the young ladies won't have you for breakfast after all. We will see.'

She wished him good day and returned to the main part of the house, retracing her steps to the parlour by following the sound of voices and laughter. The door was ajar. She knocked and gently pushed it open. Lady Faraday was standing by the fire, wearing a dark green gown. Her younger daughter was at her side, engaged in animated conversation. She had a girlish figure and blonde curls piled up on her head. Agnes coveted her dress, which was made from red and blue silk with pagoda sleeves and the fullest skirt she had ever seen.

The elder one, dressed in brown, sat in the chair opposite with her legs folded up beneath her and a small black and tan King Charles spaniel in her lap. Her hair was long, blonde and straight, and appeared to reach down to at least her waist. She looked towards Agnes, then back to her mother.

'Mama, there is someone here to see you.'

Lady Faraday frowned before some sign of recognition crossed her face.

'Oh, Miss Linnet, I'd quite forgotten—' She recovered

herself quickly. 'Let me introduce you to my daughters, Miss Faraday – Charlotte, look up when I'm speaking to you.'

Agnes frowned, then realised Lady Faraday was addressing her elder daughter.

'And this is my younger daughter, Miss Elizabeth Faraday.'

The younger girl, who must have been about fifteen years old to her sister's seventeen, smiled at her new governess, revealing a set of perfect white teeth.

'It's delightful to make your acquaintance,' Agnes said. 'I thought, though, that I had arranged to meet you both in the schoolroom at nine. We have plenty to do.'

'I'm sorry for your inconvenience, Miss Linnet,' Lady Faraday said without a hint of regret in her voice. 'My daughters must have their beauty sleep, so ten o'clock would be far more suitable in future.'

'Of course. I'm more than happy to arrange lessons around the family's timetable.'

'We don't want to go back to the schoolroom,' Elizabeth said. 'It is insufferably dull.'

'Miss Linnet is employed to finish your education,' their mama said. 'You must do as she says. She comes highly recommended.'

'By whom?' said Charlotte.

'By her previous employer. Miss Linnet, I should appreciate a weekly report of each of my daughters' progress, something I omitted to ask for with our previous governess.'

'I can certainly do that for you,' Agnes said.

'Girls, you must go,' Lady Faraday decided.

After a prolonged farewell between Elizabeth and her mama, and Charlotte's slow remove from the chair with the dog in her arms, they finally left the parlour and made their way to the schoolroom. Agnes decided not to insist on leaving the dog outside on this occasion. She'd always wanted a lapdog, but not in her schoolroom, she thought.

'The dog may accompany you if he sits on the floor while you concentrate on your studies.'

'Oh, he never sits on the floor. And he has a name – he's called Sunny,' Charlotte said.

'Isn't he the sweetest thing you've ever seen?' said Elizabeth.

'Not really, but he seems like a nice dog,' Agnes ventured, softening towards the creature. 'But you must put him down on the floor so that he doesn't lose the use of his legs. Now!' she said firmly. She would not have rebellion in the schoolroom. 'Take a seat and write your names on the paper in front of you.'

She watched her charges as they argued over who should take which place. Elizabeth won, taking the seat nearest the window. Agnes smiled to herself. She would have to watch that she didn't get distracted by what was going on outside. She turned, listening with one ear for any disruption, while she wrote the plan for the day on the blackboard.

'Etiquette?' she heard Elizabeth sigh. 'We have already done etiquette to death.'

'In that case, you can show me how well you deport yourselves during the day. I look forward to learning something from you.'

They sat, one in silence and the other pouting while the dog chewed its paws and licked itself rather indiscreetly in the middle of the floor.

'Please push your tables close together so you are side by side.' Agnes took the Bible and opened it. 'I should like you to copy this passage in your best handwriting.' As she saw Elizabeth open her mouth to protest, she glared at her. 'It's so I can see where you are with your learning and find out what you need to help you to improve.' She could hear Nanny's words ringing in her ears. She thanked God that she had had such a conscientious governess for her education.

'We have no ink,' Elizabeth said. 'We never have any ink.'

'I filled the wells you have in front of you earlier this morning. It will not have dried out quite yet.' Agnes was amused at her wiliness. 'Go on. Try them. Charlotte? You as well.'

Elizabeth reached out her pen and dipped the nib into the well in front of her and withdrew it. She touched the nib to the paper and the ink flowed. She looked up at Agnes and smiled.

'You see. Now, it's your turn, Charlotte. Let us see who can write the quickest and neatest.'

Charlotte's pen scratched across the paper as she wrote, her tongue sticking out between her lips as she concentrated. Elizabeth was slower, but she finished first. Agnes's forehead tightened. How could that be? She walked across and looked over the girl's shoulder and began to read.

'You have missed out a whole paragraph here,' she said, running her forefinger down the page. 'You have been either careless or deliberate. Which is it?' When her pupil didn't respond, she went on, 'You had better do it again. From the beginning.'

She noticed how Elizabeth's spine stiffened. 'I will not waste my time,' she said.

'And you will not waste mine with any more silly tricks,' Agnes said sternly.

'I will tell Mama, if you make me do it again,' Elizabeth said, getting up from her chair.

'You may do whatever you like. You may go running off telling tales and hiding behind your mama's skirts like an infant or you can apologise for your insolence and return to the task I have set you. I would strongly advise you to take the latter course of action, or be considered a telltale. Go on. Do as you wish.'

Elizabeth's eyes flashed with rebellion and for a moment Agnes thought she would call her bluff and run to her mother, but she changed her mind, sat down at her desk and picked up her pen.

'Thank you.'

'You are very strict, Miss Linnet.'

'Knowledge is important. You never know when you might need it. When you have finished, we will go out for a walk. Charlotte, Sunny may accompany us.'

'Oh no, why on earth would we want to do that?' Elizabeth exclaimed. 'It has been raining. We'll get mud on our shoes.'

'Fresh air and exercise are good for the constitution. A healthy body is a prerequisite to a healthy and receptive mind.'

'How can you have any idea about what is good for you when you are barely a year older than Charlotte?'

'I don't know who gave you that impression.' Agnes had told Lady Faraday that she was twenty-one. 'All I will say – because it's inappropriate for a person in my position to reveal how old she is – is that I have always looked younger than my age. There you are – I'm proof of the principle. Come on. A breath of country air will bring the colour to your pale cheeks, Charlotte, and a walk will settle your restlessness, Elizabeth.'

'It sounds like an improvement on lessons, I suppose,' Elizabeth said with some semblance of a smile.

'I would prefer to remain at home and read my book,' Charlotte said.

'You can read later. You do recall that I have to make

a report each week to your mama, demonstrating your progress?'

The young ladies nodded.

'You wouldn't dare put anything bad in it, or derogatory, or Mama will send you packing,' Elizabeth said.

'I will write and speak the truth,' Agnes said.

'I think she means it,' she heard Charlotte whisper.

'Yes, I most certainly do. You will complete the task I have set within the next twenty minutes. If you are not finished, that will go on your report. Then we will put on our walking shoes and coats and go out.'

'I don't see the purpose of copying out the Bible,' Elizabeth tried again, reminding Agnes of her own attempts to divert Nanny in the past.

'I will ask Lady Faraday for some more books,' she said.

'What would we want with those? I should much prefer a new dress,' Elizabeth said lightly.

'Oh, you are so superficial,' Charlotte retorted. 'Have you no interests apart from the purchase of clothes and the pursuit of young gentlemen?'

'That is unfair.'

'I've seen you with that friend of Felix who came to stay last summer. Oh, George, shall we take a turn around the room? Oh, George, do you play croquet?' Charlotte mocked, and then, like a snail sensing danger, slid back into her shell of silence.

'Is Felix your brother?' Agnes enquired, thinking of her brother Henry.

'Yes. He is away at university, studying philosophy. He wishes to follow in Papa's footsteps – it is something to while away his time until he takes over the running of the estate,' Elizabeth said.

Agnes wondered why a son should have so much opportunity compared with daughters who were merely waiting to make advantageous marriages and produce heirs and spares.

'I'm diverting you from your work,' she said, and she waited patiently while Elizabeth finished the task she had set, and turned a blind eye when Charlotte picked up the dog and placed it on her knee.

'It's done. I hope it's to your satisfaction,' Elizabeth said.

'Thank you.' Agnes perused her efforts. 'It is a good start. I'm pleasantly surprised. You will do very well if you apply yourself.'

Elizabeth flushed as though she was unaccustomed to such praise.

'Do either of you have a favourite subject of study?' Agnes asked.

'We have no need for learning.' Elizabeth sat back in her chair and dropped her pen on to the table.

'You need enough knowledge to be able to listen attentively – it isn't right that you think that the pinnacle of womanhood is the renunciation of intelligence.'

'But I don't want to grow up odd and eccentric,' Elizabeth protested.

'How about you, Charlotte?' Agnes said.

She refused to look up and meet her eye.

'You must speak when you are spoken to,' Agnes said, feeling frustrated. 'You are, what, seventeen years old? Where are your powers of speech?'

She shrugged.

'She can't help it.' Elizabeth was suddenly protective of her older sister. 'She is naturally shy.'

'Let her speak for herself. The more you practise, Charlotte, the easier it will become. Tell me, what do you like to study most?'

She peered out from beneath her fringe, which fell forward from a central parting.

'I like to read,' she whispered.

'Thank you. I shall recommend some suitable books to help improve your confidence.'

'I like to choose my own reading material,' Charlotte muttered.

'She likes to bury her head in novels,' Elizabeth said scathingly.

Agnes's heart sank. Teaching was going to be harder work than she had imagined. How was she to teach the young ladies of Roper House if they had no interest in anything? How was she to inspire them? She began to have doubts about whether she was up to the job. She was, as her ladyship had suggested, too young and inexperienced, but she had no choice but to go on. If she gave up, she would be out on the street.

She was under pressure for the first time in her life. It was her responsibility to look after herself and her interests. She could no longer drift and make up stories, or paint at leisure, or watch the light changing on the marshes. She was a working woman.

She pictured the long-drawn-out days continuing one after the other with the insufferably spoiled young ladies until such a time that her ladyship no longer required her services and she had to move on to another place and do it all over again.

She had felt free and in charge of her own destiny when she had made the decision not to marry Philip. Now, she felt trapped by her new circumstances from which there appeared to be no means of escape.

# Chapter Thirteen

## *An Education*

She woke one morning with a start as someone knocked on the door. She slipped out of bed and grabbed a gown to cover her shoulders.

'Who is it? What time is it?'

'It's only me, Evie.' The maid pushed the door open. 'Oh, I'm sorry, Miss Linnet.'

'It's all right. Come on in. Are you early today? You caught me sleeping.'

'So it appears. It's my usual time, but I can go away again.'

'No, don't.' She had felt isolated at Windmarsh Court, but here at Roper House, it was ten times worse. She had been with the Faradays since early in May. It was late June now and she hadn't got to know anyone. 'Come in, and call me Agnes, not Miss Linnet. I must hurry – I'm expecting to meet the young ladies in the schoolroom in half an hour.'

'I think it's unlikely – Elizabeth is still abed,' Evie said.

'Oh, I see.' Agnes smiled ruefully, wondering how Nanny had managed to remain so patient. 'I shall be having words with her.'

'You would be so bold as to do that?'

'I'm her governess. I've been given authority over that rebellious young woman and she will listen to me.'

'I hope so. She is a law unto herself, that one. I don't think she's ever taken notice of anyone. Her mother spoils her so. I hope you don't mind me saying, but you look a little weary.'

She didn't like to complain about her lot, when Evie was on her feet from six in the morning until eleven at night. At least when Lady Faraday gave her other tasks, such as sewing to fill in the quiet times when her daughters were with her, she could sit with her feet up.

'You have it far harder than I do,' she said. 'How long have you worked here?'

'I went into service when I was thirteen years old. I was lucky – my younger sister started at nine. I found it tiring at first, but it's got easier, although we are supposed to act invisible and neither sing nor laugh. It's very strict here, and Mrs Cox takes money off your wages for breakages.' She changed the subject. 'How about you? Are you settling in?'

'Yes, I think so.'

'I expect you're used to it. I've heard that you worked in London before.'

'Yes. Yes, that's right.'

'Pell has bin telling us about you. He said he'd bin making enquiries about your previous employment. Oh' – she flushed – 'I wasn't sure if I should say anything, but I couldn't have it on my conscience to keep it back. You must watch out for that man. He's trouble.'

'What do you mean?' Agnes bit her lip. The last thing she needed was the butler digging up her past.

'He took against one of the footmen not long ago, and set him up as a thief. He planted two silver spoons in his pocket then accused him right in front of the master.'

'Didn't somebody say something?' Agnes said, aghast.

'The rest of us wanted to keep our places. Besides, who

would have believed us against Pell? He is a snake lurking in the grass.'

'Well, thank you for warning me, Evie.'

'Make sure you keep it to yourself. I don't want him thinking I've bin gossiping behind his back.'

'I won't tell a soul,' Agnes promised and Evie changed the subject.

'I wonder . . . when you 'ave the time, if you could screeve a letter on my behalf? I've never l'arned to read and write, and I'd like to send word to my dear family to let them know I am well, and find out how they are. I haven't sin them for ages, you see. It's too far to visit them on my days off. I won't 'ave a chance to see them until the summertime. Oh, I'm sorry. Listen to me going on. You are busy and I mustn't hold you up.'

'It's all right. It seems that I have a few minutes spare to give Miss Elizabeth time to prepare herself.' Agnes opened her writing slope, took out a piece of paper, an envelope and a pen and removed the lid of the inkwell. She dipped the nib in the ink. 'What would you like me to say?'

'Let me see. How about, "Dear Father and Mother, I hope you are quite well. Please send me news of my dear sisters. I am sorry to be so far away from home, but the thought that my wages help you out in your old age consoles me a little. The family do not make any trouble, but the butler and the housekeeper are strict and not often good-natured. Don't worry, though. I know I must put up with a good deal in return for my . . ."'

Agnes added the word 'remuneration' although Evie wasn't sure her parents would know what it meant.

'"A new governess has come to do for the young ladies. She has very kindly helped me to write this letter to you. God bless you, my family. Your affectionate daughter, Evie."'

'Now you make your mark,' Agnes said, handing her the pen. Evie made a cross at the bottom of the letter, Agnes blotted it and folded the paper. She placed it in an envelope and wrote the address which Evie dictated to her. Then, with the flickering stub of a candle, she dripped wax on to it to make the seal, letting it set before she handed it to Evie. 'All you need now is a one-penny stamp.'

'I'm ever so grateful.' She smiled. 'I hope they will reply. You know, you are making changes around here.'

'I hope so,' Agnes said. She felt a little better, having made a friend in the maid, although she ached with guilt for not being honest with her. She couldn't afford to let down her guard, not now, not ever. She would never be able to be herself at Roper House.

She spent all day in the schoolroom, trying to engage the young ladies in their education. Elizabeth made a fair attempt at a watercolour landscape of the parkland at the front of the house, but solved only four of the arithmetical problems that Agnes had set. As for Charlotte, she felt that the dog had probably learned more from her lessons than she had. When she was supposed to be reading a book of poetry, Agnes found a novel hidden underneath.

It was no use, she thought. She wasn't getting anywhere with them. It was infuriating. She wanted to throw her hands up and walk away, but she couldn't because she had nowhere to go.

Instead, she waited for them to clear their tables.

'Why is it that you have no desire to improve your minds?' she said when she had their attention.

The clock struck four and Miss Elizabeth was up on her feet.

'Where are you going?'

'Lessons have finished for the day. Mama will be expecting us for tea.'

'Oh no, you must wait until I have finished speaking—'

'Oh, you are such a prig, Miss Linnet. Where on earth did you come from? You brag about your knowledge yet you are the dullest, most miserable creature I have ever met. The sight of your face would turn milk sour.'

'Elizabeth, I will not tolerate your rudeness. Sit down!'

'I will not,' she said with an insouciant smile. 'I shall do as I please.' She spun on her heels and left the room with a flounce of her skirts. Charlotte stood up and followed with the dog trotting along behind her without a backward glance.

Agnes didn't know what to say, what to think. How dare they flout her authority?

She felt sick to the stomach. How had Nanny managed to make teaching look so easy? She looked around the schoolroom and sighed. She had wanted the place to be an oasis of calm, but it had turned into a battlefield.

Was it because her lessons weren't engaging enough? Elizabeth had said she was dull.

She took a look around the house, searching for resources she could use for her teaching. She walked along the landing to the master's study and knocked gently on the door. There was no answer so she turned the handle, but the door was locked. She moved along to the next room, the library. The door was ajar so she pushed it open and looked inside. It was empty and the curtains were drawn to protect the books' leather spines from the sunlight. There were shelves along two walls, full length from floor to ceiling, and innumerable volumes set out in numerical and alphabetical order. She found it a little strange that Miss Elizabeth was not at all bookish when there were this many books in the house, and that Charlotte was only to be found reading novels, not more serious tomes. It was the finest library she had ever seen.

She walked across to the nearest shelf and took down a volume. She blew off the dust, opened it and started to read. *Physical Geography: A Treatise*. This was what she was looking for: maps and engravings to stimulate the young ladies' interest. She took a second volume down and carried them back to the schoolroom, along with three illustrated books on botany. All she needed now was a globe.

She returned downstairs to find Pell or Mrs Cox, and Cook.

Cook was not impressed with her request but softened when Agnes explained that it was for the young ladies' benefit.

'Have Evie bring it up to my room with breakfast in the morning,' she said.

'Haven't I already got enough to do? The pork griskins aren't ready, and the aspic hasn't set.' Cook tut-tutted and shook her head, but she agreed to carry out the task as long as she had some red cabbage or beetroot available.

'Shall I go and ask the gardener?' Agnes asked, determined not to be defeated.

'No, that won't be necessary. I expect there's something suitable in the scullery. Miss Linnet, may I ask what you are planning?'

'I'll let the young ladies show you themselves the day after tomorrow.' She smiled. 'I'm very grateful for your trouble.'

Pell was in his room, polishing the silver salvers for the dinner table.

'I'm sorry to disturb you,' she said.

He looked up, frowning.

'What do you want?'

'I have come to ask if you can help me – I want to expand the young ladies' experience of geography, and wondered if there is a globe anywhere in the house?'

'A globe?'

'A map of the world,' she explained.

'Oh?' He rubbed his chin. 'Let me think. I may have seen one in the attic. You can tell one of the footmen that I've said they are to assist you in your search. Take a lantern and be careful how you go.'

'I shall go by myself.'

'As you wish.'

She dug around in the dark and dingy attic room at the end of the house above the west wing, brushing cobwebs and dust from her clothes as she made her way between the pieces of furniture and belongings that the Faradays had discarded there. There was an old clock on its side, its carcase open and its insides tipped out. There were some boxes of china and several framed paintings leaning against a wardrobe, and – she suppressed a cry of joy – a small globe on a table.

She picked it up and carried it to the landing into the light. It wasn't the finest, and some of the writing on it had been scuffed, but the outlines of the countries were intact. It would do, she thought.

She took it downstairs to the schoolroom, cleaned it up and oiled the workings so it would spin freely on its axis. Tomorrow, she thought, they would study Italy, and with the dye from the kitchen and their botanical specimens, practise a kind of alchemy.

In the morning, she met the young ladies in the schoolroom.

'You are late again. This will not do.' She noticed how Elizabeth smirked and it riled her, but she would not be angry. She reined in her emotions and took a deep breath. 'You will stay an extra twenty minutes this afternoon.'

'Mama will not allow it,' Elizabeth said.

'You will have to apologise to her and explain why you are delayed meeting her in the parlour.'

Elizabeth bit her lip.

'Now, push your tables together and sit down.' Agnes turned away and picked up the globe under its muslin cover and placed it in front of the sisters. Aware that they were watching her with some consternation, she took the corner of the muslin and swept it off with a flourish.

'Oh!' Charlotte exclaimed. 'It is a map of the earth.'

'What do we want with that, Miss Linnet?' Elizabeth said.

Agnes ignored her, sensing that the more she paid attention to her, the more she played upon it.

'Which of you can find Italy?'

'I'll look,' Charlotte said quickly, snatching the globe away. She peered at it closely. 'There it is,' she said in triumph.

'Where?' Elizabeth asked.

Charlotte showed her.

'I could have found that, if I'd had a chance.'

'Show me,' Agnes said. 'Let me spin the globe and then you can find Italy.'

It took Elizabeth longer than her sister to find it.

'Now show me Sicily, Elizabeth,' Agnes said.

'I don't know where that is.' Her cheeks began to turn pink. Agnes recognised the signs of frustration building inside her pupil, like a volcano about to erupt.

'Let me give you a clue – the toe of Italy has kicked Sicily into the Mediterranean Sea.'

'I cannot see it.' Elizabeth gazed at the globe. 'Ah, yes, I can. There it is.'

'Well done. Now I'm going to show you the map in the book – we can draw it out together and add the capital of Italy, and the floating city, and the site of the Ponte

Vecchio.' Agnes recalled the thrill of Nanny's teaching, and it must have shown in her voice because the young ladies applied themselves to the task with great enthusiasm, and by the end of the day they were planning their Grand Tour of Europe and plotting how they would persuade their father to fund it.

'Can we stop now?' Elizabeth said when Agnes had checked their work. 'We can take Sunny for a walk.'

'We will take a diversion through the garden on our return from our daily constitutional as we need to prepare for tomorrow morning's lesson in botany,' Agnes said.

'Can't we do more geography?' Charlotte said.

'We can't study the same subject all day every day,' Agnes said lightly. 'Make haste and prepare for our outing. The sun is shining.'

'I should like to go into Canterbury today,' Elizabeth said. 'We could turn it into a nature walk if we went via Rough Common.'

'Since when have you been so interested in nature and long walks?' Agnes asked.

'She wishes to study the nature of officers in more detail,' Charlotte interrupted.

'I beg your pardon. What did you say?' Agnes was taken aback.

'It's true,' Charlotte said. 'When we're in town with Mama, my sister can barely walk for swooning at their uniforms.'

'Oh, you do exaggerate,' Elizabeth exclaimed crossly.

Agnes gathered that Charlotte's revelation might have some truth in it, in which case she was determined to avoid the town like the plague. She had to confess that she'd been nervous when she'd discovered how close Roper House was to Canterbury. It worried her that the occupants of the house had business there with tradespeople and family, but she reassured herself that it was unlikely that anyone would be in contact with the Cheeverses at the tannery. It would be too much of a coincidence. However, she still preferred to remain in the environs of Upper Harbledown and Chartham Hatch nearby for safety.

'It's too far for what remains of this afternoon – at least a two-hour round trip. We will walk around the grounds and pick some flowers.' Agnes had her eye on some carnations she had spotted in among the beds in the kitchen garden. The gardener had started them in the glasshouse and planted them out when all risk of frost had passed.

They walked through the village, past the white cottages, the oasts and the inn and through the orchards and back via the woods along the sunken footpath before diverting to the garden.

'I should like you both to pick three white carnations,' Agnes said. 'Let's see who finds them first.'

'Which are they?' Elizabeth looked at her to glean clues as to their whereabouts.

'It is up to you to find them.'

'I don't know what they look like,' Charlotte muttered.

'If you both paid attention to your surroundings, you would know. I'm not going to help you.' Agnes took a seat in the arbour beside the pond in the middle of the garden and watched the fish while she waited. There was a net across the top – the heron had taken the last shoal for his dinner. Every now and again, she stood up to check on her charges who were wandering desultorily around the flower beds. 'Have you found them yet?' she called.

'We have found all kinds of white blooms, but can't tell which is which,' Elizabeth said.

'So you have narrowed it down. That's a start. How will you identify the carnation? Without asking anyone,' she said with a smile. 'Have you ever heard of a library?'

'Of course. We have one in the house. Everyone has one,' Elizabeth said. 'Oh, we could look in a book. Miss Linnet, I'm too exhausted to return indoors and come back out here again. I'll have to send one of the maids. Besides, I'm not ranging about in the mud – I'll get my dress dirty.'

Agnes's heart began to sink again. She'd thought they had been making progress. It would have been easier to give in to the younger sister's tantrum, but she remained firm.

'The sooner you apply yourself, the sooner it will be done,' she said.

'Come on, Elizabeth,' Charlotte sighed. 'We'll do this together.'

'I shall wait for you here, I think,' Agnes said, enjoying the sunshine on her face. Mama and Nanny had never allowed her to expose her skin to the sun's rays for fear of ruining her complexion.

'You aren't going to keep your beady eyes on us?' Elizabeth said, surprised.

'I'm trusting you to do as you've been asked. You are not children any more.'

'You aren't like our previous nanny – she made us do embroidery every day until our eyes hurt.'

'Go on then.' Agnes waved them away and took advantage of a few precious moments of quiet. She breathed in the scent of stocks and watched the bees, laden with pollen, clambering on the roses.

If only she could win the young ladies over, then she could lead a relatively comfortable existence – the food was more than adequate, and although the wages were poor and her room was intolerably small and badly furnished, she had escaped an unwanted marriage. The trouble was that she still yearned to be the spoiled young woman who didn't have to think about what she would teach the next day, and constantly worry about being recognised or hounded out as an impostor. She wished for peace of mind.

She glanced up at the windows that overlooked the garden – she thought she caught sight of Lady Faraday, her figure drifting across the parlour window. She would never know what it was to earn her living. She was married – happily, Agnes thought from the way she had seen her with her husband at dinner. Sir Richard was a baronet and landowner – he spent most of his time away from the house, shooting and carrying out his daily business on the estate. His wife had plenty to occupy her with running the house, but she had a goodly team of servants to carry out her orders. She adored her daughters and her future was certain.

Agnes envied her.

She was soon distracted from her thoughts by the sound of the young ladies' voices.

'We have discovered them, Miss Linnet,' Elizabeth called. 'How many did you say you wished us to collect?'

'Three each,' Agnes said, standing up from the bench as the dog came trotting over, wagging his tail. She followed him to where the sisters were working out how to pick the carnations without stepping on the earth and dirtying their dresses. Charlotte found a board leaning against the wall behind the gardener's wheelbarrow. She laid it on the flower bed and Elizabeth stepped on to it and reached down for the white carnations, choosing six stems.

'I should have preferred the yellow ones,' she said. 'They are far more cheerful, don't you think?'

'They have to be white,' Agnes said. 'We are going to carry out a scientific experiment. It will take but five minutes of our time.'

Back in the schoolroom, they put the carnations into the red cabbage juice that Cook had provided that morning.

'I wonder if you can use that to put a blush on your cheeks,' Elizabeth said, dipping her finger into the cup and applying it to her face. 'What do you think, Charlotte?'

'It makes you look ridiculous,' she said, grimacing as Elizabeth ran out of the room.

'Where are you going?' Agnes called after her.

'To find a mirror,' she laughed. Eventually, she returned, rubbing her face with a handkerchief. 'Look, it has a remarkable effect.'

'It is the rubbing, not the juice,' Charlotte pointed out. She wrinkled her nose. 'It makes you smell of cabbages.'

'Oh, I hadn't thought of that,' Elizabeth said.

'I don't suppose you'll try that again,' Agnes said, suppressing a smile. It served her right for wanting to preen herself. 'We are finished here.'

'Is that it?' Charlotte said.

'We are late for Mama,' Elizabeth said. 'Where has the time gone?'

'Yes, that is all. You may go now. We will look at the flowers in the morning. Make sure you are here on time.'

She returned to her quarters before taking her evening meal there. Despite Pell's observation on the day of her arrival that she would generally be dining with the family, this was not strictly followed in practice. The food was good, basic fare of bread and mutton dripping, hash and hot vegetables, bread, butter, cake and gooseberry jam. She was favoured with a supply of tea and sugar as governess, but the other servants didn't have such luxuries because of the cost. She shouldn't complain about her lot, she thought, but she did miss her hot chocolate.

The next morning when Agnes saw how the blooms had turned pink, a symbol of a mother's undying love, a tear sprang to her eye as she thought not of Mama Berry-Clay, but her true mother who had missed her all those years after giving her up. She wished she hadn't dismissed her with such upset and anger. She wished she had asked her more questions. She wished she'd had a mother like Lady Faraday who loved her daughters.

'You have played a trick on us, Miss Linnet,' Charlotte said when she and her sister turned up in the schoolroom.

'There is no trick.'

'They are very pretty now,' Elizabeth said, her eyes wide with wonder. 'How do you explain this miracle?'

'I'm going to ask you to explain it from what you read yesterday,' Agnes said, knowing full well that neither girl had studied the lesson. Charlotte had been reading her novel again, and Elizabeth had been gazing out of the window. 'Perhaps you would like to have another look at it this morning to remind you. The answer to the mystery of the colour change is in the pages that I've marked.'

'Yes, that's a good idea,' Charlotte said quickly.

'I thought we would take them out of the water and dry the stems to show your mama later. I think she will appreciate a gift of a small posy of pink carnations, especially when you tell her how they started off.'

Elizabeth smiled and took her seat. When she opened the book at the bookmark and began to read, Agnes hoped that she'd taken a step in the right direction.

When they had both finished the required passage, she asked them to explain to each other the process of how the dye had made its way into the blooms, and then write it up with drawings of the flowers. It was a most successful lesson, and Agnes followed it up with a brief spell of algebra and a walk in the park.

She sat back later and breathed a sigh of relief. If only they could be like this every day. It had been hard work, though, and she wasn't in the most receptive mood when she received a request from Lady Faraday to meet her in the parlour that evening before taking dinner in her room.

'I thank you for what you have taught my daughters today.' Lady Faraday was wearing the latest fashion, a blue bodice and wide skirt, along with sleeves that flared out like funnels from her elbows, requiring her to wear white undersleeves. 'Charlotte is much more talkative and Elizabeth has produced some proficient drawings. The carnations were a sweet idea too, although I'm not sure how their creation can be described as educational.'

'It was an experiment to demonstrate an aspect of botany.'

'I see.' Lady Faraday shrugged as if she couldn't see at all. 'Anyway, I'm delighted to see that they are progressing at last, thanks to you. It seems that I was right to have taken a risk in taking you on as their teacher.'

'I am very pleased with how they have applied themselves to their studies.' Agnes beamed with pleasure at her employer's praise.

'I would appreciate it if you would fill up your spare time when you aren't teaching by making yourself generally useful,' Lady Faraday said.

'I believe I do that already,' Agnes said.

'There is always sewing to be done.'

'I've done the needlework that you asked for.'

'It wasn't very neat,' Lady Faraday sighed. 'In fact, I had to give it to one of the maids to unpick and do again. I was disappointed.'

'I don't know why you're surprised. I'm a governess, not a seamstress. I'm better acquainted with the theory of sewing than the practice.'

Lady Faraday frowned. 'You must own that as I pay you a fair wage with meals and accommodation, I expect a fair day's work in return. I note that you have many hours when you are unoccupied. I merely wish to have my money's worth.'

Agnes had an answer. She wasn't lazy. Far from it. She had become used to work, but she found the other chores she had been given distracting, which made her temper short.

'I'm afraid that whatever draws me from training your daughters is a loss to them. I should be teaching all day by word and example. Lady Faraday, if you wish to employ a seamstress, then do so. I have a proper sense of the importance of my calling and I wish that you had a better appreciation of my position. I can't achieve your aims for your daughters if I'm caught up in sewing when I'm supposed to be planning their lessons. I have made progress. It would be a sorrow to me if you should permit me to fail now.'

'I thank you for your opinion, Miss Linnet. You have spoken in a most mature manner. I wish you had had Felix when he was of a tender age. I believe that you would have made a difference to his temperament. He might have been more sensitive to his mama's tender reproofs.' She smiled. 'Elizabeth says you are quite the professor. She is doing well with her painting, but I'm a little concerned that she isn't making the same progress with her singing.'

'A wise parent such as yourself will acknowledge your daughter's strengths in watercolour and drawing, and encourage her in this pursuit over singing. She cannot excel in every subject.'

'You are right, I suppose,' she acknowledged. 'May I confide in you for a moment?'

'Yes, of course. You have my complete discretion.'

'I know that.' She smiled. 'You've turned out to be a real asset. Anyway, I want both my daughters to do well, particularly Charlotte. It will be hard to find a suitable match for her, I think, whereas with Elizabeth – every young man falls in love with her. I know she is only fifteen, but she always attracts attention when we're in company.

'My son has sent word that he will be visiting Roper House with a friend of his, George Moldbury. I should be most grateful if you will remind Elizabeth of the behaviour expected of her in George's presence. He is a polite, well-mannered young gentleman, and she was quite taken with him the last time he came to stay. I don't want any goings-on that might tarnish her reputation, if you know what I mean.'

'I think I do, Lady Faraday.'

'Make sure that you chaperone them at all times.'

'Of course.'

'To that end, I should like to invite you to join us for dinner tomorrow evening when our house guests arrive for the weekend. It will be a formal occasion with myself, Sir Richard, my sister and brother-in-law – Mr and Mrs Thomas, George Moldbury, Felix, Charlotte and Elizabeth.'

Agnes thanked her. She looked forward to meeting the young ladies' brother at last.

She made sure to read some passages from the book on etiquette to her charges the following day, including the piece about allowing a gentleman to take one by the arm, but never two gentlemen at once. She went on to say that flirtation didn't have a place in society and finished with the premise that a woman of delicacy should never entertain a sentiment towards a gentleman by whom it had not been solicited.

'You will show us how to behave by example,' Charlotte said primly.

'Of course she will – Miss Linnet is not interested in young gentlemen,' Elizabeth said with a giggle.

Agnes didn't comment. She had already run out on an engagement to a man in whom she'd had no romantic interest. Had she ever felt tempted to flirt with anyone? Not really. She might, if she was honest with herself, have felt an attraction to Oliver Cheevers, but it had been fleeting and certainly nothing that she would have acted on. Smiling to herself, she gazed fondly at her innocent charges. If only they knew.

# Chapter Fourteen

## *Pistols at Dawn*

'Felix is home,' Elizabeth said joyfully, running to the window in the schoolroom as a carriage drew up on the drive. Charlotte joined her, and Agnes, torn between duty and curiosity, went to stand behind them. She looked over Elizabeth's shoulder as she leaned across and waved at the two men who disembarked.

'You are overwrought, dear sister, and it has nothing to do with our brother's return and everything to do with his friend, whom I confess I find rather uninspiring.'

'Hush, Charlotte. You can't say that. He is most handsome.'

'He is a fop. He spends ages on his appearance and still manages to look the same.'

'Miss Linnet, we will find out your opinion of him at dinner tonight, if not before,' Elizabeth said.

'It isn't seemly for refined young ladies to discuss a young man's attributes.'

'May one be at liberty to think it quietly in one's head?' Elizabeth said. 'What do you think, Charlotte?'

'As long as one's thoughts aren't revealed on one's face,' Charlotte responded.

'I believe that even thinking of such things goes against the spirit of feminine behaviour,' Agnes said, seeing that she would have to ensure that she kept Elizabeth occupied for however long George was staying at Roper House. 'It is unacceptable.'

'Oh, you can be so dull,' Elizabeth sighed. 'You should hear George play the pianoforte – he is a music scholar and his fingering is exquisite. I shall ask him for a duet.'

'Oh, for goodness' sake,' said Charlotte.

'You must let him ask you,' Agnes said.

'We must go down and greet them.' Elizabeth turned to Agnes and looked her straight in the eye. 'It would be impolite not to.'

'I'm sure your mama will be waiting for them. Now, we have dallied long enough. You haven't completed your writing.' She was teaching them how to write letters of thanks for a gift and acceptance of an invitation.

'Surely they can wait,' Elizabeth said.

Agnes wouldn't allow anything, even the arrival of a much loved brother, to interfere with their studies. If she gave in to Elizabeth on this occasion, she would always be on the back foot, she thought. However, it took more than an hour for the young ladies to finish their task – Elizabeth daydreamed, while Charlotte couldn't think of anything to write.

After another half an hour, Agnes suggested that they go to the drawing room to practise some pieces for the evening's entertainment in an attempt to concentrate her charges' minds. Elizabeth met this suggestion with great enthusiasm. Charlotte tagged along with the dog.

As they approached the drawing room, Agnes heard voices, which was unusual at that time of day. She paused at the door then pushed it open, at which a gunshot rang out, echoing around her head.

Elizabeth screamed. Charlotte scooped up the dog and ran for cover, sheltering under the side table on the landing, rocking the vase on the top. Agnes stood stock-still.

There was a young man in breeches and a tweed coat standing on one of the chairs with a smoking pistol aimed towards the corner of the room. She followed the direction of the muzzle to the hole that had been blasted through the leather Chesterfield, taking out the horsehair stuffing.

'What are you doing?' Agnes exclaimed.

The young man turned slowly to face her.

He was remarkably handsome, she thought – tall with a mop of dark curls and a square chin. His eyes flashed with intelligence and his mouth was lively with humour and wit.

'Who wants to know?' he said.

'You are wearing your boots indoors,' she observed. They were long black hunting boots with tan tops.

'Who are you? This isn't your house.'

'She must be a new friend of your sisters,' said another voice.

She glanced to her left to find another young fellow, leaning against the wall with one booted foot against Lady Faraday's silk wallpaper. He was well built, a little on the short side to be considered a match for the perfect male physique, but his clothes were well cut, his brown hair was brushed smooth back from his face, his lips were full and his eyes large and blue.

The first man lowered the pistol and jumped down from the seat. He strode across and prowled around her, making her feel like an exhibit at a menagerie.

'Allow me to introduce our governess, Miss Linnet,' Elizabeth said, coming to her side. 'Oh, George, it is good to see you. Charlotte, you can come out now. It is only our brother and George.'

So this was Felix, Agnes thought as he stopped right in front of her.

'Please forgive us for scaring you ladies half to death.' George grinned. 'Felix was hunting the rat.'

'I can assure you that we are not easily frightened,' Agnes said.

'From the sight of my sisters' white faces, you are speaking only for yourself,' Felix said.

'Did you kill it?' Agnes asked.

'Of course – I never miss. Although I might have been a little carried away on this occasion.' He waved towards the Chesterfield. 'I'll get one of the footmen to clear up.'

'I should prefer it if you removed the poor dead creature presently,' Agnes said. 'For your sisters' sake. We are just about to have a lesson.'

'Well, I never. Governesses have become much younger and prettier than when I was a boy.'

'You are most impertinent.' She wasn't sure how to address him. She settled on, 'Master Faraday.'

'I apologise, Miss Linnet,' he said coolly. 'It's just that we can be no more than a year or two apart in age.'

Charlotte gasped. 'You must never comment upon a lady's age. You will have to apologise for a second time.'

Felix didn't say sorry. 'You've come out of your shell, Charlotte,' he said. 'You appear to have grown a tongue while I've been away.'

'Don't be mean,' Elizabeth said. 'Why don't you two stay? We are about to rehearse for tonight. Charlotte, you can sing. George, you can duet with me.'

'Oh no,' Agnes said quickly.

'I'm sure he has much to teach me.'

'I won't have anyone, music scholar or not, gate-crashing our lessons.'

'Oh, Miss Linnet. This is an exceptional day – it calls for exceptions to be made. Charlotte and I have studied very hard this week. We deserve the rest of the day off.'

'You will not twist me around your little finger.' Agnes smiled and turned to the gentlemen. 'It's been lovely to make your acquaintance, but I would appreciate it if you would take your pistols elsewhere, preferably outside where they belong.'

'Of course.' George gave a bow of his head. 'Good day to you.'

'We will see you at dinner,' Felix said to his sisters. 'And you, Miss Linnet?'

'I have accepted your mother's invitation. What about the rat?' She nodded towards the corner of the room. With a sigh, Felix gave in to her unspoken demand, walked across, picked it up by the tail and carried it out. Agnes winced. He caught her eye and smiled.

'I am sorry if this offends you, but George and I have achieved our aim. We have saved you from further dismay and disruption. The rat is dead.'

'I am grateful, but couldn't it have been done another way?'

'And what do you suggest, as an avowed expert in vermin control?'

'I thought it could have been trapped and released, perhaps,' she said.

He laughed. 'What would be the point of that? It would have run straight back inside. I don't think one should have any scruples when it comes to rats. They are dirty creatures.' He gazed at her. 'You appear to have led a sheltered life, Miss Linnet.'

'I don't think so,' she stammered as events from her past flashed through her head: the days she'd spent in the schoolroom with Nanny and Henry; the evenings in the drawing room with Mama and Papa; the fateful visit to Faversham where her life had begun to unravel.

She hoped that she hadn't let her guard down. His

presence disturbed her. She tried to put her feeling of unease down to the fact that the young gentleman who was standing uncomfortably close to her with a pistol in one hand and a dead creature in the other, would one day be master of the house. She should defer to him, she thought, but her governess's instinct took over.

'I would expect you to be more circumspect about shooting indoors in future,' she said sternly. 'Good day, Master Faraday, and you, Master Moldbury.'

'You can call him Felix,' Elizabeth said.

'I shall address him as I see fit. Come along, Elizabeth. And you, Charlotte. We are wasting time.'

The young gentlemen bowed as they left the room.

'Isn't George wonderful?' Elizabeth said as Agnes closed the door behind them.

'He seems quite ordinary to me,' Agnes said, moving across to open the pianoforte. 'Now, who will play first?'

Charlotte sat down on the stool with Sunny on her lap. She fiddled with the music book on the stand in front of her. Elizabeth stood alongside her sister. As Charlotte played, Elizabeth sang and Sunny joined in, howling at the top of his lungs.

'Oh, this is no good,' Agnes said. 'The dog will have to go outside.'

'No,' Charlotte said, crashing her fingers down on the keys. 'If Sunny goes, I go.'

Agnes was out of her depth again. There was no exemplar, no one to advise on how to handle this situation. How did you instil obedience in young ladies who were so wilful? It didn't help that their brother seemed just as impulsive and forceful in his opinions. He was no role model for his sisters.

'I shall not let the dog out of my sight while Felix is at home – I'm afraid he will shoot him dead.' To Agnes's surprise a tear rolled down Charlotte's cheek. 'He wouldn't do it deliberately, but it could happen by accident.'

Agnes gazed at the dog. She didn't like the idea of him suffering.

'I wish to continue,' Elizabeth said.

Agnes made her mind up.

'Charlotte, return to the schoolroom with the dog. You can read for a while. Elizabeth and I will practise our music for another half an hour then we'll meet you upstairs.'

'Thank you, Miss Linnet.' Charlotte stood up with the dog in her arms. 'I'm very grateful.'

Agnes played the piano while Elizabeth sang and then they played a duet together. She wasn't sure if either of them was concentrating, though, for there were many wrong notes. She guessed that Elizabeth was thinking of how to impress George that evening, while her own mind kept wandering on to the subject of what she should wear for dinner.

Later, when she had finished for the day, she returned to her room. She looked down at her navy dress. She recalled the conversations she had had with Nanny and the young ladies about modesty and not drawing attention to oneself, but a vision of Felix crossed her mind, and she decided to throw caution to the wind. Charlotte and Elizabeth would be wearing their finery. She would stand out like a sore thumb in the serge.

She washed her hands and face, revelling in the warmth of the water and the rose-petal scent of the soap, a recent extravagance of hers. She brushed her hair and trimmed the ends with scissors before putting it up. She slipped her scarlet dress over her undergarments, fastened the buttons and looked at herself in the mirror. The little weight she'd put on since she'd last worn it had improved the fit. Was the red too much? It hadn't been for Miss Berry-Clay of Windmarsh Court, but what about a member of staff at Roper House? She left it on, refusing to be a shrinking violet.

She was late for dinner, she realised when Pell ushered her into the drawing room where the other guests and the family were already assembled.

'That's a very fine dress, Miss Linnet, too fine for a lowly governess and a terribly vulgar colour. It's most unsuitable for a woman in your position and if I were Lady Faraday, I'd be having second thoughts.'

'Then it's fortunate that you are only the butler,' she said.

'I have bin unable to trace Mr and Mrs Norbert.'

'Perhaps they have moved away from their previous address. It's only the provincial who remain in one place all their lives.'

'There is no such address,' he said quietly. 'I've warned you before – I'm watching you. If the young ladies weren't so happily engaged with your lessons, I would have bin straight to Lady Faraday with my suspicions. As it is . . . well, if you so much as put a foot wrong, I'll have you.'

A tingle of fear ran down her spine, but she pulled herself together quickly.

Evie's favourite footman, John, approached, carrying a tray of glasses.

'Wine, Miss Linnet,' he said with a smile.

She thanked him and took a glass for courage. Where were Charlotte and Elizabeth?

She noticed Felix first and then George, and then the young ladies assembled beside the window in animated conversation. She yearned to be part of their circle, but she was the governess, not a friend.

'Miss Linnet, come and be introduced to the Thomases,' Lady Faraday said, interrupting her plan to join the young people.

'Good evening,' Agnes said. 'Mr and Mrs Thomas, I'm so glad to make your acquaintance.' Mr Thomas was grey and wizened, much older than his wife, who reminded her a little of her Aunt Sarah.

'The feeling is mutual. Lady Faraday has sung your praises to us in the most effusive terms. It is lovely to meet you,' Mrs Thomas said.

'Be careful. My wife is plotting to whisk you away to our house to teach our daughter, Isobel. She is most envious of Lady Faraday for having found such a treasure.'

Agnes blushed.

'She has been putting ideas into my daughters' heads,' Sir Richard said. 'They have asked if they can go on the Grand Tour of Europe to see Italy and France in particular.'

'They must go,' Mrs Thomas said. 'It could be a most excellent experience for them. In fact, if you are planning that Miss Linnet accompanies them as chaperone, I wouldn't be averse to Miss Isobel joining them.'

'I don't believe that it's good for them to travel. It is unsettling,' Lady Faraday said. 'It will make them discontented. A young woman's role is to marry and run the house, not fret about distant climes. Exposure to strong sunshine will mar their complexions for life. And what the eye doesn't see, the heart doesn't grieve over.'

'I'm surprised, considering how enlightened you are about the importance of education for girls, that you feel that way, my dear wife,' Sir Richard observed. 'When you were convincing me of the benefits of employing another governess, you presented quite the opposite opinion, that young ladies these days should be aware of the world beyond England's shores. Britain governs

Canada, and large parts of India and Australia. We cannot ignore it. We trade with countries from all four corners of the world. A woman – Queen Victoria herself – rules the British Empire. You can't tell me that she would allow her daughters to remain in ignorance of the rest of the world.'

'What I'm trying to say is that knowledge can breed discontent,' Lady Faraday said.

'What do you think, Miss Linnet?' Sir Richard asked.

'I follow the example of Her Majesty,' Agnes said, not wishing to take sides in an argument between husband and wife. 'Any young lady should receive education in world affairs so she can play her part in the drawing room.'

'Oh, I am very fond of you, Miss Linnet,' Sir Richard guffawed loudly. 'You make perfect sense.'

'I want my daughters to be educated, but I'd prefer them not to travel,' Lady Faraday insisted. 'I would miss them. And I'd worry.'

'You will have to let them go one day,' Sir Richard said.

'I know, but they are young yet, too young to leave their mother's care.' Lady Faraday glared at her husband. 'Shall we change the subject? We should make plans for your stay tomorrow. We usually attend church on a Sunday morning. You will not go off shooting on the Sabbath as you did last time, Sir Richard.'

Just as Agnes was thinking this could be a cue to blend into the background, Sir Richard turned to her.

'Which church did you used to go to?' he asked. He appeared to have surprised himself, taking an interest in the governess all of a sudden. Or was he distracted by her scarlet dress? Agnes thought, feeling somewhat ashamed. She had dressed for Felix's benefit, not his father's. She had forgotten there would be other gentlemen present.

'I didn't used to go very often. Mama – when she was alive, God rest her soul,' she added quickly when she remembered that she was supposed to be dead, 'didn't like to leave the house. It was her nerves. They are – they were very sensitive.'

'How did she keep her faith?' Sir Richard asked.

'The reverend used to come to the house on occasion in return for dinner.' She didn't know what to say. Her audience, the Faradays and Thomases, were staring at her, waiting for her to go on. 'He ended up a very corpulent gentleman,' she said, suppressing a giggle.

'How very odd,' Lady Faraday said.

'I haven't heard of that before,' Mrs Thomas observed.

'Aren't their stipends fattening enough without feeding them extra?' the master laughed.

Agnes scolded herself as Lady Faraday and her friends turned away. She felt so at ease with the family, she had forgotten to keep her distance. She would have to be far more careful, she thought, as she noticed Pell watching her closely.

'Miss Linnet. Over here.'

She turned to find Elizabeth beckoning to her.

She smiled and walked across to join the young people.

'I adore your outfit,' Elizabeth said. 'You must tell Mama which dressmaker you use.'

'I don't know where it came from. It was a gift.'

'It changes your appearance. I hardly recognised you.'

'It makes no alteration,' Felix said. 'Miss Linnet is as pretty as ever.'

Her heart missed a beat. He looked more handsome than before in his evening dress and with his hair falling in soft waves over his forehead. How could she keep her composure?

There was an awkward silence until Charlotte ventured to mention that she had done well in geography.

'We have begun on America,' she said.

Felix sneered and laughed.

'I see. Your brilliant governess has just discovered America. Oh, sister, self-praise is not a virtue.'

Charlotte fell quiet again. Agnes noticed her brushing a tear from her eye, and the ire rose in her throat. How dare he undo the progress she had made? How dare he denigrate his sister's achievements! She had no hesitation in confronting him, even in the drawing room.

'That was unkind, Felix,' she said.

'What is it to you?' he said rudely.

'She was making conversation. Where are your manners?' He flushed. 'A gentleman would apologise . . .'

'And that is what I shall do,' he said quickly. 'I'm sorry, Charlotte, and Miss Linnet. I overstepped the bounds of polite opinion.'

'Thank you,' Charlotte muttered.

'That was very graceful of you.' Agnes glanced towards Elizabeth, who was gazing up admiringly at George and hanging on his every word. 'Do tell us about your favourite music, Master Moldbury,' she said, interrupting their conversation, having decided that this sacrifice of the finer points of etiquette was worth it to maintain Elizabeth's reputation. 'Tell me, are you a follower of Beethoven or Haydn?'

'I don't have a preference,' he said, his eyes on Elizabeth. 'I find that all music can be quite stirring as long as it is performed with feeling.'

'Indeed. You are very wise, George,' Elizabeth simpered.

Agnes bit back her annoyance and suppressed an urge to send her charge straight to bed. Luckily Pell rang the gong for dinner so they made their way to the dining room, where she was seated between the coquette and her willing suitor. Felix sat opposite, between Charlotte and Mrs Thomas, and the meal passed without incident. They had consommé, cod sounds and Florentine of rabbit stuffed with a forcemeat of bread, anchovy, wine and herbs and served with a white sauce. After that, they ate burned cream – an egg custard with a flamed sugar topping served with wild strawberries.

Afterwards, they retired to the drawing room where Felix came over to sit next to Agnes on one of the chaises. The young ladies showed off their prowess at playing the pianoforte and singing, before George was urged to take over the keys and show off his musical training.

'Would you like a seat closer to the piano, Miss Linnet?' Sir Richard said, getting up from his chair.

'Oh, no thank you,' she said, a little shocked at this breech of the rules of social propriety. Nanny had always been most adamant that it was rude of a gentleman to offer his seat to a lady when the cushion may still be warm. He had coarse manners, she thought. The whole household had an unruly, excitable atmosphere compared with the predictable gentility of Windmarsh Court.

Felix shifted closer to her.

'Miss Linnet, what has given you this air of superiority?' he said in a low voice. 'Where does it come from?'

'I have acquired it from observation and practice,' she replied.

'You are quite fascinating, and very beautiful too – if you don't mind me saying.'

'You can say what you like to me as long as it's the truth,' she said boldly, putting his attentions down to convention. He could hardly ignore her, could he?

He leaned back and stretched out one long leg.

'My little sister is making a fool of herself over George,' he sighed.

'I'm doing my best,' Agnes said sharply. 'Perhaps you can have a word with him, and advise him not to encourage her.'

'Anything to be of service,' he said with a smile. 'I wonder if in return you might give me some instruction in the French language.'

'Oh?' she said, flummoxed by his request. 'I don't know. I'd need to seek approval from her ladyship.'

'I can't think that Mama would have any objection. I'm intending to travel abroad – it would be useful to develop the art of conversation in another tongue. I shall speak to my mother and let you know so we can make arrangements. I'm also planning a trip into town while George is here, and thought I'd better ask you if it's all right for my sisters to take a day off their lessons. I've heard you are a tartar.'

'Is that what Charlotte and Elizabeth have said?' She couldn't help smiling.

'You've made quite an impression on them.' He smiled back. 'Of course, you would have to accompany us. Mama would never let them go unchaperoned.'

She raised one eyebrow. 'I would have thought that their brother would have made a perfectly suitable chaperone.'

'My mother knows me too well.' He stood up. 'I will wish you goodnight, Miss Linnet. George and I are planning to go out shooting first thing in the morning.' His eyes glinted with humour when he added, 'Before church, of course, and outside, rather than in the drawing room this time. I look forward to seeing you again.'

The guests began to retreat, retiring to their beds.

Agnes made her excuses and returned to her room, but she couldn't sleep for worrying about Pell and what he would do, and for thinking about Felix. It meant nothing, of course. It was merely empty and meaningless drawing room conversation. For a moment her mind flashed back to the Cheeverses, their genuine warmth and affection, unpretentious talk and meaningful occupation. She wished . . . Oh, what was the point of wishing? She had to make the most of what she'd got.

# Chapter Fifteen

## *Like a Rose Embowered*

The young gentlemen didn't make an appearance at church, being caught up in their other pursuits. Lady Faraday was most unhappy about it, but her husband was more forgiving. Agnes had to confess that she was disappointed not to see Felix that morning. She missed him too in the afternoon and evening when the family went on an outing with their guests, leaving her at home to occupy herself with some painting in her room.

Her paintbrush slipped from sky to hillside and muddied the colours. She scuffed the paper, spoiling it with the bristles, and threw the brush down. She felt dull. It seemed that the arrival of the young gentlemen had stirred up some restlessness and rebellion in her breast.

The presence of visitors in the house had a similar effect on Charlotte and Elizabeth, who were late for their lessons the following morning.

'I find it difficult to provide any occupation that holds your attention for more than five minutes, and you don't help at all. You do not set yourself to any employment, Elizabeth,' Agnes said. 'You seem content to sit with Sunny on your knee, talking about George and soldiers. It is frustrating because you're an intelligent young woman. Where were you this morning? I was expecting you in the schoolroom.'

'Felix sent us on an errand.'

'To do what?'

'To find him a pair of cufflinks. And then to take a note to Mama.'

'Why could he not undertake these tasks himself?'

'Because he's my brother and it's expected of us.'

'Why did you not explain that you were unavailable? I should like to add that when we are in the schoolroom, we should be considered to be out of the house and be strangers to everyone within it.'

Charlotte joined in. 'We aren't able to give our undivided attention to anything when Felix is at home. He is a distraction. I love him, but I find that I would prefer to be with my books.'

He had been taught by his mother and father's example that every vice might be forgiven in a man and every virtue was expected from a woman. That all girls' interests should be subservient to his was natural. Boys first. The young ladies were expected to wait on him without complaint.

'Sit down, both of you. Let us get on.'

They worked through their lessons, and later they went out for a walk. Lo and behold, the young gentlemen appeared in the woods, strolling towards them with Sir Richard's rangy black gun dog wandering alongside.

Sunny, who was trotting along at Charlotte's heels, came darting out from behind her and growled.

The gun dog's hackles went up. He dived on to the smaller dog and grabbed it by the neck.

'No!' Charlotte screamed. 'He will kill him!'

It was George who was the hero. He waded in and grabbed the black dog by the scruff, which took him by surprise. In yelping, he let go, and Sunny ran up Elizabeth's dress to the safety of her arms.

'Oh, my poor dear,' Charlotte exclaimed as Elizabeth pushed the dog into her sister's arms.

'Are you all right, George? You aren't hurt?' she said. 'It was a very brave thing to do.'

'I am quite well, Elizabeth,' he said, smiling. 'And I'd hardly describe it as an act of courage.'

'Where are you going?' Felix asked. 'Would you permit us to join you, Miss Linnet?'

'If you wish,' Agnes said.

'It is rather quiet here at Windmarsh when you are used to Oxford and its entertainments.'

'I thought you were supposed to be studying there,' she said archly.

'We are. In a manner of speaking. But you can't study all day, every day, can you?'

They walked together. Elizabeth took up position beside George while Charlotte walked the other side of him. The dogs were ignoring each other now. Agnes dropped back a little. So did Felix.

They walked through the estate in the summer sunshine until they reached Wingate Hill.

'It's strange that you and Master Moldbury have turned up like bad pennies. Anyone would have thought that you were lying in wait for us.'

'Elizabeth made it known that you usually take the air at this time.' He smiled. 'I think that was for George's benefit, but it has advantages for me as well. It is very pleasant walking with you and my sisters. You seem out of sorts, Miss Linnet. Is it something I have said?'

'Oh no, it isn't you.'

'Is it about another gentleman? You have a special friend?'

'No.' She smiled. 'It has nothing to do with affairs of the heart.'

'I'm surprised that you are not already engaged.'

'I am a governess. I work for my living. I'm not in a position to be married.'

'I don't think you will be left on the shelf for long.' He paused before continuing, 'Forgive me. I speak my mind. There is no point doing otherwise. By the way, I've spoken to Mama about the French conversation and she is in full agreement. She said to ask you when it would be convenient.'

'I look forward to that. How about tomorrow at eleven?' It would tie in with the French conversation she had planned for the young ladies. The more the merrier, she thought.

The party continued along Faulkner's Lane and on to Pilgrim's Way before entering the orchard, where they climbed over one stile, and then another. They passed alongside a row of cottages and a hop garden where the bines were at the top of the chestnut poles. They walked on into the woods and back through the fields to Upper Harbledown.

Agnes was glad of Felix's attentions, the way that he included her in his plans, and made her feel like a friend of the family, not a governess. She was fascinated by him and found herself thinking about him far too often during the remainder of the day.

She looked forward to their lesson with more than a little trepidation, unused to being in the company of a gentleman and unsure how the young ladies would perform in his presence. Would Charlotte be tongue-tied with shyness in front of her brother and would Elizabeth show off?

The next morning, there was a sharp rap at the schoolroom door. She glanced at the clock. He was early. Her pulse bounded a little faster as he opened the door.

'Good morning, ladies,' he said, entering with a flourish of his hand. *'Bonjour.'*

'Come in and sit down, Master Faraday,' Agnes said.

'Oh, let's have none of this Master Faraday nonsense. I am Felix to you.'

'I am the governess, not one of your sisters,' she said, amused.

He remained on his feet to address Charlotte and Elizabeth.

'Mama requests your presence in the parlour. She wishes you to meet with the milliner.'

'Oh? I thought that Charlotte and Elizabeth would take part in our lesson.' Agnes hadn't entertained the idea that they might be left alone together.

He cocked one eyebrow. 'I prefer to have you all to myself – when it comes to conversation, Charlotte is mute and Elizabeth talks of nothing but which gown she'll wear when George is here for dinner.'

Agnes glared at him.

'Oh, I see,' he said, seeming to look right into her soul. 'My dear sisters. I apologise for what I've just said.'

'Are you willing to accept your brother's apology?' Agnes said, turning to the young ladies.

'He deserves some kind of penance for his low opinion of us,' Elizabeth said. 'What do you suggest, Charlotte?'

'We will consider forgiveness when he has waited upon us hand and foot for a whole day,' Charlotte said with a smile. Agnes smiled too. Charlotte had lost the girlish plumpness around her face and was beginning to bloom as a young woman. Her mama wouldn't find it as hard to marry her off as she'd imagined. Agnes watched how she stood with her back straight and head up, no longer scared to speak in case she said something out of turn. Her efforts in deportment had served her well.

'Shall we have George wait on us as well?' Elizabeth giggled.

Agnes sighed inwardly. All her lessons in modesty and etiquette had done little for the younger sister.

'I believe that an hour of your brother's time will be adequate compensation. You'd better run along to your mama. Sit down, Felix. Charlotte, leave the door open, please,' Agnes added quickly as Charlotte made to close it behind her.

'Don't fret, Miss Linnet. What on earth do you imagine I am going to do with you?' Felix said softly. 'All you have to do if I touch one precious hair on your head is scream, and Pell will be here within seconds.' He pulled the chairs out and placed one each side of the window so they were facing each other. He held out his hand.

Agnes hesitated, her heart pounding so hard it felt as if it would jump out of her chest.

*'Venez vous asseoir, mademoiselle.'*

*'Merci beaucoup, monsieur.'* She stepped across, avoiding taking his hand, and sat down. He took the other seat, pulling it up so close that their knees almost touched.

'You are blushing.' A smile spread slowly across his face, revealing his even white teeth.

'It is the sun coming through the window.' She touched her cheek.

'Then allow me to move your chair,' he said, getting up again and straightening his coat tails before moving round behind her.

'This really isn't necessary,' she said, flustered by the attention. She was a governess, the teacher, and therefore she should be in control of the situation, yet she felt far from it. She stood up as he placed his hands on the back of the chair. He moved it into the middle of the room.

'I am most grateful,' she said, trying to maintain an air of calm as she sat down again and he brought his chair alongside hers.

'There is a draught,' he decided, and he strode across and pulled the door closed. 'That's better. I believe we are ready to begin.' He sat down.

Silence fell as she wondered what on earth to say. Suddenly, she felt awkward and tongue-tied.

*'Vous vous intéressez à la météorologie, monsieur?'* she said.

*'Non,'* he said, his eyes sparking with humour. 'I am interested in you.'

'You are very direct,' she said in a low voice. 'Your mama has entrusted me with improving your use of the French language.'

*'Vous êtes tres jolie, mademoiselle.* Is that right?' he entreated.

*'Oui, monsieur,* but this isn't a suitable topic of conversation.' She couldn't help smiling. She knew that he knew very well what he was doing. 'We should talk about Paris.'

'I've heard that the ladies there are very beautiful, but I don't see how they can be as charming as you.'

'I insist that you apply yourself to your studies immediately,' Agnes said sternly.

He looked her straight in the eye. She didn't flinch.

'Elizabeth said you were very strict.' She thought she noticed a glimmer of capitulation in his expression.

He sat back, but in the process turned slightly on his chair so that his feet were perilously close to hers.

'Tell me what you know about Paris,' she said.

*'Les mademoiselles—'* he began. She opened her mouth to protest. He backed down and changed the subject.

'Forget Paris. Let us talk in general,' she said and she began to ask him questions in French about his pastimes, hunting, his horse and his ambitions for the future.

'Oh, this is so very dull,' he said eventually, reverting to their mother tongue. 'I don't mean you, I mean talking about me.'

'I'm surprised to find that you are already quite proficient in the use of the French language.' Agnes looked at the clock. 'That is the end of today's lesson.'

'I look forward to the next one.' He stood up and took his leave. '*Au revoir.*'

He exited the schoolroom just as his sisters returned in high spirits because Mama had let them choose new hats. Agnes let them talk and play with the dog. Their chatter set her nerves on edge. She had grown to love them, but today she was finding their company after their brother's a little tiresome.

Felix had reminded her who she was and how she'd been brought up to be a lady. She hadn't been snatched from her real mother and brought up in splendid isolation to teach flibbertigibbets for the rest of her life. She was aware of what Felix saw in her – a lightly turned ankle, youth and an ability to talk to him as an equal. As for Agnes, she found him vibrant, and interesting.

He was fascinating, and unlike the other men she had met – apart from Philip, of course, who'd done all he could to help poor Papa, and Oliver, who was a hero, rescuing Arthur from drowning. They were both interesting in their own way, she owned, but neither was as handsome as Felix. He was a real gentleman of wit, humour, and – she wasn't afraid to admit it – good fortune. What was he worth? She couldn't imagine, but it had to be more than Philip, Oliver and Papa put together.

There was one element of the day that had confused her, though.

She had expected from the way he had spoken before that he was in need of a considerable amount of coaching, but that hadn't turned out to be the case. Her suspicions that he had engineered the situation so that he could spend time with her were confirmed later when she found out that it was Pell's half-day off. Felix hadn't been entirely truthful with her, had he?

She looked forward to every day with renewed enthusiasm now that Felix was at home. She admired his rebellious streak, his dry wit and the way he dressed in the latest fashions. He was mostly respectful to his mother, and treated his sisters better under Agnes's civilising influence.

She was invited to dine with the Faradays the day after Felix had come to the schoolroom to speak French. Everyone was gay at dinner and afterwards they retired to the drawing room, where Elizabeth called George to the piano to accompany her. Charlotte sat with her mama and quietly discussed a book they had both read, while Sir Richard sat drinking brandy and stroking his dog's ears. Sunny the lapdog was sleeping on a cushion on one of the armchairs.

Agnes was about to take a seat near the piano so she could chaperone Elizabeth. She had decided she would intervene if the distance between singer and piano player closed to a less than a respectable distance. The family seemed very relaxed about social protocol, but Agnes felt responsible and couldn't stand by. Before she could sit down, though, Felix caught her very lightly by the hand.

She glanced at him fiercely. They were in company.

'Oh, I wish you wouldn't look at me like that,' he said, smiling. 'Your expression would turn a flame to ice in an instant. Please, I only wanted to attract your attention while everyone listens to the entertainment.' He continued, breathless. 'I wanted to ask you if we could continue our lessons in French conversation. I am planning to travel to Paris and I have all but forgotten what I learned the other day.' He lowered his voice until she could barely hear him. 'You have this effect on me . . .'

'I don't know how,' she stammered. 'I have done nothing.' She searched her conscience and found no stain or blemish. She hadn't encouraged him in any way. 'I'm engaged here to teach your sisters. I'm willing to continue our lessons, but only in their presence.'

'I wish to be alone with you. I'm sure I would make much better progress.' He raised his eyebrows in a silent plea.

'No, Master Faraday.' She was aware that Pell was watching her as he moved around the room, serving more brandy to the master, who was beginning to remind her of her uncle with his red face and purple nose. 'I will not compromise my position or my reputation.'

'You are turning me down, Miss Linnet.'

She stared at him, feeling like a rabbit must, caught in the sight of his gun. This wasn't merely about French conversation, was it?

'We will discuss it tomorrow,' she said rather sharply. 'Come to the schoolroom at ten o'clock.' Charlotte and Elizabeth would be there. It would be perfectly safe. She pressed her hands together to control the trembling in her fingers.

'I will not give up my pursuit,' he said quietly.

'I shall pretend that I didn't hear that comment and we will carry on as before.'

'As if nothing has happened?' he said with sarcasm. 'Miss Linnet—'

She cut him off with a curt nod, turned away and walked up to the piano.

'Miss Linnet,' Elizabeth called. 'Come and sing with us.'

'Oh no,' she said.

'But our voices blend so harmoniously. George kindly said so when he heard us practising the other day.'

'You are a natural singer, Miss Linnet,' George said. 'You have perfect pitch, as does Miss Elizabeth.'

'Indulge us,' Felix said.

'Sing, Miss Linnet,' Sir Richard bellowed from his chair.

Reluctantly, she took her place alongside Elizabeth, and they sang. She noticed how Felix stood leaning against the wall, frowning darkly. He was sulky, spoiled and bad-tempered, she decided. He reminded her of the young Agnes Berry-Clay who had – to her shame – exhibited a similar sense of entitlement.

She was attracted to him, of that she was certain, but at that moment she wasn't sure that she liked him. She wished he had remained at Oxford for the vacation, not come to Roper House to disturb her peace of mind.

He didn't join her and her pupils in the schoolroom the following morning, having been tempted outside by the promise of good weather for riding, but he and George walked straight into the schoolroom unannounced that afternoon.

'Your sisters are attending to their studies,' she said reprovingly.

'Oh, it is all so dull. Come out with us – the air will put the colour back in your cheeks.'

Agnes glanced at Elizabeth – she had no need of more colour. George's presence had brought a flush of scarlet to her face.

'We have much to do. Please leave, gentlemen,' Agnes said.

Felix walked across to Charlotte's desk. He picked up the book she was reading.

'Poetry?' he said, looking at the gold lettering on the

spine. 'What piffle and poppycock is this?' He opened it to a page.

George looked over his shoulder. 'It's Shelley.'

'"To a Skylark",' Felix read. He recited the poem, his voice lingering as he reached, 'Like a rose embower'd/In its own green leaves,/By warm winds deflower'd . . .'

'Stop there,' Agnes ordered. 'Please desist.' She wouldn't have chosen this poem for her charges. It wasn't suitable. She had led a sheltered life, but she knew enough to understand that the poetry was inflammatory, especially the way Felix was reciting it – with passion. She blushed with embarrassment. He stopped but held her gaze, a wicked glint in his eye. What should she do? Remonstrate and make too much of it? Or let it go?

Keeping his eyes on her, he put the book down.

'Thank you.'

'About that French lesson,' he said.

'I have half an hour while Charlotte and Elizabeth complete the task I've set. If you and George would like to sit and make conversation, now is convenient.'

He opened his mouth as if he was about to protest, but she gave him a look, one she'd perfected in her role as governess, and he seemed to change his mind.

'What do you think, George?' he said, turning to his friend.

'I think we should be grateful to Miss Linnet for her offer,' he said, beaming.

'In that case, we will take you up on it,' Felix said, and he went off to find an extra chair.

Agnes sat down with him and George while Charlotte and Elizabeth continued studying at their desks.

'*Merci beaucoup pour*—' George began.

'Really?' Felix interrupted, raising one eyebrow. 'I thought we were going to confirm our plans for our day out in town.'

*'En Français, s'il vous plaît,'* Agnes said sharply. She would have discipline in her schoolroom, whoever was in attendance, but Felix . . . he had this way with him. She tried to suppress her amusement at his antics, but she couldn't stop herself smiling. Their eyes connected and he smiled back as though he knew exactly what she was thinking.

# Chapter Sixteen

## *An Awkward Encounter*

Evie was bubbling with excitement when she brought Agnes's breakfast tray to her room one morning a few days later.

'Good morning, Miss Linnet.'

'Same to you, Evie.'

'It's a beautiful day.' The maid opened the curtains, letting in a stream of light. 'A letter came for me yesterday – I wonder if you can read it to me. I can only make out my mother's mark at the bottom of the page.'

Agnes slipped out of bed.

'Pass it to me,' she said, perching on the edge of the mattress.

Evie took a crumpled letter out of her pocket. Agnes opened it up. It was written in a tidy hand, down the page and back up the other way to make best use of the space.

'"Dear Evie,"' Agnes read. '"We are well and very happy to hear your news."' There followed a long story about how Evie's favourite cow had had her calf, and broken into the garden. 'What a lovely letter.'

'It is indeed. I shall keep it under my pillow to help me dream of home every night.' Evie changed the subject as Agnes gave it back to her. 'Miss Linnet, I beg you to be more careful in your dealings with Master Faraday.'

'What is it to you?' Agnes said rudely, forgetting that

she wasn't a child talking to one of the maids at Windmarsh Court. Evie frowned.

'I thought we were friends. I thought I could speak openly to you.'

'I'm sorry, Evie. You are the only friend that I have.'

'You 'ave no idea about friendship,' the maid exclaimed. 'You're clever with letters, yet you're careless with people. You speak before you think.'

'Please accept my apology . . .' Agnes's voice trembled. 'I'm begging you.'

'I'm not sure that I should associate with you in future. Mrs Cox has forbidden us to speak to you because she is worried about a scandal. It has bin noticed that you are spending time with Master Faraday.'

'Only because he wishes to spend time in the company of his sisters.' Agnes felt a pang of regret as she got up to make her tea. 'He and George are going to Paris later in the summer and then they'll return to Oxford. You can't blame him for wanting to make the most of his time here. It is a little distracting – for Elizabeth in particular.'

'There seems to be some kind of attraction, a flirtation between you and Master Faraday, though. He isn't that special – I empty his piss pot and the turds float on the top just the same as everyone else's.'

Agnes shrank back at Evie's coarse language.

'It is just gossip.' Her palms grew damp as she began to pour hot water from the teapot on to the pinch of leaves in the bottom of her cup. She was lying to herself. 'I'd never put my reputation at risk. You know as well as I do – as governess and moral guide – that I have to be beyond reproach. These rumours, observations, whatever they are, are scurrilous and untrue.' She was angry at the way she had laid herself open to them. She would have to be far more careful in her dealings with Felix in future.

'I have no feelings for him, except for the normal regard one has for a member of one's employer's family.'

'I'll take your word for it.' Evie put her arm through Agnes's. 'Let's not say any more about it. Let me read your leaves in return for you reading my letter to me.'

'I don't believe in them – it isn't scientific.'

'My mother swears by it. She doesn't leave the house without checking the leaves first.' Evie stripped the bed while Agnes finished her tea.

'What do the leaves say, then?' Agnes said, handing her the cup.

'It's a little strange – my eyes make out the shape of a bat in the bottom.'

'And what is that supposed to mean?'

'It says you are going on a journey in the future. A short distance – it was a small bat.'

'Well, that's a surprise,' Agnes said with sarcasm. 'That will be our day out into town. Felix, George and the young ladies are going to Canterbury today.'

'That's why they're all up and about so early,' Evie said, smiling.

'What are your plans?' Agnes asked.

'The usual. Cleaning, fetching and carrying.'

'I don't mean your plans for today. I mean, your dreams? What are your hopes for the future?'

'I don't think it's my place to 'ave them,' Evie said.

'Why not?'

'I'm a maid and will remain one until I marry or retire, but if I had a choice, I would like to advance my position.'

'You mean be raised to housekeeper.'

'Oh, I should like that. But then I should also like to marry and 'ave children. Wouldn't you?'

'Yes, of course. One day . . .'

'It must be almost time for you to leave. The carriage is waiting.'

They could have walked, but Elizabeth had thought that they might have shopping to bring back with them. Agnes recalled the last time she had visited the town with Nanny, and how Oliver had rescued the little boy, Arthur, from the river. Her anticipation of the day trip was rather clouded by her fear of running into someone she knew. Reason told her not to worry – Canterbury was a big place and they would be keeping to the main streets.

'You aren't listening.' Evie snapped her fingers. 'You are in a trance, Agnes.'

'You're right. I'd better hurry.' She dressed, put on her coat and collected her outdoor shoes from under the bed. She put on her shoes and went downstairs and out to the front of the house, where Pell opened the door for her.

'Good day,' he said, his voice like acid, etching another layer of guilt into her conscience.

She thanked him and stepped outside into the sunshine. Was Pell still pursuing his quest to find out her true identity? She felt sick with nerves. Was this how it was going to be? Was she always going to be on edge?

'Make haste, Miss Linnet,' Felix called from where he stood beside the carriage.

'Where are Charlotte and Elizabeth?' she said, telling herself to calm down.

'They are here, ready to go. Elizabeth says she has been up and dressed for hours.' He smiled and held out his arm as Agnes approached. She took it and he helped her up into the carriage, his other hand somehow finding her waist and lingering there much longer than was necessary. Her pulse thrilled at the contact. What did it mean? What was he trying to tell her?

Elizabeth sat next to George, which necessitated Felix sitting next to her – she felt uneasy when the horses set off, jolting the coach. She gripped the seat to prevent herself being rolled against him by the movement.

She felt very differently about him than she had about Philip. When he was in the same room, she felt that she was walking on air. When he was away from her, she thought of him fondly every second of every passing hour. The occasions when the family didn't invite her to dine with them caused her great grief. Sitting in solitary confinement in her room, knowing that Felix was nearby, was torture.

'What shall we see in Canterbury?' Charlotte said.

'There is the cathedral,' Agnes said, looking out of the window at the orchards and hop gardens to avoid Felix's gaze.

'Only a governess could say that,' he said. 'The town has other attractions.'

'It is most historic,' Agnes argued.

'We have been inside it before,' Charlotte said.

'There would be no harm in seeing it again, then we can take a walk across the Dane John and climb the monument to look at the view.' She avoided any mention of the river.

'I would much prefer to look at the shops,' Elizabeth said mutinously. 'Wouldn't you, Charlotte?'

'No, I don't think so,' Charlotte said.

'You are so dull,' Elizabeth exclaimed. 'How can you be my sister?'

'Let us not have any disagreements today,' Agnes said.

They disembarked in the centre of Canterbury and walked across the bridge. Felix and George picked up stones and competed to see who could throw them the furthest along the river. Agnes felt uncomfortable.

'You are drawing attention to yourselves,' she said.

'We're only larking around,' Felix said, smiling, but she couldn't help thinking that he was showing off his athletic prowess for her benefit.

'Please think of your sisters.'

'Of course. We apologise, Miss Linnet,' George cut in. 'Let's move on.'

They walked along Mercery Lane, mingling with a crowd of the military in their red coats, and a gaggle of ladies dressed in their finery and feathers. Agnes glanced at her charges, and her breast filled with pride. She hadn't been born to be a governess, but she could teach. She was still convinced that she was destined for a better station in life, but for now she was content. She had done better than she'd expected after leaving Windmarsh.

They moved on along the street where the upper storeys of the buildings leaned in towards each other, blocking out the sunshine, and all of a sudden, she caught sight of Oliver Cheevers. She was sure it was him.

She tried to hurry the party along, but Miss Elizabeth was distracted by a display in the haberdasher's, and within a heartbeat, Oliver was upon them.

He hesitated and frowned, and just as she was about to breathe again at the thought he was going to move on without recognition or comment, he approached her.

'Good afternoon, Miss Berry-Clay. How lovely to see you,' he said with a genial smile. 'You and your friends must come and take tea with us. You will be surprised to see how little Arthur has grown. Bert has turned into rather a cocky young man, and I worry about him, but—'

'I'm sorry, sir,' she said, trying to hide her trembling. 'We have not met.'

'Don't be silly. It's me, Oliver Cheevers from Willow Place.'

She shook her head almost imperceptibly.

'I apologise,' he said, red-faced. 'I am mistaken. You reminded me of a young lady with whom I was once briefly acquainted.' He gave a bow. 'Good day, madam.'

'Good day, sir.'

'What a fool!' Felix exclaimed.

'Idiot,' George agreed.

'He really seemed to think that he'd already made your acquaintance,' Elizabeth said.

'I can assure you that I have never set eyes on him before,' Agnes said.

'He looked like a ruffian,' Felix said superciliously.

Agnes wanted to defend him, to tell everyone that Oliver was a well-meaning and decent young man who worked for his living, cared for his grandfather and helped the poor. He didn't spend his days riding and ordering his sisters about. But she daren't expose her identity.

She shivered as they walked on. She had been a whisker away from discovery.

'Do you think you have an identical twin out there?' Felix said.

'Stop teasing our dear Miss Linnet,' Elizabeth said kindly. 'You heard what she said.'

'That's told you,' George chuckled when Felix fell silent on the matter.

They strolled around the cathedral precincts, deciding against going inside. George had a sister on each arm. Felix walked with Agnes, his hands behind his back, his shoulders slightly bowed as he made conversation. He talked some more about his studies in philosophy. He talked much about himself, she thought, slightly disappointed because they appeared to have little in common. She wished she could share some of her history to make the time pass more easily, but she didn't dare.

They continued towards the Dane John – Agnes steered them away from the slums down by the river. They joined the wealthy of Canterbury and the nannies pushing prams, promenading along the walkway on top of the grey stone walls. They walked up the mound, following the narrow path that spiralled its way up to the top. Agnes noticed how George took Elizabeth's hand in pretence of helping her up the slope.

She glanced towards Felix, who was scanning the view of the city in the afternoon sunshine. It was hot, she hadn't eaten, and she felt a little faint, so she was relieved when they soon made their way back down again. As they returned through the gardens, they came across a woman dressed in rags with a snotty babe in her arms. She stepped across their path.

'What is the meaning of this?' Felix said.

The infant started to bawl.

'Please, sir, a shillin' for the child,' the woman begged.

Felix stared at her. George and the young ladies stood watching.

'A penny, then. A ha'penny will do. Anything. My husband has gorn.'

Agnes couldn't stop herself. She pulled out her reticule and took out a couple of coins, pressing them into the woman's hand.

'Thank you, miss,' the woman said.

'No, Miss Linnet. There's no need for that.' Felix moved up beside her. 'She is a fraud, one of the many who haunts the streets, begging for a living.'

'She is desperate. Can't you see?' Agnes said as the woman scurried away, baby on her hip.

'She's a professional. I've seen it before. You've been had.'

'Master Faraday, I thought better of you.'

'She'll go round the corner, give the child back to its mother and spend your money on gin.'

'I would rather judge her kindly.' Her cheeks grew hot as she recalled the incident with Oliver and Bert when she had had to hand over the coins that Papa had given her as a punishment for releasing the golden linnet from her cage.

'You are a philanthropist as well as a governess?'

'I hate to see people suffer,' she said simply. She thought of her true mother and how she might not be alive today if people like Papa hadn't shown some generosity. Admittedly what he'd done for Agnes, lying about her beginnings, had been wrong, but he'd given her the chance of a good life and her true mother the means to support herself. 'I did right by that poor woman.'

'So you say, but I still maintain that she was undeserving of help. If she was truly destitute, she brought it on herself.' He wrinkled his nose. 'She was disgusting, dirty and of low morals.'

'How can you deduce her morality from her appearance?'

'Women like her are all the same,' Felix said. 'There's nothing you can say that will change my mind. I recognise a whore when I see one.'

'Master Faraday!' she exclaimed. 'I'm shocked by the way you speak. Think of your sisters.'

'I'm sorry. I should have spoken with more delicacy, but I was only telling the truth.'

'Then we must agree to disagree on this.' She turned away abruptly, and rejoined the others. Felix had rather taken the shine off the day. She avoided speaking to him for the rest of the day and the journey back, and he barely looked at her.

She had been surprised to discover his true feelings

about the plight of the poor. Was his lack of compassion a result of ignorance or arrogance? She scolded herself for thinking badly of him when she had felt the same in the past. It had taken Oliver's gentle admonition and explanation to open her eyes to the truth.

When they returned home, Felix caught her on the landing as she passed by the drawing room to take her dinner tray back to the kitchen. She hadn't been invited to dine with the Faradays that evening.

'Miss Linnet,' he called, moving close to her.

She held the tray between them like a barrier.

'You aren't still cross with me?' he said.

'A little, but I overreacted. Your attitude reminded me of how I used to be,' she confessed.

'I'm sorry for offending you earlier. You saw fit to give that money. It was your choice and I shouldn't have contradicted you. You're a kindly soul and I hold you in the greatest regard.'

'Thank you,' she said.

'I was wondering if we can spend a little more time together.'

'You gave me the impression the other day that you weren't all that interested in the French language,' she said lightly.

'What you taught me the other day has completely fled my mind.' The cutlery rattled on her tray as he continued, 'I find your beauty, your perfume and your presence fascinating. In fact, I think I have fallen in love with you.'

'Oh, Felix, no. Do not speak in this way. It is ungentlemanly.'

'Why are you always finding fault?' he said. 'It gives me the impression that you have strong feelings for me in return.'

She gazed at him. It was true. Her breast seethed with fondness and dislike in equal measure.

'I regret to inform you that you're wrong,' she said.

'You're lying.' He lowered his voice. 'I've seen the way you look at me – your eyes caress my soul.'

Had she really let her emotions show? Had she not managed to rein them in sufficiently? She didn't know what to say. She wasn't used to being pursued by young men.

'For goodness' sake. It cannot be.' She recalled Nanny's admonitions. 'I can't afford to risk losing my place and reputation by acting upon feelings.'

'Oh, Miss Linnet. Allow me to call you Agnes.'

Her heart began to melt, but she steeled herself. Her reputation was the most precious item that she possessed. No matter how strong the attraction, she would not take another step along that road.

'You will continue to address me as Miss Linnet, and we will forget this conversation ever happened.' She glanced towards the drawing room where Pell was silhouetted in the doorway. 'Goodnight, Master Faraday.' She could hardly bear to see his face, his expression dark with anger and hurt at her rejection. This time she felt that his mood was justified, although she reproved him for it.

Once again, she passed a sleepless night. She tossed and turned as a pair of owls called to each other outside. She couldn't stop thinking about Felix and the strength of his passions and opinions.

# Chapter Seventeen

## *An Unlaced Boot*

Agnes found a letter that had been slipped under the schoolroom door the next morning.

*My dearest Agnes –*

*I hope that by now we are on familiar enough terms for you to permit me to address you as such. Please excuse me for writing to you like this. I had to let you know how ashamed I am of how I behaved when I left you last evening. I was vexed by your insistence on doing the right thing, of maintaining your perfect innocence.*

*Till we meet again, when I will throw myself down at your feet to beg your forgiveness.*

Her heart beat faster. He had explained his behaviour. He had been frustrated by her rejection. This had nothing to do with her lecturing him on his attitude to the poor in Canterbury and everything to do with how he felt about her. She was grateful, happy and excited all at the same time, her mind a heady swirl of anticipation and affection. Was it love?

*Tell me how I can win your heart.*

*Felix*

She didn't have to tell him anything – he had already won it.

Agnes folded the note and tucked it away in her pocket. She looked out of the window across the park, catching sight of two riders and their horses galloping across the pasture. They were racing. She recognised Felix's horse – the chestnut mare. He was leaning forwards in his saddle, urging her to extend her stride as she drew level with George, who was borrowing a grey. The horse went ahead by a nose. Felix raised his arm in triumph and they pulled the horses down to a walk, puffing and blowing as they returned across the park. The groom wouldn't be happy, she thought – he didn't like the horses being ridden hard.

She chewed on her lip, wondering how she could keep her emotions in check. How did you maintain an air of composure when you were filled with uncertainty and hope? She had never felt like this before.

'Miss Linnet, we are here,' called Elizabeth. 'Have you not noticed us? We have been at our desks for the past five minutes while you've been staring out of the window.'

'I don't know why when there is nothing to see,' Charlotte joined in.

'I'm sorry. I was preoccupied.' She walked across to the cupboard and opened it. The papers and books fell out on to the floor. 'Oh dear – it's going to be one of those days.' Charlotte stood up and helped her put everything away.

'Perhaps we should forget about lessons, then,' Elizabeth said. 'George says he and Felix are going on a railway trip today. I should love to go with them.'

'On another occasion,' Agnes said.

'Oh, but they won't be here for ever,' Elizabeth said. 'We should entertain them.'

'They are entertaining us with their antics. We do not need to return the favour. I for one will be relieved when they embark on their travels.'

'Oh, Miss Linnet. How can you say that? I will be heart-broken,' Elizabeth cried.

'Don't be ridiculous. This attachment that you feel for Master Moldbury is puppy love, that's all.'

She didn't mean it. Her heart wrenched at the thought of her admirer's absence. Did she dare hope that he would write to her?

'What do you know about love?' Elizabeth said.

'Very little, to tell you the truth, but I do know that you are far too young to be setting your sights on someone.'

'But George sings and plays the piano very well, don't you think? He has a beautiful voice, and his eyes . . .'

'You are sounding like a character from Charlotte's novels,' Agnes scolded. 'Now, pick up your pens.' She handed out some paper. 'I would like you to write a summary of what we learned about Canterbury Cathedral when we visited yesterday. I hope you committed some of your observations to memory.'

'No, that is too hard. I cannot do it,' Elizabeth said.

'You will sit here until you complete the task to my satisfaction.' Agnes was stern with them. 'The sooner it is done, the sooner we can go out for a walk.'

Elizabeth's pen fair flew across the page, and from then on, the hours passed quickly.

When they were out walking, they inevitably ran into the young gentlemen, and as usual, Felix dropped back to walk beside Agnes. After Evie's recent suggestion that his attentions towards her had been noticed, she felt exposed and uncomfortable.

'You received my note?' he said.

'Yes, thank you.'

'Will you meet with me tomorrow?' he asked, his head bowed and his hands behind his back. 'I thought we could walk together. I found out from Charlotte that you have a half-day.'

'I'm sorry, I can't. I use my free time to prepare lessons.'

'Oh, don't tell me you work every hour that God sends. I don't believe that you're really such a serious person, Miss Linnet. If I were a medical man, I'd recommend that you took some time off. You will make yourself ill.' He looked up.

'Thank you for your concern for my health, but I can assure you that I am quite well, and intending to remain so for the foreseeable future.'

'I'm very glad of that.' He was smiling. 'George is going into town tomorrow, so I will be all alone. I fancied some pleasant company and intelligent discourse, that's all. Does that reassure you?'

'What about what you said in your note?'

'Ah, I hope that you will permit our conversation to touch on our feelings when we are alone.'

'What about your mama? What would she think of this . . . invitation?'

'She doesn't tell me what to do. Agnes, how old do you think I am?' He didn't pause to let her answer. 'I'm twenty-two years old. I'm a grown man, not a boy tied to his nanny's apron strings. You are a respectable young woman to whom she has entrusted the moral education of my sisters. There is hardly better recommendation of your character than that.'

She stared at him. What was she afraid of?

'Don't worry. Your reputation will be quite safe with me.'

'I'm worried that people are talking about us. This will only add fuel to the fire.'

'It's all perfectly proper. It's your day off and you are

entitled to do as you wish on that day – unless you have other plans, apart from work.'

'Oh no,' she said quickly. She thought of Miss Treen – she knew exactly what she would have said about the situation.

'Then say you will walk with me,' he said.

She smiled. Why shouldn't she grasp a little joy when it came her way?

The next day, Agnes dismissed Charlotte and Elizabeth from the schoolroom at midday so they were free to meet their mother to call on a neighbour who had recently moved to the area. George had gone to Canterbury and Sir Richard was out on estate business.

Agnes wore her pale grey dress, bonnet and summer shawl, and her outdoor boots, because it looked as if it might rain before the afternoon was out and she didn't want to spoil her shoes. She ran down the stairs to the back of the house and crept along the corridor to the rear entrance, hoping that she wouldn't meet anyone on her way. She placed her hand on the latch.

'Miss Linnet, you are going out?'

She turned at the sound of Pell's voice and her heart sank.

'Are you going anywhere in particular?'

It wasn't any of his business, but she didn't like to say so.

'I'm going to take the air for a while,' she said brusquely.

'Hmm,' he said. 'You seem nervous, like a cat on hot bricks.'

'I don't know what gives you that impression.' She opened the door and stepped outside, impatient to get away.

'You are in a hurry?'

'I wish to make the most of my free time, that's all. Good afternoon.'

'Good afternoon, Miss Linnet,' he called after her as she fled across the yard.

She slowed down to a walk when she reached the garden. She followed the path between the flower beds filled with marigolds, lavender and mint. She turned left at the beech hedge, opened the iron gate and went through the arch into the park. She glanced behind her. There was no sign that she was being followed.

Was she doing the right thing? There was still time to change her mind, she mused as she hesitated. She had agreed to meet Felix as friends, but what did it matter if their assignation should lead to anything else? She had thought that it was impossible that she should ever meet a suitable match, but then her and Master Faraday's paths had crossed. Like Evie, she'd had low expectations about how she would spend the rest of her life, but Felix was master of his own destiny and she was a lady of quality. He was a baronet, and highly eligible. She was attracted to him, and he was attentive towards her. She was more than qualified to be mistress of Roper House.

Why shouldn't she go on to marry him?

It wasn't often that a young man of his standing married a governess, but it did happen. He was also slightly mad, as evidenced by his shooting of the rat and the way he tore about the countryside on his horse, but she put that down to youthful impulsiveness. She hoped that he didn't possess too many of the eccentricities of his father. If she ever became mistress of Roper House, she would insist on the hunting trophies, the stags with their glassy stares and the pheasant and hare facing each other in the box, being put away in the attic.

She walked on up the sweep of short grass to the top

of the hill. Her heart beat faster as she spotted a figure waiting with a dog at the foot of one of the tall chestnut trees on the ridge. Behind them, a white-topped thunder-cloud was slowly spreading across the sky.

'No one saw you leave?' he asked anxiously when she reached him.

'Pell did,' she said.

Felix frowned.

'Does it matter? You said that meeting like this wouldn't be a problem.'

'I'd rather he hadn't seen you, that's all. Oh, don't worry about it.' He whistled to the dog and a pheasant flew up from the undergrowth. 'We'll go this way. There's a game-keeper's hut over the other side of the hill. We can take shelter there if it rains.'

'Oh no,' she faltered.

'Or we can walk in the garden, up and down in full view of the house, and run indoors at the first sign of a shower,' he said. 'I have no fear of our association.'

'We'll go towards the hut,' she decided.

'One day, not too soon, I hope, I shall be master of all this,' he said, raising his arms and spinning around on the heel of his boot. 'I will not be answerable to anyone.'

Agnes couldn't help laughing. He looked vaguely comical as he came to a stop, his hair caught up by the breeze.

'You are very fortunate,' she said, thinking how differently her life might have worked out if she had been born a boy. Perhaps she would have been in line to inherit Windmarsh Court, instead of Henry? Or would she have been cast off when Henry came along because she was the Berry-Clays' adopted son?

'Let's walk,' he said. 'I can't bear standing still.'

They reached the top of the hill and began to stroll down the other side.

'May I venture to take your hand?' he asked. 'There is no one watching except for the birds and the deer.'

She supposed it would be all right. She felt his fingers touch and entangle with hers. His skin was smooth, his grip was firm. She felt sick with longing, but for what she wasn't sure. He strode out more quickly, taking longer strides. She hurried along, trying to keep up with him, but as they turned off down an avenue of trees, she caught her foot on a tussock of grass and tripped.

'Oh,' she cried out, as a pain shot through her ankle.

He stopped and turned to her.

'Agnes, what has happened? You have hurt yourself.'

'It's all right. It's nothing.' She touched her toe to the ground and winced.

'You must sit down and rest for a while. I'm sorry. I was walking too fast for you.'

She hopped on one leg as he supported her with his arm around her waist, the contact seeming to burn through to her flesh. He guided her to a fallen trunk and she sat down.

'Allow me,' he said, sinking to his knees in front of her, and taking hold of her foot. She froze. He moved his body close to hers so that their arms were touching and then their thighs through her dress. She was painfully aware of his breathing, the way his breast rose and fell, quicker than before. His cheek was flushed and his eyes dark, his pupils dilated.

He began to unlace her boot. She didn't argue, transfixed by the sight of his face, his concentration and the dexterity of his fingers. He gently pulled off her footwear, making her gasp with a mixture of pain and longing.

'There is no bruise,' he said, examining her skin. 'I don't think you have broken any bones.'

'How can you tell?' she said. 'You are not a doctor.'

'I've taken many a tumble from my horse. I can recognise a break when I see one.' He looked up at her, his expression soft. 'Shall I carry you back to the house?'

She smiled at the very idea. 'No, I shall be all right in a few minutes.'

A drop of rain fell on to one of the curls on his forehead as he slipped her boot back on and retied the laces loosely around her ankle.

He cursed lightly as another drop fell. 'We will have to go back.'

'I think that would be for the best.' She was having second thoughts.

'Why did it have to rain now?' he went on.

She reached out for his arm and pulled herself up. She touched her toe to the ground again. The pain was immense, but she managed to limp two steps with Felix's support.

He hesitated for a moment, leaned down and pressed his mouth to her cheek.

She gasped.

'I hope I haven't offended you, my dear Agnes.'

She wasn't sure. She touched her cheek as she turned slowly to face him.

The rain pattered down, but she hardly noticed as he leaned closer and his lips found hers.

'One kiss,' he said softly, 'for the pain. Do you feel better?'

She nodded. Her heart was pounding and she ached for more, but Felix returned to her side. He offered her his shoulder to lean on, and they made their way back to the house.

'I've told you about how my future is mapped out,' he said. 'How about you? What do you wish for? Are you going to teach young ladies like my sisters for the rest of your life?'

'That depends. My wish is to save some money so I can set up a school for less fortunate girls.'

'You have noble intentions, but you are misguided. People misrepresent themselves as disadvantaged, if they think they will benefit by it.'

'I thought we'd agreed to disagree on that,' she said with half a smile. She felt sore that she couldn't talk about where she'd come from and the experiences she'd had. The pain in her ankle was nothing compared with the pain she felt at having to pretend she was someone other than her true self.

'What if you can't build up enough of a reserve to start your school?' he asked. 'It seems unlikely that you'll manage that on your wages.'

'If I can't do it by myself, I hope to find a patron who will set up a charitable trust.'

'So you are not thinking of marriage?'

'Of course, I wish to make a good match one day,' she said. 'I expect that your mother has someone in mind for you.'

'Oh, she is full of ideas. There's Lady Bottes' daughter who laughs like a horse. And the very dull Miss Lawrence of Selling.' He held her gaze. 'She will never convince me to marry either of them.'

The rain stopped and the sun came out. Her heart soared like the buzzard that owned the sky above their heads, as Felix walked and she limped back down the hill to the house. When he'd said that he wouldn't marry either of his mother's suggestions, he'd hinted – yes, she was sure that he had hinted that he was free to marry another. Her, perhaps? She hobbled on through the garden.

Pell was waiting at the back door.

'Look who I found,' Felix said loudly.

'Miss Linnet,' Pell said, his expression inscrutable.

'It was a lucky coincidence – she has fallen and twisted her ankle in the park. Will you help me take her to her room? And have some hot water sent up so she can apply a compress?'

She was relieved that Felix had turned out to be a good liar. He seemed to have convinced Pell that their meeting had been totally innocent. She wasn't sure that they should make another arrangement in the future. It was too dangerous, she thought later, as she ate dinner alone in her room. The trouble was that, torn between duty and desire, she would find it well nigh impossible to resist.

# Chapter Eighteen

## *Be Careful What You Wish For*

They met once again on her next afternoon off. This time, she managed to escape the house without Pell seeing her – at least, she thought so. She met her beloved at the top of the hill in the shade of the chestnut tree, where he pulled her behind its mighty trunk and kissed her. She felt that she would burst with joy.

'We will go to the hut,' he said, taking her hand. 'I have a surprise for you.'

'I mustn't be out too late.'

'I'll have you back before dusk. Trust me, my love.'

'Oh, my dear Felix,' she sighed, feeling overwhelmed and weak with a desire for more kisses, to meld with him, body and soul. He loved her. He'd said so and she would love him back with all her heart.

They ran down the hill and into the woods, following a path between the hazel trees and chestnut underwood. She hesitated when they reached a clearing in the middle of which stood a tumbledown timber hut. He took her hand.

'Come on in,' he said, leading her towards it. 'I took the trouble to check for spiders beforehand, and I've left a blanket and a basket of provisions inside.'

She followed him through the door which was sagging on one hinge, into a single room with an earth floor on which he had spread a tartan blanket. It had a strong odour as if it belonged to one of the dogs. There was a basket to one side, and a broken window that was partly obscured by brambles.

'Sit down with me,' he said.

She consented and they sat down side by side. Felix poured her some of his father's sherry. Even after one sip, she felt light-headed.

'Have some more,' he said.

'No, thank you.'

'Oh, go on.' He rested his hand on her knee and tipped some more from the bottle into her glass. She put it aside. 'Tell me about your family,' he said. 'I still feel that I don't know you very well.'

Agnes gazed at his profile, reminding herself of the way his hair curled down over his forehead.

'It is difficult,' she said. 'I am not sure I can speak of it.'

'You will have to . . .' he lowered his voice ' . . . if you are to satisfy my dearest wish and become my wife.'

'You mean . . . ?' Her heart leapt and hot tears sprang to her eyes.

'I have admired you from the first time we met, and since then my affection for you has grown. I adore you.' He took her hand. 'Do you think you can ever feel the same about me?'

'I-I-I don't know. I mean, I do . . .'

'Prove your love for me,' he whispered.

'How can I do that? Isn't my word enough for you?'

'Show me . . .'

'How?' Her belly felt alive with butterflies.

'Lie with me,' he begged urgently. 'Give yourself to me.'

She touched her throat. 'Shouldn't we wait, at least until we are formally engaged?'

'Oh, we are past that. We are here alone together and I think of you fondly as my fiancée.'

'Do you? Do you really?' she marvelled. It wasn't what she expected. She had dreamt of a proper proposal, whatever that was, when the gentleman went down on one knee and offered his hand in marriage. This was the second time when it hadn't gone to plan.

It crossed her mind that she should mention Philip and her previous engagement, but as she felt his hand on her shin, she realised that it probably wasn't a good time.

'Your parents are happy with our arrangement?' She could hardly speak now as her dress was riding up her thighs.

'Hush, Agnes,' he whispered. 'I've been patient. But now I have to have you. You are driving me mad.'

'Are you sure?' she gasped. It felt wrong. It was wrong. They were promised to each other, but they weren't married.

'Don't worry. It's perfectly natural. And if anything should happen, I'll look after you. I have the means, and the intent.'

'Felix, I don't think—'

He silenced her with a kiss, obliterating her doubts. She loved him, wanted him, ached for him . . .

Afterwards, Agnes pulled down her skirts and watched him fasten his breeches, and then they lay together, their bodies entwined. Agnes's eyes filled with tears.

'I'm sorry,' she sobbed, unsure why she was crying.

'Didn't you like it?' he asked, rolling over and leaning on his elbow. His face was a sheen of perspiration.

'Oh, yes, I think so,' she said, biting her lip.

'It always hurts the first time.'

She didn't ask him how he knew.

'When will we be married, do you think?' she asked.

'Oh, not yet. I have to finish my studies.' He smiled. 'I can't marry before then.'

'Is that what your parents have said?'

'Oh no, I haven't spoken to them yet.'

'What?' Agnes sat up abruptly. 'You said that we were engaged.'

'I said that we should consider ourselves engaged. We can't say anything just yet. I have to speak with Mama and Papa first, then we can be open.'

'Why did you let me think you had?' She wouldn't have lain with him if she had known otherwise. 'You misled me.'

'Oh my dearest girl, of course I didn't. It was your imagination that led you to think this way.'

'Felix, what if I am with child?' She was filled with sudden panic.

'I've said, don't worry about that. It's very unlikely.'

She thought of Mama and how it had taken her years to conceive, and felt a little reassured.

'My parents respect you. Mama is most impressed with the way you've brought my sisters to heel.'

Which was all very well, she thought. It didn't qualify her to be a wife.

'I need to know more about your family and where you come from,' he went on. 'I have to be armed with all the answers when they start interrogating me. They will expect me to justify my choice, but I can't see any reason why they should disapprove.'

Agnes did. Would the Faradays still be as fond of her when they knew her history? At least, though, if it was out in the open, she would have no more trouble with Pell. It was a chance that she had to take. She wondered how much she should say, and when.

'What are you thinking now?' he asked.

'That we should go,' she said quietly.

'We will walk back separately,' he said. 'I can see this upsets you, but I can't expose you to gossip and speculation. I have to choose the right moment to speak to my parents,' he went on. 'Until then, we'll continue to meet in secret. Not a word. Don't worry, Agnes. When I want something, I get it. Haven't you noticed?' He grinned as he helped her up, and planted a kiss on her cheek when she was back on her feet. He grasped her around the waist and kissed her again before letting her go.

'I wish we could stay longer, my dearest love,' he whispered as he led her out of the hut and forced the door shut behind them. 'Until next time.'

They parted and she watched him saunter away with a piece of grass stuck between his lips like a country fellow.

When he had disappeared over the brow of the hill, she felt more alone than she'd ever been at Windmarsh Court. Did he really love her? Could she take him at his word? She recalled her true mother and what had happened to her, but her situation had been different. From what Agnes had gathered, she had been parted from her betrothed by an unexpected circumstance. There was no reason for history to repeat itself.

She dismissed any doubts. All would be well because Felix had said so. She trusted him. She had no reason not to. They were engaged.

The next morning, when she went into the schoolroom, she found a rose and a note on her desk.

*To my dearest Agnes xx*, it read. *Burn this.*

She pressed the paper to her lips and then set it alight, watching the flame lick across his words of love before they crumpled to ash. It was right to be discreet, she thought. He needed time.

She wondered how they would present their news to his sisters. She would no longer be their governess once she was married – there would be no need. They would live on Felix's allowance until such time as . . . well, she didn't like to think of Sir Richard being taken up to Heaven like Papa, not yet.

She blushed whenever Felix caught her eye and she couldn't concentrate on giving her lessons. The rest of the month of August seemed to crawl by, but she consoled herself with the fact that she would soon be able to give up her burden of teaching. She would celebrate by burning the dreaded manual of etiquette.

Agnes and the young ladies were in the schoolroom one afternoon when one of the footmen – the one who was sweet on Evie – called to speak to her.

'I hope I'm not disturbing you, Miss Linnet, but I 'ave a message from Mr Pell asking you to meet him in his room after lessons,' he said.

'What can he want?' she wondered aloud.

The footman smiled. 'Can I tell 'im you'll be there?'

'Yes, of course. Thank you.' Agnes returned to the lesson.

'Are you well, Miss Linnet?' Elizabeth said. 'You have gone quite pale.'

'I'm grateful for your concern, but there is no need for it. Charlotte, please continue with the next paragraph.'

She was reading out a page from a tome called *A General History of Quadrupeds*, about the Great White Bear of the Arctic. It seemed odd hearing about an animal which lived in the frozen wastes of the north, when the sun was shining, showing up the dust that billowed from every surface. The schoolroom wasn't a priority for the maids at Roper House.

'Oh, let's finish there,' she sighed. 'We will go on to drawing.'

Elizabeth clapped her hands together. 'I'll finish my picture of Sunny. Miss Linnet, you are more like a friend to us than a governess.'

Agnes was touched, but she wouldn't be inveigled into time-wasting chatter about the value of friendship.

'Charlotte, what about you? What subject would you like to draw?'

The older sister settled on a still life, created from items they had in the schoolroom: a book, wooden rule, pen and inkwell.

Agnes paced up and down while they applied themselves. She should be writing up their reports for Lady Faraday, but she was too distracted. What if Pell had found out who she really was? How could she persuade him that he was mistaken, if that turned out to be the case? The air was hot and stifling, even with the windows open. She felt oppressed.

She would do anything, say anything to keep her place here. She couldn't bear to be set adrift for a second time.

As the clock on the mantel chimed four, Charlotte and Elizabeth put their pencils away before bidding her a good afternoon.

'Are you expected at dinner tonight?' Elizabeth asked.

'Not this evening.'

'We will miss your company.'

Agnes smiled. 'I thought you would have had enough of it.'

'No, not at all.' Elizabeth almost danced out of the room. Charlotte followed.

Agnes remained in the schoolroom, tidying up to delay her appointment with Pell for as long as possible, but she couldn't put it off for ever. She trudged down the stairs and went through to the front of the house, past the paintings of the Faraday heirs in their pink hunting coats with their dogs and guns, all bearing a marked resemblance to Felix. The last thing she needed was for Pell to spoil things for her now.

The door to the butler's room was open. Sick at heart, she knocked.

'Come in.'

She stepped inside. Pell was standing at the table, counting out the silver for dinner: soup spoons, dessert spoons, fish knives and forks. He picked up a knife and rubbed it with a white cloth before examining it closely. It glinted in the light from the window. Once it had passed muster, he placed it on the table with the rest of the cutlery, then turned to her slowly. His mouth twisted into a smile.

'Close the door and take a seat, Miss Linnet. This needn't concern anyone else as yet.'

She pushed the door. It clicked shut behind her.

'Tea?' he asked as she sat down at the table.

'No, thank you.' Her hands grew damp with perspiration.

'I expect you are wondering what this is about.'

She didn't respond. He was clearly intending to draw out her ordeal for as long as possible, like a cat playing with a mouse.

His gold signet ring looked as if it had been set into the fat little finger that he used to beckon his staff.

'I won't beat about the bush. I've always taken pride in my work and put my employers first. The Faradays have rewarded me generously for my loyalty and attention to detail.' He rested his hands on the table. 'I have evidence.'

'Of what, Pell?' She feigned weariness.

'That you are a fraud.'

She tried to hide the jolt of shock that shot through her body.

'Your accusation is false, therefore you cannot possibly have proof.'

'There's no need to keep up the pretence.' He pulled a letter from his waistcoat pocket. 'I took the liberty of keeping your post aside for you. Oh yes, it is addressed to a Miss Linnet, but unfortunately the seal was not secure and the paper unfolded to reveal its intriguing contents.'

'How could you? It's private.' Who on earth had written to her? Who knew of her address?

'It is my business to know about everything that goes on in this house. I make no apology, Miss Berry-Clay.' He spread the letter open on the table. Agnes cast her eye across it. She recognised the handwriting immediately. Nanny! Why had she done this, when she had been the one who had suggested that they shouldn't contact each other?

*Dear Agnes*

*I hope this letter finds you well. Please don't blame me for breaking our agreement, but I thought that enough time had elapsed by now for you to be comfortably settled at Roper House. I had to let you know that I have found a new situation in Whitstable . . . After you left Windmarsh Court, I found it intolerable to remain. Henry is well and looking forward to going to school.*

*I have heard that Philip is happily embarking on his studies. I thought you would like to know.*

*I have enclosed my address. I would love to hear your news. I miss you.*

*Kind regards,*

*Marjorie*

'You can't deny that this letter is addressed to you.'

She shook her head.

'It didn't take me long to make enquiries about the house at Windmarsh. I made contact with the housekeeper there – she told me the whole story. Now, I'd have thought that the servants would have been under pressure to keep the scandal quiet, but she was more than happy to discuss it, especially when I told her of my fears for the Misses Faraday.'

'You're going to tell her ladyship?'

'I will manage this information as I see fit. I can see you are doing wonders for Charlotte and Elizabeth and I should hate to distress them by causing their governess to be sent away, at least for now. I think that a small honorarium, a percentage of your wages, would help me maintain my silence.'

'No, that isn't fair.'

'You have no right to be the judge of what is fair, or not. You are an impostor, a cheat and a liar.'

'If I don't agree to pay?'

'Then' – he shrugged, his fat neck creasing above the collar of his shirt – 'I have no choice but to speak to Lady Faraday and have you dismissed.'

'This is blackmail.' She realised that Evie had been right about Pell. She had underestimated him.

'Call it what you will. I consider it as an insurance for your immediate future, and a little investment on my part.'

She was furious with herself, with Pell and with Nanny for breaking her word.

What choice did she have other than to pay the butler?

If she could keep him sweet until such time as the engagement was settled, all would be well. Felix would be obliged to protect her, not only out of love, but for the sake of his reputation. A gentleman would never break his promise of marriage. She had to admit that her plan was devious, but what else could she do?

'You will give me one quarter of your income, a regular weekly payment,' Pell said.

'As much as that?'

'I should have thought you'd be more than happy to

settle on that amount for my silence.' There was a blob of spittle on his fat lip. He'd won, she thought. For now.

'I agree,' she said softly.

'I'm glad we see eye to eye on this matter. By the way, in addition to the money, I expect you to end this dalliance with Master Faraday. It will come to nothing.'

Agnes took a deep breath and walked to the door with her head held high.

She would do nothing of the sort.

'Do not cross me,' she heard Pell say as she left the room.

She headed up the stairs, reaching out to hold the oak handrail to steady herself. It had been smoothed by years of use by the Faradays. She surveyed the paintings and hunting trophies, the Wedgwood vases in Portland blue, and the Axminster carpet underfoot. This would be her house. She belonged here, and she would play along with Pell's nasty plot for as long as it took for Felix to settle their engagement.

A week passed without progress. She paid Pell the first of his instalments, but she didn't trust him and worried that he would let her secret slip at any time. She revelled in her memories of the afternoon she and Felix had spent in the hut: his expressions of love; his proposal of marriage; his sherry-laced kisses and the force of his body. They met in secret once more, this time in the hayloft above the stables. Felix reached for her hand when she arrived a little later than planned.

'You have the radiance of an angel,' he breathed softly against her ear. 'You are the queen rose in a garden of ordinary blooms. Let me undress you, my love.'

He unfastened the buttons on her blouse and released her stays before taking her into his arms and laying her down in the soft bed of hay. The moonlight slanted in between the slats of weatherboard, illuminating her lover's face as the intensity of his embrace forced the breath from her body.

When it was over, he pulled away and rolled on to his back. She rested her head on his chest.

'Did you hear that?' Felix whispered.

'What?' She strained her ears, but all she could hear was his heartbeat and the sound of a horse chewing its feed in the stall below.

'That,' he said, sitting up abruptly. He reached for his shirt and slipped it back on. 'We should go.'

'So soon? I thought we were going to spend some time together.' She sat up too, straightened her clothing and ran her fingers through her hair to remove any stray fragments of hay.

'George will be starting to wonder where I am, and I'm worried that Pell is on to us. He keeps following me around as if he's about to say something. I don't like it. I don't want him speaking to Mama.'

She was concerned about Pell too. Should she mention that he was blackmailing her? She and Felix shouldn't have secrets between them. She held her tongue, though. She would tell him soon enough.

She looked forward to writing back to Nanny to tell her that everything had worked out for the best.

'I'm not concerned about Pell.' He would keep his silence while she continued to pay him. 'I shall be proud to call you my husband in the future.'

'Oh, Agnes, you are very sweet.' Felix touched his forehead against hers so she could smell the sweet taint of his breath. 'Be patient. I promise I won't let you down.' He pulled back. 'Now, we really must go before someone catches us out. I'll go first.'

He helped her down the ladder from the loft and she

waited in the shadows while he walked across the yard to the back of the house. After a few minutes, she took the same route.

Pell caught her on the way in past the servants' hall.

'Where have you bin, Miss Linnet?' he said. 'Why are you wandering the house at night?' His eyes fixed on her skirt. She glanced down and quickly brushed away a stalk of hay, but it was too late.

'I went out for a breath of fresh air – I couldn't sleep.'

'You would do well not to walk out alone on a night like this,' he said. 'You never know what dangers lurk for the unsuspecting.'

'Thank you for your concern, but it is none of your business.'

'I find that having a clear conscience helps me to slumber more peacefully,' Pell said. 'I wish you goodnight.'

# Chapter Nineteen

## *A Problem Shared is a Problem Halved*

She had no further doubts of Felix's constancy and intentions. He seemed keen to deepen their association, because when she was next invited to join the Faradays for dinner two days later, he made sure that he was seated beside her at the long mahogany table. She had learned her lesson about modesty and had chosen to wear her pale silk dress. George was opposite her with Elizabeth at his side. Charlotte and her parents made up the rest of the party.

Agnes glanced towards the older Faradays, looking for clues in their expressions. Had Felix talked to them yet about their engagement?

'I hope that you will permit Felix to come and stay with us at the Moldbury residence,' George said. 'I'm very grateful for your hospitality, Sir Richard and Lady Faraday, and I have no wish to outstay my welcome.'

'There's no risk of that,' Sir Richard said. 'It's been a pleasure. I've been glad of your company. My wife and daughters have no interest in hunting.'

'You make it sound as if you're thinking of leaving us,' Lady Faraday said.

'George and I are travelling to Paris tomorrow,' Felix said as Pell moved around the table, filling their glasses with Bordeaux.

Agnes heard Elizabeth's gasp of shock and gave her a hard stare. It was unbecoming for a young lady to express disappointment at the thought of a gentleman's absence – but she felt the same. Why hadn't Felix told her of their plans before? She'd known that he intended to go to France, but not so soon.

'That's all rather sudden,' Lady Faraday said. 'I was under the impression you wished to stay for a few more weeks, at least for the rest of the summer.'

'We think it's for the best,' George said firmly, looking at Felix. 'We've been distracting the young ladies from their studies for long enough.'

'You've been here for less than a month!' Elizabeth turned to Agnes. 'Please, tell Mama how we haven't been in the slightest part diverted by their activities. George, you must stay.'

'It's already been decided,' Felix said.

'But you will come back to Roper House?' Elizabeth said. 'We will miss you.'

'I shall return if I am invited,' George said jovially.

'Of course you are,' Lady Faraday said. 'As my husband has said, we have enjoyed your company. The house comes to life when you and Felix are here, although the furniture suffers terribly.'

'I'm sorry about the Chesterfield,' Felix said.

'We should never have worn our boots indoors,' George said.

'Your mother has been looking for an excuse to redecorate the drawing room.' Sir Richard dropped a lamb chop into the gun dog's open mouth as it sat at his feet. It crunched on the bone just once and swallowed it. 'It will be done by the time you return,' he said, addressing Felix.

'When will that be?' Elizabeth asked.

'We plan to return here from Paris towards the end of

September, and travel on to Oxford so we're there in time for the start of the Michaelmas term,' Felix said.

Agnes glanced towards him. She couldn't bear to think of the house without him.

'One more year and we'll have to start thinking about what you're going to do with your time,' Sir Richard went on.

'I thought I'd take a year out to travel, Pa,' he said. 'It would be a good opportunity to look at making some business investments abroad. I was wondering about India or the South Americas.'

Agnes's heart plummeted. What was he thinking of?

'I don't see why not,' Sir Richard guffawed. 'It would do you good to sow your wild oats. What do you think, George?'

George blushed. 'I really don't know, sir.'

'Don't embarrass him,' Lady Faraday said. 'George, do have some more of the duck.'

The evening went on. It seemed interminable to Agnes when all she wanted was to spend time with her beloved. She sang to George's accompaniment, but Elizabeth declined, saying that she had a headache. She grew paler and paler and eventually fled from the drawing room.

'I'll go after her,' Agnes said, excusing herself. 'You stay, George,' she added as he made to rise from his seat.

She found Elizabeth in her room, lying on her bed face down, sobbing.

'Oh come on,' she sighed. 'I can guess what this is about.'

'It is the end of the world,' Elizabeth cried.

'Sit up,' Agnes said. 'I will lend you my handkerchief. Please, Elizabeth, this is most unseemly, and unnecessary.'

The distraught girl sat up on the edge of the bed, the fingers of one hand playing with the fringe of the coverlet.

'What will Master Moldbury think of you?' Agnes said,

giving her the handkerchief from her pocket. 'You are but fifteen years old.'

'I'm almost sixteen.'

'You are behaving worse than a child.'

'I'm in love with him, his manners, his countenance, his smile.'

'You are far too young to know anything of love,' Agnes scolded. 'This is an infatuation, that's all. George doesn't feel the same way about you.'

'Of course he does. You've seen how attentive he is.'

'That's because he doesn't want to hurt your feelings. There are times, I believe, when he has become weary of you and wished you to leave him alone, but he is too polite to say so.'

'You are lying, Miss Linnet.' Elizabeth's eyes flashed with anger. 'How dare you say such a thing?' She stood up from the bed and tossed the handkerchief on to the floor. 'Did Charlotte put you up to this? She's always been jealous of me.'

'No, she didn't. This is me, speaking as the guardian of your good character. Don't make a fool of yourself in front of your mama and papa, and most of all, the object of your affection.' She took a step back. 'You are quick-witted and light of heart. You would soon grow tired of him.'

'Are you saying he is dull? He's the most interesting person I've ever met.'

'What do you think is the most important thing in George's life? Which flame burns most passionately in his breast? Music? Hunting? His friendship with your brother?'

'How do I know?' Elizabeth said after a pause. 'I can't read his mind.'

'Exactly. You assume that you are well acquainted with Master Moldbury, but that isn't the case. You have no understanding of his motivations and deepest thoughts.'

She hesitated for a moment, thinking of Felix. Wasn't she guilty of the same thing? Had she been foolish, succumbing to the idea of love at first sight? 'He isn't courting you. He is humouring you. Please, Elizabeth. I speak the truth.'

Elizabeth sat down again, her expression turning from anger to distress as Agnes's words began to sink in.

'I would have thought that a young gentleman who was deeply in love with you would have discussed his plans for the rest of the summer with you first,' Agnes went on. 'I'm sorry if what I say upsets you. It's little consolation, but one day you will meet someone who has the same regard for you as you do for him.'

'Miss Linnet, I'm so sad.' Tears rolled down Elizabeth's cheeks, making Agnes want to cry for her. She was relieved that her pupil seemed to have grasped the reality of the situation, but regretted that she'd had to be so brutal in her assessment of it. She wished that George had never shown his face at Roper House.

'It will take time for your heart to mend, but you will recover,' Agnes said gently.

'You are very wise. Thank you.' Elizabeth sniffed.

'Wash your face and get yourself ready for bed. You will feel a little better in the morning.' Agnes hurried away and returned to the drawing room, hoping to catch Felix. She had much to say to him before he went away on the morrow, but the party had dispersed. Charlotte was straining her eyes, trying to reading a book in the flickering light of a candle while her father continued to sip at his brandy. Lady Faraday had retired to her room. The young gentlemen were nowhere to be seen.

She didn't know what to do.

'Is my sister feeling better?' Charlotte said, looking up.

'She has a headache – she will be better in the morning.' Agnes excused herself, collecting a candle from the table outside the drawing room to light her way back to her room. It was after ten o'clock and the heat of the August evening was stifling. Was she going to have the chance to speak to Felix before he left? Her footsteps echoed hollowly on the boards along the corridor. On reaching her door, she slipped the key into the lock and turned it.

'Agnes, it's me.'

She turned to find Felix's shadow right behind her.

'I've been waiting for you. I needed to see you, to feel your lips on mine before I go,' he said softly, his hand on her waist as he propelled her into her room and closed the door behind them.

'You cannot stay here,' she said, breathless.

'I don't care. Oh, I need . . .' His words faded to a guttural sigh.

'No, Felix.' She pushed him away and placed the candle on the washstand. 'This is too much of a risk. We must wait until we are married.'

'You didn't think that before,' he protested, making her feel a little hurt by reminding her of their indiscretion. 'It will be all right. No one knows I'm here.'

'It's impossible. If you love me you will do as I ask. Your sister sleeps on the other side of the wall, and the butler prowls the corridors of Roper House day and night.' He would be more than happy to have an excuse to extort more money from her, she thought – or worse, reveal her secrets.

'All right. I understand, but . . .' He strode across to her and took her in his arms. 'Oh, I will do anything for you, my darling, even though it causes me great discomfort.'

'I'm sorry,' she said. 'There's nothing I want more than to lie in your arms again, but not here, not in the house.' His hands were on her waist. 'I suppose that you are here to tell me that you haven't spoken to your mother.'

'I'm afraid that a suitable opportunity has not yet arisen.

Believe me, I'm as disappointed as you are that we aren't in a position to announce our engagement. Part of me wants to climb up and shout it from the rooftop, but we have to set out on the right foot with my parents. To that end, I need to avail myself of a time when my mother is in a more receptive mood. She's been unhappy with me since she found out that I brought my father's best horse back lame the other day. It wasn't my fault that it put its foot down a rabbit hole, but she didn't see it that way.'

'You make it sound as if she will disapprove of our liaison,' Agnes said. He wasn't exactly filling her with confidence.

'I have to tread carefully. If I married you against my mother's wishes, she would make sure that Papa disowned me and I would lose all of this.'

'Wouldn't you give up your inheritance for love?' she asked softly.

'I'm the only son. If anything happens to me, the estate is entailed to my cousin, and my sisters will lose out. If I inherit, I will make sure they are provided for – if they are not married off by then, of course.' He paused, his brow furrowed. 'It is a pity that you have no pedigree as such. My mother is impressed by social connections and good breeding.'

She felt concerned. No amount of beauty or intrigue or accomplishment in the arts of the drawing room would ever compensate for her origins, but that was the least of her worries at the moment. She felt uneasy. With Pell after her money, and Felix leaving Roper House, it was imperative that the matter of their engagement was settled.

'Why did you not tell me when you were going to Paris?' she asked.

'We just did, at dinner. It was a spontaneous decision. George suggested it. Oh, Agnes, I argued against it at first, but I'd promised to accompany him. I couldn't let him down.'

'What about me?' she said. 'Didn't you consider my feelings? I care about you, Felix.'

'As I care deeply for you. We will have to spend the rest of our lives together in the future. There's plenty of time. Perhaps we could plan a bridal tour and visit France together when we are married?'

'I would have no objection to that,' she said, smiling at last. 'When will you be back, so I can count down the days?' she asked, realising that she couldn't change his mind about his trip to Paris.

'We will drop by at Roper House on our way back to Oxford to tell you all about our adventures,' he said. 'I'll be able to beg an advance on my allowance from Pa at the same time,' he added with a grin. 'George and I aren't planning to stint ourselves.'

'And what about this idea of yours of travelling the world when you've finished your studies?' she said, remembering the conversation at dinner.

'Oh, don't worry about that. Let's take one day at a time.'

'Will we write to each other?' she asked.

'Yes, when I'm back in Oxford,' he said. 'There is no point in exchanging letters while we are in France – we are there but three weeks, that's all, not a lifetime, my love.' He took her face in his hands and kissed her passionately, then abruptly turned and left the room, as if he was hiding his sorrow at their parting, she thought.

From then on, time seemed to pass intolerably slowly. The atmosphere in the schoolroom was subdued. Elizabeth spent hours staring out of the window while Agnes waited for Felix's return. Three weeks later, in the middle of

September when the young gentlemen were due back from Paris, they received bad news. Felix and Master Moldbury would not be making an appearance in Upper Harbledown. They were travelling post-haste straight back to Oxfordshire. Lady Faraday announced this to her daughters, who told their governess when they next met to pursue their studies.

'We will write to them,' Agnes said, trying to hide her disappointment. All she really wanted to do was run away and cry in private.

'Oh, can I?' Elizabeth said more cheerfully. 'I will ask after George.'

'Why would I write to Felix?' Charlotte complained. 'He has no interest in my affairs, as I have no interest in his.'

Agnes gave out paper while the young ladies retrieved their pens and ink from their desks.

'Do you know your brother's address?' she asked.

'I will ask Mama,' Elizabeth said. 'Will you write to Felix, as well?'

Agnes turned away to hide the blush that rose up her neck.

'I don't think so.'

'You can write to him in French,' Elizabeth suggested. 'That way you can continue with your lessons.'

'I think he must have more than enough to do with his studies at Oxford,' Agnes said, but her pupil did have a point. Pell or one of the footmen always collected up the post to be sent from the house, but if she wrote in French, Pell wouldn't be able to read her letters even if he should intercept them. She would write once to remind Felix that she was thinking of him.

She sat down at her table to compose a note to her beloved while the sisters wrote their letters. She found that she didn't know what to say: that she missed him dreadfully; that she was well, apart from a little sickness that she blamed on having eaten some mouldering cheese the day before. It sounded so inane and dull that in the end she merely asked him about his adventures in Paris and signed off. Nanny had always given her the impression that she was an intelligent and interesting young woman, but she was beginning to wonder if her attributes were really enough to hold Master Faraday's attention. She felt that she had done nothing of consequence in her life, nothing that she could share with him, anyway. The thought pained her.

'Have you finished yet, Elizabeth?' she asked, getting to her feet.

'No, I have much to say.'

'Charlotte?'

Charlotte leaned down and picked up the dog from the floor. She cuddled him to her cheek.

'Yes, I've finished mine. Please may we go out for a walk?' she said. 'I can't stand being inside all day while my sister mopes. You don't seem very happy either, Miss Linnet.'

'I am a little tired,' she said. Pell had demanded another payment that day, reminding her, as if she needed it, that he still had a hold over her. How she wished that Felix had come home as he'd intended. Hadn't it occurred to him that she would be waiting for him?

She folded and sealed her letter with drips of hot wax from the vermilion taper, moving it to form a small circle of wax. She let it set, remembering her life at Windmarsh when she had had her own seal with her initials in silver intaglio relief. This time, she used a button to impress the seal.

'Run and ask your mama the address, Elizabeth,' she said. 'We'll keep a note of it in the schoolroom so we can write again.'

'I'll go,' Charlotte offered, and she disappeared with Sunny, only to reappear shortly afterwards with the address of the college at Oxford scribbled on a piece of paper.

Agnes thanked her and quickly memorised the address before handing it to Elizabeth.

She wrote the address on the front of her letter and blotted the ink.

When Elizabeth had completed hers, she offered to put Agnes's downstairs with the outgoing post, but Agnes declined.

'I'll post this on my day off,' she said.

'Who are you writing to?' Elizabeth said.

'One should say, "To whom are you writing?"' Agnes said, tucking her letter into her pocket. 'If you really must know, I'm writing to my former nanny.'

'Ah, what is she like? You haven't talked about her before,' Elizabeth said.

'She is one of the loveliest, kindest people I've ever met. I spent many happy years with her.' A tear rose in her eye at the memory of Miss Treen. In spite of the letter she had sent, making the problems with Pell worse for her, Agnes had forgiven her the transgression. She could afford to be forgiving when she was engaged to be married to Felix.

The following week, Agnes and the sisters took their usual promenade in the grounds of the house. They strolled through the gardens and along the path to the gate giving on to the park where she had once hastened up the hill to meet her lover. The leaves on the chestnut trees were changing colour, turning orange and yellow. Agnes thought she caught sight of a pair of deer moving along the ridge and down towards the copse where she and Felix had taken shelter from prying eyes. She felt sick with yearning. He had been gone for five weeks, and it seemed that it would be at least another thirteen before he returned for Christmas.

'I received a letter today, Miss Linnet,' Elizabeth said.

'Oh?' Agnes's heart missed a beat. She had heard nothing.

'It was from Felix,' Charlotte said. 'She is a little disappointed that it wasn't from Master Moldbury.'

'What did he say?' Agnes asked, trying not to sound too eager. If Elizabeth had received a letter from her brother, it wouldn't be long until she received one herself.

'Oh. Nothing much.' Elizabeth bit her lip. 'He says that he and George are well and that they have been to evensong at Merton College and out beagling. He says that George looked a picture in his green coat and velvet hunting cap. And they miss us and wish they were back at Roper House.'

'Anything else?' Agnes asked.

'Oh yes, he asks after you, Miss Linnet. It is just a line, enquiring about your health.'

October and November came and went. The leaves fell from the trees, the days shortened and an east wind blew across the countryside. It rattled windows and slammed doors. It was so cold at the beginning of December that they moved downstairs to a smaller room, where they sat in front of the fire with blankets across their knees. The sisters looked forward to their lessons, and Lady Faraday seemed content with their progress, which meant that Pell gave Agnes no bother, except when he collected his regular payments.

Agnes wondered why her lover hadn't thought fit to write back to her. Perhaps he was too occupied with his studies, or his letter had been lost in the post. He would have written, she felt sure of it, but his answer never came, and she didn't persist with her attempts to get in touch with him because of her fear of Pell's prying eyes. She was a little out of sorts for a while, but her spirits and state of health began to improve as she counted down the days until Felix's return.

By the end of the first week in December, she was on tenterhooks waiting for him. It was also her birthday. As she washed and dressed in her room, she remembered how she had looked forward to last year's occasion, how proud she'd felt wearing the scarlet dress, and how her joy had quickly turned to sorrow. Poor Papa. She stifled a sob. She thought of Henry and happier times in the nursery, and wondered if he still thought of her as fondly as she did of him. How was Mama? And Nanny? Was she happy in Whitstable?

That was all in the past, she told herself. She had to look to the future now, and find joy and contentment in that.

'How are the tea leaves today?' she asked Evie when she turned up with the breakfast tray.

'You are mocking me, Miss Linnet,' the maid said, but she was smiling. 'Only last week, I read Mrs Cox's leaves and told her she would hear good news very soon, and guess what? She has had a letter from her brother to say that her niece is fully recovered from a broken arm.'

'I didn't know she had a niece, or a brother.' Agnes regretted that she didn't have a bond with the other servants.

'How are you? You've bin poorly.' Evie swept the ashes from the grate. 'You aren't . . . ?' She glanced towards Agnes's midriff.

'Aren't what?'

'In the family way?' Evie whispered.

'No, you mustn't speak of that kind of thing!' Agnes exclaimed. 'It's private. It isn't something one should speak of.'

'Why not?' Evie looked shocked. 'It is perfectly natural and it isn't something that will go away if you don't speak of it. Me and my sisters talk about personal matters all the time. Annie, the oldest, got herself into a situation, as you might call it, when she was only fifteen.'

'I beg your pardon?'

'You heard right. She was walking out with this boy, not much older than her, and he got her into trouble behind the church.'

'Oh dear,' Agnes sighed. 'What happened to her?'

'Ma guessed and Pa gave her what for, then he went round to the boy's house and had a few beers with his pa, who agreed that they should keep the baby. Annie and the boy are married now, and the child lives with them, but when he was small, he stayed with us.' Evie smiled. 'He was like the little brother we never had.'

'Wasn't there a scandal? I mean, the infant was born out of wedlock.'

'Oh, people talked, but it soon blew over. It wasn't long after that when Mr Watkins murdered his wife in her bed. That kept tongues wagging for a fair while because it turned out that she'd bin having relations with another man.' Evie returned to the subject of Agnes's condition. 'It's all very well being secretive, but sometimes it helps to share. I promise I won't say a word to anyone.'

Agnes's eyes filled with tears. She wished she belonged to a family like Evie's where people didn't mind so much about what they said to each other. She recalled the atmosphere at Willow Place, how the Cheeverses didn't stand on ceremony, and generally said what they meant and in turn meant what they said.

'You were sin gallivanting with Felix before he left, even though you promised me you weren't. Pell said so,' Evie went on.

Agnes blushed. Was it possible? They'd only connected twice.

'I can't tell a lie,' she said eventually.

'It is possible then?' Evie persisted, as though she could read her mind. 'What will you do? 'Er ladyship won't 'ave you here if you're with child.'

'I don't think I can be.' Agnes looked down at her stomach – her dress was tight around her waist. She'd had to leave one of the buttons undone.

'Well, it's either that or you've bin eating too much dessert. You're looking quite matronly if you don't mind me saying.'

'I do mind a little,' Agnes admitted.

'And you had the sickness something terrible on and off for at least a month.'

That was true, but she'd blamed the first bout on the mouldering cheese, the second on the marbled veal at dinner being too rich, and the next on the rice pudding she'd eaten being off. Through the swirl of thoughts in her head, Agnes accepted it now as a certainty. She was with child.

'Evie, you won't say anything?' she urged.

'So it isn't just possible? It's more than likely.'

Agnes nodded. 'I'm afraid so.'

'Oh, Miss Linnet,' Evie gasped.

'It's all right. I'm going to marry Felix. We're as good as engaged.'

'Oh? Is that what he actually said, or what you think he said?'

'He told me so in no uncertain terms.'

'You know that it's impossible.'

'No, he promised me.'

'What use are a young man's promises? They are like paper buckets – they don't hold any water.'

'I will talk to him.'

'He doesn't know?'

'Not yet, but he won't mind.' She gazed down at her hands to avoid Evie's searching gaze. 'He is aware of the possibility. He loves me.' His passion for her knew no bounds. 'He would never let me down. I will speak to him when he returns from Oxford.'

'It's a shame I didn't know before – there are ways—'

'Of doing away with it?' Agnes interrupted. 'There is no need for that.' The child was her insurance. She hadn't wanted it this way, but it would pressure Felix into marrying her sooner than he would have done otherwise. It was only hastening the inevitable, and she didn't mind that at all because she was looking forward to giving up her teaching and doting on her husband. She was tired and needed a rest. She wasn't used to working all the hours that God sent. She was fed up with paying a quarter of her wages to Pell to keep him quiet.

'Felix won't 'ave you now,' Evie said quietly.

'Don't say that!' Agnes exclaimed. 'There's no need to blacken his character out of jealousy.'

'I'm not jealous. I wouldn't want to be in your situation.' Evie paused before continuing, 'I've heard that you can apply to a magistrate for assistance if the father should deny paternity.'

'Oh, Evie, he won't do that. He wouldn't do that to me.' Agnes was furious at Evie's slurs. 'Go away. Get out of my room!'

'I'm sorry for upsetting you.' Evie was almost in tears. 'I'm your friend, your only friend by the looks. I won't judge you – or Master Faraday, for that matter. Let me stand at your side in this matter.'

Agnes relented.

'You did something kind for me by writing that letter

to my parents. It's my turn to look after you. If you ever need to talk, you know where I am. You can trust me to keep your secret. I will not tell a soul.'

Agnes thanked her. 'I don't know what I'd do without you. When I'm mistress of Roper House, I will make sure you get your wish to become housekeeper.'

'It is very kind of you to say so,' Evie said, 'but I'm afraid that you will never get to be my mistress.'

'Please, don't say that. I must have hope or I shall die.'

With a shiver of fear, Agnes thought of her true mother and the fate that had befallen her. How ironic it would be if history should repeat itself. She took a deep breath and mustered her inner strength. She would lace her stays up tight, and be patient. She had found the other half of her heart in Felix and she wasn't going to sit back and risk losing it.

# Chapter Twenty

## *Spirit of Hartshorn*

Agnes overheard Mrs Cox arguing with Cook. The point of disagreement was whether they should have turkey or goose for Christmas dinner. Cook declared that Felix preferred the former. Mrs Cox said that she was mistaken, and then Cook said they should ask him in person, which meant only one thing. He was back. Felix had returned to Roper House in time for the festive season. Agnes's heart leapt and her breast flooded with relief.

She'd made her mind up to forgive him for returning to Oxford without telling her. She put it down to one of those thoughtless impulses of youth. He had said he loved her – there was no reason for him to come back and repeat the sentiment. And he would have been too busy, too caught up in his studies, to have time to write letters.

She bit her lip to bring the blood to the surface and brushed back a stray lock of hair, then rushed off to find him. He was in the library, lounging on the chaise with his legs stretched out in front of him. He was dressed in his shirt and breeches, and his hair was tousled as if he had not long ago been out riding.

'There you are, Felix,' she said, smiling with joy and happiness to see him. 'It isn't like you to find solace in books.'

'I'm not reading – I wanted to be on my own for a

while. I intended to ride out, but the groom forbade it because of the frost. The ground is too hard for the horses, apparently. He mollycoddles them too much. They'll get fat and lazy.'

Agnes didn't care about the horses. 'The housekeeper said you were back. Why didn't you send word that you were coming?'

'I did.' He frowned.

'Oh, I've missed you.' Her heart fluttered in her chest, so fast and shallow that she thought she might faint. She moved across to him and reached out her hand to touch his shoulder. He shrank back. 'What is wrong?' she exclaimed.

'I've missed you too, but we can't talk here. We mustn't be seen together, except in company,' he muttered. 'I'm afraid that we have to act more circumspectly for a while.'

'Why?'

'I don't want to see your reputation besmirched by the gossips.'

'That is very thoughtful of you, but there are things we need to discuss.'

A brief smile crossed his lips as he looked her up and down.

'Oh, you are more beautiful than I remember. Although you look as though you've been eating a few extra pastries,' he said bluntly.

'There is a reason that I look more voluptuous,' she said nervously, but she wasn't sure he was really listening to her. She was consumed with anticipation at being back in her fiancé's embrace, although she wasn't entirely looking forward to giving him the news that would inevitably reaffirm and hasten preparations for their wedding. She didn't think he would welcome it with open arms, not at first anyway.

'I've dreamed of you, you know. Every night.' He stood up and took her hands, chafing them in his. 'Oh,' he swore, 'I can't resist you.' He glanced at the clock. 'Meet me at twelve in our usual place. You can do that? You can make some excuse for my sisters?'

'Make it two o'clock – they are going to call on the new neighbours with your mama.'

'Even better.' He grinned. 'How I've missed your sweet kisses.' He frowned suddenly. 'Did you receive my letters? I was expecting you to reply.'

'Letters? You wrote to me?' She was confused. 'I wrote to you too, but I didn't receive a reply.'

'I heard from my sisters and Mama quite regularly.'

Something had happened to their correspondence and she could take a good guess at what that was. Pell. It had to be down to him. She couldn't tell Felix of her suspicions, though – she didn't want to have to explain her reasoning and reveal the butler's wicked plot to blackmail her over her identity, not until they were formally engaged at least.

'I thought you might have changed your mind about . . . us,' he went on.

'Of course I haven't,' she said softly.

'I'm glad,' he said. 'I'm very fond of you, Agnes.'

'As you should be, considering that we are engaged.'

'I'm sorry.' He released her hands and strode to the window, opened the curtains and gazed outside. 'We are not engaged.'

'But we agreed . . .' Her heart in her mouth, she moved up behind him until she could smell the masculine scent of musk and the outdoors emanating from his skin. 'Nothing has changed on my part.' She looked out on to the parkland where the chestnut trees and oaks stood stark and bare of leaves against a grey sky.

'I'm a young man, enjoying my time at Oxford. I'm not ready for marriage.'

Agnes was overwhelmed with confusion. It was as if her Felix had gone away and been replaced by someone else. Had he suffered from a concussion? Had he lost his mind?

'Only recently, you whispered sweet words of love into my ear, you held me close,' she said.

He turned abruptly.

'I thought we could continue as we were.'

'As lovers?' She was appalled.

'There is no reason why not.'

'There are all kinds of reasons why I can't possibly accept that arrangement. I'm with child. Your child,' she added in case he had any doubt. 'Here.' Trembling, she held out her hand for his to place it upon her belly, but he moved away, out of reach. His cheeks were flushed. His eyes glinted with what she thought was fear. 'Please, say something,' she begged.

'Mama doesn't know?'

'Of course she doesn't. I wouldn't let on until after we're married.'

'That's a relief at least.'

'Don't look so worried, my love. All will be well. Speak to your father and we can be married within the month.'

'That's impossible. It can't be done.' A sound from the corridor interrupted him. He looked towards the door and quickly released her hands. 'Go,' he whispered.

But it was too late. Pell strode into the library unannounced.

With great presence of mind, Agnes moved to the shelves and took down one of the books on botany.

'Ah, here it is,' she said, holding the volume to her

breast. 'This will help guide the young ladies with their drawings later.' Whether she had convinced Pell of an innocent reason for being in the library at the same time as Master Faraday, she wasn't sure.

'There's no need to pretend any more, Miss Berry-Clay,' Pell said. 'I think it's time that Master Faraday and her ladyship knew of your lies. I'd suspected you were with child. Now, I have the proof from your own lips. I can't allow this state of affairs to continue. I will not let you trap my employer's son with any more falsehoods. The folly of your fancied passion is truly laughable. Your status is an insuperable objection to a marriage between you and him. Who's to say that this infant isn't somebody else's bastard?'

'What's the meaning of this?' Felix demanded. 'Pell, tell me. Who is Miss Berry-Clay?'

'I am,' Agnes said, her voice sounding harsh in her ears. 'My name is not Miss Linnet.'

'Really? No, you are making this up.'

'I'm not, Felix.'

'You mean you are a fraud?'

'I took a false name, that's all. I did it to secure a position – I had no way of obtaining a reference because I hadn't been a governess before.'

'You've tricked me. You've deceived everyone.' Felix ran his hands through his hair.

'I'm the adopted daughter of the Berry-Clays of Faversham.'

'I've never heard of them,' he said. 'Although . . .'

'I can prove it.' She looked towards the butler. 'Pell has the evidence in the form of a letter from a former acquaintance of mine. I had everything, just like your sisters do – a governess, beautiful clothes and jewellery.' She still prayed that she could turn the situation around, using Pell's accusations to her advantage. 'My parents brought me up to have high expectations of marrying well, but when my dear papa died suddenly, my mother arranged for me to be betrothed to my cousin, a match that neither party wanted. I couldn't go through with it so I ran away.'

'When were you going to tell me of this?'

'I-I-I was waiting for the right time,' she stammered.

'I don't believe you. You were going to trap me with your secret. Pell is right. How do I know that you haven't lain with somebody else?'

'Felix!' Her heart was shredded, as though someone had ripped it from her chest and let the dogs on to it. 'This is our child, I swear. Don't you care at all?'

'There's no proof. It could be anyone's. And you can go running to Mama if you like, but who will she believe? Me or you?'

She knew the answer to that. Felix was a spoiled child, the heir, the only son.

'I don't even know who you are any more,' he added, his face red with rage.

'I'm the same as I was before,' she insisted. 'My feelings haven't altered.'

'You'll have to leave the house. You won't be able to stay here.'

'Where will I go? What will I do?' She began to panic. She would have nowhere to stay, no roof over her head, no position and no money. She was ruined. She blamed Felix. She railed against herself for not listening to Evie, and at her own arrogance, born of her upbringing at Windmarsh Court. What had she been thinking, that life was one big fairy tale? She turned away and opened the door.

'Where are you going?' he said quickly.

'To speak with her ladyship.' She wasn't afraid. It had

to be done. She was more than a governess to Lady Faraday. She was well acquainted with her. She would throw herself on her mercy.

'Oh no, you must not. I beg of you not to upset my mother with this. She will hate herself for employing you in error.'

'You have given me no choice. Lady Faraday will be sensitive to my situation. Unhand me!' she went on as he grabbed her by both arms and tried to pull her back. She felt his strength and the heat of his body, reminding her of what had gone before. 'Let me go. I insist.'

'Lower your voice, please,' he hissed. 'You are showing yourself up.'

'You are afraid that I will show you up in front of your family, your sisters.'

'I'm not afraid of anything, Miss Linnet.'

'You are a lily-livered, cold fish of a man. I didn't think you were a coward, but that's what you've turned out to be. Where is the son who was in charge of his own destiny?'

'Felix, is that you? Miss Linnet, what is going on?' Elizabeth appeared in the doorway, still dressed in her gloves and bonnet, having returned from the neighbour's house. 'Felix, you must release Miss Linnet this very second.' He relaxed his grip and Agnes staggered back, unbalanced, against the wall. Elizabeth reached for her hand to steady her. 'Oh, you are crying.' She turned to her brother, her eyes wide and mouth open with shock. 'What have you done to her?'

'She has made a false allegation against me. Go away. Run back to the shelter of Mama's skirts. This is none of your business.'

'Of course it's my business. You appear to have made our governess cry. What have you said to her?'

'Nothing. Absolutely nothing. She is deluded and hysterical. She is with child, and like some common street-walker, she doesn't know who the father is.'

'Cover your ears, Elizabeth.' Agnes glared at him. How dare he expose his younger sister to such horrors!

'You are talking nonsense,' Elizabeth said, half smiling. 'Our dear Miss Linnet is the most virtuous of women. She has tutored us many times on the perils of succumbing to the wiles of unscrupulous gentlemen. Why on earth would she go against her own teaching?'

'Ask her,' Felix said. 'Go on.'

'Ask her what?' Charlotte said, joining them. 'What is all the commotion?'

'I don't believe you, Felix. You are always making trouble.' Ignoring her sister, Elizabeth reached her arms around Agnes's shoulders. 'Miss Linnet,' she went on tenderly. 'There is no need to be ashamed of something you haven't done.'

'She has deceived us all,' Felix interjected. 'Her name isn't Miss Linnet. It's Miss Berry-Clay – just as her old friend addressed her when they met in Canterbury. She told him he was mistaken, but she's finally confessed the truth, and Pell has confirmed it. She has been employed here under false pretences all along. She wasn't a governess before she came here.'

Charlotte gasped, her hand over her mouth. Elizabeth gazed at Agnes.

'That cannot be. You have taught us well, better than any governess or nanny we've had before.'

'What your brother says about my identity is true,' Agnes said, her voice breaking. 'I came here with a forged reference in the expectation that I would prove myself to be a good teacher. You wouldn't believe how many times I wanted to reveal the truth – it's been very distressing having to pretend, especially when you and Charlotte accepted me willingly into your family and treated me almost as a sister. I wished I could be open with you and be entirely myself.'

'The child, though?' Elizabeth said, her voice hardening. 'What's this about a child?'

'She can't possibly be with child – she never goes anywhere without us,' Charlotte said. 'Even on her days off, she is here, reading her books and writing her lessons.'

'Felix, this discussion is entirely unsuitable for your sisters' ears,' Agnes said.

'They're going to know soon enough,' he said in mocking tones. 'One look at your belly and they can see you're in pup.'

'Don't speak of her like that!' Elizabeth exclaimed. 'Miss Linnet, please tell me this is all some kind of joke on my brother's account.'

'I can't do that. Not any more,' Agnes said. 'My name is Miss Agnes Berry-Clay and I am with child. The man in question seduced me with fine words and protestations of eternal love and affection, and now I am left with the unfortunate consequence.'

'He must marry you then,' Elizabeth said matter-of-factly.

'It isn't that simple,' Felix growled. 'Who would pledge their hand in marriage to an impostor?'

Elizabeth turned to her brother. 'If you know who the father is, you must speak to him and make him marry her.'

'I can't believe this. It's all such a shock,' Charlotte said weakly. 'What is Mama going to say? She is very fond of you, Miss Linnet. You have betrayed us all.' She grew pale and began to sink to the floor. Felix caught her swooning.

'Look what you've done,' he snapped, looking at Agnes.

'I'll fetch the smelling salts and a fan,' Agnes said quickly. 'Sit her down on a chair.'

She hurried to the parlour.

'Lady Faraday, may I borrow the smelling salts? Miss Charlotte is in a faint.'

'Oh, my poor child,' said Lady Faraday. 'Shall we call the doctor?'

'I believe it is a passing occurrence and she will be well again in a short time.'

'Miss Linnet, what would we do without you?'

'I would very much like to speak to you about that as soon as she is revived.' Agnes rushed back along the landing to the library, where she handed the vinaigrette to Elizabeth. Charlotte was sitting on a chair with her head back against the antimacassar. Felix had obtained a fan from somewhere and was waving it in front of her face.

'Open it and place it under her nostrils so she can inhale the vapours.'

Gradually, as Charlotte breathed in the astringent scent of hartshorn, the colour began to return to her cheeks.

Agnes, seeing that her charge was going to make a rapid and complete recovery, hastened back to the parlour. She had nothing to lose. Felix followed close on her heels, then pushed past her and rushed to his mother, falling dramatically to his knees at her feet.

'Mama, I wish to say as your loving son, that whatever Miss Linnet alleges I have done, I am wholly and completely innocent.'

'Really, Felix. What is this all about? First I hear that Charlotte is having a fainting fit, then that you are claiming not to have done something you are accused of, which usually means quite the opposite.'

'Not in this case. I shall not accept responsibility for Miss Linnet's condition. She is only trying to put the blame on to me so she can extort money and sympathy.'

Lady Faraday, her face lined with concern, turned to Agnes.

'What is the meaning of this?' she asked.

'Don't listen to her,' Felix interrupted. 'She has been lying to you all along.'

'As you have to me, your mother,' she said. 'Pell gave me your sordid little love letters. I didn't read them – I had them burned.'

'Mama, how could you?' he stammered.

'He warned me of your dalliance. You're an impressionable and impulsive young man – I knew it wouldn't last. I was only hastening the inevitable. As it is, it seems that my interference wasn't necessary.' She turned back to Agnes, who was trembling. 'When Pell came to me before with his doubts as to your identity, I was prepared to ignore them because you were so sweet and kind to my daughters, but I cannot see past this. You seduced my son.'

'He seduced me,' Agnes protested. A tear trickled down her cheek. 'I thought he was fond of me. He was – until I found out I was carrying his child.'

'Well, that makes it ten times worse. I'm shocked and deeply disappointed.' Lady Faraday held up her hand. 'No, let me speak. I have no desire to hear the details. You must pack your belongings – I shall call one of the maids to help – and leave forthwith. You will not say goodbye to anyone, least of all my daughters.'

'But what will you tell them?' Agnes pictured their distress when they found out that she had gone.

'I'm not sure yet. I shall either hold you up as an example of how easy it is for a woman to fall from grace, or make some excuse that you have had to return to your family, whoever they are. Your character was a forgery – a good one, but a forgery all the same. It's all right. I suspected that you were too good to be true. Don't expect me to write a reference for you after this. I will make sure that you never work as a governess again.'

Agnes made one desperate last attempt to appeal to her employer.

'This is your grandchild, your own flesh and blood. Have you no compassion?'

'Not one shred. To think that I entrusted someone like you with my daughters' moral education! As for you, Felix, let this be a lesson to you too. I shall keep silent on this matter from now on and you would be wise to do the same. Please ask Pell to see Miss Linnet to her room.'

Agnes was sick with shame and anger. Felix had let her down. Her cheeks burned as the butler escorted her to her room in silence. She walked past him and stood waiting for him to close the door behind her.

What had she done? She had been too open, too trusting and ridiculously naive, measuring the depth of Felix's love by the force of her own passion. She had thrown caution to the wind out of her affection for him along with the expectation she had been brought up with: that she would marry well. She had gone against every principle that she had instilled in the young ladies, and she had lost everything.

There was a knock at the door.

'Come in,' she said, keeping her face averted.

'Afternoon, Miss Linnet.' She turned at the sound of Evie's voice. 'I've bin told I 'ave to help you pack your belongings. Oh, what is wrong? Of course, they 'ave found out?' She walked across and hugged Agnes, wiping away a tear with her handkerchief. 'It is all over the house that Felix has gone out riding in a temper, even though the groom has told him not to because the ground is ringing. I pity the partridges today.'

'He is upset?' Agnes asked.

'I think he is truly shocked.'

She hoped that he felt something – remorse for leading her on and letting her down, and regret for what might have been.

'Thank you for not saying I told you so.' Agnes forced a brief smile. 'It is possible that Felix will call after me. He could neither say nor do anything in front of his mother.'

'Listen to me. You need to face up to the facts. Master Faraday can't do anything to help you. He's the only son of a wealthy family, and you're just a governess. He cannot marry you. It's the way it is.' Evie's voice grew soft. 'Now you 'ave to make the best of a very bad business.'

'Oh dear, you are such an optimist. There is nothing left to make the best of. Don't you see? I am ruined. I shall never be a governess again. Lady Faraday will make certain of it.'

'It may be that you will find yourself employment in Canterbury. If not, you'll 'ave to call upon the parish for help.'

'Not the workhouse,' Agnes said with a shudder. She thought of her true mother, who had loved her father, who in turn had loved their child even before she was born. 'No, I'm sure it won't come to that.' Felix wouldn't allow it. He would have some respect for her and their unborn child, surely?

'Where are your bags, miss?'

Agnes pointed towards the bedstead and Evie dragged them out. She put them on the bed and opened them up.

'Go on, then,' she said. 'Pull yourself together and fetch your things. What are you waiting for? I'm your friend, not your servant.'

'Oh, Evie, I wasn't expecting you to . . .' Agnes bit her lip until she could taste blood. If the truth be told, she had slipped back in time to her previous existence when everyone had served her every whim. Slowly, she took down the clothes that were hanging on the back of the door, and the garments from the trunk beside the dressing table and began to pack them. She rolled up her jewellery in a pair of gloves. All she had left was a necklace, ring and bracelet. She would pawn them to pay for lodgings if necessary. She had a little money saved – three gold sovereigns and a few shillings. It wouldn't last long, she suspected – and she doubted that Lady Faraday would offer to pay her outstanding wages.

'Evie, you have been a good and loyal friend to me. I was so caught up in trying to be part of the family that I was inconsiderate to you. I'm sorry.'

'Agnes, please don't worry about me. I am anxious for you and—' She stopped abruptly.

'The infant,' Agnes finished for her. 'It's all right – I can acknowledge it. I have no choice.' She checked the drawers in the mahogany chest and gazed at the luggage on the bed. There was no way she could carry everything with her to Canterbury in one go.

'I expect I could 'ave them sent on after you,' Evie said. 'If you can let me know a forwarding address . . .'

'I don't know where I will end up.' She felt another rush of panic.

''Ave you anyone you can stay with? I wish I could ask my family on your behalf, but—'

'It's all right, Evie. I understand. They struggle as it is. I couldn't impose on them.'

'They would put you up if they could.'

'I know. Thank you. You don't know how grateful I am for your kindness.' She was a maid from a poor family, and she was offering to do all that she could, while others who had the means to help her stood back, ignoring her plight.

'What about the friends you mentioned? The ones at the tannery?'

'Oh, I couldn't possibly.' Agnes was too embarrassed. 'They aren't really more than acquaintances. I only know them through my former governess.'

'Surely, they would offer you a room for a night or two at least?'

She shook her head.

'I would not bring my shame to their door. They're respectable people, and Mr Cheevers is unwell. No, I'll leave you some money to cover your costs, and send word with the address when I know where I'm staying.' She wondered briefly about calling at Windmarsh Court, but she knew that it was no use in applying to Mama for help.

'I shall look after your belongings as well as if they were my own.' Evie gave her a warm hug.

'Thank you, my dear Evie,' Agnes said tearfully.

She picked up a bag and a small suitcase. That was all she could manage.

Pell entered the room without knocking.

'You have outstayed your welcome. I have my instructions from Lady Faraday to see you off the premises forthwith,' he said abruptly.

Agnes lugged her bags down the stairs and past the rest of the staff, who were watching from the servants' hall, to the rear entrance of Roper House. She struggled to open the door while Pell looked on, with Evie standing behind him.

'Farewell,' Evie called. 'Please take good care of yourself, Miss Linnet.'

'Hush, child,' Pell said. 'There's no need to make a scene. This is what happens when a young woman takes a wrong turn. She deserves her punishment.'

'But it is so very cold and dark out there,' Evie protested.

Agnes closed the door behind her. What next? she wondered. Where should she go?

She scurried past the side of the house and along the drive in the shadows of the trees. When she reached the gatehouse where the drive met the road, she turned and looked back at the house, which stood out against the pale lemon moon. She had been happy there. She had stood on her own two feet and made her way, albeit with a forged reference. She had proved herself.

The two Misses Faraday had blossomed under her tutelage, but now they would remember her for all the wrong reasons. As for Felix – the tears streamed warm and wet down her cheeks, because in spite of what he'd done to her, her love for him still pulled at her insides.

She blamed herself. She had been a victim of her own feverish romanticism. Hadn't he told her that she had the radiance of an angel and was the queen rose in a garden of ordinary blooms? He had wanted to unwrap her body from the layers of her clothes and release her from the hoops and stays that restrained her curves. She had let him. She had fallen into his arms and she had enjoyed it.

One wasn't supposed to find pleasure in the congress of a man and a woman, but she had. She had fallen in love with him and then he had rejected her in the cruellest of ways at a time when she had needed him most.

She forced herself to concentrate on each step, as the road was rough and slippery with ice, but she couldn't suppress the turmoil of her thoughts. What chance was there that he would remember her? Would he ever wonder what had happened to her and the child? Would he even care?

# Chapter Twenty-One

## *It's an Ill Wind that Blows No One Any Good*

Agnes walked slowly as the bitter wind blew the clouds across the moon and snuffed out the remaining light, along with any optimism she'd had that Felix might have a change of heart. She struggled to find her way past the cottages and down to the crossroads where the road joined Watling Street.

Something rustled in the underwood. She stiffened and held her breath. Who was it? What was it? A shadowy creature passed by.

'Pull yourself together,' she muttered to herself. 'It's only a deer.'

She made her way into the woods and sat herself down on one of her bags at the base of a chestnut tree, where she shivered and shook – and prayed – until dawn crept through the sky, slowly revealing her hiding place. She dragged herself up and set off again. What would she have given for a pitcher of hot water and the luxuries of her dressing table? It was not that she cared what she looked like, but simply for comfort. She was lucky she hadn't frozen to death.

She picked up her bags and slid down the muddy bank on to the road. A horse and cart trotted past, and an elderly couple walked arm in arm ahead of her. She took one last look behind her in the direction of Roper House.

Her heart lifted as she caught sight of the Faradays' carriage.

He had come for her after all.

'Felix,' she gasped, but the carriage continued past and she realised that she had been mistaken. It was the family's transport, but if Master Faraday was inside it, he'd had no intention of stopping to rescue her.

She cursed the Lord above. Had she not prayed long and hard enough? Was this His retribution for her pride and arrogance, her blithe thoughtlessness and refusal to obey Mama and marry Philip? He had taken Papa, her protector, up to Heaven and forced her to part from Nanny whom she loved and missed more than anyone. Why had God not seen fit to grant her any mercy?

She had lost Felix, along with her hopes and dreams of restoring her fortunes. She had held those in a social position equal and superior to hers in high esteem, yet at Roper House, she'd learned that the possession of wealth and a certain level of class wasn't enough to inspire her regard. She felt more respect for hard-working Evie who had been kind to her than for the man who had let her down.

Her faith in love had been destroyed. She recalled the touch of her lover's hand against her face, how he had cupped her chin so tenderly and planted that first kiss on her lips. She had loved him and now she regretted her folly and grieved her loss. She hated him for what he had done to her.

In despair, she trudged on to Canterbury, towards the cathedral that rose up from the plain below as though in judgement on her. She continued through St Dunstan's and past the Westgate Towers as far as Mercery Lane, where she had once strolled with Nanny. She wondered about stopping for sustenance, but she felt too unkempt to enter the eating house, so she bought a pie and hot tea from one of the market stalls. She tucked the pie inside her cloak so as not to be seen eating on the street. She still had standards, after all, she thought bitterly.

She stood on King's Bridge over the Stour, in front of the weavers' house with its blacked timbers and mullioned windows. A ducking stool jutted out over the river from the side of the building. Nanny had once told her that it had been used in the olden days for scolds who talked too much and for women suspected of being witches. If they drowned, they were innocent.

She felt uneasy in the crowd of people with grey skins and greasy hair, who passed by in their unwashed clothes. She had a sense that she was being followed, but when she looked around to check, she saw nothing suspicious. She felt for the purse at her waist, and the sovereigns tucked in a handkerchief inside her coat.

She wandered the streets, looking for 'Wanted' adverts in the shop windows, and then, when she had exhausted those, she started knocking on doors, but the answer was the same wherever she went. A supercilious stare, a smirk or a look of horror as if she was the plague itself.

What could she do? How on earth was she going to support herself and the child? She couldn't possibly apply for a situation as a governess in her condition. She wondered about taking up lodgings and advertising that she could provide tuition to young ladies, but she was about to give birth out of wedlock. Who would entrust their daughter's education to someone like her?

She didn't dream of riches, of white kid gloves and hot chocolate, of elaborate French dishes and scarlet dresses. She dreamed of a modest, yet comfortable home with her own privy and enough money for food and clothing. She prayed for the safe delivery of her child, her health and some kind of peace of mind. She wasn't sure about happiness. That was a dream too far.

Someone pushed past her, knocking her off her feet. She went flying, falling with a bump into the gutter. Her first thoughts were for the safety of her child. She stroked her belly and pulled her skirts back over her ankles.

'I'm sorry, miss,' a man's voice said.

She looked up into the dazzling winter sunlight. She could just make out the figure of a gentleman dressed in a long coat and top hat.

'Let me help you.' He offered his arm.

She took it, and let him assist her on to her feet. As she straightened, his hands were on her cloak.

'Look at you. Your clothes are dirty and it's my fault. I was in too much of a hurry—' He smiled, showing his teeth and gums, like a snarling dog.

'Don't worry, sir.' She stepped away from him. 'There are no bones broken.'

'Thank goodness. I would hate to think that I'd caused you any harm, Miss Berry-Clay.'

'Who? How do you know my name?'

'Ah, we have a mutual friend in Mr Pell. He said to wish you the worst of times on his behalf in return for the harm you've done to the Faraday sisters. He will never forgive you.' The man slipped one hand inside his coat pocket and touched his hat with the other as he wished her good day.

She watched him turn and walk away, his footsteps quickening as he disappeared around the corner into Bargate. How dare Pell send a messenger to scare her witless! What did he think to achieve by it?

She rearranged her coat. Something was missing – the gold sovereigns. More than that. The gloves containing her jewellery were gone as well. The encounter had been a ruse. She broke into a stumbling run. Where was he? Her heart hammered and her lungs hurt as she checked the streets and side turnings, but it was too late. Pell's associate was long gone, and so were her valuables.

Agnes cursed beneath her breath, using words that she'd heard Felix use. She should have been more careful.

She began to cry, then remembered one of Nanny's sayings – it's no use crying over spilled milk – but it didn't help. She cried some more as she walked along looking for a policeman. She had to ask for help from a boy who was pushing a 'barrer' along the pavement, and he gave her directions to the police station on Pound Lane beside the Westgate Towers. Here the police constable, assuming that she was a lady of some consequence from her refined speech, called for the superintendent, who asked her many questions. What was she doing alone in Canterbury? Where was she staying? Where was her evidence of her identity? What proof did she have of the existence of the valuables she claimed to have been carrying?

He had long black handlebar mustachios and smelled of tobacco smoke.

'I regret that I can only give my word on both matters,' she said, frustrated by all his questions. 'I'm travelling to find work here or in the vicinity, and I don't have an address as yet. I don't carry an inventory of my belongings on my person either – it would seem most odd to do so.'

'It would seem most odd that you cannot give me any details of who you are and where you come from. You sound like a lady, but you cannot vouch for it. Have you any friends or acquaintances who can corroborate your statement?'

She thought of the Cheeverses. Surely they would vouch for her.

'I have acquaintances at the tannery,' she said. 'I am sure that Mr Cheevers will confirm the truth of my story if you go and ask him.'

The superintendent arched one of his dark bushy eyebrows.

'Oh, he will say anything to help a person in distress. He is the patron of lost causes.'

She began to see that she was defeated. She tried once more.

'I've been robbed of my jewellery and sovereigns.'

'So you've said, by a well-dressed gentleman according to your account. We have some rogues around here, but none of that description. If you are who you say you are, you can always place an advertisement in the local paper with the inducement of a reward for the finder, Miss, er . . . ?'

He knew she wasn't married, she thought. He had guessed. She felt ashamed.

'Mrs Linnet,' she said.

'I shall place the list of your missing items as Lost Property. That is all I can do. I wish I could do more, but without evidence, I can't pursue this further. I'm sorry, Mrs Linnet. I wish you good day.'

She was upset at the realisation that she had no hope of getting her jewellery and sovereigns back. She still had two bags of clothes, but they wouldn't help her buy food or pay rent. She was in dire straits unless she could sell them or find work.

She wasn't sure which way to turn when she emerged from the police station.

She went down to the river where the dray horses were being led down to drink, churning up the muck at the bottom and bringing up the sulphurous smell of bad eggs to add to the stench of the tannery. It crossed her mind to throw herself on the mercy of the Cheevers family, but she couldn't bear to show them how she had been brought low – or rather, she corrected herself – how she had let herself be brought low.

Oliver had thought her rather shallow. Why would he give sanctuary to a fallen woman who had known wealth and security, and thrown it away through her stubborn refusal to marry for convenience, not love, and her stupidity in not being able to tell the difference between flattery and the truth?

She took a turning down one of the narrow alleyways to try to avoid a man who was walking towards her, carrying a bucket of stinking waste. Everything that could be used was for sale in Canterbury, even the dirt that the dogs had left behind on the streets, and everyone was looking for a way to make money. A boy of about ten, wearing rags, came across to her.

'Let me carry your bags for you, missus.'

'No, thank you.'

She kept walking.

Dusk was beginning to fall, when a house with a sign in the window caught her eye. 'Screevers wanted. Apply within.'

Her spirits lifted a little as she knocked at the door. She could write, if nothing else.

The door came ajar, revealing a middle-aged woman with long silver hair, pale blue eyes, rabbit-like yellow teeth and a receding chin.

'You have an advert for screevers in the window. I've come to offer my services, Mrs . . . ?'

'Mrs Spode.' The woman opened the door a little further and looked Agnes up and down. Her glance was furtive and darting, her expression one of suspicion. Agnes wished that she had a calling card to give her.

'My name is Mrs Linnet.' It sounded refined, she

thought, and respectable. She had thought that it was as easy to be trapped into wealth as it was into poverty, but she realised now that wasn't quite true.

'You'd better come in.' Mrs Spode showed her through into a room that was sparsely furnished with a fireplace, six stick-back chairs and a table, and floorboards that creaked underfoot. The air smelled of burning incense and oranges that disguised the odours of the street. There was a gentleman, a clerk perhaps, sitting at the table and writing a letter while a young man waited, leaning against the wall with his hands in his pockets.

'There are lots of people who've come along here claiming they can screeve, but they can scarcely make their own mark on the paper, let alone write a charming and persuasive turn of phrase.' She stared at her through narrowed eyes. 'Where are you from, Mrs Linnet?'

'Faversham. I have recently made the move to Canterbury where there is more opportunity for a lady to find work.'

'Have you bin a screever before?'

'I have experience of writing letters and teaching the art of handwriting to young ladies,' Agnes said quickly. 'I'm prompt, reliable and hard-working.'

From the corner of her eye, she caught sight of the screever at the table getting stiffly to his feet to hand a piece of paper to the young man. Mrs Spode turned fast as lightning and snatched it away.

'You must pay before you can make your mark,' she said crossly. 'You know that, Mr Fletcher. How many times do I have to tell you to take payment first?'

'I'm sorry, Mrs Spode.' The screever bowed deeply, revealing the bald circle on the top of his head. He had to be at least sixty years old, Agnes thought, and he looked weary, his skin pale and of a yellow hue. He addressed the young man: 'Mr Taylor.'

The young man counted out his coins on to the table. Mr Fletcher placed the paper on the table and handed him a pen, having dipped it slowly in ink.

'Make your mark,' he said.

'I am most grateful for your service,' Mr Taylor said as Mr Fletcher handed the coins to Mrs Spode, who slipped them into a purse on a belt at her waist. Mr Fletcher took his place and extracted a fresh piece of paper from his leather portfolio, picked up his pen, dipped it in the ink again, and began to write. Mr Taylor left and Mrs Spode set Agnes to a test of her competence.

'Sit down. There is paper and a pen. Write a letter from a woman fallen upon hard times seeking pecuniary assistance from a benefactor.'

Agnes frowned.

'Don't worry. I shall add the names and addresses later. All you have to do is screeve the body of the missive.'

Agnes's fingers trembled as she picked up the pen. She hadn't had any sleep and the events of the previous days had rendered her weak and weary. She made to dip the nib into the inkwell that stood in front of Mr Fletcher, but he grabbed it up and cradled it against his neck, scowling at her.

'That belongs to me.'

'I'm sorry.' She looked up at Mrs Spode, who was standing over her. 'Please may I have some ink with which to scribe.'

'I suppose you must.' Mrs Spode walked to the side of the room and picked up a small bottle from the side table. She opened the top and held it while Agnes dipped her pen into the ink inside. 'Mind you don't waste it.'

Agnes leaned forwards and touched the nib to the paper. The ink flowed along with the words across the scratchy surface, and a few sentences later, having blotted the ink, she had completed the task to her satisfaction and, she hoped, to Mrs Spode's, although she doubted from the way she pursed her lips as she picked up the letter that she was a lady who was easily satisfied.

'"Dear . . ."' she read aloud. '"I write to you today to inform you that that through no fault of my own, I have fallen upon hard times. I am a proud and respectable lady, as you know, and it distresses me deeply that I am forced to seek financial assistance in this manner." Oh, Mr Fletcher, Mrs Linnet exhibits a fine turn of phrase, don't you think?'

'Harrumph!' Mr Fletcher grunted.

'"I am grateful in advance for your compassion and generosity." This is more than adequate. Who would have thought? "I hope that this letter finds you well. Yours sincerely."'

'I've left room for the lady's signature,' Agnes said.

'This is a gracious hand, if ever I saw one. Curlicue of the finest quality. I think you'll do very well. Mr Spode,' she called. 'Come and meet Mrs Linnet. Mr Spode!'

A door hidden in the panelled wall opened and a man ducked his head and stepped through from the room beyond. He was short, rotund and wore a colourful waistcoat that reminded Agnes of one of Papa's, and a bow tie, and velvet slippers. He looked round his wife's shoulder, slipped his spectacles on to the end of his nose and read the letter.

'Well, I never did. She has the gift of persuasion through the written word, but can we count on her discretion?' He removed his spectacles and stared at Agnes. 'Our customers generally prefer their business to remain anonymous. Their privacy is our priority.'

'I can assure you that I know how to hold my tongue, sir.'

'I will have to believe it for now – the proof of the pudding will be in the tasting.' He reeked of pickled onions. 'I shall draw up a contract listing terms and conditions and percentages. Drop by tomorrow.'

'I can start today,' she said quickly, not wanting to waste any time.

'We are about to close, and by the way, it's piecework, not regular. Sometimes we are busy, sometimes we are not.'

'Oh, I see.' She was depending on a more reliable and secure occupation. Couldn't they see that?

'Office hours are nine until six, six days a week. I assume that your husband will be happy with this.'

'I am a widow,' she said, a wave of sorrow washing through her as she remembered her foolish hopes for her marriage to Felix Faraday. 'I have no husband to answer to.'

'To lose a husband sounds like carelessness to me. It is my mission to keep mine in the best of health,' Mrs Spode said. 'Return at nine o'clock sharp, Mrs Linnet. We charge for all paper, pens, ink and blotting paper that our employees use – don't worry, we take it off your pay at the end of the week. It is to save on waste. If you've paid for the paper, you take more care. Look, how the waste-paper basket is almost empty.' She pointed to the basket beside the fire.

'How many screevers do you have in your employ?' Agnes asked, wondering if she was going to have enough work to keep herself.

'A goodly number,' said Mrs Spode. 'That way no one feels they are indispensable. It keeps their wits sharp. They don't slide into complacency. Is there anything else?'

'I wonder if you know of any suitable lodgings nearby?'

Mrs Spode looked from Agnes to her bags and back. Agnes guessed what she was thinking, that it was unusual for someone to be looking for work while dragging their worldly goods along with them.

'There is a room available in a house not far from here. The landlady is well thought of.'

'And you are sure it is a respectable house?' Agnes was apprehensive. People seemed to have varying ideas on what respectability was.

'It is indeed.'

Agnes glanced out through the dusty window at the darkening sky. 'Then I will take it, according to your recommendation.'

'Before I give you the address, there is a fee of introduction. One shilling and six should cover it.'

Agnes frowned as Mrs Spode continued, 'It is the accepted custom around here. Both time and knowledge are precious.'

Agnes realised that she had no choice if she wasn't to end up tramping the streets that night, along with the muggers and pickpockets and other unsavoury characters. Reluctantly, she dug about in her purse for the money then handed it over to her new employer.

'Ask for Mrs Hamilton.' She gave her the address. 'Tell her that Mrs Spode sent you.'

'I am very grateful for your kindness,' Agnes said.

'I shall see you in the morning.'

She heard the coins chinking in Mrs Spode's hand as she turned away, picked up her luggage and left the screevers' office to walk the streets once more, searching for the address she had been given.

She found it a few minutes later along a narrow alleyway down to the river where there was a stench of rotten eggs, privies and unwashed clothes. Number six was one of a row of houses made from timber and tiles, roughly assembled, as a cobbler might make a cheap pair of shoes. It had three storeys, the top window being tucked into the eaves. Water dripped from the gutter at the base of the roof where a few of the tiles had been replaced with a canvas sheet.

Why would Mrs Spode send her here? She must have made a mistake with the address. Surely anyone could see that this wasn't what she was used to?

The door was open. She knocked but nobody came, so she stepped inside. The corridor was dark and damp, requiring a coat of whitewash, in her opinion. As she walked a few steps towards the first door, two youths came running towards her, pushing her aside.

'Please, be careful,' she said, guarding her belly.

'Oh, you're a fine lady, all upon the hoity-toities,' one of them said.

'Listen to how she speaks,' the other joined in. 'She thinks she's the Queen. Maybe she is.'

'Excuse me,' she said. 'I'm looking for a Mrs Hamilton.'

They ran away laughing.

'Can I help you, miss? I mean, Mrs . . .'

She turned to find a woman of about thirty-five following behind her, weighed down by a basket of laundry. The hem of her blue dress was muddied and torn, and her apron was soaked through.

'I'm looking for Mrs Hamilton,' Agnes said.

'She'll be in her flat.' The woman nodded towards the door. 'Are you looking for lodgings?'

Agnes nodded.

'If you ever want any laundry done, I'm on the next floor. The name's Mrs Fortune.'

'Thank you.'

'Well, I'd best be getting on.'

Agnes watched her go, lugging her basket up the stairs at the end of the corridor. This was the worst, most godforsaken place she had ever experienced. She felt bereft.

'Oh, Felix.' She bit her lip as a tear rolled down her cheek. 'If only you could see what your thoughtlessness has brought me to. You would soon change your mind, not leave me here to rot in misery.'

She pulled herself together and knocked on the nearest door.

'Who goes there?' a woman's voice said as the door creaked open. An arm thrust a candle through the gap into the corridor.

'Mrs Linnet. You have been recommended by Mrs Spode, the screever.'

'What's she up to? She knows I 'aven't any spare rooms at the moment. Only this morning, I said, Mrs Spode, I am full right up to the rafters.' The door opened wide, revealing an elderly woman dressed in dark clothing, with a long cream shawl around her shoulders and fingerless black knitted gloves.

'I'm sorry to have disturbed you,' Agnes said, noticing a small crop of white whiskers curling from the woman's pointed chin. 'I can see that I've been sent here under false pretences.' The smoke from the tallow candle swirled across her face, stinging her eyes.

'You've paid her a shilling for it, 'ave you?'

'A shilling and six,' Agnes confessed, embarrassed by her own naivety.

'By all rights, you should 'ave come straight to me as I'm the landlady here.'

'I will take my leave. Goodnight, Mrs Hamilton.' Agnes began to turn away.

'No, wait a minute. Let me see what I can do. There is room in my abode for one more as a temporary measure.

Mr Kemp who rents the room in the eaves isn't a well man, and dead men don't pay rent.' She cocked her head to one side.

'May I see the room?' Agnes said tentatively.

'Of course. You won't be disappointed.'

She did feel a little let down. It was dark, sparsely furnished and reeked of roses and lavender vying to overpower the smell of the privy which backed on to it. There were dried flowers in vases, shedding dust, and cobwebs dangling from the ceiling.

'You may keep a fire lit at your own expense or you can share my parlour of an evening. There is a meat safe where you may store the basics, but nothing edible is to be left out anywhere because of the rats. They are as big as cats around here – they've grown monstrous fat on the pickings left lying around.'

Agnes shivered.

'Oh, look at me. You are exhausted. Can I get you a nog of sherry? And a bowl of stew and some bread for an extra sum?'

'Just the stew and bread, thank you,' Agnes sighed. She was starving and felt too weak to go out to find an eating house.

'Give me a deposit then,' Mrs Hamilton said, smiling. Her jaw seemed to have sagged from its attachments, making her mouth slack and wet.

Agnes counted out more coins from her purse.

'Thank you, ducky. That will do for now.'

When she had unpacked, Mrs Hamilton showed her to the small pull-out table in the kitchen where she sat down to take the weight off her feet. Her landlady wanted to gossip.

'So you 'ave a place with the screevers,' she said, slapping a ladle of stew into a bowl and handing it to Agnes. It smelled of turnip and onion. If there was any meat in it, she couldn't find it. 'Are you a long way from home?' Mrs Hamilton sawed off a hunk of bread from a loaf.

'I have been cast off by my family,' Agnes said, not wanting to reveal too much.

'Well, it doesn't make any difference to me. As long as you pay your way, you can stay as long as you like. I don't mind the child when it comes providing it doesn't bawl all the time.'

'I hope that I will have found more suitable accommodation by then.'

'Oh? Is my home too 'umble for you, Mrs Linnet?'

'I didn't mean to offend you. It just isn't what I'm used to.'

'Do you really think you will be able to afford anything better working for the Spodes? Or are you expecting the young man who had his way with you to come and rescue you?' Mrs Hamilton smiled gently. She wasn't being unkind. 'It happens all the time. It's their nature.'

'I pray that he will be sorry one day, and come and find me. I think God will encourage him to search his heart and find the right answer.'

'If I had a shilling for every wretch who has thought that, I would be a wealthy woman.'

'You are not married?'

The old lady laughed raucously. 'Who would 'ave me? No, I value my independence and the money I've made for myself. I have three properties, all let. I have no wish to hand over my empire to a husband.'

'Why do you call yourself Mrs then?'

'To fend off unwanted amorous advances.' Mrs Hamilton's eyes flashed with humour. 'It happens all the time. The trouble is, I know that those men are after my wealth, not my body, so I make out that I'm taken. They aren't so keen when they think there's a husband lying in wait to fend them off.' She changed the subject.

'Would you like second helpings? I see that you've finished.'

'No, thank you. I shall retire to my room now.'

'Would you like me to knock for you in the morning? It's a halfpenny a week.'

'Yes, that's a good idea,' Agnes said, afraid that she wouldn't wake in time to be at the screevers' for nine o'clock.

She returned to her room and tried to open the window, but it was jammed shut. She checked the mattress and a nest of baby rats fell out with the stuffing. The bedding was dirty. She wore her clothes in bed, but she couldn't sleep for the cacophony of sounds that rattled through the building as though it was alive. She could hear her landlady snoring through the flimsy partition between their rooms, the creaking of the rafters above and the scuttling of vermin across the floorboards, people crying, shouting and laughing and a baby bawling its eyes out.

She yearned to be back at Windmarsh with the sound of the gulls and the wind. She wished for the routine of lessons with Nanny and her dear brother Henry. She missed seeing Miriam every day, turning up to the nursery with the breakfast tray and making some comment on the weather or whatever drama was playing out in the kitchen.

She stroked her belly. The infant inside her kicked back as though blaming her for the fact that he or she would never have a good life after what she'd done. She hoped her little one wouldn't cry. She wanted him, or her, to be happy, but she couldn't see how the way that she had to live now, from hand to mouth and in such dirty and desperate conditions, could ever bring any joy to anyone.

# Chapter Twenty-Two

## *Pen and Ink*

'A screever's life is a happy one in general. Some of the jobs are dull, others are more interesting, and when you get the hang of it, Mrs Spode lets you give free rein to your imagination. My name's Jeannie Cotton, by the way.' The woman who stood beside her as they waited for Mrs Spode to let them into the office the following morning was about forty, Agnes guessed from her matronly appearance. She wore a large bonnet over her greying hair, and a cape that spread over her voluminous figure. 'Nice to meet you,' she went on smilingly.

'The feeling is mutual,' Agnes said, relieved that here was someone with whom she might get along. 'I'm Mrs Linnet, but you can call me Agnes.'

'Well, Agnes, you stick with me and you'll get along fine. Have you brought anything for nuncheon?'

She shook her head. She had had weak tea and a slice of toast with lard for breakfast.

'Good morning, ladies.' A young man with dark, oiled hair and dressed in a suit with a cravat introduced himself as Mr Riley.

'Morning, cock,' Jeannie said in a familiar manner which surprised Agnes, who was used to more formal kinds of address. 'This is Mrs Linnet who's come to join us.'

He touched the forelock plastered to his forehead, and smiled.

Agnes couldn't bring herself to smile back. He didn't seem like a gentleman.

Mrs Spode came across to unlock the door. Agnes caught a glimpse of a patterned carpet, a shiny table and shelves filled with books as the door swung closed on the Spodes' private quarters behind the office. She thought the contrast with the office rather odd. Wasn't it usual to impress with the condition of one's offices? Papa had certainly thought so.

They sat down and Mrs Spode allocated tasks to each of the four screevers who were present: Agnes, Mr Fletcher, Mr Riley and Mrs Cotton.

'I've assembled a pack of items for you, Mrs Linnet.' Mrs Spode slid a paper packet across to her, and handed her an inkwell and bottle. 'I'll take the cost from your wages.'

'I should be grateful if you can tell what the deduction will be,' Agnes said. 'I might wish to purchase the items more cheaply elsewhere.'

'It depends on how much more you need in the way of screeving supplies. If you don't like it, you can lump it. Mr Spode and I have to pay to keep this place, and settle our advertising costs, collection, delivery and postage as required. As it is, we make little profit from this enterprise. We pray for riches in heaven, rather than on earth, and find joy in helping the poor seek donations from the wealthy as part of our work. We live very frugally, as you can see.' She held out one hand as though to demonstrate. A large ruby shone from the silver fretwork ring on her finger.

'I apologise for mentioning it,' Agnes said, taking up her pen and a piece of paper. She noticed that Jeannie had folded hers into thirds and used her fingernails to deepen the indentation before tearing it into sections. She did the same.

'I'm glad to see that you understand how to economise, but the letters you will be concerned with this morning require that you use whole pages, not parts.' Mrs Spode gave her a letter to copy out.

The work was hardly bearable. It didn't help that Mr Fletcher was sitting next to her, gazing at her as he wrote slowly and carefully, turning out letters without blots and splashes. She kept making mistakes: her pen seemingly incontinent of ink, then completely dry and scratching holes. She began to worry how much it was costing her in materials.

It was a far cry from when she had been in the nursery screwing up sheets of paper and throwing them into the fire for the slightest defect in the symmetry of a line, or mistake with a single letter of the alphabet.

'Mrs Linnet, you have to write a short letter to confirm the alias of the bearer. The name is here.' Mrs Spode gave her a piece of paper with the name written out in full. 'Copy it down exactly the same so there can be no confusion.'

But Agnes was confused. How could she confirm an alias when she had never met him?

'This is no time for scruples,' Mrs Spode said, pre-empting her question. 'What are you waiting for?'

It was wrong, but she didn't have a choice. It was a lie to add to the ones she had already told. She had promised herself she wouldn't repeat any more falsehoods. She would live as an honest woman as she had been brought up to be, but the more trouble she found herself in, the more desperate she had become, and the more she seemed to have to depend on committing to untruths.

Her palms became damp as she removed another piece

of paper from the packet and began to write. When she had finished, she blotted it with blotting paper and handed it to Mrs Spode, who gave her another task.

'Here's one for you – to write a letter from a decayed gentleman, a distressed scholar, asking only for the money to cover coach hire so he can take up his new appointment in Bermondsey or Wandsworth, or wherever you will so long as it's in London. I shall need at least five copies, identical.'

'Why?' Agnes asked.

'One as a record for our business, one record for himself, and one . . . never you mind. You'd do well to mind your own business.'

Her pen fair flew across the paper by the time she was writing the third and fourth copy, and she was just completing the fifth, when she felt a pressure against the toe of her shoe. She looked up to find Jeannie shaking her head almost imperceptibly and frowning with disapproval. She waited until Mrs Spode had left the room and whispered, 'It isn't right that you go so fast. Think of me, Mr Riley and Mr Fletcher here.'

'Oh? Oh dear.'

'We have an agreement to share in the work. That way we all get paid at the end of the week. It can get very unpleasant if one person should act selfish and spoil it for the others. Do you get my meaning?'

'Yes. I'm sorry.' Agnes bit her lip as Mrs Spode returned through the door. She blotted the fifth copy and handed all five to her.

'Now, let's see you provide a fakement. A gentleman of my acquaintance has asked for a petition complete with witnesses and supporters.'

'Where will I go to find these people?' Agnes asked.

Mrs Spode laughed, and even Mr Fletcher quirked an eyebrow.

'Why, you are a strange young woman. You write them yourself, all in different hands, of course. The gentleman who asks for the petition hasn't the time or inclination to go and ask for that many signatures. He's prepared to pay two guineas to have it filled in for him.'

'I can't be part of this deception,' Agnes exclaimed. 'It's wrong. It's immoral.'

'It's a living, and a good one at that. And it isn't hurting anyone. If we don't screeve for these people, they will find someone else to do it. The gentleman is very much occupied with his other business. He cannot do everything himself. He would do if he could, I am sure of it.'

Agnes couldn't believe her ears. Why didn't anyone say anything? Remembering though that she had to pay her rent and find money for food, she kept her mouth firmly shut.

Later that day when Mrs Spode had shut up shop, she walked back along the road towards the centre of Canterbury with Jeannie.

'Don't you think that it's dishonest to write fakements with forged signatures? And begging letters?' Agnes asked quietly.

'Inviting a person who has so much income they cannot possibly spend it in their lifetime to spend a few guineas? I can't see anything wrong with that,' Jeannie said. 'That's the way the Spodes do things. That couple have had thirty years on the monkery.'

'But doesn't it make you feel uneasy?' Agnes went on. 'How do you reconcile it with your conscience?'

'Ha!' Jeannie exclaimed. 'I cannot afford to have a conscience. None of us can.' She frowned. 'You aren't going to report this to the authorities? I don't want to lose my position because someone has squealed.'

'Oh no, I'm not intending to do any such thing.'

'That's good to hear, Agnes, because this is our livelihood.

We and our families depend on it. I work hard on weekdays and Saturdays, and on Sundays I go to church and pray for a dose of forgiveness for any sins I have committed during the previous seven days. It's worked for me so far.'

Agnes didn't know how she got through the first week, sitting at the table in the screevers' office all day, six days a week. By Sunday, her back ached and her eyes were sore, and she'd only just recovered from the week before when she had to start all over again.

On the Monday evening after work, she ran into a small boy on her way back into the lodging house. He was struggling to carry a bucket of flies and sticky, rotting flesh.

'Arthur?' she said, holding her hand to her nose.

'Yes, missus. Oh—' He peered at her, the whites of his eyes bright against the grime on the rest of his face. 'I know who you are.' He grinned. 'You're a friend of Miss Treen's and the Cheeverses at Willow Place. You was there when I almost drownded.'

She recalled Oliver diving into the water and bringing the boy back in his arms.

'You were very lucky that day. What is that in your bucket?' she asked.

'Trimmin's. Ma said to bring them home so she could see if she could do anything with them, but she says they're only fit for the dogs.' His eyes began to glaze with tears. 'It's all above board, miss. I'm not a thief.'

'I wasn't suggesting for a moment that you were.'

'I have a proper job at the tannery like my brother 'ad – Mr Cheevers pays me for the work I do.'

'How is your brother?'

''E's gorn to seek his fortune in London. You know, missus, you look very different from when I last saw you.'

'It's true. I'm much changed,' she said.

Arthur sniffed and wiped his nose on the back of his hand. 'I live upstairs with Ma.'

'Mrs Fortune?' Agnes surmised.

'That's right. Why, your hands are dirty. The last time we met you were wearing white gloves.'

'It is ink,' Agnes said, showing him her palms.

'You are a screever. You are working for the Spodes – sometimes, if I'm lucky, I run errands for them. I shall tell Mr Cheevers that I've sin you.'

'No, please don't. I would rather remain anonymous. I am seeking a quiet life.'

'You don't want anyone to know where you are? What happened to your grand house and fine clothes?'

'I lost them,' she said.

'That was very careless of you,' he said severely.

'It was,' she agreed, thinking of all the mistakes and wrong turns she had taken on her way to the slums of Canterbury. She hoped he would keep quiet about her turning up there. The last thing she wanted was for the Cheeverses, and Oliver in particular, to see how she'd fallen on hard times.

Agnes continued to work at the screevers' and lodge with Mrs Hamilton. It was barely tolerable, but Mrs Hamilton turned out to be kind in an odd sort of way. She seemed to take pity on a lost soul, although she charged her for everything.

The next rent day, having screeved for another week, she paid her landlady, counting out the shillings from her purse.

'Will there be any change?' she asked.

'Of course there won't,' Mrs Hamilton said, smiling. 'You look shocked, dearie.'

'I thought I would have a little more left to tide me over for the rest of the week.'

'They don't call rent day black Monday for nothing,' Mrs Hamilton said. 'You are an intelligent woman, Mrs Linnet. Mrs Spode said so when I called on her the other day.'

Agnes had spotted her in the screevers' office. She had paid for a fakement of some kind that Jeannie had written up for her.

'I won't pry into what you are paid, but as an example, when you work for six or seven shillings a week, and you pay five shillings in rent, what does that leave you?' Agnes waited for Mrs Hamilton to continue, 'It's a case of simple subtraction, one minus the other.'

'One or two shillings, of course.'

'That's for the rest, wittles, beer and laundry. Oh dear, you seem to 'ave led a sheltered life. You get down to the market on market day, and buy the cheapest items you can find, the end of a cheese, onions that are on the turn and offal, the sweetbreads and plucks. Barter before you hand over your precious coins, and walk away if they don't come down on the price. Pawn your jewellery if you 'ave any, and sell anything you 'ave to spare. Make sure you pick up any rags and rubbish from the streets – the law of finders keepers applies around here.'

'I don't think I should like to do that,' Agnes stammered.

'Beggars can't be choosers. It's what everyone has to do in order to scratch a living.' Mrs Hamilton glanced towards Agnes's belly. 'You can always give up the infant after it's born. I could use a worker, someone to help me around the house. I mean, I'm not growing any younger. A small child will 'ave an appetite to match its stature, and will take up little room. I like that idea. A sweet and joyful companion. Oh, I can see that you are not partial to the suggestion, but you'll soon change your mind when you 'ave a squalling brat with a dirty bum.'

'Thank you for your offer, but no. I will manage.'

'Well, you say that now . . . There, I've given you my advice. Like it or lump it. It's up to you.' Mrs Hamilton gazed at her through narrowed eyes. 'If you're expecting to rise up again to where you was before, like cream to the top of the jug, you'll be disappointed. I'd recommend that you make every effort to find contentment with your lot, or you'll be unhappy for ever.'

Agnes returned to her room and cried. She would have liked a clock, one that chimed the hours and gave comfort through its steady ticking, and a rug to cover the cold stone floor, but she knew that she'd never be able to afford them if she stayed working for the Spodes and remained at Mrs Hamilton's paying out all her income on food and rent.

She followed the example of some of the other residents, smoking herrings in the privy. She bought a shawl for work from the market, something less ostentatious than her usual attire. She also purchased a few rags and did some sewing in the evenings to create clothes which she then sold on at another stall. It didn't bring in much extra, but it helped. She needed a nest egg for when the baby came.

She made watercress soup, and bought sheep's trotters from the trotter sellers, and the cheapest bread she could find, a few days old and blue with mould. All the food she ate tasted sour, but beggars couldn't be choosers, she thought bitterly.

What had been the point of learning about Paris and Rome? The thought of the heat of the sun on her back, and the delicacies that could be sought abroad, made her even more discontent with the slim pickings that she managed to obtain in Canterbury.

She wrote to Evie with her address in the hope that she would send one or two of her belongings to her – her house slippers and the etiquette book which Nanny had given her. She needed the slippers to keep her feet warm on the cold floor at her lodgings and she thought she might be able to sell the book for a small sum. She disguised her handwriting in an attempt to fool Pell, who no doubt would be up to his usual tricks, censoring the mail at Roper House. She posted the letter and waited, unsure if she would ever receive a reply.

For the first time, she understood what Catherine, her true mother, must have gone through, alone on the streets and with child. Now Agnes was just one step away from the workhouse with her own child growing in her belly. In spite of the rather blunt reassurances that Mrs Hamilton offered at every opportunity, Agnes was scared for her future. What would happen when she was too far gone to work? How would she support herself and her baby then?

# 1859

# Chapter Twenty-Three

## *Powers of Persuasion*

By March, Agnes had been settled in Canterbury for almost three months. One morning, she sat with Jeannie, Mr Riley and Mr Fletcher at the screevers' office, her table empty of work.

'It is quiet again,' Jeannie remarked.

'It is getting worrying,' Mr Fletcher said as Mrs Spode emerged from the back room, carrying a stack of newspapers.

'We are short of work,' Mrs Spode said. 'We will have to use our initiative. Mr Riley, you are no longer required.'

'Oh?' He frowned.

'There's no point in you sitting here twiddling your thumbs. I'm doing you a favour. I could keep you here until business picks up, or I can let you go so you can find more lucrative employment.'

'I don't want to leave. How am I going to pay for my tobacco?'

'That isn't my problem,' Mrs Spode said.

'Whatever happened to the principle of last in, first out?' he went on, his cheeks high with colour. He stared at Agnes. 'It's her who should be gone.'

'She is our best screever, I'll have you know,' Mrs Spode said. 'Mr Spode has looked at the figures, and Mrs Linnet's techniques of persuasion bring in a far better return than yours do. When she writes, she puts herself in the shoes of the person who has fallen on hard times with great conviction. Her letters to potential wealthy patrons induce substantial benevolence. They are utterly believable, while yours are rather amateur.'

'That isn't fair,' Mr Riley said. 'Screeving is my profession and I take great pride in my work. If you let me go, you'll be cutting off your nose to spite your face.'

'It's a case of pure economics,' Mrs Spode insisted. 'Goodbye, Mr Riley.'

Agnes felt uncomfortable as her colleague packed his pens and paper and stood up to leave. Poor Mr Riley – she didn't like him much for his cocky attitude, but she felt sorry for him. She was wracked with guilt as well at having to practise such deception.

As soon as he was out of the door, Mrs Spode dropped the newspapers in his place at the table. She sat down and put on her pince-nez. She took the first paper and opened it, checking through the pages.

'Ah, here is another poor soul recently departed from us.'

'The obituaries are a goldmine of opportunities,' Mr Fletcher said.

'Indeed. Mrs Linnet – I require you to write a letter to the dead gentleman himself to appeal to his family's conscience and generosity, along the lines of, "Dear kind and honoured benefactor of mine. The money you sent me last is all expended. Our child is in need of clothes and education. A few hundred pounds will be all that is needed for now. Please send care of Mr Spode of Canterbury where we have settled as you requested, out of sight, but not out of mind, I trust. Your ever loving friend, Helen Gray."'

'But you have obtained the name from an obituary – this imaginary lady's benefactor is dead.'

'Which is perfect for our ends. I know of this man – he

was generous in life and his relatives will wish to honour his memory by continuing that after his death. The grieving relatives cannot question the deceased about what could turn out to be one of many indiscretions that he committed during his life.' Mrs Spode turned to Mr Fletcher. 'I think you should apply to the estate for a donation to a charitable trust of your choice, and of your imagination.'

He smiled and took up his pen.

'Mrs Cotton, I think a distant relative, or a long-lost acquaintance, might be in touch to apply for aid.'

'Of course, Mrs Spode,' Jeannie said with a smile.

'I will read you the addresses to which you will make your applications.'

Agnes grabbed a piece of paper and her pen, and dipped the nib in the inkwell.

'Mrs Linnet, you will apply directly to Mr Samuel Cheevers . . .'

Agnes felt sick. The kindly Mr Cheevers was dead. Nanny's uncle, the head of the happy family at Willow Place, was gone, and now she was being forced to insult his memory by making up a lie against him.

'I too know of this man,' she said.

'It isn't surprising. He's been well known in this area for many years,' Mrs Spode said. 'He's always been poking his nose in where it's not needed.'

'He has done many good works,' Agnes said, defending him. 'He would never have done what you're suggesting.'

'Whether he's done it or not is irrelevant. You will screeve as I have requested, or you know what you can do. You have a rebellious streak, Mrs Linnet. Don't make me regret sending Mr Riley on his way.'

She didn't know what to do. Black Monday would be upon her after the weekend and the rent would be due. If she refused to write the letter, she wouldn't be able to pay Mrs Hamilton and she would be out on the streets. If she continued to give in to Mrs Spode's wicked demands, she was as bad as she was. If they were caught, she would go to prison, and at the final day of judgement, she would go to Hell. She shuddered as the baby squirmed inside her, reinforcing the seriousness of her predicament. Either way, she thought, she was damned.

She glanced towards Mr Fletcher, who had his head bowed over his paper, and his tongue sticking out as he concentrated on his piece of fakery. She turned to Jeannie.

'Mr Cheevers wasn't short of a bob or two,' she said. 'Where there's muck there's brass.'

'Well said, Mrs Cotton,' Mrs Spode said. 'He took pleasure in sharing his good fortune. Now, Mrs Linnet, are you with us on this?'

What could she do?

'Yes,' she said.

'I trust that this really is the end of this nonsense and you will not breathe a word of our work here when you are away from the office.'

'Of course.'

'Good.' Mrs Spode shook her head, dispersing a cloud of powder from her hair. 'Some people don't know which side their bread is buttered.'

Agnes bit her tongue. She couldn't afford butter, only dripping to spread on her bread.

She began to write. What had happened to Samuel? He hadn't been well when she'd last seen him. She wished she could have paid her respects, but that would have been impossible. Someone – Nanny, Temperance or Oliver – would have recognised her at the graveside. Her sentences blurred in front of her. She brushed away a tear. The Cheeverses had given her a glimpse of a happiness that she would never forget.

Yet here she was in the middle of a concerted attempt to defraud them.

'Mrs Linnet,' Mrs Spode's voice cut in. 'You have blotted your work. That isn't good enough. Start again.'

She put the spoiled paper aside and took a fresh piece. She wrote, her pen like a weapon against the Cheeverses. She was sullying the good name of a true gentleman who couldn't defend himself. She was stripping Oliver and Temperance of their inheritance because she knew that they would do the right thing by a poor woman who had been taken advantage of. They would give her the benefit of the doubt, she thought, and pay up. She wondered about the tannery and the workers there. The money that came in by their efforts would go to feather the Spodes' already luxurious nest.

She wrestled with her conscience as she continued to write. If she squealed on the Spodes, Mr Fletcher and Mrs Cotton would be obliged to find other employment. They'd been lucky not to have been caught out before. It occurred to her that she could set up a new, honest screeving business with them. They could work anywhere – they wouldn't need an office at first, then when they became known and demand grew, she could rent one in the High Street.

She finished the letter and signed it, 'Your ever loving friend, Agnes Berry-Clay'.

She blotted the ink, folded the paper and sealed it with wax and a wafer. She wrote the address on the front and handed the completed missive to Mrs Spode.

'Thank you, Mrs Linnet. I'm glad you've seen sense. We will send this one by the penny post, and await the response. If it is positive, then maybe another bastard child or two may find their way out of the woodwork.'

The boy, Arthur, came to collect the letters a little while later.

'He is the perfect errand boy,' Mrs Spode said as he left the office with the post tucked in a bag which he carried over his shoulder. 'Reliable, quick, available, and best of all, he can't read to save his life.' She began to peruse the newspaper again. 'It's a good time of year for us. I see that the senior partner at the solicitors on Bargate Street has dropped off his perch – we must make hay while the sun shines.'

Agnes continued writing. She had done her best. If Oliver or Temperance opened the letter, they would recognise her name. It would certainly make them question the facts as laid down according to Mrs Spode. She hoped that it would be enough to stop them throwing their money away at least.

When she went back to her lodgings, Mrs Hamilton was all of a flutter.

'A woman called here today, looking for you. I kept my silence, Mrs Linnet – I wasn't sure you wanted to be found.'

Who was it? Could it be Evie sent from Roper House? Had Felix had a change of heart? No, of course not. She chastised herself for thinking of him. Why was there still a tiny part of her that wished he would come when she knew that it was over and she would probably never see him again?

'She gave her name. Now what was it? Oh yes – Miss Treen.'

It was Nanny, Agnes thought, her spirits lifting at the mention of her name.

'You were right not to reveal my whereabouts,' she said.

Her landlady seemed to be expecting something, a gesture of appreciation, perhaps. Agnes gave her a coin from her reticule. Mrs Hamilton smiled.

'While you're at it, I could do with an advance on your board and lodging – the butcher has sent me his bill. If you see your way to . . .'

'Of course,' Agnes hesitated, 'but just to confirm that it is an advance.'

'Don't you worry, I'll write it down in the rent book. You are too kind, Mrs Linnet.'

She was too considerate for her own good, she realised as she examined the remaining contents of her purse, because in doing Mrs Hamilton a favour, she had run herself short.

Several days passed. At the weekend, Agnes searched for Samuel's grave, finding it in the cemetery at Thanington. On the last Monday in March, she paid the rent and went to work as usual on the Tuesday, when Mrs Spode gave her a petition to write, including signatures, numbering at least fifty.

When she was halfway through, the doorbell jangled and the door flew open. Three men and a boy came rushing in.

'Stay in your seats,' one of the men shouted. 'Where are the Spodes?'

'Through there,' Jeannie said, pointing to the door into their inner sanctum. She grabbed up her papers and stuffed them into her bag. 'I haven't done nothing wrong.'

The first man went through to the Spodes' living quarters.

The second man moved towards the table and snatched up Agnes's paperwork.

'Here's another fake petition,' he said.

The third man, Oliver Cheevers, leaned back against the exit door to block the way.

'Do as you're told and no one will get hurt,' he said.

Agnes began to panic. She was in the mire now, along with the others.

'We're all going down. Someone has snitched on us.' Mr Fletcher tore his paper into tiny pieces, and stuffed them in his mouth.

'Who can that be?' Jeannie stared at Agnes, but she didn't flinch. 'You've gorn and done it now.'

'None of you are in trouble,' Oliver said. 'We want the Spodes.' He acknowledged Agnes with the briefest of smiles, then addressed the second man. She had a vague memory that she had seen him before, one of the workers at the tannery.

The first man reappeared with Mrs Spode walking meekly behind him.

'Where is your husband?' Oliver asked.

'He has taken to his bed with the shock of your false accusations,' she said. 'We run our business with the purest of motives, to provide a service to those who cannot screeve themselves. I don't understand this interruption at all.'

'I've served the papers on them, sir,' the first man said. 'They will come voluntarily in front of the court as arranged.'

'What if we don't agree with your papers?' Mrs Spode said.

'Then you'll be arrested,' Oliver said. 'You are accused of fakery, fraud and corruption. I have proof that you have tried to extort money by preying on dead men's estates with lies and falsehoods. It is well known around here that you provide fake petitions and set up new identities for crooks.'

'We do nothing of the sort. Now, go away. You are causing a stir outside.'

Agnes glanced towards the window, where a small crowd were looking in, pressing their noses against the glass as they pushed and shoved to get a better view.

'In that case, you will attend court to clear your names,' Oliver said.

'Everyone out,' Mrs Spode said. 'Go! All of you.'

Agnes made her way out of the office and on to the pavement with Mr Fletcher and Mrs Cotton. Mr Fletcher spat out the paper that was left in his mouth. Agnes and Jeannie looked back at the door where Oliver's associates came out first, followed by Oliver himself.

'Thanks for that,' Jeannie said. 'What am I supposed to do now? I have a sick husband at home. I need the money.'

Oliver stepped across to them, put his hand in his pocket and pulled out a few coins. He handed them over to her.

'I'm sorry,' he said. 'Those people have taken advantage of you as well, leading you into their life of crime, and taking all the profits.'

'I'm an honest woman,' Jeannie cried. 'Thank you for your kindness, sir.'

'Go home,' he said gently.

Agnes looked around. Mr Fletcher had gone, disappearing into the crowd. Arthur had vanished too.

'Don't take pity on that snitch,' Jeannie hissed. 'It has to be her who done it, told on us. We was all right till she came along. Since then, Mr Riley got the push and now you've turned up. It's no coincidence.'

'She is no traitor,' Oliver said.

'She is a whore,' she heard Jeannie go on. 'She has a bellyful of child, and if she knows who the father is, she won't let on. She pretends to be one of us, but she i'n't. She's snootier than Queen Victoria herself.'

'You don't know her,' Oliver said, his voice fading as Agnes retreated along the street, pulling her hood over her head. She was deeply ashamed and embarrassed. What's more, she had lost her position and any chance of making a living. Why did doing something right to make up for her previous transgressions feel so very wrong? And, on a more prosaic and practical note, what on earth was she going to do instead?

# Chapter Twenty-Four

## *The Darkest Hour*

She made her way back to her lodgings to find Mrs Hamilton waiting for her on the doorstep with her arms folded across her chest and Agnes's bags in front of her. The landlady was wearing a scarlet dress which looked strangely familiar.

'I've heard that you are recently unemployed,' she said.

'How?'

'News travels fast around here. The boy came running back to tell his mother. She passed it on to me, knowing that I would 'ave an interest.'

'Why have you packed up my things?' Agnes feared that she knew very well why, but she asked anyway.

'Because you're out on your ear'ole, I'm afraid. I'm sorry, but I l'arned a long time ago that you 'ave to put yourself first. Nobody else will.'

'I've paid up for at least one more day, and I'll go back to fetch the wages I'm owed tomorrow. Mrs Hamilton, you can't do this to me.' Agnes clasped her hands together and begged her landlady to reconsider. 'My name isn't Mrs Linnet—'

'Well, I'd guessed that already,' Mrs Hamilton interrupted. 'Don't tell me – you're the long-lost daughter of a wealthy family and your father will come and pay me in gold and silver. I wasn't born yesterday, ducky. I've heard it all before. Now, don't waste my time. I'm sorry for you,' she repeated, 'but I 'ave another family ready to take your room.' She tipped her head to one side, her eyes gleaming with avarice. 'And I've managed to negotiate an extra shilling over the usual rate.'

'What can I do? Where shall I go?'

'It's nothing to do with me. You may go wherever you like.'

'I am without help.'

'I would help you if I could, but I'm terrible hard up at the moment. I've had to take the liberty of divesting you of some of your belongings to settle your bill from the extras you've had from me.'

Agnes tried playing on her compassion for a mother heavy with child, but Mrs Hamilton wouldn't be swayed. She didn't entirely blame her – there was no way she could find the rent money for the next week without her work at the screevers', and Mrs Hamilton had been offered extra in the way of rent. She had sacrificed her survival and that of her child for the truth. Had it been worth it? At this point, she doubted it. She had paid a heavy price for giving the screevers away to make up for her sins.

'Be gone then.' Mrs Hamilton began to shoo her away.

Agnes picked up her bags. The scarlet dress had disappeared. Now she realised why Mrs Hamilton's dress looked familiar. The hem had been dragged through the mud and the seams had burst at her waist. There was a piece of grubby lace untidily stitched to cover her bosom. There had been a time when Agnes would have been upset to see the dress in such a state, but now she didn't care. Mrs Hamilton was welcome to it. She didn't think she would have any need of it in the future. She wasn't sure she could see a future.

She hurried away as quickly as she could, feeling sick

and giddy, but something – sheer stubbornness and the will to survive – drove her on. Once or twice, she thought she heard someone following close behind her, but when she turned, there was no one there. She was tired and in shock, she thought. Her mind was playing tricks.

She tried to obtain a room at the Rose Hotel, but the manager refused her admission.

'We don't have women like you here,' he said.

'I'll have you know that my name is Mrs Faraday. I'm married to the heir of Roper House in Upper Harbledown.'

'Really.' The manager raised one eyebrow. 'Pull the other one.'

'But it's true.'

'Go away, miss. We run a respectable establishment. We don't want you here, disturbing our guests. Try Nunnery Fields, where you belong.'

'Where, sir?'

'Nunnery Fields – the workhouse.'

She might have been born in a workhouse, but she wasn't going back there. She would rather die than stoop that low. Her mother had been so desperate to escape the degrading conditions that she had sacrificed the bond between her and her child. She had given Agnes to the Berry-Clays for the chance of a better life, and Agnes knew very well that her mother's sacrifice would have been for nothing if she ended up back inside with the elderly, the infirm and the mad.

'I'm sorry for bothering you, sir.' She turned away and walked back along the street.

The rain began to pour down, obscuring her vision and soaking through her clothes, as she wandered, looking for shelter. She was accosted by soldiers who mocked her appearance. She bought coffee and a roll with cheese from a costermonger, and ate it on the street without a thought about who might be watching. She had lost her pride, and been careless with her money. She could have drunk water from the public water cock near the court hall and saved a few pennies.

She staggered on through the back alleys by the river, breathing in the foul odours from the tanneries and the glue factory. Night fell. She felt sick, weak and exhausted. Even the men looking for whores took one look at her and walked away.

She had lost everything: her wealth, status and self-respect. At the foot of the Westgate Towers, she sank to her knees. She tipped forwards and lay with her head against the wall and her feet in the gutter. The passing carts and carriages ignored her.

This was her darkest hour, she thought as she closed her eyes and begged the Lord to let her die quickly. The cold seeped into her bones. Her fingers and toes grew numb. The baby kicking inside her grew still. She must surely be dead, for when she opened her eyes there was no light, and the Hand of God was on her shoulder, shaking her, and saying, 'Miss, wake up. Please.'

She felt a pair of strong hands on her arms, rolling her on to one side until she could see the flickering lights of Heaven through her eyelids.

'That's her, sir,' she heard a boy say. 'I followed her like you said. She led me a merry dance all the way round Canterbury.'

'Well, I'm very relieved that you stayed with her,' said a man's voice. 'There'll be another shilling or two in this for you, if you can help me assist her back to the house.'

So it wasn't God, then, she thought. The heavenly lights were the flickering flame of a lantern and there were two people – not apparitions – present.

'She has opened her eyes,' the boy said.

'Leave me alone,' she mumbled. 'I wish to die.'

'You are young yet, and with child. Fight for the infant who grows inside you. You mustn't give up. I won't let you,' the man added fiercely. 'Come with me. I promise I won't hurt you.'

'Mr Cheevers is a good man, a gentleman of the first order,' the boy's voice rang out.

'Thank you, Arthur. That will be enough comment upon my character.' She thought she detected some humour in the man's voice. She recognised him now. Oliver Cheevers. She wished she was already dead. What humiliation! Hadn't she suffered enough without exposing her fall from grace to someone whom she respected beyond measure? 'Arthur will accompany us – you have no reason to fear.'

'No, sir.' She coughed a racking, sobbing cough.

'This isn't done out of charity,' Arthur said, 'it's done out of the goodness of 'is 'eart.'

'I will stay here and accept my punishment. I have committed the most terrible sins.'

'No,' Oliver said, 'you've suffered enough. We all have. Poor Arthur is shivering to death. I will hear no more of this nonsense. You will come home with me and we will sort out the whys and wherefores later. I will have to drag or carry you if you continue to resist. Arthur, help me lift her.'

She drifted in and out of consciousness as the man and boy helped her to her feet. When she next came round, Oliver's arms were supporting her as he carried her through the streets.

'Run ahead of us with the lantern, boy, so that we can see where we're going.'

She must have been quite a weight, but Oliver didn't complain once, although his breathing was coming hard and heavy by the time they reached Willow Place. She heard him grunt as he handed the boy a key to unlock the front door.

The door latch clicked and Oliver carried her over the threshold into the house. He tried to let her down, but her legs trembled, unable to hold her weight, and he caught her up again and held her against him, her head against his chest. She could hear his heartbeat, slow and steady.

'Light the candles. There are spills and matches in the box over there. We will take her straight upstairs – she can have Samuel's room.' He carried her up the spiral staircase to the top of the house and placed her gently on the bed. 'Arthur, light the fire and fetch hot water from the kitchen. And find another blanket or two – they should be in the linen cupboard on the landing.'

'Steady on, sir. I can't remember all these instructions at once.'

'One thing at a time, then.' Oliver smiled. At least, Agnes thought he was smiling from the sound of his voice. As she sank back into the pillow, she felt the foot of the mattress sink too. She looked along the bed. Oliver's hands were at her ankle, unlacing her boot.

'Please, don't,' she said weakly. She might be dying, but she refused to die of embarrassment by revealing the sight of her flesh to him.

'Your stockings are soaked through, and there is no woman in the house,' he said matter-of-factly as she heard the boy strike the tinderbox.

'Where is your housekeeper?' she asked.

'Ah, Mrs Hill has left.'

'This is most improper, then. You have put yourself in a situation by taking me in. Your neighbours will talk.'

'Let them,' he said. 'You aren't the first waif and stray that the Cheeverses have taken in.'

'But I'm the worst, the most immoral and dishonest.'

'I'm not saying that I don't care about my reputation.' He placed her boots on the floor and moved round to the head of the bed. 'But I'd rather be known for my compassion than a blind eye. I can't let you back on the streets at this time of night and in your condition – I couldn't have it on my conscience. You may leave in the morning, if you must, although you are more than welcome to stay on until you are well and have some means of supporting yourself. In fact, I'd recommend the latter course of action.'

The scent of coal-smoke began to fill the room.

'What would Marjorie say if she found out that I'd let you go?' She felt fingers holding her lightly around one wrist. 'Look at you – you have no flesh on you at all.'

'How long shall I 'ave to stay?' she heard the boy ask.

'Oh, your ma will be wondering where you are,' Oliver said. 'Forgive me. I'd forgotten that she will be sitting up alone and waiting for your return. Why don't you take some pie from the larder, and then make your way home?'

'Thank you, sir. And the shillings?'

He smiled softly. 'It's all right. I hadn't forgotten.' He slipped his hand into his pocket and took out a couple of coins which he dropped into Arthur's outstretched palm. 'Come back to the house first thing tomorrow morning. I'll need you here, not at the yard.'

Agnes didn't remember much else from then on. She drifted off, then woke to find someone encouraging her to drink from a cup of warm, sweet tea, before she fell asleep again. The next time she woke, a searing daylight had found its way between the drapes. She turned away to face the wall and threw off the bedclothes as a wave of heat swept through her body. She felt the baby move inside her and knew nothing more until she heard voices. She didn't know how long she had been lying there, insensible, but she was half awake now and aware that there were two people in the room with her.

'What were you thinking? You should have left her – she's too far gone.'

'She was in a better state than this when I picked her up from the gutter,' Oliver said. 'She's gone downhill since.'

'She should be in the Kent and Canterbury hospital,' came a woman's voice. 'They will take her if you agree to sponsor her.'

'I was hoping that you would take it upon yourself to nurse her,' she heard Oliver say. 'I can't do it myself, considering the circumstances.'

'Indeed. You have got yourself into a bit of a bind, my dear brother. What were you thinking of? She's a dirty whore.'

'Temperance, I told you, this woman isn't a stranger to us. She's Miss Berry-Clay. Marjorie used to be her nanny. We saw her only recently, within the past year.'

Agnes curled herself into a ball. Temperance was right. She had as good as sold her body, offering it up to Master Faraday in return for his love, and ultimately, his fortune.

'Oh, her?' Her tone was one of disbelief. 'How can that possibly be?'

'She's fallen on hard times. I told you before – Arthur found her working for the Spodes.'

'I don't care what she was doing. What if this is cholera? There has been one outbreak after another. You have no right putting us all in danger by bringing her here.'

'She's half-starved and exhausted,' Oliver argued. 'She has caught a chill. She needs warmth, good food and a little compassion.'

'You are a fool,' Temperance said. 'Nothing good will come of this.'

'Sometimes I wonder how you can be my sister.'

'You are too soft. She won't appreciate your generosity. She's been brought up a spoiled young woman.'

'I will treat her like everyone else of our acquaintance – fairly and with kindness. She must be terrified, poor soul.'

'She's to blame for her situation. If I'd had money to give away and fine clothes, I'd have done everything to hold on to them. Look how she's wasted the opportunities she's been given.'

'She must have had her reasons for choosing the path she's taken. When she's fully recovered, I'll find her some kind of employment so she can get back on her feet and look after her child. It's what our grandfather would have wanted – and expected.'

'Then you are even more stupid than I thought.'

'If you won't help, then I'll ask Arthur's mother, Mrs Fortune.'

'Oh no, don't do that. I'll do it in Grandpa's memory, under sufferance.'

'Thank you. Please, send the boy to fetch a doctor, and go out and buy the ingredients to make a gruel: a chicken and some carrots from the market. I'll stay with her until you return.'

Agnes heard the swish of her skirts as she left the room, but she was aware of little else that day. She had the vague impression of a doctor attending to bleed her, and of Temperance washing her face and arms to reduce her fever.

'I've got better things to be doing than saving the life of a guttersnipe,' she grumbled. 'You'd be better off dead with a child on the way and no husband. I've told my brother – he's wasting his time and money. *Our* money.'

Agnes couldn't bear to hear any more. She hadn't chosen to impose on Oliver's hospitality.

She was grateful, though. It had occurred to her on the

night that he and Arthur had rescued her, that she might have lost the baby, but since then it had kicked and squirmed inside her, an innocent child who deserved the chance of life. She began to pray that God would have mercy on her and the infant, and she would make a full recovery.

Within three days, Agnes felt better. Her limbs were still heavy with the after-effects of the fever, but she was on the mend. She pulled herself out of bed with some difficulty. She was only about eight months gone, but she felt like a beached sea creature. She smiled to herself, recalling the natural history book from the library at Roper House, which had contained an engraving of an enormous blue whale. She wondered how the sisters were, and Felix. No, she wouldn't let his legacy taint the rest of her life. She would make up for her sins, one way or another.

Her clothes had been laundered and left on the chair beside the bed. She got dressed and then looked in the gilded mirror on the wall. Her reflection stared back.

Mrs Agnes Ivy Linnet. A widow. Twenty years old. She ran her fingers through her long dark locks and put them up into an untidy plait.

She pulled the curtains open and looked out at the sunshine and the weeping willows at the river's edge at the bottom of the garden. There was a magpie sitting on the railings. One for sorrow . . . she thought. Then another landed beside its mate. 'Two for joy . . .'

She headed downstairs, hoping that she wouldn't run into Oliver or Temperance.

'Where are you going?'

She stopped in her tracks when Oliver appeared in front of her in the hallway.

'I'm going to get the money I'm owed from the Spodes.

I owe you for my board and lodgings,' she stammered. It was true. She'd been planning to drop it off at Willow Place before moving on.

'You aren't going anywhere. You aren't well.'

'I'm well enough.'

'Besides, I have bad news on the Spode front – the day after the magistrate served the papers on them, they packed up their belongings and fled. They took a coach to London, I believe.' He sighed. 'I'm afraid they'll set up another office there and go on as before. We did our best to stop them, but it wasn't enough.'

'I can't stay here, Oliver, imposing on you and your sister. It pains me that I am a source of discord between you and Temperance.'

'Don't worry,' he said lightly, 'there is nothing that we agree on.'

'What I've done is unforgivable,' she went on. 'As I've said before, you've put your reputation at risk by letting me stay here.' She gazed at him, her throat tightening with emotion. He was a good man, far too good for the likes of her.

He chuckled. 'And I've told you before that I don't care what people think of me. My grandfather taught me that it doesn't matter. Those that deserve your regard are those who in return have a high regard for you. To admire where admiration has not been earned is a waste of time and energy.' He grew serious again. 'Of course, it's easier now that Temperance is married. I wouldn't have wanted anything to affect her chances of making a good match.'

'What about you? What about your chances of marriage? I think that your sweetheart would find it hard to accept that you have an unmarried woman living in your house.'

'I have no sweetheart, more's the pity. My grandfather once had his eye on a young lady for me, but there were too many obstacles in our way. She was set above me in society and we met rarely, only on a handful of occasions. I was – I still am – very fond of her and hold her in high esteem, but I have no idea how she feels about me. I don't think that it would ever cross her mind that I'd be a possible match, considering the stink in which I make my living.'

'I wish I had come back to see Samuel,' she said softly.

'I miss him. I try to think of his passing as a blessing – he was suffering terribly.' His eyes glittered with tears. 'You could have come back,' he said, recovering his composure. 'Arthur said that he'd seen you in Can'erbury, but we didn't believe him at first. He's very fond of making things up. But when he said again that he'd met you at the screevers' while he was running errands for Mrs Spode, I made some enquiries.

'Everyone knew they were on the take. Everyone – except for my grandfather and the poor blighters who were being conned – turned a blind eye.' Oliver frowned. 'You've made mistakes. We all do that. It's part of the human condition. If you don't make errors, how can you learn to do things right? I'm grateful for what you did, signing that begging letter with your true name. It alerted my attention and gave me the proof I needed to take to the magistrate. My grandfather had railed against the Spodes for years, begged them and tried before to close down their business, or at least get them to resort to honest screeving to make a living.'

'They've lived a comfortable life on their ill-gotten gains, and I'm sorry that I was part of it.' Agnes hung her head. 'I was taken in at first. It seemed an honest profession and one that I could take up.' She looked down at her belly – there was absolutely no hiding it now, stays or no stays. 'Within a day I'd realised my mistake. They asked me to fake a petition and scribe a begging letter copied out five times. I am ashamed that I continued working there so long, but – it is no excuse – I was trapped. I had no money, no resources to fall back on. The Spodes directed me to Mrs Hamilton's lodgings and naively, I let her charge me over the odds. I didn't know any better – I wasn't brought up to be streetwise like the other tatterdemalions around here.

'Oh, I'm not saying I'm better than them,' she added quickly, in case he had misunderstood.

'I know,' he said.

She gazed at him. His eyes were dark and soft. There had been a time when she would never have shared any personal details about her life, but she felt safe with Oliver because she knew that he would hold his tongue. She trusted him.

'Come and sit down in my grandfather's study. We can talk,' he said, and she followed him into the room where he plumped up the cushions on the window seat. 'Sit down.'

She took her place in the window. The sunshine streamed through the glass, and a duck quacked outside.

'Tell me more,' he said, turning the desk chair round to face her and sitting down.

'I wish I'd looked further for work. By the time I'd paid Mrs Hamilton for board and lodging, and bought the materials I needed from the Spodes, I had little left over.'

'I understand your reasons for doing what you did. You are with child. You would do anything for the infant's sake.' Her eyes flooded with tears as he continued, 'I believe that the love a mother feels for her child is one of the most powerful feelings in the world.'

'I don't deserve your forgiveness, sir.'

'For goodness' sake, call me Oliver. Let's have no more of this "sir" business.'

'Thank you. I brought this all upon myself. When I left Windmarsh, I thought I was making the right decision—'

'Marjorie came to stay with my grandfather, if you recall. She told us a little of why you were leaving – that you'd left Windmarsh because you had been betrothed against your will to your cousin.'

'Philip wished to become a doctor and it would have been a torment for both of us to have been forced into being husband and wife according to his father's wishes. I had no choice but to walk out on my old life. Nanny was a good friend to me. She found me my place at Roper House.' It was ironic to think that she could also have been the means of her leaving it through the letter she'd sent, if Agnes hadn't become involved with Master Faraday. 'I let her down with my subsequent actions, which were entirely of my own free will.'

'You did take up the position of governess?' Oliver said. 'I saw the advertisement – my aunt didn't keep anything from us.'

Agnes nodded. She was even more ashamed when he continued, 'I remember that day when you refused to acknowledge me. You were walking through Can'erbury with two young ladies—'

'Yes, my charges,' she cut in.

'And two rather obnoxious gentlemen,' Oliver added.

She blushed. 'I'm sorry for my rudeness.'

'I'm sure you had your reasons.'

'I've been very stupid. I allowed . . . the young master . . . to seduce me. I knew it was wrong, but I thought it was love. Alas, it turned out not to be on his part. He offered marriage – I thought I was promised to him – but when he discovered I was with child and my true identity, he cut all ties. He promised me the earth and gave me nothing but grief. He has betrayed me and disowned the child.'

She pulled her handkerchief from her pocket and dabbed her eyes. 'I must apologise for my weakness, in revealing too much of myself.'

'You're still fond of this man,' Oliver said gently.

'No, not after what he's done to me. I've been a fool, but I thought . . . Oh, what's done can't be undone. I shouldn't have been so frank with you. I can see that you are disgusted.'

'Not at all. I'm rather disturbed that there are men out there who purport to be gentlemen yet turn out to be cads. It gives us all a bad name. You aren't the first to be deceived and you won't be the last by a long way.'

'Nobody is perfect,' she said.

'That's true. When I first saw you as a girl with my cousin, and dressed all in white, I thought you must be the sweetest, most generous person, incapable of having a single bad thought, but' – he smiled wryly – 'your attitude to Bert, Arthur's brother, soon disabused me of that idea.'

'I harboured wrong inside me. I blamed the poor for their poverty. I despised them for their dirty hands and faces, and their ragged clothes. And I'm truly repentant now, because I know what it is like to have nothing. I've lived from hand to mouth. I've mended my own clothes.'

'I didn't mean to be critical. What I was trying to say is that you're right. Everyone has their imperfections. That's what makes us human.' He lowered his voice. 'It's our differences that make us . . . well, endearing, I suppose.'

'You are too good, Oliver.'

'I'm an ordinary man,' he said.

Far from it, she thought. He was special. He wasn't some shallow young gentleman, only interested in his own pleasures, like Felix had been.

'You must stay and rest some more,' he went on. 'There

is food in the larder. Treat my house as your home for a while longer.'

'I'm very grateful, but what can I do in return for your hospitality? I have to do something.'

'Not today, Agnes. You mustn't think of lifting a finger until you are fully recovered. Put your child first.'

Oliver turned and left, closing the door behind him. She looked out of the window at the neatly trimmed lawns, the borders filled with daffodils and hyacinths, and the painted veranda with the clematis coming into bud. She couldn't take advantage of Oliver's gallantry for much longer. He had more than enough to do, running the house and the tannery, and continuing his grandfather's charitable works. In the meantime, she had to make a plan, but the longer she sat there, the more hopeless her prospects seemed to become.

# Chapter Twenty-Five

## *One for Sorrow, Two for Joy*

One thing was certain – she wouldn't depend on Oliver Cheevers for any longer than necessary. The next day, Agnes slipped out after he'd left for the tannery. She tied the ribbons on her bonnet and made her way down to the gate and on to the street where the overnight rain had washed away some of the dirt and filth. She had nothing, neither money nor anything else to exchange or barter with, and as she continued along St Peter's into town, she couldn't find anything she could pick up to sell.

She looked in the shop windows for work. There was one place for a baker, but when she walked in to apply, the owner laughed in her face. Shaking her head, she left and walked back along the river, hardly noticing the stench as the noxious gases bubbled up through the silt. She felt restless – no longer did she yearn to live a life of quiet repose. She wanted – no, needed – to keep busy. She was a young woman who had much to give.

Returning to Willow Place, she hesitated at the tannery gates.

She spotted the boy, Arthur, helping one of the workmen haul a heavy hide out of the pits. He looked small, scrawny and hungry, she thought. When the hide was submerged in the next pit along, he came over to her.

'Hello, missus,' he said, shading his eyes from the sun. 'You look better.'

'And it's thanks to you,' she said. 'I know that you followed me that night and that you ran back and told Mr Cheevers of my plight. But for you, I would have died in the gutter. One kindness deserves another, but I don't know how to reward you.'

'A shillin' would be useful,' he said hopefully. 'I 'aven't had anything to eat since last night.'

'I have no money, but I'm sure Oliver won't mind if I bring you some food from the house.' At least, she hoped not. She would pay him back as soon as she could.

'Are you sure? I wouldn't like you to get into a bind.'

'I'll be back shortly.'

Agnes went back to the house and looked in the larder. Finding a plate and a knife, she cut off a hunk of bread from the loaf and a slice of ham from the joint, and made tea, then carried the provisions back to the tan-yard. She waited for Arthur as he helped drag another hide from one pit into another. When he saw her, his face lit up, and he came running over, splashing through the black puddles. Eyes glinting, he couldn't wait. He snatched the bread from the plate and stuffed it in his mouth.

'Arthur, where are your manners?' she scolded.

He put the bread back on the plate, crumbs spilling from his mouth.

'Oh, don't worry about them now. You're starving. Ugh, and your hands are filthy.' She held the plate towards him. 'Here, take it.'

He wolfed the rest of the bread and cheese, gulped the tea, and wiped his face with the back of his hand. 'Thank you, missus. I'm much obliged.'

'Go back to your work,' she said, allowing herself a smile. Perhaps there was still a little happiness to be found.

She went back to the house and washed the plate, knife and mug in the scullery sink. Then she found a broom in the adjoining closet, and swept the floors, before retiring to the window seat in Oliver's study.

She heard him come in at the end of the day.

'Agnes?' he called. 'Are you there?'

'Yes,' she said, heading out to the hallway to greet him.

'The fairy godmother has visited, I see,' he said. 'You have done the floors.'

She nodded.

'I have to do something. I have a confession to make – not only do I owe you for my keep, but I fed the boy, Arthur, this morning. He was starving – he hadn't eaten since last night. Oh, Oliver, I'm sorry. I raided the larder.'

Oliver smiled gently. 'Don't worry – that was a kind thing to do.'

'I think he and his mother must struggle very much.'

'I send our laundry to her, and I employ the boy as far as I can. His brother – Bert – has gone to work elsewhere, to seek his fortune in London as a bricklayer's apprentice, according to Arthur. They have lost his support.'

'How could he do that? How could he abandon his family?'

'I believe he got himself into some kind of trouble with some petty thievery. I don't think it was entirely his fault – he got in with the wrong crowd, hoping to make some extra money to help his mother.'

'I see,' Agnes said. 'Under the circumstances, he had no choice.'

'Indeed. I wanted to help him, but he was too ashamed to look me in the eye. He left without a word to me, which is a pity when he'd worked here for so long. Listen, I'd be grateful if you would give Arthur food every morning.'

'Are you sure?'

He nodded.

'What will he do when I've left Willow Place?' she said.

'Agnes, without pride, one would lie down and give up,' Oliver said, sounding exasperated, 'but you can have too much of a good thing. There is nothing wrong with taking on an offer of help until you're back on your feet.'

'It is my fault that I'm in this position. I don't deserve your charity.' She grew tearful. 'You are too kind.'

'Please don't think of it,' Oliver said. 'I'm a busy man. I work at the tannery every day of the week, supervising the workers, the operation of the tan-pits and the milling of the oak bark. I don't have time to look after the house, and I've been thinking – I'd like to offer you some work, a position as housekeeper. It's been hard since Mrs Hill left – she couldn't bring herself to stay on after my grandfather passed away. She was very fond of him. They had an understanding, so to speak.'

She bit her lip. What was he saying?

'They weren't married, but they had a deep attachment to each other. Oh, Agnes, you make out that you're such an innocent. What I'm saying is that they shared a bed.' He glanced up towards the beamed ceiling. 'There, that wasn't so bad, was it? The sky hasn't fallen in. The world hasn't come to an end. You see, my grandfather wasn't perfect either.'

'But it didn't matter because he loved her all the same,' she said.

'He left her a tidy sum of money and some jewellery which belonged to my grandmother. Anyway, that's by the by now,' he sighed. 'What do you think of keeping house for me?'

She blushed nervously. What was he suggesting?

'Oh, I don't mean—' he said quickly. 'I'm not saying that we should share a bed.'

Of course not. She was carrying someone else's child. She was a fallen woman and Oliver Cheevers was, and always would be, far too good for her.

'I'd love to work here, but it won't be long before—' She glanced down at her swollen belly.

'I'll ask Temperance to send her maid in to help with the chores while you're temporarily indisposed.'

'I don't believe that I'd make a good housekeeper,' she said. 'I can't cook or launder. I've always depended on others to do those activities. We had servants, a cook and then a French monsieur in the kitchen.'

'You aren't stupid, though – I'm sure you can learn the basics.'

'I'll try.' She stood up and brushed down her skirts, and straightened the antimacassar.

'Where are you going?'

'To make a start.'

'No, please sit down. I should like to continue our conversation for a little longer.'

'Wouldn't you like me to fetch you some tea? Have you any darning you would like me to do?' Her questions seemed to irritate him.

'You are here to keep house, not wait upon me hand and foot. I've managed without a housekeeper for some time now. Mrs Hill spent most of her time in recent months caring for my grandfather, rather than dealing with the other day-to-day activities.'

She sat down and rested one hand on her belly, feeling the baby move beneath her fingers.

'I'm sorry for coming between you and your sister.'

'Temperance has aspirations to a better life – it didn't help when she first met you because your situation was exactly the one she wanted for herself. The trouble is that her ambitions have made her bitter and dissatisfied with her lot. She has a loving husband who works for me at the tannery as our clerk and treasurer. Unfortunately, my sister has been married for several months and there is no sign of a happy event.'

'That isn't long. My adoptive mother took many years until a miracle happened.' Agnes wondered how Henry was. 'Temperance would have had good reason to envy me once, when I was a young girl and the apple of my father's eye. I was adopted by the Berry-Clays as an infant, as you likely know from Marjorie.

'Papa was a charitable gentleman. He was on the Board of Guardians for the workhouse and gave snuff and oranges to the inmates every Christmas, but he also flaunted his wealth. Mama was profligate with Papa's income from the brewery – she allowed the servants to misspend it right under her nose. Papa spoiled me with presents, and I'll never forget how he once rented a pineapple to show off to his guests on the occasion of my brother's christening.' She couldn't help smiling. 'What would I do to have the money that he spent on it now? What a terrible waste when there are families like Arthur's suffering here without proper housing, clothes and food.'

'You've changed, Agnes. You speak from the heart.'

'I've been told that I have but half a heart.'

'That isn't true,' he said, his eyes seeming to gaze into her soul. 'You are kind and compassionate, even though you've been through so much.'

'It's because of it,' she corrected him.

'Let me continue to help you, at least until the child is born. I don't see it as an imposition. It is something I wish to do.'

She glanced away at the clock on the mantel.

'I'll make a start on the dinner,' she said with a smile.

'There is a book on the shelf in the kitchen on domestic

management. I believe it has many chapters on how to prepare and cook meals. You will have to make do with what's in the larder tonight, but when you are more confident, we can send out for other ingredients. We will keep to a budget, though.'

'Of course.' She stood up and made her way to the kitchen, where she put on the apron that she found hanging on the hook behind the door. Where on earth should she begin? She thought back to the elaborate dishes she'd eaten at Windmarsh and Harbledown. Some of them had taken the cooks hours to prepare. She had no time to do one of those now. She looked in the larder and found a bag of flour with a few weevils in it, some salt and a block of lard that was melting around the edges. She had an idea that she could make a pie, but what to fill it with?

There were cold meats – some ham and beef – along with apples and some rather rubbery carrots. She pulled the book off the shelves and opened it up, searching through the index for recipes. She followed the instructions for making pastry to create some semblance of a pie. She filled it with slices of cold meat, then put it in the oven, having fed the range with more coal. She left the pie to cook for an hour then opened the oven, releasing a plume of black smoke.

She took her handiwork out quickly and placed it on the side.

It didn't look pretty, but she thought it might do. She trimmed off the burned rim of pastry and, realising that she'd forgotten to cook anything to go with it, she chopped up a carrot and dropped the pieces in boiling water.

'Is it ready?' Oliver asked, coming to the kitchen door. 'I wouldn't normally rush you, but I have a meeting to go to later.'

'You are going out again?' She wiped her hands on her apron.

'I'm expected to join the trustees of one of the charities my grandfather set up before he passed. He was Chair of the Sanitary Society.'

'Go and sit down at the table then,' she said. 'I'll bring your dinner.'

'You are going to join me?'

'I'd like that,' she said, feeling a little awkward. 'I'm not sure where I stand,' she went on. 'Am I not your servant?'

His brow furrowed. 'No, of course you aren't. You're my guest,' he said, putting her at ease.

She delivered the plates of food to the dining room and placed Oliver's in front of him.

He looked at it.

'That looks . . . interesting and very accomplished for someone who has no idea how to cook. It's beautifully arranged on the plate.'

She sat down and picked up her knife and fork after he'd said grace. She watched him saw into the pie, open the crust and manfully force the prongs of his fork into the filling, sending a piece of carrot flying across the table. With a faint splosh, it came to rest in his beer.

'Oh, I'm sorry,' she cried out.

He looked from the plate to the glass, then up at Agnes. His frown of surprise turned to a smile, then laughter. She felt the tension drain from her body. He wasn't cross. It was going to be all right. She began to laugh too.

'I couldn't have done that if I'd tried,' he chuckled as he scooped the carrot from his beer. 'Oh, Agnes. Your efforts have cheered me up. When I'm sitting in that meeting later tonight, I'll think of this. It will help me get through it.'

'I'm glad to have been of assistance, even if it was quite unintentional,' she said lightly. 'Shall I fetch some bread and cheese?'

'I'll get it,' he said, rising to his feet.

'I don't see how I could possibly go wrong with slicing some bread.'

'Whereas I can imagine all kinds of possibilities.' He grinned. 'Sit back, Agnes.'

She cleared the dishes later and washed up while Oliver went out to his meeting, and had retired to bed by the time he returned.

The next day, she placed his laundry and bedsheets in the basket for Arthur to take to his mama. On the following afternoon, it came back, clean and fresh-smelling, the shirts ironed and collars starched. She felt uneasy handling the clothes that Oliver had worn against his skin – it didn't seem right. She prepared a stew for dinner – onions, brisket of beef, carrots and turnips. She fair boiled the life out of it to make sure the vegetables were soft, but by the time it came for Oliver to eat it, they had turned to mush.

'It makes an excellent soup,' he said at the table. 'Maybe you should add a tater or two next time.'

'I'll do that,' she said, feeling stupid. She was a dolt when it came to the kitchen.

'How long do you think you have before the child is born?' he asked, changing the subject.

She placed her hand on her belly. 'I reckon I have another two or three weeks.' She was scared, not knowing what to expect, except for the pain that went along with childbirth. She gazed at her benefactor and wished that time would stand still so she could live in the moment for ever.

Agnes looked out for Arthur every day so she could give him some breakfast, knowing that he wouldn't have eaten at home. Today she had brought a slice of bread with cheese wrapped in brown paper for him.

She saw him in the tan-yard, dressed in his coat with a piece of string tied around the middle and his cap pulled down, shading his eyes. He held his bucket in one hand, his knife in the other, but even though the hides were being unloaded fresh from the carts, stiff as boards with frost, he stood immobile, not darting about to obtain the trimmings of flesh as he usually did.

'What's wrong, boy?' Agnes asked, walking across to him. 'Are you hurt?'

'Me ma, she's gorn,' he sniffed.

'Gone?'

'I tried to wake her this morning, but she won't stir. I think she's dead.'

'Oh, Arthur. Why didn't you say something before?'

'I didn't want to disturb you and Mr Cheevers.'

'We must go and find out what's happened.' She thought of Mrs Fortune, the kindly laundry woman. She wasn't that old. Why had she died? She felt as if she should have checked up on her and the boy before.

'Is everything all right?' Oliver asked as she made her way back across the tan-yard with Arthur crying at her side.

Agnes explained. 'I must go to her. I'm hoping and praying that he's wrong, but I suppose he has seen enough of death to know . . .'

'Indeed,' Oliver said. 'I'll go. You stay and keep warm. I don't want you falling ill again.'

'No, I must come with you for Arthur's sake.'

He didn't argue.

They accompanied the boy to the slum, and went up the stairs to find Mrs Hamilton standing at the door to the Fortunes' room.

'It's most inconsiderate, her dying like this. What am I to do? I can't move her, and she has no family as far as I know except the little boy. The older one has done a runner.'

'It's all right, Mrs Hamilton,' Oliver said. 'God forbid that you should change your character now and show any compassion. I'll take care of this.'

'Well, it's all right for some who can afford to show compassion. I feel sorry for the boy. His brother was a little tyke, but Arthur's a sweetheart, always willing to run an errand in return for an apple or a ha'penny.'

'Please, leave us. This isn't the time,' Oliver said.

'What about my rent? The next lot's due tomorrer. I 'ave people queuing up for the room, and I want it vacated by the end of today. I can't afford to 'ave it standing empty.'

'Just go, Mrs Hamilton,' Oliver said crossly as Agnes tried to restrain Arthur from pushing past. She couldn't hold him back. He ran and threw himself down on his mother's bed where she lay with her eyes wide open, staring at the mouldy ceiling.

'Ma,' he sobbed. 'Come back to us. Please.'

Agnes remembered how Philip had checked her father's pulse and breathing. She plucked up the courage to feel for the woman's wrist, but she knew from the cold chill of her skin that it was too late. She had definitely passed.

'Oh, Arthur, God has taken her up to Heaven on the wings of His angels.' Her heart ached for him, and again for her papa who'd been snatched away from her so suddenly.

'I tried to close 'er eyes,' he said.

'You did what you could,' Agnes said. 'She would be very proud of you.'

'Agnes, take Arthur back to Willow Place,' Oliver said,

coming across to the bed. 'I'll make sure that everything is settled here. We will decide what to do later. As far as I know the boy has no other relatives.'

'What about his brother?'

'I 'aven't seen Bert for ages,' Arthur said.

'Can we send word to him?' Oliver asked. 'Do you know his address?'

'He told Ma he would get in touch with her as soon as he was settled. He didn't do it, though – I think her heart broke, not knowing where he was.'

'Don't worry about it now, Arthur. I'll place an advertisement in the papers and see if we can find him. He needs to know of his mother's passing. Agnes, take him to Willow Place, please,' Oliver said firmly.

'Come with me,' she said, gently taking Arthur's hand.

He gave his mother one last kiss goodbye and walked slowly from the room and down the stairs, watched by women and children curious to know more about the demise of their neighbour.

Agnes took him back to Willow Place.

He reeked of the tannery and had lice crawling through his hair. His clothes were stiff with dirt and his socks – she insisted on him removing his shoes before he entered the house – had gone into holes, revealing his dirty, overgrown toenails.

'I'm sorry for your loss, Arthur, but you can't stay here like that,' she said. 'You must have a good wash.'

'I'll only get dirty again.'

She started to fill the tin bath in the kitchen with hot water.

'You can undress behind the screen,' she told him as she lugged buckets from the pump outside the back door ready to adjust the temperature. The hotter the better, she thought, looking at the state of him.

'I'll keep my clothes on, ta very much.'

'You can't get into the water with them on,' she exclaimed. 'Do as you're told.'

'I don't want to,' he said stubbornly, 'and you can't tell me what to do. You aren't my ma.' He burst into tears.

'Oh, Arthur,' she said softly. She remembered how she had persuaded Charlotte and Elizabeth to do as they were told by offering inducements.

'If you take your clothes off, get into the water and give yourself a good scrub with soap, I'll make you eggs on toast. If you let me comb those nits out of your hair, I'll find you a piece of cherry cake.' Whenever she made it, she thought of Henry and how it was his favourite. It wasn't the best cake in the world, but her baking had improved.

'Really?' he said, wide-eyed.

'Really. Your ma is looking down from Heaven – I'm sure she's pleased to see how you're behaving like a young gentleman.'

'Thank you, missus,' he said.

'Hurry up then, before the water gets cold.'

She wasn't sure how you bathed a child. She recalled how Nanny had instructed her to wash and then checked behind her ears for cleanliness. In spite of his protests, she did the same for Arthur before handing him a towel to dry himself. She went through his clothes, holding them in a pair of fire tongs so she didn't have to touch them. He couldn't possibly put them back on until they'd been laundered. She put them in a basket in the scullery.

'What 'ave you done with my clothes, missus?' Arthur said.

She stared at him. He still had smudges of filth across his cheeks. She had looked behind his ears and completely missed the fact that he hadn't washed his face. She sighed inwardly. It wasn't easy looking after a small boy.

'I'll find you something else to wear.' She went up to the linen cupboard and found one of Oliver's shirts. It would have to do. They could tie a belt of some kind around his tiny waist, she thought as she went back downstairs and slipped it over his shoulders. He looked very sweet, dressed in a white shirt that was far too big for him. 'We'll find somewhere for you to sleep. I'll ask Oliver, I mean, Mr Cheevers.'

'Can't I go home?' he said sorrowfully.

'I'm afraid not.' She guessed that Mrs Hamilton's new lodgers would already be settled in the room. 'I'm sorry. You're sure you have no one else who can take you in?'

'No, missus. I'm an orphan and I'll 'ave to look after myself. I can, you know.'

'I know that you can, but it isn't right. You're far too young.'

He shivered.

'Let's get you some food. You're cold,' she said. 'Come along.'

She watched him devour plateful after plateful of eggs, toast and cherry cake, until she was afraid that he would be sick. He didn't care that the eggs were like rubber and the toast was black. Agnes frowned. She wondered how Mrs Fortune had managed to keep her son's belly filled. He was like a chick, with his beak constantly open for food.

Where would he stay? What happened to boys of his age who had no parents?

Tears filled her eyes as she pictured him lost and alone, and subjected to the cruelty and deprivation of the workhouse. It had been said that her papa had made the Union in Faversham too comfortable for the inmates, but it wasn't necessarily the same elsewhere.

'I wish Ma hadn't bin taken up to Heaven,' he muttered. 'Maybe she's with Pa now. She used to cry her eyes out every night over what happened to him. Mr Cheevers – the young one, not the old gent – found him drunk and pulled him out of the liquor in the pit by his feet, but it was too late. He'd gorn. The old one paid for him to be buried proper like, in the churchyard with a headstone and all with his name writ large on it,' he added proudly. 'I had an aunt – I don't remember her. And I had a sister, but I don't recall her neither.'

Oliver returned to the house after she'd put the boy to bed in Temperance's old room.

'How's Arthur?' he asked.

'He washes up well,' she said. 'I borrowed one of your shirts. I'm sorry.'

'It doesn't matter. I've brought what little he had left at the lodgings house – Mrs Hamilton is a vampire of the poor, sucking the lifeblood out of them by forcing them to live in that overcrowded hovel.'

'Without her, they would have nowhere to stay,' Agnes pointed out. 'She did show me some kindness when I lodged with her, although her manner was very abrupt.'

Oliver shrugged. 'Anyway, I've brought the clothes and few possessions that Arthur's ma had left. I've had to leave it all outside, though – it's riddled with fleas.'

'I'll go through it in the morning. Oliver, I wonder if . . . Please, let me know if I'm overstepping the mark. I mean, it's your place to offer, not mine, but I wonder if we should take the boy in – for a few days, or a week at least.'

Oliver gazed at her, his eyes gentle. 'Oh, Agnes, that is exactly my sentiment. As long as you are happy to look after a lost soul . . .'

'Of course I am. He needs mothering, but can you manage with another mouth to feed? He eats like a horse.'

'I'm sure we can stretch to accommodate one more.'

'Oh, thank you. It will put my mind at rest. I don't suppose that Temperance will approve.'

'It's none of her business,' Oliver said. 'Don't worry about her.'

Temperance vented her opinion the next day when she discovered Arthur had moved into Willow Place. Agnes overheard her talking while she was back in the kitchen, trying to work out how to pluck a whole chicken that she had bought from the market, thinking it a bargain.

'You can't raise a guttersnipe from the gutter,' Temperance told Oliver.

'I think something can be made of him,' her brother insisted.

'I've just seen him snivelling in the yard.'

'He's just lost his ma. Don't you remember how we felt when we were orphaned? I don't know what would have happened to us if Grandpa hadn't taken us in. He was a widower, living on his own and already suffering from the ague. He had plenty of excuses not to.'

'He'll take advantage of you, you mark my words.'

'He'll make himself useful,' Oliver said.

'And how about Agnes? Is she making herself useful?' Temperance said snidely, without waiting for her brother's reply. 'People are talking, as I said they would.'

'Oh, what do you know about it?' Oliver said. 'Let them say what they like. It's like water off a duck's back to me.'

'I wish you could see what's going on here. She's trying to trap you into making an honest woman of her.'

Agnes felt the heat rush up her neck as she pulled ineffectually at the bird's plumage.

'She isn't. And if she was, well, I like her – I like her very much.'

Agnes found herself with a handful of feathers. Her heart was pounding. He liked her – he'd said so.

'You are being ridiculous,' Temperance exploded with rage. 'You cannot marry a whore.'

'If you repeat that allegation once more, I shall ask you to leave my house and not come back. She's a good woman. She's kind, which is more than I can say of you.'

'She is carrying somebody else's child.'

'A fact of which I am painfully aware,' he said, his tone filled with regret. 'Now, go and don't show your face again until I've had time to calm down.'

Agnes was even sorrier now that she'd taken so many wrong turns. No one would consider marrying her now, least of all someone she admired as much as Oliver.

Temperance no longer visited Willow Place or sent her maid to help Agnes out with the housekeeping. Arthur stayed on, though, and the three of them took to sitting in the parlour or the study in the evenings. Agnes would sew and mend while Oliver read or wrote letters, and Arthur looked through picture books and talked. It was so very different from when she'd been at Windmarsh Court at the same age – seen, but not heard.

'Would you like to learn to read?' Oliver asked Arthur one day.

'It looks like too much trouble, sir.'

Arthur looked quite the dandy, Agnes thought. She had altered some second-hand clothes to fit him and cut his hair.

'Perhaps Agnes can teach you. She has been a governess.'

'I'd like that.' She wondered how long she would stay, and how much progress he would make in that time. 'You must go to bed now, Arthur. You have work in the morning.'

'I'd rather stay up late,' he said.

'Listen to your elders and betters, young man.' Oliver sounded stern, but he was smiling.

'All right, I'll go.' Sighing, Arthur got up and stomped out of the room.

'Goodnight,' Agnes called after him. 'Don't forget to say your prayers.'

'I won't, Ma,' he called back.

'Ma?' Oliver raised one eyebrow. 'Since when did he start calling you that?'

'That's the first time I've heard it.' She smiled and shifted in her chair as the baby kicked. 'Has anything been decided about dredging the river?' she asked, remembering that he'd been to another meeting of the Sanitary Society the previous evening.

He shook his head. 'It was suggested that I paid for it to be done, but it would bankrupt me. One of my great-great-grandfathers set up the tannery with a shop across the road and there have always been complaints about the stink, but what can I do when I employ ten people? Isn't it more important to provide a living for those who would otherwise be unemployed than worry about noxious odours?'

'Well, I would agree with you on that.'

'The tanneries and the dye factory can't stop using the river – we depend on the water for washing and disposing of by-products. It's been suggested that an alternative would be to lay drains that empty further downstream.'

'Won't that merely pollute the water for the villages outside Canterbury?' Agnes said.

'You're right,' Oliver said, sounding taken aback.

'Are you surprised by that?' Agnes asked. She refused to bite her tongue.

'I apologise. Sometimes I forget that you've had the benefits not often granted to your sex of education and common sense. We are easily equals in intellect.' He blushed to the roots of his hair. 'I'm always pleased to hear your opinions. You remind me of my cousin in many ways. In fact, I've received a letter from our dear Marjorie. She's hoping to call on us shortly.'

'Oh,' Agnes gasped in dismay.

'I thought you'd be pleased to see her again,' Oliver said, frowning.

She couldn't possibly meet her beloved Nanny, not in her condition. She had gone against her teaching. She had let her down, especially after all she had done for her in helping her find her place at Roper House. Nanny had given her the opportunity of making a comfortable living and she had thrown it away.

'I've written back to let her know that you're here,' he went on.

'I wish you hadn't,' she sighed.

'She called on you once when you were at Mrs Hamilton's, but you were out. She'd been to see me and Temperance, and Arthur happened to mention that he knew where you were living. She was disappointed that she didn't get to see you before she returned to Whitstable.'

'Whereas I was relieved,' Agnes confessed. 'I'm so ashamed – I wouldn't be able to bring myself to look her in the eye.'

Oliver smiled wryly. 'She doesn't care what you did or how you came to be here. She's desperate to see you again. She's always talking about you. She misses you like a daughter.'

'I miss her too.' She brushed back a tear as she remembered the days they had spent in the schoolroom and out walking. She often dreamed that she and Nanny were back at Windmarsh.

'I don't like the idea that I'm an extra drain on your resources,' she said, changing the subject. 'I've been thinking.'

'Again?' He rubbed his temple with his forefinger. 'I

don't like the sound of that. The last time you said it, you told me you were leaving.'

'Well, you won't want me here with a child.' She forced a smile. 'They can cry a terrible lot. When my little brother was born . . .' Her voice tailed off at the memory of when she'd first consoled him as a babe in the nursery while Mrs Pargeter snored in her bed.

'His name was Henry,' Oliver said. 'Marjorie was his governess until he was sent to school.'

'That's right.'

'I know that babies bawl, and create untidiness, but I'm more than happy for you to remain here. In fact, I insist that you do. Agnes, I can't see another child brought into the world disadvantaged through no fault of its own. Arthur's fond of you and needs a woman's care at this time of his life.'

She was fond of Arthur too and touched that he had called her Ma.

'I can't help noticing that the time of your confinement isn't far away and I think it would be useful to call in some extra help. You'll soon have an infant to care for on top of everything else. Do you know of anyone, a girl who might be in need of a place?'

She thought for a moment.

'Don't worry about whether or not I can afford it.' He smiled. 'I'm happy to pay for a decent cook. I'm not being unkind – I'm being practical.'

'I'm not sure how much experience this person has of the kitchen, but I know she'd be a good, honest worker,' Agnes said.

'Who would that be and how do I contact her?'

'I'll write to her on your behalf.'

'There is paper and a spare pen in my desk. You can use that.'

'I'll write straight away,' she said, making her way to the study, where she composed her letter.

*Dear Evie,*

*I pray that you will find someone to read this letter to you. I hope you are well.*

*I have some news that may be of interest to you. I know of a position for a maid with good prospects. When the master of the house where I am staying in Canterbury asked me if I could recommend a suitable person, I thought of you.*

*Please send word that you will at least come for an interview.*

*Your ever loving friend,*

*Agnes Linnet*

'Do you think your friend will come?' Oliver asked later when she returned to the parlour to wish him goodnight.

'I sincerely hope so,' she answered. She would like to see Evie settled at Willow Place as a reward for her friendship and loyalty.

'If you left, I'd miss you more than I can say,' he said softly. 'You will stay on?'

'For now,' she said, her heart silently breaking.

# Chapter Twenty-Six

## *Three for a Girl, Four for a Boy*

'There's a lady askin' for you, Ma,' Arthur called from the front door a few days later. 'It's a Miss Potts and she looks very well.'

'Evie.' Her heart leapt. She had come. She waddled down the hall to greet her.

'Hello, Miss Linnet.' Evie's hair was plaited up under her bonnet and she was dressed in her Sunday best and a pair of gloves. 'Thank you for your letter – John read it to me.'

'The footman?' Agnes enquired.

'Yes.' It was a bright May morning and the sunlight turned her dark blue eyes a shade of violet. 'The position? It is still available?'

'Of course, but unfortunately the master of the house is at the tannery.'

'I'll run and fetch him,' Arthur said.

Agnes thanked him and he put on his boots and disappeared.

'There's no way you'll be running anywhere.' Evie smiled. 'You look very well. Oh, Miss Linnet, I've bin so worried about you.'

'I've made it through some hard times, but I'm still here. I've lots to tell you,' she said. 'Do call me Agnes, though.'

'I thought I should speak proper seeing I'm here to impress.'

'There's no need for ceremony. Mr Cheevers – Oliver – is a kind and considerate man. He's my former nanny's cousin who took me in, and let me live here in return for housekeeping duties. The trouble is, I'm no good at cooking – Oliver almost broke his tooth on my first attempt at pastry.'

Evie smiled again. 'It seems that you've 'ad to l'arn quickly considering you were a governess at Roper House, not a maid.'

'How are the young ladies? I feel very bad for what happened. I'm not sure I shall ever live it down.'

'Oh, don't worry about them. Elizabeth cried and refused to eat for three days unless Lady Faraday had you reinstated, but as soon as she heard that Master Moldbury was returning to Roper House for a few days in the New Year, she was back to her usual self. Charlotte was quiet for a while – she took it worse. They 'ave a new governess, but she is like a mouse and will not last long. The ladies run rings round her.'

'And what about . . .' she lowered her voice ' . . . Master Faraday?'

'Ah, he is . . . I'm not sure you'll want to hear this.'

'Go on.'

'He is engaged to be married. Sir Richard called him a loose cannon, I believe, and said it was time he stopped sowing his wild oats and settled down.'

'Oh?' She thought for a moment about Sir Richard's hypocrisy. It was exactly because he'd wanted Felix to sow his oats that he'd encouraged him in his plan of going abroad to look for investments once he'd finished his studies.

'I hope the news doesn't upset you.'

'Not in the slightest.' It didn't. She didn't care for him any more, only for his child who was growing every day in her belly.

'Are you and this Mr Cheevers . . . ? Well, you know?'

'Oh no.'

'I'm sorry. Of course, you aren't.' Evie's lip trembled. 'I 'aven't wrecked my chances, 'ave I?'

'Don't be silly. Not with me, you haven't.'

'I want this job. I can't stand being at Roper House a moment longer.'

'I had thought you were rather fond of John the footman.'

'Yes, I am. We're walking out together.' Evie's cheeks turned pink. 'No, it's Sir Richard. There's bin a plague of rats in the attic. I was creeping up to bed when this gun went off in my face. I've never jumped so high. My screams woke the whole household. Anyway, I can't live like that, in fear of my life. And those dogs of his. You clean the floor until it's gleaming and a few minutes later it's covered in muddy pawprints, and you 'ave to start all over again. He has no respect for anyone except his slavering hounds.'

Like father, like son, Agnes thought.

'Anyway, I'd rather be out of there, and when you said in that letter that there were prospects, I jumped at it. I only hope that I can persuade this Mr Cheevers to take me on.'

'Just be yourself and you'll win him over.'

'I 'aven't asked Lady Faraday for a reference.'

'Don't worry about it. I've already given Oliver my opinion of your character. Come into the study and take a seat. Would you like some tea?'

'No, thank you. I'm too nervous.'

Agnes heard Arthur's footsteps as Evie sat down at the desk.

'He's on his way,' Arthur yelled as he came into the study, red-faced and breathless from running.

'Hush,' Agnes said. 'You are very loud.'

'I'm sorry, Ma, but it's to get attention. If you don't

shout, you won't be heard. That's what Ma used to say.' His face creased suddenly.

'Oh, Arthur.' She put her arms around him and pressed her lips to his hair, which smelled sweet and clean.

'I hear that we have a visitor.' Oliver strolled into the room, ducking his head under the beam just inside the doorway. 'Oh dear,' he added, noticing Arthur's distress.

'I'll take him into the kitchen. Oliver, this is Evie – Miss Evie Potts.'

'Greetings,' he said with enthusiasm. 'Welcome to Willow Place.'

'Good afternoon,' she said, then stammered, 'Oh dear, that's gorn and done it. It isn't past twelve o'clock yet. You won't want a maid who doesn't know the time of day.'

Oliver smiled and took a seat opposite Evie. Agnes backed out with her hands guiding Arthur by his skinny shoulders, and closed the door behind them.

'I have cake,' she said, leading him to the kitchen. 'I made it last night after you'd gone to bed.' She cut him a slice of raisin loaf.

'It's delicious, Ma,' he said, chewing valiantly.

'You should always tell the truth,' she said. 'Take it from me – honesty is a virtue.'

'I'm not lyin',' he said, grinning as the tears dried in grimy tracks down his cheeks. 'This is the best cake I've ever 'ad.'

'Well, thank you,' she said, gratified.

When he had finished the third slice, Evie came through to the kitchen. She stood in the doorway, beaming.

'You'll never guess, but Mr Cheevers said I can 'ave the position of maid. If I do well, he'll promote me to housekeeper within six months.'

'Oh, congratulations, Evie. When do you start?' Agnes said.

'In a week or two, as soon as I've worked out my notice. You look like you can do with some help.' Evie eyed Agnes's belly.

'I'm struggling. It won't be long until the baby comes.' A shiver of fear ran down her spine. 'To be honest, I'm scared.'

'There's no reason to be. All will be well in the end.'

'I wish I had your faith.'

'You've bin in my prayers every night since you left the Faradays. Oh, Agnes, I can't wait to be here. We'll be two friends together again.'

Agnes smiled wryly. She didn't enlighten Evie that she wouldn't be staying at Willow Place for ever, only until the baby was born and she could find employment elsewhere. It wasn't merely because she didn't want to impose on Oliver any longer than necessary, but because she was falling hopelessly in love with him. And it *was* hopeless, because even if, by any stretch of the imagination, he decided to commit to her, a fallen woman with a bastard child, she would never allow it. He'd said they were equal in intellect, but she was inferior to him in every other way, in generosity and goodness.

Evie returned to Willow Place a week later, and her arrival wasn't a moment too soon, because the next day Agnes was standing at the scullery sink washing the pots when a dull pain dragged through her belly. She must have gasped out loud because Oliver came to her side.

'You aren't well, Agnes,' he said, his voice filled with concern.

'I'm fine,' she said through gritted teeth as a wave of pain, stronger than the first, took the words from her mouth. 'What are you doing here? Aren't you supposed to be at the tannery?'

'Well, yes, but I saw Evie go out to the market and I thought I'd better stay and keep an eye on you. It's a good thing I did.' He held her gaze as she looked up at him. 'Let me help you up the stairs.'

'No, really. I'm perfectly . . .' She pressed her hand to her belly.

'Oh, my dear. I can't bear to see you like this.' He swore out loud. 'I wish I knew what to do.'

'Just hold my arm while I make my way to my room,' she said.

'Of course. Anything,' he muttered. As he walked her to the foot of the stairs, she heard voices and the sound of the front door opening.

'Oliver?' Evie called.

'Oh, what is it now?' he said.

'You 'ave a visitor,' Evie announced. 'She says her name is Marjorie.'

'Everything is happening at once,' Oliver said, his voice filled with relief. 'Greetings, dear cousin. You've arrived just in time.'

'My mistress released me from my duties a day early.' Agnes looked along the hallway at the familiar tone of the person she had loved and grown up with. 'The family is going away on their annual holiday and I have two weeks to myself. Thank you for writing to me. Where is she?'

Oliver kept hold of Agnes's arm as he introduced Miss Treen to Evie, and although she wanted to greet her too, Agnes could hardly concentrate as another pain began to build in her belly.

'She is ready for her confinement?' she heard Nanny exclaim.

'I think the baby will be here very soon,' Oliver said.

'Help me get her to bed. Evie, bring some refreshments – we will all need to keep our strength up.'

This was not how Agnes wanted Nanny to see her: about to give birth to her illegitimate child in the Cheeverses' home. But that was the least of her worries right now because the pain made her want to scream, and in suppressing that impulse, she recalled her mother's screams as she laboured with Henry. She couldn't go through with it, she thought. It was too much.

Oliver and Nanny helped her up the stairs to her room, and sat her on the edge of the bed.

'Now, Oliver, you must go about your usual business,' Nanny said sternly. 'This is women's work.'

'I don't think I can leave her,' he said.

'All will be well. Trust me,' Nanny said, shooing him away. She helped Agnes out of her apron.

'The child is coming.' Agnes rocked back and forth to ease the next pain, wondering how she could have ever been so naive as to have believed the story of the stork and the chimney. 'I'm so sorry.'

'There's nothing to be sorry about. Oliver has explained a little of what's happened in his letters to me, and as far as I'm concerned, it's all water under the bridge. The important thing now is to concentrate on helping this child into the world.'

'Have you delivered an infant before?' Agnes asked tentatively.

'No, but I'm sure we'll manage.' Nanny sounded apprehensive, Agnes thought. 'All you have to do is stay calm and breathe through the pains. We have Evie to fetch and carry, and we can call for a doctor if there are complications.'

She laboured for seven hours. When she thought she couldn't go on any longer, and was wishing that she'd been left to die in the gutter at the foot of the Westgate Towers, she was at last safely delivered of a baby girl.

She could hardly look at her at first for fear that she

would see Felix in her features, but she couldn't put it off for ever. As the infant yawned, she forced herself to examine her face.

'She is very beautiful, the image of you, dear Agnes,' Nanny said, and she began to point out all the ways in which she resembled her mother. 'I recall when you were eight months old. Your hair was like that, and your nose was a similar shape, like a button. Oh, you are most fortunate to have a healthy infant. I wish . . . Oh, never mind.'

'Do you really think she looks like me?'

'There is no mistaking that you are mother and daughter. Ah, she is perfect, a gift from God. What will you call her?'

Agnes pressed her lips to her forehead, inhaling her warm, milky scent. She wanted to call her by a name that had no associations with her past, something pretty and entirely her own choice.

'Rose,' she said softly. 'Rose Agnes Ivy Catherine Linnet.'

'Catherine? After your mother? Are you sure?'

Agnes nodded. She felt it would go some way to making up for how she had treated her true mother when she had met her just before her nineteenth birthday.

'What a lovely idea,' Nanny sighed fondly. 'I couldn't have chosen better myself. By the way, I have something to return to you. It seems like an auspicious moment.' She disappeared from the room and returned a short while later. 'Here,' she said, holding out her hand on which lay the half a sixpence on its silver chain which her mother had given her on that fateful day in Faversham. 'I found it under the bed at Windmarsh Court.'

Agnes remembered throwing it across the room in a fit of temper, and her eyes filled with tears at what she had done. She knew now, sitting propped up against the pillows with her daughter cuddled up against her breast, that her mother must have been truly desperate to have handed her over for adoption. She could never find the strength to give her own baby away, even if she knew she would be certain of a better life. Maybe it was selfish of her to think that way, she thought, but she couldn't do it.

'I will wear it until the time is right for me to hand it over to Rose,' she said.

Nanny placed it around her neck and fastened the clasp at the back without disturbing the baby.

'I believe that your mother married your father's brother in the end – he is a blacksmith in a village called Overshill. He had the chain made for her.'

'How do you know this?'

'I did a little investigation of the address from which she sent the letters asking me to arrange the meeting.'

'I see.' Agnes touched the rough-edged half a coin at her neck, marvelling at how something so small and financially worthless had become her most precious possession. 'Thank you, Nanny.'

'Isn't it time you started calling me Marjorie?'

Agnes smiled.

'Pull up the chair and tell me what you have been doing,' she said.

'I'm nannying for a family in Whitstable. The children are still very young, but I'm enjoying the sea air. We walk along the clifftop every day.' Marjorie sat down on the bedside chair.

'When did you leave Windmarsh?'

'Not long after you did. My services were no longer required when your mama sent Henry off to school. Miriam and I have corresponded since.'

'Everyone is well?'

'Your mama is even more reclusive and the house is neglected because she doesn't give the servants any guidance. Henry is growing up to be a fine boy – he looks more like your father than ever. He used to speak of you – we used to say you had sailed away and we would wave at the boats in case you were on one of them.'

'Wasn't that rather cruel, to raise his hopes and dash them?'

'I couldn't bring myself to tell him the truth. I may have been in the wrong, but I think he coped with the loss of his sister better that way. He still had hopes that you would return one day.' A shadow of regret crossed her face before she continued, 'Miriam is just the same.'

'And Philip? Did you hear anything more of him?'

'He got his way. He's taken up his studies in medicine.'

Agnes fell silent, happy that her cousin had been able to follow his dream.

'Listen to me – I'm wearing you out with all this talking.'

'We have so much catching up to do.'

'And you need to sleep,' Marjorie said firmly.

Aching and exhausted, Agnes tried to doze off with the baby in the crib beside her – Oliver had brought it in from the shed outside. It had been his and Temperance's when they were babies, and his grandfather hadn't been able to bring himself to give it away when he'd cleared their parents' cottage. She felt compelled to keep checking on her daughter. Was she still breathing? Was she too hot, or too cold? She reached over and touched her cheek. She snuffled, opened her eyes and closed them again.

'Oh, my darling Rose,' she whispered, overwhelmed with love.

A little while later there was a knock at the door.

'It's me, Oliver.'

'Come away from there right now.' Agnes smiled as she heard Marjorie's voice on the landing. 'What do you think you're doing?'

'Arthur and I wanted to meet the new arrival,' she heard him say.

'You must be patient. Mother and baby need to recover their strength before they receive visitors.'

'I'd like to see her too,' Evie's voice joined in from the other side of the door.

'No, absolutely not.'

'Oh, Marjorie, you are cruel.'

'I'm being cruel to be kind. I'll let you know when you can visit.'

It was three days before Nanny let Oliver and Arthur meet the baby. Agnes remained confined to her room, but that morning, Evie helped her dress to receive her visitors. She brushed her hair and checked her reflection in the mirror on the dressing table. She pinched her cheeks to give herself some colour, then smiled at her vanity.

The door burst open.

'I'm sorry, Ma. I couldn't wait any longer.'

'Oh, Arthur,' she exclaimed.

'Is she sleeping?'

'She is awake,' Marjorie said.

Agnes glanced towards Oliver, who had followed Arthur into the room. He smiled as Marjorie showed them to the crib where Rose gazed up at them.

'She's gorn squinty-eyed,' Arthur said in an awed whisper.

'Look at all that hair.' Oliver turned to Agnes. 'Can I hold her? Is that allowed?'

Agnes leaned into the crib and picked the baby up. She placed her in Oliver's arms and showed him how to support her head. His fingers caught hers very briefly. She glanced up. He did the same, caught her eye, and as if he felt guilty for doing something that he shouldn't, he looked away.

Her heart melted as she watched him bend down to give Arthur the chance to stroke the baby's head.

'Isn't she beautiful?' Oliver whispered.

'She's very pretty,' Arthur breathed. 'I can't wait for 'er to grow up and be a proper sister. I'll be able to take 'er outside and show 'er the ducks.'

'It's going to feel like an awfully long wait,' Oliver said, grinning.

Agnes swallowed against the lump that formed in her throat. She wished that the next months and years weren't quite so uncertain. What did the future have in store for her and Rose?

It was one evening in late September, long after Marjorie had returned to her employment. Evie had gone out walking with her young man, and Agnes had made sure that Arthur had washed and retired to bed before she fed Rose. She put her in her crib upstairs with the door open so she could listen out for her cries, but she was a good baby. She already slept through the night, possibly exhausted by the entertainments that Arthur provided, showing her pictures, singing to her and reciting rhymes, some of which were suitable for the nursery and some of which were not. Rose entertained him in return, smiling when he shook her coral rattle in front of her. When he dropped it, it would go rolling across the sloping floor of the room in the black and white timber-framed house.

Agnes and Oliver were alone together in the parlour, sitting side by side but apart on the chaise to make the most of the heat of the fire. Some apple wood was burning in the grate. Every so often a log spat, sending a glowing ember on to the rug in front of the fireplace, at which Oliver would reach out one foot and stamp on it before its flame could take hold.

'Shall we play cards tonight?' Agnes asked him. He had taught her the principles of whist and draughts, and how to play Old Maid.

'Not tonight,' he said. 'I thought we could talk. We don't often have the opportunity . . .'

'What would you like to discuss?' she asked.

'The future.'

She felt apprehensive. Was he beginning to tire of her presence? She wouldn't blame him. Perhaps she had outstayed her welcome.

'As soon as I'm able, I'm going to start paying my way,' she said. 'I'll advertise as a teacher for boys and girls up to the age of ten.' She felt confident that she could teach the basics to that age group, rather than have to undergo the trials of teaching rebellious and privileged young ladies the accomplishments required for them to shine in the drawing rooms of great houses. 'I'd make places available for children like Arthur who wouldn't otherwise receive an education.'

'That is admirable.'

'I have to do something useful. I cannot be idle.' She could see too that she and Rose were a considerable extra burden on the household. 'Nanny – I mean, Marjorie – taught me well. Circumstances forced me to find out what I was truly capable of, and I've proved that I can teach. Oliver, I've found my calling, and I wish to pursue it.'

'Do you mean that you want to set up a school?'

'Eventually, I hope. I'll have to start on a small scale – I can't afford to rent a suitable site yet.'

'I can help you with that. One of the cottages opposite the tan-yard is empty. It needs a little work.'

'Oliver, I can't possibly accept. You've done more than enough for me already.'

'No, this is something I'm interested in doing.' He paused for a moment. 'Agnes, you show great restraint when it comes to expressing your wishes and feelings, but I wish you'd let me into your heart.'

It was true. She had built a wall around her from the bricks and stones of suffering and betrayal.

'I notice that you're wearing some jewellery,' Oliver said.

'I wear it all the time. Why haven't you asked me about it before?'

'I thought it might be a gift or memento from Rose's father. I didn't want to upset you.'

'Oh, Oliver.' She showed him the half a sixpence on the chain around her neck. He leaned in close. She could smell his breath, fresh and warm. She could feel the glow of his skin close to hers. 'Marjorie returned it to me. It's all I have left.' She forced a smile. 'The rest of my jewellery was stolen from me when I arrived in Canterbury. Not that it matters. Gold and silver have lost their shine for me.'

'What is it, then?'

'It's half a sixpence, given to me by my mother, the woman who gave me up.'

'Do you recall your true parents?' he asked.

'My mother gave this to me when I was buying dresses for my nineteenth birthday – that's the only time I can remember meeting her.' How foolish she felt, thinking of the scarlet dress and how proud she had been to order it. She didn't care now for silk parasols and ostrich-feather fans, or black lace mantillas and reticules decorated with silver beads. They were fripperies.

'What was she like?'

'She seemed pleasant, rustic.' She remembered her long dark hair and tear-filled eyes, and her joy at seeing her. 'My father . . .' she hesitated ' . . . he was falsely convicted of the terrible crime of murder and transported to the other side of the world. I should have liked to have known more about him, but I dismissed her in a hurry because I was in shock at the sudden discovery of my lowly start in life. I regret that now.' She sighed. 'She told me that the half a sixpence was a good luck charm, and a memento of my father. Someone out there – my father, perhaps – has the other half. I wonder if he may return to find me one day, if he is still alive. I won't hold my breath, though.'

'What a strange story,' Oliver said.

'I don't think it's any odder than the way that I've ended up here with you. And Arthur, of course,' she added quickly, her cheeks warm at the idea that he might draw the wrong conclusion. She bit her lip, suppressing her emotion as Miss Treen had taught her to do. She didn't deserve Oliver's affection, even if she was more than willing to return it.

'I found you intriguing from the very start when I met you as a boy of – what was I? About sixteen?' he said.

'It feels like a lifetime ago,' she observed.

'It wasn't until the last time you visited Willow Place that I felt attracted to you, but you were betrothed by then to your cousin.' He shrugged. 'I knew anyway that I didn't stand a chance.'

She frowned as he went on, 'Times have changed, though, and I'd be honoured if you and the children would take my name. That way, we can have Rose baptised – and Arthur as well. His ma was a God-fearing woman, but I don't think she would have had her boys christened.'

'It's a generous offer, Oliver,' she began. She had led an unconventional life up until now, but she wasn't sure that she was prepared to change her name for a second time. 'However, I do have my pride, and I don't want you to do anything that will jeopardise your chances of marrying in the future.'

'You are too kind.' Was she imagining it, or was his tone laced with irony? He stood up and paced the room, then stopped in front of her. 'I'm not going to rake up the past. It is dead and buried as far as I'm concerned. But,

Agnes, be honest for once. What are you feeling? Right now? Sometimes you are a complete mystery to me.'

She took a moment to collect herself, then realised that this wasn't what he was asking for. He wanted her to let go of her self-restraint.

'Please,' he begged, his eyes dark with emotion.

'I feel—' she began. 'This is hard for me. I've been brought up not to reveal my feelings.'

'But you do feel something? Affection? Regret?'

'I feel happiness – I've never been as happy as I have been staying here with you, Rose and Arthur. And Evie, too.'

'And?' he pleaded.

'I feel a great fondness towards you, dear Oliver.'

He blushed and her pulse fluttered. She had grown fond of him, fonder than she would admit. She thought of the way he lined up his cutlery at dinnertime and stacked his papers on his desk – he could be quite particular at times. She smiled.

'Then you have given me hope, dear Agnes,' he said, going down on one knee.

'Hope?' She hardly dared to breathe.

'That one day we will become man and wife,' he said simply.

She glanced down at the half a sixpence that glinted from her breast. It had brought her good luck after all.

'What do you think? Please, don't keep me in suspense.' He paused, then blundered on, turning away to put another log on the dying fire. 'I am being too forward. It is too soon. That's fine. I can wait. Or maybe you can't find it in your heart to accept me as your loving husband?'

'Oliver, slow down. This declaration has come as a shock to me. I have never allowed myself to think that I could ever be more than a friend to you. I came here a fallen woman with an illegitimate child. You picked me up from the gutter. How can you possibly wish to marry me?'

He turned back to face her. 'Because in spite of all the possible obstacles in our way, I've fallen in love with you and nothing will change that. I don't care about your past.'

'Oh,' she whispered. 'It is a miracle.'

'We are well suited, equals in every way. You are a wonderful mother to Rose and Arthur, and I hope that one day they will both call me Father. I already think of the boy as my son. Our son. We are a patchwork family, stitched together by circumstance, but there's nothing wrong in that.' He frowned. 'What is your answer, my dearest woman? Will you marry me and be my true and proper wife and companion in life, and in my bed? Will you make me the happiest man who's ever lived?'

'Yes, my darling, of course I will. Yes.'

'We shall be inseparable, like our beloved Queen and her prince. We will hold our heads high and promenade along the Dane John with the best of them.' Smiling, Oliver got to his feet, then sat down beside her with his arm around her shoulders. The log in the grate smouldered and burst into flame. Agnes turned to her dear friend and husband-to-be, her hero, and smiled back softly. His love and kindness had made her half a heart whole.

# *Acknowledgements*

I should like to thank Laura at MBA Literary Agents, and Viola and the team at Penguin Random House UK for their enthusiasm and support. I'm also very grateful to my friends and family for their patience while I've been researching and writing Agnes's story.